Prince George
& Master
Frederick

Prince George & Master Frederick

✝

Rosalind Freeborn

Rosalind Freeborn
February 2025

APP
Alliance Publishing Press

Alliance Publishing Press

www.alliancepublishingpress.com

Published by Alliance Publishing Press Ltd
This paperback edition published 2024
Copyright © Rosalind Freeborn 2024
Rosalind Freeborn asserts her moral right to be
identified as the author of this book.

ISBN: 978-1-8382598-5-3

Typeset in Adobe Caslon Pro
Book & Cover Design by **WORKSHOP**65

Biography

Rosalind started her career as a book publicist and went on to promote a variety of arts organisations including the London Philharmonic Orchestra and several high-profile charities.

While her family was young she established her own consultancy before becoming a director within a PR Agency working in the fields of art, design, retail and architecture.

In 2002, Rosalind followed her childhood dream and went to City & Guilds of London Art School, acquiring a Higher Diploma in Fine Art. However, having learnt how to paint in oils, she found herself drawn to paper collage and concentrated on that medium.

She is now a commercially successful artist, regularly exhibiting and showcasing her work.

She was prompted to write **Prince George & Master Frederick** after investigating a family story suggesting that she might, in some way, be related to George III. Researching the real-life history of Frederick Blomberg was so fascinating that she was compelled to write this novel. This is her first published work.

Rosalind lives in north London, is married to Simon Battersby, a film editor, has four grown-up daughters and five grandchildren.

For Simon
and our daughters
Hannah, Matilda,
Florence and Imogen

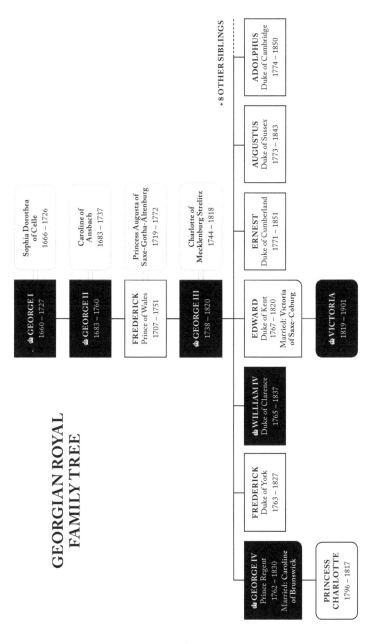

GEORGIAN ROYAL FAMILY TREE

♔ GEORGE I 1660 – 1727 — Sophia Dorothea of Celle 1666 – 1726

♔ GEORGE II 1683 – 1760 — Caroline of Ansbach 1683 – 1737

FREDERICK Prince of Wales 1707 – 1751 — Princess Augusta of Saxe-Gotha-Altenburg 1719 – 1772

♔ GEORGE III 1738 – 1820 — Charlotte of Mecklenburg Strelitz 1744 – 1818

♔ GEORGE IV Prince Regent 1762 – 1830 Married: Caroline of Brunswick

FREDERICK Duke of York 1763 – 1827

♔ WILLIAM IV Duke of Clarence 1765 – 1837

EDWARD Duke of Kent 1767 – 1820 Married: Victoria of Saxe-Coburg

ERNEST Duke of Cumberland 1771 – 1851

AUGUSTUS Duke of Sussex 1773 – 1843

ADOLPHUS Duke of Cambridge 1774 – 1850

+ 8 OTHER SIBLINGS

PRINCESS CHARLOTTE 1796 – 1817

♔ VICTORIA 1819 – 1901

Prologue

Extract from a diary story in *The London Gazette*, 15th June 1765

The curious tale of an apparition delivering a message from beyond the grave has reached our ears. According to our source, two English officers based in the Caribbean in 1764 had retired to their shared barracks when a shadowy figure entered the room. Colonel Stewart shouted out in anger at the surprise appearance of his fellow officer, Major Blomberg.

Speaking in a grave voice, the figure confirmed his identity, adding that he had died, and had an urgent instruction for his commanding officer. He bade him seek out the orphan child of his secret marriage and convey news of his son's whereabouts to King George III. The apparition then disappeared.

Searching the barracks, no trace of the officer could be found. The following day, after much ribbing from colleagues about the amount of port enjoyed at dinner, a message arrived from an adjoining island confirming that Major Blomberg had died during a battle with the French, just at the time of his appearance in the officers' room.

Chapter One
A Royal Governess Visits a House in Dorset
July 1765

"It's here," shouted Frederick, bouncing on the bench and pointing at the cloud of dust rising from the sandy lane. The carriage wheezed to a halt outside the cottage and the driver lowered the step to the passenger door. He helped down a small woman swathed in a cloak and bonnet despite the warmth of the afternoon.

"Ooh, lacy gloves!" cried Harriet.

"Four horses," breathed Frederick.

Jumping down from their perch, Frederick kept his distance whilst Harriet pressed herself into her mother's skirts as they stood by the gate.

"Mrs Cotesworth, I presume?" said Margaret Poulton, holding out her hands in greeting.

"Indeed, pleased to meet you, Mrs Poulton." Both ladies curtsied whilst the children stood staring with saucer eyes. "You must be Frederick," she added, looking at the little boy.

Frederick nodded mutely, making an awkward bow. Harriet, bobbing a curtsy, raised her chin and, in a clear piping voice, said, "I'm Harriet, Fred's cousin. Pleased to meet you, ma'am. I'm five and a half."

"Do come in," said Margaret Poulton and the children followed the lady up the path to the door. "Your driver is expected at the stable down the lane. Simon, the lad, will give him refreshment and water the horses."

"Most thoughtful, thank you."

Lowering her head to avoid snagging her bonnet, Mrs Cotesworth entered the cottage with the children following closely. The lady glanced over her shoulder at them, smiling, as she walked across the rush-strewn stone floor of the parlour and looked around the modest living space.

"Madam, are you content to stay here?" asked Mrs Poulton.

"Yes, most suitable. Thank you."

"Let me show you to your room," said Margaret.

Beckoning the lady to follow, the children scampered up the narrow stairs. Frederick felt bubbles of anxiety rising in his chest. Why had Joan, their housekeeper, dusted every surface in readiness, he wondered, and why was everyone wearing their best clothes? And why was this lady staying in Aunt Margaret's room?

Running ahead to the window of her mother's bedroom, Harriet jumped on the spot, pointing to the precious piece of soap in a saucer bought especially for their guest, and patted the fresh linen folded on a chest of drawers nearby.

Margaret pulled back the curtain to an alcove at the side of the bed where she kept the commode and Mrs Cotesworth immediately disappeared behind it. Covering their mouths to hide giggles at the sound of water tinkling on porcelain, Margaret shooed the children out of the room, and they ran back downstairs snorting with mirth.

"Did you see her fancy hair?" said Harriet. "She wears high heels and smells like roses."

Frederick nodded in agreement, sensing only threat from the visit.

Back in the parlour both children ran circles around the table until Aunt Margaret caught them and forced a comb through their brown curls.

"I want you both to be on your best behaviour, d'you understand?"

Frederick nodded and Harriet shrugged in silent assent.

"But why is she here?" Harriet asked.

"To meet you both, well, Fred in particular, because some important people want to help us."

"Can we go to the stable and look at the carriage?" said Frederick. "I want to see the picture painted on the door."

"Yes, children, you can, but do what Simon the stable lad says, and don't go anywhere near the horses' hind legs."

Dashing out of the kitchen, through the garden gate, Harriet stopped as they approached the lane, pulling Frederick back. "No, not the stables. Come back to the house and listen to the lady."

Together they ran back and crouched beneath the window to the parlour.

When Mrs Cotesworth came downstairs, she had shed several layers and was now wearing a plain blue dress revealing her small figure. A lacy shawl encircled her shoulders and was tucked into her bodice. A ribbon choker with a cameo pinned to it circled her throat and a lace headdress replaced the bonnet. She warmed her hands by the range although the day was pleasant and sunny.

"Please do sit down, madam. Would you like some tea?"

Margaret poured tea into her best china cups. "I trust your journey was comfortable?"

"Tolerable. We stopped at Winchester overnight and it was a relief to get out of the carriage. The roads can be very rough despite the dry weather."

"So I understand," said Margaret. "I've rarely left Dorset. I've only ever travelled to and from my family farm in Kent. I've never been to London."

"Never been! Oh, my dear, I'm sure you would enjoy the city and all the society it affords. I have travelled a great deal in my life, especially on the Continent. One cannot underestimate the value of a well-sprung carriage and a driver who is willing to stop whenever you knock. The discomfort of waiting to reach an inn or a coach post can be unbearable. I have no need of a lady's maid like other members of the royal household; I'm very independent."

Mrs Cotesworth settled back in the chair, sipping her tea. "I'm sure you don't want to hear about me. You want to know why I have come."

"Yes," replied Margaret Poulton, patting the piece of paper on top of a pile of books on the table next to her chair. "I was very surprised to receive this letter from Lady Charlotte Finch, on behalf of Their Royal Majesties. Just as I was surprised to receive that mysterious visit from the two soldiers in the spring."

"Yes, I'm sure it must have been a shock. I was sorry to hear about poor Major Blomberg. Did you know him well?"

"A little," replied Margaret. "He was married to my sister, Melissa, as you know, God rest her soul. He visited us just before his regiment went to the Caribbean, when Frederick was about two. My poor sister died giving birth to Fred and I've done my best to be a mother to him. He is very close to my daughter, Harriet, who is a year and a half older, yet they are often mistaken for twins. He's happy here with his family. More tea?"

Margaret rose to fill her guest's cup, watching as the lady took a small phial from the pocket in her skirts and poured some liquid into her cup.

"Medicinal, my dear," she said, taking a sip and licking her lips. "I can see that you have looked after Frederick very well, Mrs Poulton. Here is a letter you must read. It is from Colonel Stewart, Major Blomberg's commanding officer, and was sent to Lady Charlotte Finch, who then presented it to Their Majesties, King George III and Queen Charlotte. It will explain something of the visit you received from your brother-in-law's comrades, and it may disturb you."

Passing Margaret the letter, Mrs Cotesworth sat back in her chair. "And after you have read it, we can discuss how we act upon the directive it contains."

Margaret read the letter, clapping her hand to her mouth before reading it a second time. Looking up from the paper, her eyes wide in amazement, she said, "Mrs Cotesworth, I find this hard to believe. I am sure that the soldiers who visited me had known Major Blomberg. They spoke fondly of him and seemed surprised to find us here. But William told me he wanted to keep his marriage and his son, Frederick, a secret, certainly from his colleagues, and

I don't believe even his family knew. Yet these officers were given this information about Frederick in such a bewildering way and made their way here, as instructed. And then they told the King and Queen that they had found us. Why?"

"They did as Major Blomberg, or his apparition, had requested. I gather he had been a close childhood friend of His Majesty and when the King and Queen heard that the child had been orphaned, they were eager to help. Hence my visit."

"Mrs Cotesworth," said Margaret, returning the letter. "We can't tell Frederick anything about this. He is a nervous child and would be terrified. He's not quite four years old and scared of the dark. He shares a bed with Harriet, and we keep a candle burning in their bedroom through the night in case he wakes up."

A scuffling noise from below the parlour window attracted the women's attention and they stopped speaking. "Excuse me," said Margaret, rising from her chair and marching outside. Sternly addressing the two children crouched on the ground, she said, "Why are you two listening to grown-ups talking? How dare you. Come inside right now."

Ushering the children into the room, Margaret bade them stand on the hearthrug in front of their visitor. Harriet chewed her forefinger and tugged at a tendril of hair. Frederick shifted from foot to foot in his tight shoes, smoothing the sides of his breeches with sweaty hands.

"Well, children, you both look splendid," said Mrs Cotesworth. "Come closer, let me see your hands."

Both held out their hands, front and back, for inspection.

"Spotlessly clean. I commend you, Mrs Poulton. Tell me, Frederick, do you know any Bible stories?"

"I know about the Good Samaritan who looked after a hurt man."

"Very good. And Harriet, what stories do you know?"

"Jesus made a man rise from the dead."

"Excellent. I look forward to talking to you more."

"Off you go to the stables now," said Margaret.

The two children scampered outside, through the garden gate and ran down the lane.

"They are charming children, Mrs Poulton," said Mrs Cotesworth. "Frederick looks so like him. It's very striking."

"Really?" Margaret clasped her hands together.

"Now, this is the proposal. Their Royal Majesties will adopt Frederick into the royal household and bring him up with their children. George, the Prince of Wales, will be three years old soon and Prince Frederick is two. Queen Charlotte is expecting another child very soon. Master Frederick will make a good playmate for Prince George."

Margaret's mouth fell open in shock. "Goodness. They want to take Frederick. I don't know what to think. This is dreadful. We are such a tight-knit family."

She stood up and paced across the hearth before sitting down again. "No, Mrs Cotesworth, it's not possible. Frederick has lived with me for nearly four years, and he is content. I love my nephew as if he were my son." Wringing her hands, she continued, "I can't let him be taken away to live with strangers."

"I understand your reluctance, Mrs Poulton, but this is the express wish of Queen Charlotte. When Her Majesty heard of Frederick's plight, she said, and I quote her very words, 'We will take this boy.' Think what an opportunity it will be for Frederick. I can see that you are a caring and dedicated aunt, but he will be living with the highest family in the land. He will gain an education and good manners and, in time, be introduced to society. He will be a playmate for the heir to the throne. Could you deny him this advantage just to keep him by your side?"

"Madam, I realise I'm hardly in a position to refuse. I am a widow with limited resources to offer young Frederick. My family, in Kent, are farmers, and they support us. My late husband, Alexander

Poulton, God rest his soul, left me a small inheritance. Of course I understand the advantages this would offer Fred. But he's not a brave boy and he's happy here."

"I commend your concern, Mrs Poulton, and do not doubt your affection for Master Frederick, but this is a royal summons. You have little power to refuse."

Patting her flushed cheeks, Margaret paced around the room. "Oh, dear me. What to do? Before I agree to anything, I need to know that Fred would be well cared for in the royal household. Being a playmate for a prince who's a year younger is all very well, but this will be overwhelming for him. My daughter, Harriet, is far more robust by nature and he depends on her. I also need to know that I'll be able to see him as he grows up. He bears the Blomberg name. William was of good stock, an aristocrat, his forebears were barons. I want him to know the history of his family and assure him that he can hold his head up wherever he goes."

"I completely understand, my dear Mrs Poulton, and share your concerns. Let me assure you that Lady Charlotte Finch, the Head Governess, and I, her deputy, have the child's best interests at heart. Master Frederick will live like a prince. He will learn from the best tutors, and he may, in time, become a gentleman or acquire a profession. He will take his place with confidence in the highest level of society."

Mrs Cotesworth leant forward in her chair, gripping her hands together in her lap. "Mrs Poulton, there is another matter to discuss. We must establish what Frederick's father, the late Major Blomberg, provided for his son. I gather you have some documents."

"Yes. After Melissa died, I promised to care for Frederick. I'm his godmother. William gave me a box containing letters and documents which suggest that Frederick should inherit a valuable estate in Yorkshire."

"I'm glad to hear you have it."

Sighing, Margaret sank into her chair, covering her eyes for a moment. Looking up at her visitor, she said, "Oh, poor little Fred. This is of course a very generous offer, and I do understand what this means for him. What age do you think we should send him?"

"I will return to London with him tomorrow."

Margaret covered her mouth, stifling a cry.

"Mrs Poulton, Frederick will be in my constant care. I will accompany him to the nursery at Richmond Lodge where the royal family resides. He will meet young George, the Prince of Wales, and the infant Prince Frederick. The journey will take us two days with a stop at Winchester."

Margaret dabbed her eyes with a handkerchief.

"The King has charged me to bring back the box with Major Blomberg's documents. I promise you I will keep it safely in my private apartment and assure you that I, personally, will do everything possible to ensure that the inheritance is secured for Frederick."

Margaret sighed. "Do I have any choice?"

"No, Mrs Poulton, this is the King and Queen's personal command. For the love of his late friend, Major Blomberg, the King wishes that Master Frederick should receive all that he is due. I will leave it to you to explain to him exactly what will happen."

Chapter Two
Aunt Margaret Breaks the News to Frederick

"But why?"

Harriet burst into tears and Frederick howled. Sitting on the bench in the garden, he clung to his aunt Margaret, tears dripping down his cheeks. Harriet flung her arms around him, sobbing into his shirt. Margaret hugged the children and did her best to describe the excitement of travelling in that smart carriage and being treated to new and wonderful things.

"Don't want to go, want to stay here with you and Harriet." Frederick wound his arms around her waist, pressing into her body.

"Darling Fred," said Aunt Margaret. "I want you to be a very brave boy. This is an important opportunity for you. I know you're only little, and I will miss you so much, but this is a good thing."

Frederick wailed more loudly, deep sobs wracking his body. "Don't want to, please don't make me."

"Fred, we'll miss you, but think about it; you'll live like a prince. You will meet the King of England!"

"Don't want to be a prince, don't care about the King." Wiping his nose on his sleeve, he mumbled, "Just want to be me."

"Fred, you'll go to London with that nice lady, Mrs Cotesworth. You'll see the world go by from the window of that carriage. And when you get to Richmond Lodge, which is a great big house with gardens, you'll have children to play with and lovely food to eat. You'll learn grown-up reading and writing. Wouldn't you like to learn to ride a horse, or how to fight with a sword? You'll become a proper gentleman."

Frederick nodded in partial agreement, his lower lip trembling, not wanting to disappoint Aunt Margaret.

"So, Fred, we'll pack up your most important things in a box, ready for the journey tomorrow. Just think, the driver might let you sit next to him for a while and hold the whip."

"Could I?"

"We'll ask him. Come on, Harriet. You can help us pack up Fred's best clothes and his favourite toys. This is going to be exciting," added Aunt Margaret, turning away from them. But Frederick could see that she was crying.

The following morning Aunt Margaret led Frederick towards the carriage. The harnessed horses pawed at the sandy earth, nodding their heads. Lifting him up, the driver placed Frederick on the seat at the front of the carriage. Realising how high he was, Frederick yelled, stretching his arms to be taken down, and the driver laughed.

"I think that's everything," said Mrs Cotesworth, watching her trunk being loaded onto the back of the carriage and Frederick's smaller box slotted in beside it. "Frederick and Harriet, I have a special present for each of you to cheer you up."

The children stared at her, not knowing whether to trust or fear this woman.

"I'm giving each of you a guinea. Have you seen one of these coins before?"

Shaking their heads, both children watched her delve into a bag and draw out two large, shiny gold coins. "Here," she said, "I have one for each of you. It's worth one pound and one shilling. It's a special present to you both from our very own sovereign, King George III. You can see his head on the coin. Have you ever held so much money?"

The children received the fat coins in each of their clammy palms. Harriet stared at her coin and then dropped it into her mother's hand as if it had burnt her.

"Frederick, would you like me to look after your guinea for you until you have a safe place to keep it in your new home?" asked Mrs Cotesworth.

Frederick nodded silently and handed back the coin. Unable to take pleasure in the rare gift, he miserably watched her put it back into her pouch.

Aunt Margaret pushed a basket loaded with provisions onto the floor of the coach. "I've packed you some of Joan's breakfast scones and a pie. There are some early apples and a flagon of water in there too."

"How very considerate, thank you," said Mrs Cotesworth. She took the driver's hand to step in, plumping herself down on the seat facing the direction of travel. "Say goodbye, Master Frederick."

Frederick threaded his arms around his aunt's waist. "Must I?" he whispered to her.

"Yes, my darling. We will see each other again. We will come and see you in your fine new home."

Detaching Frederick from Aunt Margaret's arms, the driver lifted him into the carriage, avoiding the small kicking legs, before dropping him onto the padded velvet seat opposite Mrs Cotesworth. The door slammed shut. Frederick could hear Harriet wailing as she clung to her mother, who buried her face in her apron.

"I promise I will write," called Mrs Cotesworth through the lowered window. "He will be well cared for."

Lurching backwards as the driver unhitched the brake, the horses took the carriage's weight and set off. Frederick shuffled along the bench seat to the window, sticking his head out as far as he could to see Aunt Margaret and Harriet waving until the carriage rounded a bend and they disappeared from view. Dark clouds loomed over the thickening trees along the road as the countryside flashed by and plops of rain streaking the glass made the view blurry and abstract. Slumping back onto his cushioned bench seat, Frederick pressed his hands between his thighs, convulsed by sobs.

A few hours later, Frederick woke up and lifted his head from the seat. He realised, from the mark of dribble and tears on the padded fabric, that he must have fallen asleep. Where was he? No, he wasn't dreaming. He was still in the carriage. He looked up and saw Mrs Cotesworth on the bench opposite. She was working on some knitting and tugging fine wool from her bag. The rhythm of the clacking needles matching the clop of the horses' hooves made him feel queasy. Frederick started squirming from side to side, his legs unable to reach the floor of the carriage. Mrs Cotesworth viewed him through narrowed eyes above the glasses fixed to her nose.

"I hope you had a nice sleep, Master Frederick. Now, what is it, water or worse?"

He understood her meaning. "Water."

"Very well. We won't stop the carriage. Here, you should make your water into this." She reached under the seat of her bench and drew out a small vessel, like a tall jug. "All the gentlemen use these when travelling. We can't always be stopping, and I fear the next stage is not for several miles. Aim into the jug and then hand it to me."

Turning away from her, he undid the buttons on his breeches, reached inside for his penis and pointed it at the large spout. She seemed unperturbed by the performance. "Thank you, now hand it to me." She took the vessel, opened the window and emptied out the contents. "Well, it's my turn now," she said, replacing the small jug under the seat. She took out a different vessel, like a large gravy boat. Frederick stared as Mrs Cotesworth shifted position, hoisting up her skirts, inserted the bourdaloue between her legs and sat down upon it. He heard the unmistakeable sound of water trickling and sniffed the aroma of another person's urine. He remembered how he and Harriet had giggled together at the same sound only a day ago. Mrs Cotesworth opened the window again and threw out the contents. "That's better. Now, let's try some of your aunt Margaret's thoughtful picnic."

Frederick nodded. Although he was still terrified at what was happening, there was a sense of solid comfort about this woman. He gnawed at the piecrust and ate an apple. After the simple meal he felt his eyes droop again and considered lying down on the bench seat. He noticed Mrs Cotesworth taking a sip from her phial before pushing it into her pocket.

"Come over here and sit next to me," she said, shifting to the side of her bench, patting the soft, buttoned surface. He slid off his seat, took two steps across the carriage floor and was instantly pulled up onto the seat to sit by her side. She hooked her left arm around his shoulders to secure him and, within seconds, he was fast asleep.

After two days of constant travel in the carriage, and the terror of an overnight stay in a strange house, Frederick's head ached. He had been roused from a fitful slumber by a change in vibration as the carriage wheels rattled over cobbles. Rubbing his eyes, he looked around.

"We have arrived," said Mrs Cotesworth, her eyes beaming brightly. "This is Richmond Lodge. Richmond is a place quite close to London, which is the capital of England. You must do your best to remember this, Master Frederick. When we are in the schoolroom, I will show you on a map – that's like a picture on paper of where we live – and you can see exactly where we are, and where Harriet and Aunt Margaret are."

Frederick slid from the bench to the carriage door and pressed his nose against the window to gaze at the tall buildings surrounding him. Men in leather aprons emerged from doors and gateways and a footman in a smart uniform opened the door of the carriage, lowered the step and held out his hand.

"Go on, Master Frederick, you can descend first."

He jumped from the bottom step and watched as Mrs Cotesworth was helped down.

Allowing his small hand to be gripped by Mrs Cotesworth's, he felt the lacy roughness of her gloves. This woman he barely knew was now his only friend in the world. He still had no idea why this had happened but, more urgently, he was desperate to find the privy, the pot or whatever they had in this place.

Holding hands, they entered a cold, stone-floored hallway, climbed a long flight of stairs and turned into a shadowy corridor with thick carpet under foot. Mrs Cotesworth opened a door and drew Frederick into a vast room with a large, canopied bed close to an open window. He could see a washstand, a clothes press and colourful carpets on the polished wooden floor.

"This is your room, Master Frederick," she announced. "Do you like it?"

"Yes," he replied in a small voice. "I need to…"

"Through that door there," she said, as if reading his mind. "It's called a water closet – quite a new thing in this house. And there's a pot under the bed too. When you go into the closet, you sit on that wooden seat and do your business into it."

Climbing up, Frederick waited and finally his bowels expelled two days' worth of unfamiliar food from the long journey. When he emerged from the closet, she had gone. He explored the room, gazing at the large paintings on the walls of countryside and grand people. He circled the high bed and, gripping one of the posts, hauled himself onto it. Shuffling along the slippery satin covers to the bolster and pillow at the head of the bed, he lay back, staring up at the canopy, overwhelmed by the loneliness of this new situation.

Mrs Cotesworth returned with another woman. Sliding off the bed, Frederick did his best to bow in front of the other grand lady. She was wearing a navy blue dress with embroidery on it and the lace trimming on her white cap shook like leaves.

"Master Frederick," said Mrs Cotesworth, "this is Lady Charlotte Finch, the Head Governess. The children here call her Lady Cha, and they call me Coaty. You can call me Coaty too. She and I are in charge of the nursery, and we are here to look after you."

"Indeed, the resemblance is astounding," said Lady Charlotte, bending down to touch Frederick's face with her forefinger. "He is so very like him."

Gazing up at the elegant lady, Frederick was so overcome that tears spilled down his face.

"There, there, don't cry, Master Frederick, you will be happy here," said Lady Cha softly.

Mrs Cotesworth joined in with appeasing words, but it only made things worse. Frederick could no longer control his emotions. Heaving their way from his very core, the sobs consumed him; his face turned red, and his nose ran.

Handing him a lace-edged handkerchief, Mrs Cotesworth said, "Blow your nose, Master Frederick, and compose yourself. Then we will have some tea. Do you like cake?"

Frederick nodded, doing his best to breathe deeply. Wiping his eyes and nose, he handed the damp cloth back to her. Then, holding her hand, they followed Lady Cha along corridors and down stone staircases until they came to a bright, elegant room with tall windows overlooking a large garden.

Next to the window was a table laden with plates of bread and butter, cakes, scones, biscuits and bowls of fruit conserves. Another table held small porcelain teacups, dotted with painted flowers, a silver urn and more pots and jugs. Mrs Cotesworth picked up a plate and pointed to the delicious spread.

"Would you like bread and butter with jam?"

Lady Cha lifted Frederick onto a chair with cushions plumped up beneath and behind and he watched the food being prepared.

"Very soon, Master Frederick," said Mrs Cotesworth, "you'll meet your new playmate. He's called George. Prince George. He's the Prince of Wales and a very important boy. Remember, I told you he's going to be king one day."

Frederick was too interested in the food placed before him to bother listening. He picked up the glass beaker of milk on the table, downed it with relish and started eating buttered bread and jam before moving on to a slice of Madeira cake.

On hearing the door open, he looked up and saw a small boy being led in, holding the hand of another woman dressed in dark material.

"Ah, Your Royal Highness," said Mrs Cotesworth, "may I introduce Master Frederick. He's come to live with us. Frederick, this is George. Say hello."

"Why's he wearing a dress?" said Frederick, staring at the boy, who was about the same size as him, wearing a long, smocked frock with frilled sleeves and a lacy collar.

"And why's he got breeches?" retorted the child, pointing at Frederick's legs, his plump lips pouting and eyebrows frowning.

"Because, George, you look very handsome in your clothes," said Lady Charlotte.

George tugged at the sleeves of his dress and looked across the room to the tea table.

"Want cake."

"'Please may I have' is what we say, George," corrected Lady Charlotte. "Come and sit down next to Frederick." She helped George up onto the chair and arranged more cushions behind him. She put a small slice of cake on a plate in front of him. "Now, you two boys can get to know each other over tea and then afterwards we'll have a game in the garden before bedtime."

"Do I have to?" said George, eating the cake quickly and holding up his plate for another slice.

"Frederick is going to be your playmate, George," said Lady Charlotte. "Your father, His Majesty, has arranged it. Having Frederick here will be fun for you. You can show him your toys in the nursery too."

"Won't. Don't want to; they're mine."

"You let you little brother Prince Frederick play with them."

"He always messes them. Shan't. More cake."

Frederick could see Mrs Cotesworth and Lady Charlotte exchanging looks as George scowled, pointing to his plate. The two children sat in silence, occasionally glancing at each other. Before George had finished his third slice of cake, Mrs Cotesworth said, "Come along, boys. We'll get out the hobbyhorses and the little carts. You can run about in the garden until bedtime. It's a lovely evening, and Frederick, I'm sure you could do with some exercise after your long journey."

"Don't want to play with him," said George, tugging at the frilled collar around his dress.

"Of course you do, George," said Mrs Cotesworth. "Come along, it's still sunny and warm."

Later that evening Frederick lay in bed in his new room and, through a gap in the drapes, could see that it was still light outside. Birds sang in the branches of the poplar tree close to his window and he could hear soft voices and the tread of feet on the shingle path outside the building. Mrs Cotesworth helped him put on his nightshirt, tucked him in and bade him goodnight. Left alone in this alien place, his face crumpled as he thought about Aunt Margaret and Cousin Harriet. He was used to sleeping next to Harriet, with arms entwined, comforted by the sound of her soft breathing. Questions filled his mind as he sank into the pillow. Who were these people? Why did he have to be on his best behaviour all the time? And why was that horrid little boy George so proud and rude? Within minutes he was asleep.

The next morning, a gentle but firm shaking from Mrs Cotesworth woke him from chaotic dreams. "Good day, Master Frederick," she said, helping him slide from his high bed. "We'll get you dressed, but the palace tailors will come soon and measure you for new clothes. The King has chosen a lovely blue colour and looks forward to seeing you both in your new outfits."

"Not a dress?" said Frederick.

"No, and nor will George. We all see the time has come for him to wear breeches like you." She helped him pull on his breeches and her nimble fingers buttoned up the coarse linen shirt Aunt Margaret had made for him.

"Our cobbler will measure your feet too," she said. "And you'll receive two pairs of new shoes plus some riding boots. Now you look excellent and ready for your day. Come with me."

Holding her hand and trailing along the corridor to the swish of her dress, Frederick entered a bright, sunny room. Bookshelves lined the walls and toys were stacked in baskets in a corner. Here, the tables and chairs were smaller, a perfect size for children. Frederick saw that Prince George was already seated at a low table eating a bowl of porridge. The child looked up at Frederick with an expression of disdain.

Across the room, he could see another child, too large for his high chair, being fed the same porridge by a nursemaid, smacking his hands upon the wooden table in front of him and shouting 'shoot' between mouthfuls.

"Coaty," said George, in a whining voice, "that boy is still wearing breeches. I want to."

"George, you will be pleased to hear that your mother and father agree that you can start wearing breeches. And little Prince Frederick over there will also have new things when he's bigger. You boys will soon be the envy of all nursery children. We can talk about it again with your mother if she comes to see you this morning, or we'll go down and see her after breakfast. Do you remember I told you that she's expecting a new baby brother or sister?"

George shrugged indifference at this piece of information and continued eating.

"Come along, Master Frederick, you can sit next to Prince George. Here is your porridge."

"Look, Master Frederick," said Mrs Cotesworth, "your namesake, Prince Frederick, is enjoying his breakfast."

Frederick looked at the noisy child, who continued to shout

'shoot' as his nurse shovelled the food into his mouth. He was on the brink of saying that he didn't like porridge but resisted. He did his best to consume the contents of the bowl, remembering to say thank you, drank his milk and was about to wipe his mouth with the back of his hand when Mrs Cotesworth saw him. Shaking her head and mouthing the word 'no', she handed him a napkin, which he used to rub his face clean.

A servant brought in tea and a plate of warm muffins for the two governesses. George and Frederick viewed the adult food with envy. The two boys sat side by side at the table in silence, turning to stare at each other occasionally, whilst the two women conversed softly, sipping their tea and crunching their muffins.

"Where have you come from?" asked George.

"Dorset," said Frederick.

"Dorset, what's that?"

"I don't know; it's where I live."

"Is it on the puzzle map? Coaty will tell me. Why are you here?"

"I don't know," replied Frederick. "My aunt Margaret said the King and Queen wanted to be kind to me."

"Why?" replied the little boy, slouching back in his small chair and tapping his tummy. "I've never had anyone to play with before except my brother Frederick, and he's only just learnt how to walk. What games do you play?"

"I play with my cousin Harriet mostly, outside in the garden. I like tag, hopscotch or skittles. Sometimes we play pirates or highwaymen with our friends."

"I'd like to play highwaymen," said George. "Do you use pistols?"

"Pretend ones."

"I've got a real one."

"Aren't you scared of the noise it makes?"

"No, it doesn't fire, but you can still make it go bang. It's in the cupboard over there. I challenge you to a duel."

"Why?"

"Because I can. It's what gentlemen do."

The boys' conversation was interrupted by the sound of silk petticoats rustling as the two governesses rose from their seats, curtsying to a man and a woman who swept into the nursery. The man was wearing a large blue jacket with enormous pockets overflowing with handkerchiefs and his breeches were spattered with mud. He wore no wig on his head, just a fuzz of cropped light brown hair. The woman next to him looked enormous in a wide grey dress with some kind of smock over the top and an elaborate headdress frilled with lace. They approached the table where George and Frederick were sitting. George scrambled to his feet to bow, and Frederick copied him. The governesses moved the chairs they had been sitting on nearer to the children's table for the King and Queen to sit on.

"So, Master Frederick, what, what," said the King, flipping up his coattails behind him to avoid sitting on them and clamping his hands upon his knees. "You are Blomberg's boy, come to live with us. What think you of your new home?"

Frederick stared back at this man whose eyes seemed to pop out of his head. He had a large nose with a curve at the end and the same full lips as Prince George.

Frederick's eyes filled with tears, and he couldn't reply. Mrs Cotesworth moved behind him and patted him on the shoulder. "Now then, Master Frederick, don't take on. You've enjoyed talking with Prince George, haven't you?"

"Yes," he managed to say in a small voice and swallowed hard. "George says we are going to do a duel."

"Ha!" cried the King, slapping his thighs with his hands. "What a rascal you are, George. Let me make it clear: we will not be challenging anyone to any duels in this household."

"My dear," said the Queen in a whisper, "is it not a striking resemblance? They could be twins."

"Like me and my cousin, Harriet!" exclaimed Frederick. "Aunt

Margaret says we are like twins. We live in Dorset," said Frederick, forgetting Mrs Cotesworth's instructions never to speak freely to the King and Queen.

"Indeed," said Queen Charlotte with a smile. "How very forthright you are."

Frederick had never heard a German accent before and stared at the woman with suspicion.

"So, you boys will be going to the schoolroom soon," said the King. "I want to see some excellent writing from you both before long."

George pouted his lips and shook his head. "But I can write. You know I can." Pointing at Frederick, he added, "He can't. Don't think he knows anything."

"George, be kind," said his father. "You must welcome Master Frederick into your home, and you will enjoy sharing your lessons. It is good for you to have someone close to your own age to learn with. Master Frederick," continued the King, looking down at him. "Be assured, I will pay close attention to your progress. I hope that you make the best of the education you receive here. This is a privilege."

Frederick had no idea what the man was talking about. As the King rose to leave, Frederick felt himself nudged by Mrs Cotesworth to stand up and make a bow. He watched the King and Queen swish their way out of the room. *What strange people*, he thought to himself.

Ushering the boys along the corridor to the schoolroom, Mrs Cotesworth held open the door to a plain, white-walled room decorated with maps, prints and scenes of battles. Bookcases lined the walls, tall tutor's desks were piled with exercise books and papers, and in the middle was a large, low table, with matching chairs for children to sit on. A cushioned sofa fitted tightly into an alcove. Frederick noted the abundance of tall candles in wall sconces dotted around the room, though there was no need to light them on this bright morning.

"So, Prince George and Master Frederick," said Mrs Cotesworth, "we'll begin our day with a story and then we'll work on our handwriting. Settle down next to me on this sofa and we'll start with an adventure story."

Bunching up his long frock around his knees, George scrambled up onto the sofa. He settled himself on the padded seat, looking at his shoes, which stuck out below the petticoat. Frederick wasn't sure whether he should do likewise and approached the chaise.

"He can't sit next to me, Coaty," said George. "Give him his own chair."

"Now, George, don't be silly. You mustn't be selfish. Climb up, Master Frederick. There's room for both of you. Stop fidgeting, George, and listen to the story."

Chapter Three
Life at Richmond Lodge
November 1765

From Mrs Cotesworth, The Royal Nursery, Richmond Lodge, London
To Mrs Poulton, Field Cottage, Milton Abbas, Dorset
16th November 1765

My dear Mrs Poulton,

I write to you from Richmond Lodge where young Master Frederick is in good health and has settled into his new home very well. After three months together, he and Prince George have become friends. They play in the gardens at the lodge, share toys in the nursery and enjoy their studies in the schoolroom. Frederick is learning to ride a pony and goes out with Prince George into the park at Richmond or Kew.

As you may have heard, soon after Frederick's arrival, Her Majesty, Queen Charlotte, gave birth to a new prince, named William.

Frederick is proving to be a model student and a good influence on the Prince of Wales. He and Prince George spend all morning in the schoolroom with a break at noon for lunch, followed by a rest, further study, and then tea at four o'clock.

The King and Queen like to see the children after their dinner at six o'clock and offer them food from their own table. Lady Charlotte and I have trained them in genteel behaviour and good manners. They have a bath at least once a week unless they have become muddy from riding. Bedtime is strictly at seven o'clock. Be assured that Frederick is allowed a candle in his room. He has had some disturbed nights and is prone to tears on occasion but is comforted. He is a clever and hard-working boy.

Like all the royal children, Frederick now wears a new blue uniform, designed by His Majesty the King. The consensus from the nursery staff, and the King and Queen, is that Frederick's presence is good for all the royal children.

I'm sure you are concerned about your young nephew, but Frederick is a contented child and part of a most harmonious and well-managed household. I enclose a small missive from him, and I hope you will agree that, for a child of four years old, he is making good progress.

With kindest regards to you,

Mrs Henrietta Cotesworth

*

After living at Richmond Lodge for over ten months, Frederick had adapted to his new life. He and Prince George were now friends, enjoying creating imaginative battle scenarios with their toy soldiers, riding their small ponies together around the park and climbing trees. When no one was looking, they'd chase frogs near the pond in the park and throw mud at each other. Listening to stories read by Coaty or Lady Cha, the boys shared amusement at funny words or phrases. Sometimes, pointing at images in books, they might dissolve into uncontrollable giggles.

One morning, George and Frederick were in the schoolroom with their new governess, Mrs Cheveley. Frederick was nervous of this woman whose dark eyes stared out below heavy brows, her black hair scraped back into a tight bun. Both boys regarded her with suspicion, sensing the threat she emitted in place of the sympathy and encouragement offered by Coaty and Lady Cha.

Sitting at the low table in the schoolroom practising their writing, George cupped his hand over his mouth and whispered to Frederick that he didn't like the way she tapped her fingernails on the table and copied making the noise with his fingers on the wooden seat of his chair. Both boys chuckled.

"Why are you laughing?" snapped Mrs Cheveley, glaring at them.

"I showed Master Frederick a funny thing in the book," said

George, riffling the pages of his reader, and Frederick nodded.

Then, when her back was turned, George reached across the table and deliberately tipped over a bottle of ink. A dark puddle spread across the surface, staining the books next to it and dripping to the floor. Mrs Cheveley shrieked when she turned and saw the disaster. After mopping up the ink, she demanded who had done this.

"Wasn't me," said George, gazing innocently up at the woman's face.

"Master Frederick, how dare you blot these valuable books," cried Mrs Cheveley. "You will be punished."

"No," cried Frederick. "It wasn't me."

"Yet, Master Frederick, Prince George denies spilling the ink," retorted the governess. "There are only two children in this room. Stand up, Frederick, hold out your hands."

"Why?"

"Because you committed a crime and must take the punishment."

"But I didn't do it," repeated Frederick.

"Well, you must take the punishment. That is your place. Hold out your hands and stay still."

Squeezing shut his eyes, Frederick waited for the impact of the ruler upon his palms and winced each time his hands were struck.

"And once more for remembrance," said Mrs Cheveley, swiping his hands in a final stroke.

Frederick's cheeks burnt with indignation. He looked at George, who remained seated at the table, impassively watching the punishment.

"You may go to your room, Master Frederick," she said, replacing the ruler on the high tutor's desk. "Stay there until lunch and I will take you downstairs to dine."

Frederick tiptoed away from the schoolroom, up the stone steps into his room. Where were Coaty and Lady Cha? He loved and trusted these two women who were kind and caring towards him. Where had they gone and why was this mean-faced Mrs Cheveley now in charge of him? But what upset him most was that George had committed the crime and not owned up. He could have said it was an accident.

Crumpling to the floor next to his bed, arms around his knees, he sobbed. He missed his home desperately. Yet, when trying to picture his old parlour and the small chairs he and Cousin Harriet sat upon by the fire, the image was fading.

Had he been fooled into believing he really was cared for in the royal household? Coaty had told him he was loved and the King and Queen, when they saw him, were pleasant to him. The servants seemed friendly, and he liked playing with the princes George, Frederick and William. But why had George allowed him to take the punishment? It wasn't fair. And what did Mrs Cheveley mean when she'd told him it was his place to take George's punishment? In the short time that this new governess had been at Richmond Lodge, Frederick had learnt to fear her, trembling at the way she clapped her hands together as a prelude to cuffing him around the head for a mistake in his writing or poking him with a pencil, urging him to answer a question.

Where were Coaty and Lady Cha? When they were close he would stop feeling on edge all the time. He even enjoyed the occasional conversation with the King and Queen. Along with the other princes, he liked being brought down to the dining room in the evening before bed. Tasting morsels from the royal table and talking to the adults was a daily pleasure. When playing games with the children on the soft rugs at his feet, the King would chuck Frederick under his chin like the other boys and mutter 'what, what' at his little statements. Surely they wouldn't want this governess to hurt him?

Bending down, he felt underneath his bed for his box of treasures and, opening it, conducted a comforting audit. He examined the guinea Mrs Cotesworth had given him, safe in a soft velvet pouch. Owning the coin was reassuring and empowering. But how long would a guinea last if he were ever to leave this place? How could he leave and where would he run to, anyway? No, he couldn't imagine life beyond the walls of Richmond Lodge.

He drew out the latest letter from Aunt Margaret and Cousin Harriet, sniffing the paper, imagining he could pick up the faint aroma of country air, the smell of fresh bread and the tang of the apple drawers where the rosy fruit would ripen. He was proud to be able to read the letters Aunt Margaret wrote to him in her best and clearest hand using words he would understand. Closing his eyes, he imagined her seated at the table in the parlour, wearing a plain, rust-coloured dress and clean white apron. Tears welled in his eyes before running down his cheeks and one plopped onto the paper, causing the ink to swell and bloom like a small bud. He couldn't imagine how, if ever, he would be able to get back to them or find a way for them to come to him. Coaty had shown him the puzzle map of England made from wooden pieces cut to the shape of counties. Understanding how far away Dorset was, he couldn't think how to get there. Yes, people rode around on horses and in carriages, but he had no idea how he could make the journey.

Aunt Margaret's letter contained a note from Harriet, written in poorly formed letters, which included a picture of Biddy, the tabby cat, pawing a small animal he assumed to be a mouse. It made him smile. There were mice living in this palace too. He saw them at the end of the day when the household had gone to bed, emerging from a small hole in his bedroom wall and running at lightning speed through the door and into another hole at the end of the corridor. He knew that they were heading for the servants' stairs and down to the kitchens. If Biddy were allowed to visit this place, she would enjoy teasing and chasing the mice.

Hearing a tap at the door, he looked up and saw a small figure standing in the frame. "Can I come in?" asked George.

"Yes," said Frederick, wiping his eyes and pushing the precious letters and coin back into his box.

"I'm sorry, Fred."

"Are you, really?"

"Yes, I've had a think about it, and it wasn't fair."

"No, it wasn't. Does she know you've come to my room?"

"I told her I needed the closet and then I came up the stairs to see you."

"Oh, then she'll be looking for you. Where's Coaty and Lady Cha?"

"At a funeral. Lady Cha's daughter died. She's very sad. They both went."

"Oh." The news was upsetting, but Frederick had no real sense of its meaning. "Will they come back to look after us?"

"Oh yes."

"Good," Frederick said. "They're kind to me."

"Yes, they're much nicer than this new one. Are you hungry?"

"Yes."

"So am I. I've got something for you."

"What?"

"I went into Mama's bedroom on my way here. I found these."

Pushing his hand into his pocket, George drew out a handkerchief and unwrapped four squashed crystalized fruits.

Frederick gasped. "Jellied sweets!"

"Like the ones Mama and Papa sometimes give to us after dinner. I took them from the box in Mama's bedroom. Go on, try one."

"Are we allowed? Won't they notice they've gone?"

"No, there were lots in the box and I only took four."

Frederick picked out a plump, pink jelly and popped it in his mouth. George took a green one. They both chewed the confection, closing their eyes to savour the sweetness.

"Fred, do your hands hurt?"

Frederick nodded, holding out his palms for George to view the raised, red stripes across his fingers.

George nodded. "I've had that."

"Really?"

"Yes. My father did it to me. I told a lie. I pretended I hadn't done something."

"What did you do?"

"I peed into that tall blue pot with the spouts in the hall by the front door. Then I said I hadn't."

Frederick couldn't help laughing out loud. He pictured the tall blue and white china things standing like chimney pots by the doors to the garden. They had curious spouts you could push your fingers into. The same idea had occurred to Frederick. He put his hand to his mouth, giggling at the confession, and George giggled too – it did sound funny. The pair of them stood up, pretending to pee into imaginary containers, laughing loudly.

"Father didn't hit me as hard as Mrs Cheveley hit you. Have another jelly."

Both boys ate the remaining two jellies and George screwed up the handkerchief, pushing it back into his pocket. "I finally feel full," he cried, patting his tummy. "They never let me have enough. Why do we have to leave food on the plate 'for Mr Manners'? I'd much rather eat everything. Fred, has it stopped hurting? I am sorry. I won't do that again."

Frederick nodded and swallowed the last of the jelly. Before the boys could talk any more, the door flew open and Mrs Cheveley burst in.

"There you are. Where have you been?" cried Mrs Cheveley.

"In the closet," replied George, scrambling to his feet. He gazed up at the adult and smiled at her with false respect.

"I couldn't see you there."

"Then I came to see Master Frederick," George replied.

"Very well," replied Mrs Cheveley. "Follow me, both of you. We must go to the dining room for lunch."

Frederick gazed with admiration at George as they followed Mrs Cheveley downstairs. Here was a boy who could tell lies with absolute conviction and adults believed him. This was quite a skill and something he needed to emulate. But, at the same time, he wondered, was George someone he could really trust?

Chapter Four
Prince George's Fifth Birthday Celebration
12ᵗʰ August 1767

On the afternoon of Prince George's fifth birthday, all the children were in their bedroom being dressed for the celebration. Frederick was glad to now be part of the rough and tumble of the boys' bedchamber, having been moved out of his soulless room on the floor above. His new bed was smaller than the four-poster, but it still had a canopy embroidered with images of horses and he enjoyed lying beneath it, gazing at the galloping scenes by the light of a flickering candle on his bedside table.

The royal parents had insisted that all the boys should be presented in fancy dress for the party in the ballroom of Richmond Lodge.

"Must I wear this?" cried George, posting his arms into the sleeves of a blue jacket, held up for him by a nursemaid.

"You look quite the jolly tar, sir," she said, doing up the buttons and then tying the kerchief around his neck. "Come and see your reflection." The nursemaid directed George to stand in front of the tall cheval mirror in the boys' bedroom, setting a sailor's tricorn hat upon his head.

"Their Majesties want you to look especially handsome for your fifth birthday, young sir. Think of the party food waiting for you in the nursery after you perform your dance."

All the children were dressed in their costumes. Prince Frederick had been squeezed into a red and black diamond harlequin outfit, George in the sailor's suit and the infant William sported a feathered headdress.

"What are you dressed as, Fred?" asked George, walking towards him and tilting from side to side, sailor style.

"I'm Mercury, some kind of messenger," said Frederick, tugging at the sleeves of his silvery jacket and lifting his feet to show George the wings attached to his shoes.

"I'm some sort of sailor," said George, shrugging, "and I have to dance a hornpipe. I don't want to."

Coaty gathered the children together and escorted them downstairs to the great ballroom at Richmond Lodge where members of the royal family and illustrious guests gathered for the celebration.

Realising that he was free to explore the room, Frederick wandered through the sea of adults. Heated bodies, encased in thick and richly decorated clothing, exuded a heavy scent of expensive perfume, citrus fruits and body odour. The room was hot, despite all the doors and windows being open, and he knew that, when the tapers were brought in to light the candles, the place would become even hotter.

Intrigued by the sound of music, Frederick pushed towards the far end of the ballroom where an orchestra was playing lively tunes. Spotting a stool close to the raised platform, he climbed onto it to observe the players, staring particularly at the cellists.

The singing tone of the strings filled his young heart with pleasure. He caught the eye of one of the musicians, who nodded at him in friendly recognition, noticing that Frederick was studying the movement of his left hand up and down the fret and mirroring the movement with his fingers. A light powder from the musician's wig fell, like fine snow, upon his instrument as he vigorously moved his bow across the strings.

Frederick remained upon his high seat, watching in rapture, until the music stopped. Prince George spotted him through the crush of adults and pushed his way towards him, rolling his eyes for sympathy.

"How much longer do we have to stay here?" he groaned, holding out his hands in front of him.

Frederick patted him on the shoulder. "When you've done your dance, Coaty says we can go upstairs to play. We can have your birthday tea too."

George nodded, demanding that he too should sit on the stool, and Frederick shifted to the side of the narrow seat. A murmuring amongst the guests signalled that the King and Queen had entered the room. Spotting George, the King bade him jump down and prepare for his performance whilst the royal parents took their seats in front of the stage.

Coaty approached the boys, took George by the hand and placed him on the platform. Listening keenly for the opening notes of the dance tune, signalling the start of the hornpipe he had learnt to perform, George smiled sweetly. Hopping from foot to foot in time with the music, demonstrating the action of pulling a rope, saluting and searching the horizon for land, he concluded his dance with a flourish of high knee-kicks.

Delighted, the audience cheered and clapped at his performance. Frederick envied the praise heaped on the young prince and felt a stab of jealousy in his heart as he heard George being described as the cleverest, most enchanting and adorable child, and a credit to the King. The King rose to his feet and spread his arms in fulsome praise of his son, patting him on the shoulder and chucking him under the chin. Everyone roared with approval. Then the monarch straightened his cravat, turned on his heel and disappeared into the crowd of guests. The entertainment was over.

Coaty beckoned to Frederick for him to come and join her. It was time for the children to return to the nursery. Frederick slid from his perch, taking her hand, glad to leave the crowded and oppressive room. Coaty ushered all the children back to the nursery where the whooping boys bounced around the room, tearing off their fancy clothing before being gathered up for their birthday tea.

Frederick was relieved to be back in the safety of the nursery and away from the adults in the ballroom. He knew that guests had looked at him with curiosity and, yet again, he heard them comment on his likeness to Prince George. What was it all about? Even after all this time, he still did not truly know why King George III had chosen to take him from his home and bring him up like a pretend prince.

After two years at Richmond Lodge, Frederick had grown fond of the royal children, now regarding them as his family, but at events like these he felt at his most lonely and awkward. The guests had come to see the King and Queen and the royal children and had no interest in the small boy who trailed around the corridors of Richmond Lodge, following Prince George like a shadow.

Frederick believed he was liked and indulged by the royal servants, but every now and then he noticed a hint of contempt directed at him. Nursemaids might cease their chatter when he approached, whispering behind cupped hands, and he might hear them referring to him as the *little cuckoo*, which bewildered him. He learnt to be cautious when dealing with adults, whether they were the family, guests or servants, and could sense whether they were sincere in their friendliness towards him.

The only people he believed treated him with true kindness and genuine love were the sad-faced Lady Cha and Coaty.

*

Nearly three weeks later, on 30th August, it was Frederick's sixth birthday. The royal household made a fuss of him, but there was no huge party like the one George had been given. He enjoyed the presents, the festive food and games with the boys. But, like one of Coaty's puzzles from the schoolroom, the pieces of his life did not fit together; the image was incomplete. When awake, late at night, he wondered what his life might be like if he were back with his 'real' family.

Dutifully, Frederick wrote to Aunt Margaret and Cousin Harriet every two weeks, receiving regular letters from them in reply. He was pleased to see that Harriet could now write well and drew pictures with confidence to remind him of his old life. She often sent little sketches of the cottage, her bedroom, the animals around them and flowers in the garden. Frederick reached into the box beneath his bed where he kept the letters and read the latest one.

From Aunt Margaret Poulton, Field Cottage, Milton Abbas, Dorset
To Master Frederick Blomberg, care of Richmond Lodge, London
1st September 1767

My dearest Fred,

I hope you enjoyed your sixth birthday. Goodness, it's hard to believe that we've not seen you for two years. Harriet and I enjoy picturing you in the royal palace having tea with the King and Queen of England.

I hear from Mrs Cotesworth regularly and she is full of praise for your hard work and your patience with the younger children in the nursery. I gather the Queen has given birth to a baby girl – Princess Charlotte, the Princess Royal. I'm sure she must be very delighted to have a daughter after all those boys.

My dear Fred, I have some sad news. My father, Farmer Henry Laing, your grandfather, has died. I realise you only met him a few times, so this will not hit you hard, but it makes me very sad. He was a good father to me and to Melissa, your dear mother. But, as happens with inheritance, the farm has passed to his younger brother, my uncle Charles Laing. Uncle Charles, and his sons, your cousins Sam and Noah, will inherit the farm. I realise you are too young to understand these things, but families who have property like to pass it down to the boys in the next generation and not the girls. Harriet says that it isn't fair, and I agree with her, but that is how things work. Harriet and I will travel by post-chaise to Laing Farm in Kent for the funeral. We will stay in Kent for a few weeks and be home in time for Christmas.

We wish you our fondest love.

Aunt Margaret and Cousin Harriet

Chapter Five
Frederick Sits for a Portrait
June 1769

"Stay still a little longer, Master Frederick," said Hugh Douglas Hamilton, leaning forward and rubbing a little white chalk into the paper in front of him. Then, dipping his paintbrush into a saucer of brown pigment, he added a few brushstrokes to the portrait.

Frederick thought he'd 'stayed still' long enough and his back hurt from sitting upright on the hard chair in the schoolroom. He calculated that he'd posed in the same position for at least half an hour watching a shaft of sunshine shift across the wooden floor. It was a warm bright day, and he could hear the other children playing outside in the garden.

"There," said Hamilton with a flourish. "It's finished." He turned the drawing round so Frederick could see. Yes, there was a definite likeness. Written below the picture were the words: *Master Frederick William Blomberg, aged 7.* And at the base of the portrait was a sketch of a violin. Frederick examined the drawing, pointing with delight at the artist's inclusion of the instrument. Throughout the sitting, Frederick had chattered about his enthusiasm for music.

"Will you give this to the King and Queen?" said Frederick.

"Yes, I've been commissioned to make portraits of all the royal family, including Their Majesties."

"Is it just one picture of me you are making?"

"Yes, why, do you want to sit for another? Does this one not satisfy you?"

"Oh, it does," replied Frederick. "It's very good. But I'd like to send a portrait to someone – my cousin Harriet and aunt Margaret. They haven't seen me for nearly four years, and I think they'd like to know what I look like now."

"That's a very kind thought, Master Frederick," said Hamilton.

"Because you were so still for this portrait, I could make another of you, a quick sketch, which you can have as a present."

"Oh yes, please, thank you. I promise I won't move at all."

Frederick endured another half hour, and Hamilton handed him the finished sketch. "Make sure you use a piece of card or thin wood at the back when you send it, so it stays flat. Where do your cousin Harriet and aunt live?"

"They live in Kent now with Grandmother Laing. We did live in Dorset, but our old village isn't there any more. The owner pulled down all the houses."

"That's a very extraordinary thing. Did you like your old house?"

"I did, but I don't really remember it and now I'll never see it again. I've never been to Laing Farm. That's where my mother, who died, and Aunt Margaret grew up."

"And you haven't seen your family for nearly four years," said Hamilton, whistling through his teeth as he packed up his paper and pencils into his leather case. "Could your cousin and aunt come here and see you?"

"I don't know. I've asked Coaty, but she doesn't tell me."

"And now you live here with the royal children; very generous of the King."

Frederick looked at him, puzzled. Was it a kind thing? He'd lived so long at Richmond that he had almost forgotten his old life.

"Right, Master Frederick," said Hamilton, "thank you for your time. I now have to go downstairs and make some portraits of the younger children, The Prince of Wales and Princes Frederick, William and Edward. I doubt they'll stay as still as you. Have you met my fellow artist, Mr West? He is also here to make portraits."

"No," said Frederick.

"Benjamin West," said Hamilton, "he's American. Do you know where America is?"

"Of course I do," said Frederick. "It's across the Atlantic Ocean and is one of our colonies. It's near the Caribbean. That's where my father died. Have you been there?"

"No, never, but Mr West sailed across the ocean from America to come here. He said it took many weeks and the sea was rough. He's a very fine artist. I'm fortunate to be helping him make portraits of the family."

Hugh Douglas Hamilton closed his box of pencils and chalks and pushed the cork into his bottle of brown ink. After smoothing his paper into a folder, he stowed everything in his leather case, snapping shut the lock. "Well, Master Frederick, thank you. And because I may well be here for some time, I hope we will meet again."

Frederick nodded. He had noticed the easel set up in the drawing room and seen a man making sketches on a large canvas. Perhaps that was Mr West. Princes George, Frederick, William and Edward were often summoned to sit with their mother for a portrait. They'd all sigh with boredom at the prospect. Now he knew what it felt like. He went to the boys' bedchamber and put the precious sketch into the box below his bed. Peering out of the window, he could see the children and some of the adults in the garden. Overcome by the June heat, everyone seemed to be drifting about the palace and there were no classes. He heard the shrill voices of the young princes outside in the garden and the complaining whine of the toddler Charlotte. A new baby, Princess Augusta, had been born a few months ago and there seemed to be even more nursemaids and governesses to look after the growing family.

Frederick recalled being invited into the Queen's bedroom a few months ago, with the other royal children, to meet the latest addition to the family, Princess Augusta Sophie. There he had seen the latest family portrait. All the children were there, clustered around their parents, but they hadn't invited him to be part of the picture. He wondered why.

Frederick walked downstairs from the schoolroom, through the hallway and outside onto the gravelled path surrounding the palace. The noonday sun was high in the sky and the air was hot. Across the lawn, towards the woods fringing the park, he could see the children lolling on cushions beneath the shade of a huge tree or rolling down a slope nearby, whooping as they tumbled. He was about to run and join them when he heard an adult tread. Turning, he saw that the King was behind him.

Matching their steps, they walked towards the family.

"I sat for a portrait this morning, Your Majesty," said Frederick, thinking it might amuse the King to hear this piece of news.

"A portrait, what, what. Yes, all of us, including myself, are being drawn at the Queen's command."

"Sir, why don't I sit with the others for the big portraits?"

"Ah, Master Frederick, you are different from the royal boys and girls."

"Oh," said Frederick. "But, sir, I've always wanted to ask you, why am I here?"

"Why are you here? Dear boy, I wanted to give you a home for the love of your father, William Blomberg."

"Were you good friends with my father?"

"I was." The King mopped his brow with a handkerchief and, pausing the walk, looked at Frederick. "We'd known each other since childhood. We were a bit like you and George. He was my best friend and protector. We grew up together, adventured and rode our horses around the countryside. We had a wonderful time."

"And he married my mother?"

"Ah, the beautiful Melissa. Yes, he did."

"And then I was born. And she died."

"Yes, you were born."

"Sir, Mr Hamilton made a second portrait of me which I'm going to send to my cousin Harriet and Aunt Margaret."

"Ah, your aunt Margaret. Margaret and Melissa, I remember the two sisters well. What fun times we had together before I became king."

"Sir, my father died serving his country, defending the American colonies from the French and the Spanish. He was shot dead."

"He was a hero," said the King. "I loved him, and I was sorry for his loss, very sorry."

Continuing their walk, they approached the sprawled family, and the King detached himself from Frederick, taking a seat next to Queen Charlotte on the cushioned bench.

"My dear," he said to the Queen. "I have been talking to young Master Frederick. He has sat for a portrait."

"Good," said the Queen. "I will hang all the drawings in my bedroom next to West's portrait of our family."

Frederick bowed to the Queen, who smiled back at him before whispering something to the King. He couldn't be sure whether they wanted him in this place at all. Life at Richmond was very confusing.

Chapter Six
George and Frederick Play a Cello Duet
October 1770, a year later

"Have you heard of a composer called Wolfgang Amadeus Mozart?" asked Mr Crosdill.

George and Frederick shook their heads.

"He's a very fine musician. He started playing instruments when he was three years old. He was a child prodigy – do you know what that means?"

"Yes, I know what a prodigy is," said George. "That's what I am, a brilliant child. My uncle Cumberland told me I was one."

"Yes, Your Highness," said Crosdill, pushing his spectacles up his nose. "I'm sure you are a prodigy. Well, Mozart was a brilliant pianist, and his father took him all over Europe to play in the best palaces and concert halls. He performed for kings and queens, dukes and duchesses. And now he writes his own music. He's not much older than you two boys."

George and Frederick blinked at their tutor.

"I was fortunate enough to see him perform in London four years ago when he was nine years old, the same age as you, Master Frederick. Young Mozart is now fourteen and he has written a symphony. Well, here's a name you should know – Johannes Bach?"

Both boys nodded. "Good. We'll play this piece by Bach on the piano first. Then we'll see if we can play the same tune on the violin and also on the cello, because, Master Frederick, I know you are anxious to master this instrument."

Frederick beamed with delight. Classes with this kindly man felt blissful after the boredom of other lessons and the threat of punishment if he did not pay attention. He told himself he could endure studying Latin, Greek and mathematics as long as the music class took place at the end of each day. Crosdill tutored his students with encouragement rather than brutality. After a few months of learning their instruments, he declared that Frederick and George were both competent enough musicians to perform a piece in public. He adapted the overture 'The Entrance of the Queen of Sheba' by George Frederick Handel for them to play on their cellos and the boys practised the piece daily. Frederick was desperate to please Crosdill. Feeling his muscles moving in unison with George's as they both played was satisfying and he loved hearing the notes of their duet melding in harmony.

On the day of the concert, the King and the Queen, with the infant Princess Augusta upon her lap, took their seats in the drawing room, surrounded by the smaller children. The entire household joined the throng with equerries, grooms, pages and governesses in attendance. Frederick was terrified and George nervous but resolute.

Mr Crosdill brought his two young students onto the stage below the far window in the room. The audience settled in anticipation and, after a short introduction from the tutor, the boys sat side by side at their cellos and began to play. Frederick was so wholly absorbed in the music that he believed the world had stopped turning. He and George both made mistakes but managed to cover the small slips. The overture ended with a flourish, the notes hanging in the air like dust motes. Setting down their bows, the boys looked up at a sea of smiling faces as the room resounded to loud hurrahs, stamping feet and clapping hands.

"Was I wonderful?" asked George, lapping up the attention, flourishing his hands and bowing. Frederick, overawed, managed a stiff jack-knife bow, acknowledging Crosdill's approving nod of his head, confirming that he had performed well.

"I wish to hear it again," exclaimed the King, marching onto the platform. "You were both magnificent. Oh, my boys, how proud I am." The King hugged both children, one under each arm, patting Frederick on the back, chucking his chin and beaming with approval. Frederick was astounded. The King had referred to him as his boy as well as George. Was this significant? Could it be that, by some mysterious event, he might truly be the King's boy? So many people had commented on his resemblance to Prince George and the King, yet he could only shrug it off as coincidence. His father was Major William Blomberg. Everyone knew that. Until that moment, Frederick had doubted that his presence held much meaning for the monarch.

The Queen, still seated close to the platform, smiled at him, beckoning him to come closer. Then, to his amazement, she handed the baby to a waiting nursemaid and took his hand. Holding it firmly, she said, "Master Frederick, my dear boy, you make me proud."

Chapter Seven
Time for a Change
May 1772, two and a half years later

"I don't want to leave, Coaty," wailed Frederick on hearing the news.

"Frederick, it's not my decision. It is time for you boys to have your own household. Look how crowded it is in the Richmond nursery; you must understand. We're not being cruel to you."

"Prince George doesn't want to leave, he told me," cried Frederick. "And Princes Frederick and William don't either. And little Edward was upset."

"Think about it," said Coaty, in her practical voice. "There are now eight royal children, and you make nine. It's not suitable for you five big boys to be in the household with the young princesses and the baby prince. It's time to move somewhere of your own. But you won't be far from us; Kew is only a short carriage journey or horse ride away. Frederick, listen, you are ten and a half years old. You may still be small for your age, but you will soon be a man. You must be brave for yourself, for Princes George, Frederick, William and Edward. You will all be together, and you'll have far more freedom than you have here at Richmond, or at the other royal residences."

Frederick ran his hand across his mouth and cheek, wiping away a tear. The news of the sudden move to the redbrick mansion at Kew had been a shock. Change alarmed him and he was anxious that, yet again, he was leaving a safe place and going out into the unknown. Along with the four boys he regarded as brothers, he would move to a building he had rarely been to before with tutors he did not know. He feared separation from the two women who were his only comforters. Misery bubbled to the surface of his very being.

Moving closer to Coaty, Frederick wound his arms around her waist. She embraced him, kissing his forehead, making him feel like a small child again. The notion of adulthood seemed a distant prospect, yet he knew it was fast approaching. Prince George, at nine and a half, was already taller than him and Princes Frederick and William were catching up. He wondered what was wrong with him that he seemed unable to grow as fast as these confident young princes.

"Fred," continued Coaty, "all we have to do today is pack up your room. The porters will move you all tomorrow morning."

"I can take my box with me?"

"Of course. You'll have your own space in a large boys' bedroom upstairs. You'll have a bigger schoolroom too. The lessons will be longer and probably harder, but your friend Mr Crosdill will come with you. You'll carry on learning your instruments and you're doing so well. We all love hearing you play the cello and violin."

His heart sinking, Frederick knew that there was no choice.

"And you will come and see us?"

"Of course, Fred. We'll see each other at the drawing rooms and levees at Richmond and other palaces. You'll enjoy being at the Princes' House. And think of the space, Fred. You'll be free to run about in the gardens and look at the river, learn to sail or go fishing. And this is something very special, Fred: you can have a dog."

"A dog, of my own?"

"Yes, the King himself suggested it. What breed would you like?"

Frederick thought for a moment. This was a huge gift. "I'd like a whippet or a greyhound."

"Then I will tell the King that you would like one. We will find a litter of puppies and you can choose one. The other boys can have their own dogs too."

Frederick nodded and smiled. Coaty was right; this would be a new adventure. He must try to be brave and not fret about where he was going. He liked Princes George, Frederick and William. Even Edward, at four years old, could join in with some of the boys' games. But Frederick remained wary of the more haughty Princess Charlotte, also known as the Princess Royal, who, at six years old, insisted that everyone should call her by her title, Royal. She was proud and quick to make nasty comments about the boys. She was especially spiteful to him, criticising his clothes or his hair or teasing him about his small stature, sniggering at the way he blushed when anyone spoke to him.

Princess Charlotte also enjoyed bossing around her two younger sisters, Augusta and Elizabeth, and the latest baby brother, Ernest, dressing them up like dolls and pushing them around in her small perambulator. The young princesses whirled around the nursery in lacy dresses and dainty shoes, scattering colourful toys everywhere. Frederick agreed that Coaty was right; the girls had become the focus of the nursery. It was time for the boys to establish a new home.

Before the move from the Richmond Lodge nursery to Kew, Queen Charlotte insisted that she must have portraits of her older boys because she would miss them. She commissioned the court artist Richard Brompton to paint their portraits. Princes George and Frederick posed in Garter robes, with Windsor Castle and Westminster Abbey in the background. By contrast, Frederick wore an elaborate suit in rust-coloured silk and adopted a relaxed pose with his new dog, Jupiter, who obligingly stood on his hind legs for the sketch, with one paw resting in Frederick's right hand. The background depicted Buckingham House. All three boys wore the same cream-coloured shoes with pom-poms. When his portrait was finished, Frederick was delighted to see that the Queen had asked Brompton to include an inscription in Latin explaining his adoption into the royal family by King George III and Queen Charlotte.

George endured the process resentfully, complaining bitterly at the length of time he had been made to stand up wearing the heavy, uncomfortable robes and that his neck ached. Used to painting small children, Brompton coaxed George into staying still and holding his feathered hat by describing how these portraits would be copied and distributed as prints to anyone wishing to see how handsome the young Prince of Wales looked. The thought soothed George, and he lifted his head higher to continue the pose.

Once the paintings were finished, Frederick, George and Prince Frederick stood next to them, propped up against the wall in the Queen's private chamber, whilst she examined their likenesses, deciding where they should hang. It pleased Frederick to know that the Queen could view these portraits of her older sons and be reminded of them whilst they forged a new life away from the rest of the family.

Chapter Eight
Life at the Princes' House
16th November 1772

The new governors at the Princes' House were tartars. Now separated from the royal parents and governesses, the boys were under their absolute control. Some of them were firm but kind whilst others were brutal in their approach, believing that the principles of discipline and punishment were necessary for education to 'take'. Any perceived rudeness or failure to pay attention would be punished with a beating.

With approval from the King, the boys were restricted in further ways. Their food was kept deliberately plain and limited in quantity. Even when the sun shone brightly, early bedtime was enforced and regular exercise imposed with military vigour.

The freedom to tend each of their small gardens in the grounds of the Princes' House offered some relief to the boys. They could dig trenches, plant seeds, grow vegetables and even keep chickens. But resentment at their restricted life festered within the children and hunger was a constant subject of conversation.

One evening, after dark, all five boys were together in George's bedroom, clustered, cross-legged around their candle on the carpet, open books upon their laps. Then George began moaning that he was hungry, so very hungry, that he would waste away if he did not have any food to eat. Princes Frederick and William joined in and then Edward. They all looked at Frederick. "Go on, Fred, you're the fastest runner," said George. "Go and fetch something to eat and drink from the kitchen."

"But I'll get into trouble."

"Not if you don't get caught."

"But they'll notice if I take something."

"You'll be careful. We know you can do it. We depend on you,

Fred," said George.

Frederick sighed and pulled on his slippers before rising to his feet and tightening the cord around his dressing gown. He knew how to reach the kitchens from the Princes' House; he had done it before, but it involved a daring journey. Glancing at the clock on the wall, he calculated the success of the venture. It was half past eight on a winter's night and dark outside. He heard the boys snorting with excitement as he left the bedroom carrying the candle and tiptoed down the servants' stairs, shielding the flame with his hand to stop the draught from the door blowing it out. At the far end of a corridor was a door leading to a covered walkway connecting the palace to the kitchen building.

Pattering along the walkway, he paused for a few seconds outside the heavy wooden door to the kitchen and opened it. The place was deserted. To his left was the bakery room, enticing him in with warmth from the ovens, but he ventured further along the corridor and into the main kitchen with its high-vaulted ceiling, then ran across the flagstones to the larder. A mesh-covered open window at the far end let in cold air. Shivering, he reviewed the bottles, jars, packets of sugar, boxes of dates, dried fruit and great sacks of flour and dried peas filling the shelves, unsure of what to take. It all looked like ingredients rather than food you could eat. Then, on a lower shelf, he found several solid-looking fruitcakes wrapped in fine cloth and tied up with string. That would do.

Picking one up, he fitted it under his armpit. Then, thinking of the boys' wish for something to drink, he spotted an open bottle on the sideboard and sniffed it. Without worrying what it was, he stuffed it down the front of his dressing gown with the cake and scampered back to the bedroom.

The boys cheered on his return, George slapping him on the back and calling him a 'trooper'.

Taking a swig from the bottle, George declared it to be Madeira. "My uncle Cumberland always brings me a glass of it after dinner.

Yes, I'd say this is Madeira."

Frederick tried it and shuddered as the sweet and bitter liquid warmed his body. Princes Frederick and William pulled faces as they drank but kept taking more. Edward refused to drink it.

Frederick unwrapped the cake to the sound of gleeful shouts.

"I'll fetch my sword," said George, rummaging in the toy box for a miniature cutlass to cut into the cake, and the aroma of soft dried fruit, sweet spices and toasted nuts filled their nostrils. George cut great slices and distributed them amongst the boys. This was bliss. They ate the cake, drank, fell about, laughed, roared and howled again.

They made such a commotion that the night nurse, hearing the noise, marched into the boys' bedroom, recoiling at the sight of the children rolling around on the floor hallooing and smacking each other on the back. Spotting her, the boys looked up in fright, put down their cake, swaying as they tried to stand. Waggling a forefinger at the children, she ran out and moments later returned with Mr Holderness, the head tutor, summoned from his rooms downstairs.

"Boys, this is disgraceful," he bellowed. "How dare you behave like this. I'm ashamed and appalled. How did you get this cake, and what's this?" He picked up the now empty bottle and sniffed it. "Everyone into bed. We will deal with this in the morning. It's too late for punishment tonight. Tomorrow the King and Queen will hear of it."

In the morning Frederick confessed that he had been the one to steal the cake and the wine. He waited for the boys to admit their encouragement of the theft, but they remained mute. Mr Holderness took him to the schoolroom and administered the beating. Raining down the blows onto Frederick's back and legs, Holderness shouted out his own catechism: 'Truth is the first quality of a man. Always be truthful.'

After the beating Frederick limped back to his bed and lay down on his front. Every part of his body throbbed with pain, but most of all he felt betrayed by the boys, his erstwhile brothers, who had deserted him. He'd only done this deed for them.

A few hours later there was a tap at the bedroom door. "Come," he replied through the muffled cloth of his pillow. The boys shuffled in and stood around Frederick's bed.

"We've come to say sorry," said George. "You took it for us. We should've been beaten too."

Frederick turned onto his back, wincing as he sat up and looked at them.

"We've brought you something." George handed him a box. "Open it. Hope you'll like it."

Frederick opened the box and saw the violin.

"We know you like the cello best but thought you might like this. We told Mr Crosdill what happened, and he was very angry with us and sorry for you. He said he had a violin we could give you. We clubbed together our money and bought it."

Frederick picked up the violin and held it to his neck. He scraped a few sweet notes with the bow.

"Thank you," said Frederick, wiping his eyes and trying to smooth his tousled hair. "I like it." He picked up the bow again and played a few notes before setting it down. "You should have owned up too."

"We know, sorry."

"Don't ask me to steal any more food for you."

They all nodded, patting his shoulder where they hoped it wouldn't hurt. Then the brothers left, and Frederick picked up the bow again.

Chapter Nine
Riotous Behaviour
September 1774

From Harriet Poulton, Laing Farm, near Chartham, Kent
To Frederick Blomberg, care of the Princes' House, Kew
1st September 1774

My dear Fred,

Happy thirteenth birthday – I hope you celebrated it well. I'm back at Laing farmhouse after spending three months at the convent in Canterbury. Here is a sketch of me made by one of the nuns. Mama thinks it a good likeness.

I enjoyed my studies at the convent, but I am now a milkmaid. It's cold in the dairy early in the morning, but I like sitting on the stool with my cheeks close to the cows' warm flank, squeezing the milk into buckets. Mama is well, but she is busy with farm work and must look after Grandmother Laing, who has a strange sickness. She sits by the fire staring at her hands and doesn't know who we are now.

Mother Billington, who lives in the village, is teaching me how to forage for herbs and make medicines and visit sick people. Last week I was with her at a birth. I've seen pigs and sheep birthing but never a baby and it was shocking to watch. The woman was in terrible pain and the child took a long time to be born, but it was a perfect little girl. The vicar baptised her and wrote 'father unknown' in the big book at church because the mother is unmarried, which is shameful.

When I told Grandmother Laing about the baby, she came to life and talked about Melissa, your mother, who died giving birth to you. I now understand what it must have been like, and I feel so sorry for her. Grandmother and Mama then told me about your parents' wedding in Rochester when Aunt Melissa married Major William Blomberg. She said it had been a blustery day in April 1761 with apple blossom flying everywhere and your mother cried throughout the marriage. That's so strange – why would a bride be sad on her wedding day?

Fred, are you ever allowed to speak to the King and ask him about your father? I'm sure there's more to know. It still seems very strange that, of all the little boys in England, you should have been chosen as a playmate for the Prince of Wales. I hope you find out the reason one day.

Your loving cousin,
Harriet

Putting down the letter, Frederick gazed at the small portrait included in the envelope. It was a crude drawing of a pretty girl in profile who was almost smiling. He shuddered at the thought that Harriet was a milkmaid. He'd been taught to have little contact with the servants who looked after the royal family's needs and never to regard them as friends, let alone family.

Food was placed in front of him at the dining table and he had no idea where or how it had been made. Chambermaids tidied and cleaned his room; backstairs grooms prepared his bath and pages attended to his personal needs. Palace tailors made and mended his clothes. He could ride, fence and fire a pistol, but disliked the noise it made.

All the royal children knew good table manners and how to talk to adults. Frederick could speak French and German, understood Latin and a little Greek. By now, he thought of himself as 'royal'. Certainly, he was treated and behaved like one, even though he hadn't been born royal.

Frederick liked to copy George and be haughty. An elegant drawing-room drawl replaced his Dorset accent. He gave orders to servants with confidence, expecting his instructions to be obeyed.

His only responsibility was the preparation of meat for Jupiter, his greyhound. He loved spending time in the kennels, feeding him titbits, brushing his smooth fur and curling up next to the dog on a blanket, whispering his innermost thoughts into his soft ears.

Taking Jupiter out into the long grass of the park at Kew, he enjoyed running after him in pursuit of rabbits and hares. At his whistle, the dog came bounding back to accept a treat, be stroked and petted, his dark eyes gazing up at Frederick with devotion.

Stowing Harriet's letter in his box below the bed, he pictured his aunt and cousin living on a farm somewhere in Kent. They were yeoman farmers but still lower class and could have no understanding of the royal world he inhabited.

Life at the Princes' House continued with a relentless round of classes and gentlemanly activities. Morning rides or brisk walks were followed by hours of tedious learning. Unable to make history interesting or geography engaging, the tutors simply drilled their students in names, dates and places, expecting them to parrot back the facts.

To relieve the boredom, Prince George led the boys in the art of subversion. Finding ways to irritate tutors and disrupt classes was his special talent. He might release a mouse in the classroom or deliberately tread in dog's mess and complain bitterly about the smell. George was quick to identify weakness in a tutor, teasing and goading them with easy cruelty. Unable to confront a boy who could puff up to his full height and threaten punishment in the Tower of London when he became king, the tutors took fright and resigned. By the age of twelve, George had grown tall, and his chest had broadened. Holding his chin high, he would toss back his head and berate servants who dared deny him what he wanted with threats of dismissal when he was older.

Everyone observed that the young heir to the throne was greedy, rude and told lies with astonishing conviction. Grooms at the stable became used to comforting exhausted horses George forced to gallop at alarming speed around the park at Kew. When wine went missing, George regularly denied all knowledge, yet the servants chuckled as they gathered up empty bottles hidden behind drapes and in drawers in the boys' bedchamber.

In a bid to suppress the young princes' appetites, and to quell Prince George's taste for sweet and spicy food, the King demanded that meals at the Princes' House be kept even more plain and uninviting. Aware of his father's strategy, and to mock it, George habitually pretended that the pie on his plate was 'too salty' or complained that the sauce was 'too piquant'. Late-night sorties to the wine cellar and kitchen became bolder with George leading the expeditions. When confronted by a servant, he would reply: "What are you going to do? Nothing. Now hand over another bottle."

One evening George, with twelve-year-old swagger, wagered that he could ride a horse up the stairs of the Princes' House to the bedchamber. His brothers and Frederick mocked him. Of course a horse couldn't ride up the narrow staircase to their room on the second floor of the palace. George disappeared. Later the boys heard the noise of hooves clattering on the stone stairs. Wide-eyed they peered over the bannisters to see what was causing the commotion. George was yelling at his terrified horse, digging his heels into the beast's flanks, urging it to climb the narrow staircase, higher and higher. The horse and rider scaled the stairs, battering candles from their sconces and snagging paintings on the wall until they reached the bedroom. A groom ran after George, exhorting the young prince to dismount for fear of damage to himself, the horse and the interior of the house. Dogs barked furiously around the horse's legs whilst George dismounted in the bedroom to the sound of boys cheering and howling with laughter.

"See, I told you I could do it, so I did it," he yelled, flourishing his feathered Prince of Wales headdress and taking a swig from a brandy bottle on the floor. A groom dashed in, grabbed the horse's reins and led it back downstairs to the sound of baying hounds closely following.

"George, you've overdone it this time," said Frederick. "We'll all be in trouble."

"Sometimes, my dear Master Frederick, you have to prove a point to your presumed elders and betters. I can do what I want." George drained the brandy bottle and smashed it against the bedroom wall. Placing his hands on his hips and swaying, he threw back his head and laughed.

"The tutors have all fled. They can't stop our riots. What's the worst they can do to us now?"

All night Frederick worried about the retribution, chewing his lips and scratching his arm. Punishment came the next morning with the arrival of the King. Eyes protruding from his face in rage and pounding across the bare floor of the boys' room, he hauled up his eldest son from his bed, pushing him against the wall and shouting in his face, venting his fury at the boy and then at the others. Frederick saw servants peeping around the door, enjoying this moment and speculating on the severity of the beating to follow.

A soldier from the King's Guards was brought in to thrash all five boys on the backs of their legs. Then they were made to stand upright in the schoolroom for hours and denied any food for a day. But rather than break their spirits, the punishment consolidated their resolve. Under George's direction they made a pact, sharing a conviction that they would, one day, seek vengeance on the adults who mistreated them. George encouraged everyone to nurture hatred and plot retribution. Frederick could see how dangerous George had become. He was tall and strong, bullish and proud rather than meek and obedient. He continued to challenge those in authority over him, demanding assistance from staff and chastising servants who were slow to serve him.

Late one night, in the quiet of their bedroom, he pledged to Frederick that, one day, when he was old enough and had the power to please himself, he would change everything, adding, "If I want a pie with crust, then I will have it."

Chapter Ten
Prince George's Devastating Announcement
August 1775

A few weeks before George's thirteenth birthday, the King and Queen proposed that their son should host his first dinner party, conceding that the 'nursery riots' would be forgotten if he were willing to demonstrate his new maturity and behave in a more adult way. George, feigning gratitude and obedience, agreed.

Frederick knew that George might appear contrite to his father but, in reality, his behaviour worsened. He continued to roam the palace grounds alone or demand his horse be saddled for illicit gallops. Regularly stealing away from the Princes' House in late-night expeditions into London, under the protection of his uncle Cumberland, he learnt how to bribe any witnesses with promises of promotion when he had his own household. George had also started to notice the pretty servant girls who tiptoed around the palace, teasing kisses from them behind trees in the park or down shadowy corridors.

Whilst out riding together in the park, a few days before the birthday feast, George and Frederick paused by the pigpen in the estate's farm.

"Look at that one," said George, pointing at the boar mounting a sow with noisy grunts. "That's what all creatures do, even humans."

"Really," said Frederick, gazing with distaste at the mating. "How do you know?"

"Well, everyone knows. Don't you? My uncle Cumberland told me. He often brings me here to see the pigs at it. That big boar will mate with all the sows in the pen. He jumps onto them one by one and sticks it in them. That's how you get the piglets."

Frederick shook his head. "I can't believe humans do something like that."

"They do, Fred, believe me. How else do you think women have babies? Cumberland told me how it's done and showed me some pictures. It's called fucking." George's eyes gleamed at some secret vision Frederick could not share. "We're not allowed to do it unless we're married," he added. "The women don't like it. But there are places where the women do like it, and you can go there and do it with them."

Frederick pulled a face. Why, he wondered, was George always ahead of him in knowledge and experiences? He was a year younger yet inches taller and filling out where Frederick remained slight and lacking in muscle. It was obvious that Uncle Cumberland's influence was strong. The portly younger brother of the King liked excess in everything, and he had taken George under his wing. Frederick experienced a mixture of distaste and envy. There wasn't any man in his life wanting to take him under his wing and the thought rankled. But he was sure Coaty loved him. Perhaps he should be satisfied with that.

At his birthday dinner, George sat at the head of his own table in the dining room of the Princes' House at Kew. As guests of honour, King George and Queen Charlotte were seated at the centre of the long table, flanked by the two younger princes, Frederick and William. Silver salvers and crystal glasses twinkled in the late summer evening light. George had overseen the menu and chosen the wine. Everyone praised him for the excellence of the food, the perfection of the claret and the honeyed flavour of the champagne. Older guests patted their breasts in pleasure at the maturity of the young prince's choices, commenting on his charm, how well his colourful clothes fitted his figure and the lustrous quality of his wavy brown hair. The young prince's precocious confidence was finally seen as a virtue. Yes, they agreed, with satisfaction, the Prince of Wales would prove to be an excellent monarch when the time came.

With a shiver of excitement, everyone anticipated Prince George's speech. A feathered hush silenced the room as the young man stood up and raised his glass. He toasted the King and Queen, his brothers, sisters, uncles and aunts and all the honoured guests. Then he began to tell a story. He described a conversation he had had with his old governess, Mrs Cotesworth, whom he had met in the garden at Kew earlier that day. Raising his glass, he suggested that this esteemed lady might have taken too many glasses of brandy and was a little tipsy. He then quaffed some wine in mockery, continuing the story.

"My father, His Royal Majesty King George III, has always insisted that one should tell the truth. I agree. I have been beaten many a time for not telling the truth."

More laughter.

"However, I have discovered from my esteemed governess, Mrs Cotesworth, that my father is also guilty of not telling the truth."

Guests shifted uncomfortably upon their chairs.

"What, what?" muttered the King.

George continued. "I have discovered that I have been living a lie."

Gasps were heard around the table.

"I am not the firstborn son of our monarch."

The King thumped his fist on the table and then shook it at George, who continued.

"The firstborn son of the King is in this room, but it is not me. It is Master Frederick Blomberg."

Frederick looked up, shocked. Had George gone mad?

George puffed up his chest and continued. "Master Frederick, my esteemed friend, nay brother, is my father's firstborn son."

The King leapt to his feet and shouted, "Desist! This is folly! Madness!"

"I have it on good authority," continued George, "that my oh-so-moral and worthy father had a son before me. He had a liaison with a young lady before his marriage to our dear mother, Queen Charlotte. This lady was a farmer's daughter, who lived in Kent.

The fruit of that liaison was our very own Master Frederick. I have learnt, from my worthy governess, that my father begged his good friend Major Blomberg to marry the girl. He obligingly did. He married the mother and gave the child a name to save her reputation and also save the new king from scandal. Why else would Master Frederick Blomberg have been adopted into this family but to salve his father's conscience and bring up his son as the prince he truly is?"

Shouts of disbelief echoed around the room.

Breathing in, George continued.

"I toast my father for his moral lapse. I toast my brothers, Princes Frederick and William, Edward, the princesses and all my family. And I toast my dear Master Frederick for being a most excellent older brother whom I love and admire."

The blood drained from Frederick's face. What could George be saying? He had never heard any of this before. The news was a blow to his stomach, making him sick. Clutching his mouth, he rose from the table, bowed to the guests and fled the room. He ran to the antechamber and retched into the pot. Standing up, George's words crowded his brain, and he retched again. Was this true? How could George make up such a story? Surely Coaty couldn't have told him something so terrible? George might have wanted to humiliate his father and get back at him for all the anger he felt towards him but to say that! No, it was not true. Surely George wouldn't do that to him? He loved George and thought George loved him back.

Dashing to the hall, he pulled open the heavy front door, running out into the courtyard and round the side of the palace. Leaning over, with hands on his knees, he retched again onto the cobbles. He had to get out of there.

Chapter Eleven
Frederick Runs Away
12th August 1775

He ran out of the courtyard, past the stables, through the gate into the garden and across the dewy grass of the park as far as he could until he came to the river. The Thames drifted in front of him, a dark mass reflecting streaks of orange light from the setting sun. He followed a shingle path, keeping the water to his left. He had no idea what to do, where to go or who to turn to. All he could think of was the betrayal. George had ruined everything. Hadn't he considered the impact of his reckless announcement? Frederick thought they were friends. How could George not care? Could he really have been living a lie for the past ten years?

Hot tears gushed from his eyes, and he dashed them away with his fingers. He couldn't go back.

Running hard on the deserted path by the river, Frederick thought about George's devastating revelation. No, it couldn't be true. His name was Blomberg; his father was William Blomberg. The King had referred to his friend many times with sorrow at his death. But he had been very kind to him in a fatherly way. Then there were all those references to his similarity to George. He had learnt to shrug that off. Yet why had Coaty chosen to tell George and not him? Was she like the rest of them and had never been truthful? Everyone knew that Coaty liked to drink. Throughout his childhood at Richmond, he had smelt brandy on her breath.

Slowing down, Frederick tramped along the riverbank, spotting a jetty in the distance crowded with moored barges. Drawing closer, he could see that they were owned by Henry Thrale's Anchor Brewery and loaded with dozens of empty wooden barrels. The water lapped at the boats' sides. Noticing a small gap in the layers of barrels, a plan entered his mind. Checking there was nobody to see him, he stepped from the jetty onto a barge, which rocked slightly. Picking his way through the barrels, he found the gap and wriggled into it. The space was not comfortable, but it was dry, dark and unseen. He didn't want to go back to the Princes' House, ever. Burrowing into that space, he gave way to more tears, consumed by misery. A tawny owl on a nearby tree hooted whilst rats scuttled in the watery sump of the boat.

Frederick awoke to a moving boat, hearing the clop of the horse pulling it and guttural yells of the brewery men. Peeping through the barrels, he saw the riverbank drifting by. Beyond the towpath he noticed brick walls, buildings, trees, crowds of people and heard the sound of metal-clad wheels on cobbles, shouting, talking and children crying. He smelt food cooking, horse dung and rotten vegetables. And, most of all, he smelled the strong stink of old ale mixed with urine. Pulling himself out of his nook, he looked around. Had he slept all the way to central London?

"Oi," cried one of the men in a leather apron. "Wot you doing on board?"

"I fell asleep."

"Ooh, mister la-di-da," he replied, looking Frederick up and down. Glancing at his blue silk breeches, buttoned under the knee, and white stockings, Frederick realised he was still wearing his party clothes. He tugged down the frilled cuff of his white linen shirt and buttoned the embroidered waistcoat beneath his best three-quarter-length red jacket. Knowing he must look absurd, he stood up straight and re-tied his cravat.

"I've come from Kew," he said. "Very sorry. I didn't realise. Where are we?"

"Southwark, mate, by the brewery. You better hop it before the gaffer spots you. We don't tolerate stowaways."

"Apologies. I did not mean to take advantage."

"Get away wiv ya."

Frederick clambered over the barrels and hopped off the boat onto the cobbled landing. All around him were piles of barrels stacked outside the warehouses, presumably ready to make the return trip to Kew. He pondered going back. No, he could not.

"Thank you, sir."

"Oo, er, mister macaroni. You're very welcome, me lud. Now be off wiv yer."

Frederick walked around the giant building, staring up at the tall chimneys spewing yeasty steam. His smart black shoes topped with ribbon pom-poms were pinching his feet as he made his way along the cobbled streets. All around him people were travelling by horse, on foot, in coaches, in sedan chairs, running, skipping or staggering with a stick. He had been to the centre of London before but never to this area. On earlier visits he had travelled by carriage to places like St James's Palace or Buckingham House, always with the protection of equerries and pages to escort him.

Frederick thought about his situation objectively. He was in a place he did not know, dressed in party clothes, with no money and no plan. He might be regarded as a gentleman or an aristocrat – he looked and spoke like one – but gentlemen generally had money; they might have a cane, a sword and a hat. He had nothing.

Looking towards the sun in the east, he spun round a few times to get his bearings. In front of him he could see church towers and an idea popped into his head; he could ask for help from a cleric and then decide what to do. Picking his way through the crowded streets and narrow alleyways, he noticed the curious glances and sniggers behind cupped hands but pressed on. The vast church rose up in front of him – Southwark Cathedral. Surely some man of the cloth in the church would be able to help?

Frederick pushed through the heavy wooden doors into the gloom. Gazing up at the ceiling, his eyes followed the curved columns soaring upwards and joining at the top of the roof like hands in prayer. People wandered in and out of the cathedral, chatting and calling to each other. He picked his way past baskets filled with live ducks and hens and piles of beer barrels like the ones he had slept amongst.

"Good morning, stranger," said a man in a black cassock, who approached him. "Are you joining the party? They're about to leave."

"What party?"

"The pilgrimage to Canterbury. They are preparing to set off later this morning. Though, with respect, you might consider bringing some suitable travelling clothes."

Frederick absorbed this information; a trip to Canterbury in Kent, yes, that's where he should go. Then he should be able to find his way to Laing Farm where Aunt Margaret and Harriet lived. They had often written about trips to Canterbury for the market and Harriet had attended a convent in the city.

"How long will it take to get there?"

"On foot you should do it in a week, maybe ten days. Some of the pilgrims take their horses and even a cart. They need their comforts no matter how strong their faith."

"Would they let me join them? The thing is, I have no money."

"I see. Well, sir, can I offer you ale and some bread?"

"I'd be most grateful, thank you."

Frederick watched the kindly cleric disappear into a room at the side of the cathedral, returning with a flagon of small beer and a loaf of bread.

"Not fresh, as you can tell, but we appreciate the brewer and baker's charity and like to hand it on. Sir, if you are considering joining the party, then you should make your way to the Tabard Inn. It's on Borough High Street, just across the road from here. You'll see the travellers gathering. Return the flagon to this shelf when you've finished."

Frederick took the bread and flagon and thanked the priest. Leaving the church, he sat down on a low wall in the graveyard. The sun had risen higher, warming his back. The stale bread tasted gritty and dirty, filling the void in his stomach, and the beer was watery but welcome. Frederick started to feel better. On this bright sunny morning in London, for the first time in his life, he was in charge of his destiny and had a plan.

Chapter Twelve
Frederick's Flight
13th August 1775

By noon, his feet hurt. He'd only been walking for a few hours, but his fine shoes were rubbing the skin on his ankle, and his big toes poked through holes growing in his stockings. Joining the group at the Tabard Inn, he felt full of purpose at the prospect of walking to Canterbury with them. People chatted and laughed, comparing the weight of the packs slung across their backs. Pilgrims' carts groaned with baskets of bread, fruit, great kegs of beer and flagons of water. The atmosphere was jolly and far from religious.

Whilst his stomach was full of the poor quality bread, Frederick was happy to be travelling. But, after hours trudging along the uneven paths, he was hungry again and realised he'd not thought this plan through properly. For the first time in his life, he was independent, but he needed money. He pictured the stash of coins, and the precious golden guinea from Coaty, lying in the box below his bed at the Princes' House. He could not go back for it now.

Walking through the outskirts of London, he could still hear the distinct thrum of the city, a mix of shouts, horses' hooves, hammering, the noise mingling with the clattering of carts and carriages making their way up and down the route he walked along. Travelling further from the centre, the clamour faded, and buildings started to thin out with gaps of fields and copses between them. Behind him, the skyline revealed a jumble of rooftops and church spires, in front of him lay farmland, rolling hills and woods.

The August day was warm, so he took off his silk jacket, revealing the embroidered waistcoat. From nowhere, it seemed, the driver of a passing cart shouted 'whoa', tugging his horse's reins to come to a halt. The driver jumped from his seat and approached Frederick. The man's face was black, and the whites of his eyes glowed from his dark features. Frederick jumped away from him, alarmed at the man's sudden approach.

"Fine clothes you're wearing," he said, looking Frederick up and down. "Not the usual dress for a trip like this."

"I decided on impulse to make the pilgrimage," said Frederick, noting that this man was considerably taller than him and resembled the dark-skinned servants he used to see around St James's Palace and Richmond Lodge. Was this man a threat or just being friendly? Frederick was not used to being addressed so directly by a lower-class person. He decided that good manners would be his best policy. "Sir," he began, "do you often travel towards London?"

"All the time, with my trusty steed," he said, pointing to his exhausted-looking horse. "Not on foot, oh no."

"Travelling by cart must be a lot easier. My feet are sore."

They both looked at Frederick's dainty shoes, now filthy with dust.

"I'll buy that off you," said the man, pointing to Frederick's waistcoat. "You've got the Prince of Wales feathers embroidered into the design. It's the sort of thing you'd see the royals wearing at court but unusual for round here."

Frederick looked down at his waistcoat. He'd never bothered to examine the design before. Oh yes, it did have the three feathers sewn into the motif. He'd seen feathers on so many objects around Richmond and Kew that he'd stopped noticing them.

"What will you pay me for it?"

"Ten shillings for the waistcoat and the jacket too."

Frederick bit his lower lip. Here was a helpful offer and he needed money. But he wasn't sure that he could trust this strange-looking man. His accent was a curious mixture of a working-class Londoner mixed with lengthened vowels from the palace drawing rooms. Frederick tried looking confident but knew his face showed discomfort.

"Sir, you haven't got a sou about you, have you?" the man said, softening his voice.

"No, I didn't come out with any money," Frederick replied, shaking his head and running his fingers through his hair. "But it would be useful to have some. Where does everyone stay overnight on these journeys to Canterbury?"

"There are inns, a couple of priories, one or two private houses," replied the man, pointing vaguely in the direction of travel away from the city. "You have to pay for them though."

"Yes, of course. And would ten shillings be enough to pay for a room, or bed, at one of these places?"

"Yes and no. You'll need some food too."

"So how much money will I need?"

"I'd say at least two pounds to get there."

"Thank you. I will sell my jacket and waistcoat to you."

The young man shook his head and grinned. "You're not a man of the world, that's for sure." He laughed, patting his horse on the flanks.

"Sir, please tell me," Frederick began, "how did you know about the Prince of Wales feathers design?"

"Well, it's not that uncommon. We've had that many Princes of Wales, and they're all called George, it seems. But I have actually met the King."

"Have you?" Frederick was intrigued.

"Not this king, the one before, his grandfather, George II. I used to work at St James's Palace and Leicester House."

"Really! I… know it too." Frederick was about to reveal his connection but resisted.

"I was a page to Princess Augusta."

"The mother of King George III, our monarch?"

"Yes, I worked there when I was five or six years old. They dressed me up in a turban and I brought tea into the drawing room. I had a pearl earring." He indicated the hole in his right ear where it had been. "They also made me wear a thick gold collar which was cold and heavy. I could never look down properly. And I wore a red and gold trimmed jacket. It had a lace frill at the neck and cuffs, like yours, with a matching waistcoat. That's why I asked. I was sorry when Prince Frederick died before he could be king. You probably know this, but his father, George II, hated him; they didn't talk or see each other. And Prince Frederick hated his own son too, the George who's now king, and he hated him back."

"Our king hated his father?" Frederick had to bite his lip not to smile at the coincidence. "Sir, what is your name? We should be better acquainted if you are going to buy my clothing from me."

"I'm Raphael. I don't have a surname. I don't know my parents. So I call myself Raphael Page, for that is what I was."

"And I am Frederick Blomberg. Pleased to meet you." They shook hands.

"So, now we've done the introductions, we should complete the transaction," said Raphael. "I can only sell these fine things of yours in London."

"And that's where you are headed?"

"I am. I will give you a half guinea for the two garments. I might catch up with you in a few days' time when I've turned a profit on these and head back to Canterbury."

Raphael pulled four half crowns from his leather pouch, plus a few small coins, and placed them in Frederick's palm. Pushing the coins into his breeches pocket, Frederick took off his silk jacket and waistcoat, shivering a little as a breeze blew through his fine white shirt. Folding his arms over his chest, he told himself he needed money more than clothing.

"Why did you leave your work with the royal family?" he asked.

"I grew," said Raphael with a shrug. "They liked having little boys as pages and I became too tall." Frederick looked up at his broad shoulders and nodded his understanding.

"I was nine years old when they chucked me out of service to Princess Augusta," continued Raphael. "I didn't have any family, not that I knew of. Palace life was all I'd known and leaving St James's was hard at first. They put me into service with a tailor who did work for the royals. Very fine work. That's why I recognise quality stuff when I see it."

Frederick wanted to hear more of Raphael's story, but he could see his new acquaintance was eager to head towards London. Raphael took Frederick's jacket and waistcoat, folded the clothing into his pack and slung it over his shoulder. Waving cheerily, he turned on his heel and climbed back onto his cart.

Frederick carried on walking but kept glancing back down the London road every few minutes to catch sight of Raphael's cart until the view dwindled to a moving smudge. Frederick kept plodding on, loneliness overwhelming him. He had enjoyed the conversation with Raphael, especially since he sensed they had a great deal in common. He was now a solitary traveller with no clear vision of his journey or where it might end. He had left behind a cossetted world of food and drink and the company of people who probably despised him now. Why hadn't he seen himself as others did? Why hadn't he worked out his true identity and the reason why he was so often called the *cuckoo in the nest*? It was obvious that everyone else knew; they must have known the whole time. He cast his mind back to the sniggering, whispering and the hurtful cuffs, pinches and swipes. Yes, the truth had been apparent all the time. What a fool he had been.

Frederick pressed on, running for a while to warm up, then slowing to a steady walk. He approached a straggling group of pilgrims who'd been ahead of him, but they seemed merry and self-sufficient and not interested in talking to a stray boy who attached himself to their party. His craving for company surprised him and being alone made him nervous; Frederick realised how ignorant he was of the world.

By late afternoon, the sun was beginning its descent towards the west, and he overheard the group discussing plans to stop soon.

They tramped into the town of Dartford and Frederick trailed after them into the cobbled courtyard of The Crown. Carts and carriages emptied then filled again with people on the move.

After negotiating a bed and a meal for the night at a cost of three shillings, he handed over two of his precious crowns and pocketed the change. Embarrassed that he had no luggage, no extra clothing and no personal effects, he spent a quiet evening in a corner of the inn eating as much roast mutton and potatoes as he could fit on his plate. Bedding down on a straw-stuffed mattress in an attic room, with just a scratchy blanket to protect him from the night air blowing through an open window, he slept fitfully.

By the following morning the weather had changed, and the day was cloudy and cool. A stiff breeze carried the first drops of rain. Flags flapped on top of poles and wisps of straw and chaff skittered across the road.

Examining his money, he made a decision. He could afford an outside seat on one of the stagecoaches heading for Rochester, although that would leave little money for food. After paying four shillings to the driver, he climbed up onto the top of the coach, feeling very unsafe and exposed. He envied the travellers sitting inside the carriage out of the rain, remembering that in his old world that would have been his rightful place. With equal envy he looked at the men wearing waxed greatcoats and women in thick cloaks and broad hats. Rain spattered over him, soaking his linen shirt. Taking pity on him, the coach driver threw him a coarse woollen blanket for his shoulders. Flanked by a large woman clutching a basket of eggs and a young man with missing teeth who whistled tunelessly and sniffed constantly, Frederick wiped the rain from his eyes and hunkered down between his fellow passengers. Creaking and groaning, the great coach began its journey out of Dartford, into the countryside and east towards Rochester.

Dozing, Frederick dreamt he was running through the park at Kew with Jupiter at his side, but he was jolted awake each time the carriage stopped at the many towns and villages along the route. By the time he reached Rochester, Frederick was soaked through and shivering, with water dripping from his nose to his chest. Climbing down from the carriage, he heard his shoes squelch when he stood up in them and the driver refused his offer to hand back the sopping blanket, telling him to keep it.

It had taken all day to get to Rochester. The town was large and busy, and Frederick had no idea where he should stay. He felt in both his pockets for his money. It had gone! How? Why? Then he remembered the whistling boy who had sat next to him and the ill-tempered woman with the eggs who had sworn under her breath for the whole journey. Whilst perched up on the coach, he had appreciated the closeness of their bodies as he slept. One of them, or both, must have burrowed into his pockets and found the money. All that remained was a shilling, a tiny sixpence and two farthings. He felt sick, weak and desperate.

These limited funds were not going to get him all the way to Canterbury. He must find shelter and try to dry himself. The landlord of an inn eyed him with suspicion as he entered. Frederick handed him the sixpence and asked for bread and cheese and a pint of small-beer. He crouched on a stool as close to the fire as he dared, his clothes and blanket steaming in the heat. At closing time he stumbled out into the darkened streets. Where to sleep? He picked his way down some steps in front of a shop and found a man already curled up on a pallet in the basement, snarling at him to be off and find his own billet. Some distant memory stirred. His father, his name father, William Blomberg, had some connection with Rochester. Oh yes, he'd married his mother, Melissa, in this town. Was there an army billet somewhere?

Staggering along the dark streets until the buildings grew sparse, he came upon a woodshed. There was no one in sight and no lights in any windows of the homes nearby. Pulling open the door, he saw piles of cut logs waiting for the stove. Creeping further into the space, he found he was able to wriggle between two piles of coarse kindling when, to his horror, the fabric of his breeches snagged on something and ripped. He couldn't see the damage in the dark but knew that he'd torn his breeches from the buttons at his knee to the top of his thigh. He burrowed into the space, pulling the damp blanket around his shoulders. Cold, hungry and miserable, he dozed until the sound of a cockerel crowing roused him and he crawled out of his hiding place.

By the light of dawn, he could see that his silk breeches were ruined and his upper thigh exposed to the air. All he could do was drape the damp blanket over his right arm and hope that nobody would see. Retracing his steps back to the high street, he saw a basket of windfall apples by the gate of a house. He took one, biting into it, and, grabbing as many as he could carry, munched through them all. Anyone seeing him would regard him as a peasant or vagrant, never believing that he was the son of a king who, had circumstances been different, might have become heir to the throne. No, he must dismiss that idea, remove all thought of his previous life and now live on his wits.

Frederick wandered the streets until he spotted The Bull Inn. He'd heard the pilgrims talk about the place as an overnight stop. He took a deep breath and ventured inside. Serving women were busy wiping tables, sweeping the flagstones and stoking the fire in the great fireplace. As he sat down on a stool close to the warmth, one of the women nudged his feet with her brush. "Be off with you," she hissed. "We don't want beggars here."

"I'm not a beggar," he replied, in his politest accent. She looked at him through narrowed eyes.

"Then what are you, in fancy dress?"

"I'm lost and I was robbed whilst travelling here."

"Oh, I see. We get a lot of that."

"I need to get to Canterbury."

"Right, well, you can get the post, but it'll cost yer and I'd hazard you're skint."

"Could I do something, some work to earn money?"

"With your dainty hands, I don't think so. What are you good at?"

"I play musical instruments."

"Do you, now?" Eyes widening with interest, she wiped her hands on her apron.

"Well, my husband, the master of the inn, might be interested in that. We've got a wedding here later today and the fiddler's gone missing. Can you play a jig?"

"I don't know. I can play work by Handel, Bach, Mozart, some earlier works by…"

"No, lad, it's jigs they want. They want to dance. Here, let me fetch the fiddle we keep, and you show me what you can do."

After a few moments the woman returned bearing an old violin and a bow with broken horsehairs.

"Go on," she said, "play something we can dance to."

Frederick thought for a moment and then an air for a gavotte popped into his brain. Feeling for the right position on the fret, he pressed the strings and scraped a few notes to gauge the tone of the instrument. After tuning a couple of the strings, he started playing, half remembering and half making up the melody. The woman beamed as she tapped her foot in time with the music, patting the side of her skirt.

"Reckon you'll do. Can you stay here for the day and play all night?"

"Yes, but I do need something to wear." He showed her the gash in the fabric.

Tapping a finger to her lips, she bustled into a room at the back, returning with a pair of worn black breeches and a fresh white shirt. She then produced a green jacket with large pockets which, when he tried it on, swamped his small frame but looked presentable. "These were left behind by guests and will serve you well enough.

What a shame about these fine things," she added, fingering the lacy cuff of his shirt.

"Will I be paid?"

"Yes, and you can have your dinner on the house. I'll set you up with a mattress in the attic. I'll find some old boots for you too. Those fancy shoes have had it."

"Thank you, madam," said Frederick, bowing.

"Aren't you a la-di-da type. Takes all sorts round here. I'm Jenny, by the way. I run this place, but don't tell my husband."

Nervous at the prospect of performing at a wedding, and having no idea what to expect, Frederick took the fiddle to the courtyard at the back of the inn and practised a few tunes. Jenny came out to him with a slice of cold pie and sat down next to him on a bench.

"Where did you learn to play that thing?"

"I was…" Frederick hesitated. "I had a music tutor at my home. And I gave concerts with my fellow students."

"Then why are you here?"

"I'm travelling."

"Yeah, yeah. Young gents like you don't just turn up out of nowhere. You on the run?"

"You could say that. There was a family argument, and I left."

"Hmm, reckon there's more to it than that, but I won't press you. So, are you ready for the wedding?"

"I think I am. Will you tell me when to start? I've not played at a wedding before."

"No, didn't think you had. You'll be fine. You're a good fiddler and they'll all be too merry from ale to notice if you miss a note or play the same tune."

"Thank you, Jenny."

"You're welcome. You've helped me too. I'll show you where you can stay. It's not smart, not what I think you're used to, but you'll be safe here."

Chapter Thirteen
Frederick's Journey Continues
Late August 1775

After spending a week at The Bull in Rochester, Frederick felt established and had become a popular figure in the dining salon, playing for the visitors whilst they ate their dinners, sat in chairs or gathered on benches around the fireplace.

One evening, after hearing Frederick play, a plump woman with a leathery face shuffled towards him whilst he was resting between performances. "I likes yer music," she said. "I heard you playing last night to the guests and came back specially to talk to you. My name's Mary and I'm with the pickers. Will you come to the hop gardens and play for us? We pick during the day and then gather in the fields after work. We could do with a tune."

Frederick had no idea what she was talking about. "Hop gardens, pickers?"

"Everyone's come down from London to pick 'em, but there'd be work for a strong young man like you, and good pay."

He gazed at her, not understanding.

"Oh Lordy, I can see you've never heard of 'em." Pushing her fingers into her bag, she drew out a small handful of tiny dried-up blooms, each one about the size of his thumbnail, rubbing them together and holding fragments for him to sniff. Leaning forward, he smelt the distinctive aroma of earth combined with green leaves.

"It's the hops that gives ale its flavour. Harvest goes on for weeks and they're dried in the oast houses then sold to the brewers. I likes to keep some by and stuffs them in me pillow," she said. "They helps me sleep. But, after a day in the hop gardens picking yer bushels, you'll always sleep well. Come and join us. We have good parties in the evening, and we'd pay you to play."

"Where do you stay?" Frederick was interested in this woman's proposal but unsure whether he was ready to leave the relative security of the inn. Jenny had assured him that, if he wished, he could stay at The Bull until the autumn.

"We have a barn and some tents," said Mary. "Some of the travellers bring their covered wagons and sleep in those. If you come with me now, we can meet the hop farmer, and he'll sign you up as a worker. You'll earn sixpence a bushel, and if you're fit and quick, you can make three shillings a day. Then you can play for the pickers after work and earn more."

Playing for guests at the inn each evening had given him confidence. He was sure of a bed for the night and a meal each day, but he was not earning enough money to pay for a coach to Canterbury. Hop picking sounded like an opportunity for more lucrative employment and it would be a new experience. Frederick agreed to come.

Discussing this offer with Jenny, she understood his need for more funds and agreed that he should go with Mary to join the hop picking and allowed him to take the fiddle with him on the understanding that he return in a few weeks' time to The Bull to play at another wedding. Gathering up his few possessions and carefully wrapping the violin in a cloth sack, Frederick followed Mary to her cart and made the journey deep into the rolling countryside.

Approaching the hop gardens, Frederick stared in astonishment at a large field alive with human activity, resembling bees besieging a flowering shrub. He could see row upon row of A-shaped poles, lashed together with ropes, garlanded by vines of hops hanging down in swags.

Muscular men with rolled-up sleeves used long sticks with hooks to snag the vines, pulling them down to the ground where they lay at the base of the pointy frames. Then, into these rows, pickers trundled linked cribs, moving slowly through the arches filling them with hop florets.

Old women with sunburnt faces sat on stools whilst younger

women stood, chatting as they pulled the vines through their fists, stripping the florets and watching them fall into hessian bags inside the cribs.

Loud male shouts mingled with women's laughter and shrieks from children who ran barefoot through the gardens, whilst babies howled in baskets or slept, lashed to their mothers' backs. Everyone was working hard, yet there was a party atmosphere.

Frederick joined the men and learnt how to hook down the vines, dumping them on the ground, ready for the pickers to gather. Then, he took his turn to strip the hops he had felled, feeling the abrasion of tiny cuts on his tender hands. With satisfaction, he lugged filled sacks onto a handcart, pulling the hops to the oast houses to be weighed and dried.

At the end of the day, families and workers gathered around a bonfire in a nearby meadow. Women prepared food whilst men sat on logs around the fire, drinking ale and smoking pipes. Frederick's nose tingled in anticipation at the smell of lamb roasting on a spit and he watched women pushing potatoes into the edge of the crackling fire to bake. Mounds of ripe tomatoes were sliced onto plates, and strawberries, picked in a nearby field, filled wooden bowls placed on trestle tables.

"Come on, Master Fred," called Mary. "Come and sit down. You've earned your dinner, then we want to hear you play." She patted a space next to her on the smooth log by the fire. Rubbing his hands, he hoped his battered fingers would have the strength to find their way around the fret of the fiddle. His face was burnt red from a day in the sun and his body ached, but he was happy with the work he had done and the shillings he had pocketed. Now, he was pleased to join these people as they feasted and caroused.

Taking out the borrowed fiddle, he entertained the pickers with jaunty tunes as the sky grew darker, the moon rose and stars appeared. Later he followed the weary workers to a nearby barn and lay down in the hay. After resting his head upon his rolled-up jacket and pulling a blanket over his shoulders, he sniffed a few stray hops before pushing them into his pocket, sleeping more deeply than he had ever slept in his life.

*

After five weeks, the hop gardens were empty, and the pickers prepared to return to work in London or carry on harvesting apples and pears from orchards nearby.

Frederick travelled back to The Bull at Rochester with Mary where he bade her farewell and jumped down from the cart. He was pleased to see Jenny, tell her about his experiences and return the fiddle. Spending two further weeks at the inn, he played for the wedding and each evening for the guests in the dining salon, once again enjoying the response of the delighted audience.

One morning, in late September, he packed up his things and prepared to leave. Thanking Jenny, he promised to return one day and pay for the clothing she had given him. Jenny roared with laughter at the idea of him ever returning, grabbing him by the shoulders and giving him two smacking kisses on each cheek. Frederick blushed and was sorry to be leaving this friendly place. He knew he could easily have stayed, but he needed to keep moving and find his family, his real family. It was time to travel to Canterbury.

Hop picking and fiddle playing had earned him enough money to continue his journey. Following Mary's advice, he bought a loaf of bread and a slab of Cheddar cheese. After eating the dough, he pushed the cheese inside the crust and wrapped it in a cloth, happy to know that the food would sustain him for a day's travel.

Paying the coach driver, he climbed up to the top seat of the carriage. The journey was long, and his hipbones ached on the hard, high seat. Making sure that his money stayed in the deepest recesses of his pockets, he struck up conversation with his fellow travellers, determined not to fall asleep no matter how pleasant they appeared or how tired he felt.

Towards evening, after several stops at towns and villages along the route, the stagecoach clattered to a halt in Canterbury. Frederick gazed up at the ancient cathedral towers soaring above the roofs of the jumbled buildings surrounding it. Remembering to shake hands with the driver, he offered him a couple of small coins from his modest cache and looked around, breathing in the city, savouring the aromas of wood-smoke and cooked food. Having travelled this far, he was not sure exactly where Laing Farm was, so he decided to stay at an inn and ask for directions in the morning.

The late September warmth was ebbing away. In the sky to the south, he could see dark clouds spreading and the whiff of rain became stronger. As the first drops started falling, he rushed for cover under the awning of a haberdashery. Peering through the shop window, a thought occurred to him. He was going to see Aunt Margaret and Cousin Harriet for the first time in ten years. Jingling the coins in his pocket, he calculated that he might have enough to buy them a present. The serving girls in the shop were tidying up and preparing to close when he entered. Picking up the pretty ribbons, lace and trimmings, which he knew women loved to adorn their hats and headdresses with, he asked the price, gasping at the cost. Resolute, he chose twelve inches of fine lace and a yard of embroidered ribbon. Handing over the money, he proudly received the packet, wrapped in a linen cloth and tied with string. Leaving the shop with a spring in his step, he anticipated the pleasure he would feel giving these gifts to the women he loved.

Turning down a side street and walking towards an inn, he was about to enter when he felt a great blow to his head. Stumbling forward and putting out his hands to save the fall, the package slipped from his grasp. He crashed down upon the stone step of the pub doorway, hitting his forehead. As he tried to pull himself up, strong hands grasped him, raising him to his knees and pinning his arms behind his back. A man's hand delved into the pockets of his breeches. Frederick was conscious enough to know that he was being robbed as he was roughly shoved back to the ground, lying there, too dazed to move or cry out.

Gingerly picking himself up and standing unsteadily near the pub door, he felt blood pouring down his face. Raising his hand to his forehead, he wiped the gash, but the blood kept coming. He felt in his pocket for something to staunch the flow. Nothing. Then he spotted the precious package of lace and ribbon nearby and in despair grabbed it, holding it to his head.

Shocked by the sudden assault, and sick from the blow to the back of his head, he staggered back into the main street, slumping onto a bench outside the cathedral, below a buttress offering slight protection from the rain. He tilted his head back, staring up at the darkening sky. Lifting the package from his wound, he saw that it was soaked with his blood. How could he ever give this gift now?

Nobody stopped to offer help. Frederick was not sure how long he sat on the bench, but hearing the cathedral bell toll eight, he knew he must find shelter before nightfall. His head hurt and misery overwhelmed him. He might have arrived in Canterbury with money and a plan, but now he had become a penniless boy again with a serious head wound.

Recovering enough to get up from the bench, he approached a woman dragging a small cart loaded with bundles, asking her if she knew the way to Laing Farm. Shuddering at the sight of him and shaking her head, she moved away as fast as she could. He stopped a man in a black coat with a clergyman's collar, who peered down his long nose at him, swatting him away like a fly.

Finally Frederick spotted the town crier preparing to call the evening's news. He approached him, asking directions to Laing Farm. The crier recoiled at first at the sight of the bloodied young man but knew the place. Pointing to a street leading out to the west of the city, he told him it was about five miles along that road and then a left turn at the sign to Chartham.

No longer having any money to pay for a room or hire a horse, Frederick decided to take his chances upon the road and walk to the farmhouse. He told himself that he should be able to find it before midnight, hopefully earlier. Still dazed and feeling sick from the assault, he pulled up the collar of his jacket and set off down the road, stumbling like a drunken man. Men on horseback, carriages and carts passed him on the road. He glanced up at a few of the travellers, but the drivers, seeing his battered state, looked away, clicking their cheeks and shaking the reins to hasten their horse onwards. Pelting rain soaked Frederick to the skin; shivering and miserable, he plodded on.

After a couple of hours, a cart drew up next to him. "Whoa," cried the driver. "Sir, halt. I will give you a lift."

Frederick stopped, his body swaying as he looked at the cart and at the driver, then, with a start of recognition, he saw that it was Raphael. He was so happy to see a familiar face that tears mingled with the raindrops on his face.

Jumping down from his cart, Raphael held out his hand and Frederick grabbed it.

"Raphael, it's really you. I can't believe it."

"Master Frederick Blomberg, what are you doing out alone and in this condition? Where are you headed?"

"I'm looking for Laing Farm. I was told it's down a turning to the left, after Chartham."

"Then that's where we'll go."

Raphael helped Frederick climb into the cart, pulling his drenched coat around his chest. Delving into the box below his seat, Raphael drew out a small glass bottle, pulled out the cork with his teeth and handed it to Frederick, who took a small swig. He did not care for brandy but could feel its warming strength coursing through his body. Raphael took a bigger swig, re-corked it then set it back in the box. He then drew out a ragged cloth and shook it, suggesting Frederick should clean his face.

"Sir, what happened?" asked Raphael, glancing at Frederick as he dabbed at the wound with the cloth, using rainwater to mop away the dried blood.

"I was robbed. Two men, I think. It happened so fast and now all my money's gone."

"That money for those clothes lasted this long?"

"No," replied Frederick, wincing at the pain of his injury as he laughed. "I was robbed of that earlier."

"Oh, you poor fellow, you are a stranger in this world."

"Don't you ever get robbed?" asked Frederick.

"Oh yes, but I'm used to it. You recognise who is likely to do you wrong, or right. Besides, I have learnt to use my fists and understand the ways of the street."

"Well, I have no idea," said Frederick, rubbing his face. "But I am very grateful that you saw me, and that you stopped. Why are you going this way?"

"I often come this way. I sold your clothes in London for a pleasant profit, stayed a few weeks and then decided to return to Canterbury. And, having finished my business, I thought I'd continue to Winchester to look for more business."

"Who did you sell my clothes to?"

"That I cannot reveal, but they will enjoy a good life on their new owner. Why d'you want to get to this farm?"

"It's my family home."

"And you don't know the way?"

"I've never been there."

Raphael whistled through his teeth and shook his head. "Well, here's the junction. Can you read what the sign says?"

"It's pointing to Laing Farm. Oh Raphael, we're almost there!"

Chapter Fourteen
Frederick Finds His Family
30th September 1775

Margaret had tidied away the cooking pots after dinner and was about to take the candle upstairs to her bedroom with a book to read when she heard the horse and cart clattering into the yard of Laing Farm. She called out to Uncle Charles, who'd been dozing by the fire in the parlour. He hurried into the kitchen and together they looked out of the window into the yard.

Signalling to Margaret to stand away from the door, he took down the sword from its hooks above the fireplace and, holding it in his right hand, opened the kitchen door with his left. Margaret peeped around him and, by the light of the flaming torch in the yard, saw two figures clamber off the cart, walking towards them.

"Stand back, Margaret," barked Uncle Charles. Holding his weapon in readiness, he shouted, "Who goes there?"

Frederick picked his way towards the light above the kitchen door. "Is my aunt Margaret there," he called, "or Harriet? It's me, Frederick Blomberg."

Margaret gasped and, pushing past her uncle, rushed outside towards the stumbling figure. "Fred, is that really you?" she cried, gazing at him, wide-eyed.

"Aunt Margaret, yes, yes, it's me. I've come from London. I wanted to find you."

"Oh Fred, it is you. You're injured. What's happened? Come in, come in."

Margaret grabbed Frederick's arm and drew him into the light and warmth of the farmhouse kitchen.

"Who are you?" demanded Uncle Charles, staring at Raphael, standing by the horse.

"I'm Raphael Page, sir," he replied, pulling his hat from his head.

"I brought the young lad to you. He was set upon in Canterbury and robbed. He needs help."

"I see," replied Uncle Charles, lowering his sword. "You'd better come in."

Raphael entered and stood by the door whilst Aunt Margaret bustled around the kitchen, lighting candles and shifting chairs. A young woman in a dressing gown crept down the stairs and peered around the door.

"Harriet," cried Aunt Margaret, "look, it's Fred!"

Harriet approached, picking up a candle from the table, holding it close to Frederick's face before setting it down and flinging her arms around him.

"Be careful of his wound, dear," said Aunt Margaret. "Let's get this looked at."

"Harriet," whispered Frederick. "I've wanted to see you for so long. Your letters, your drawings…"

"Shush, Fred," interrupted Aunt Margaret. "Right now I need to clean this wound and put a bandage around your head. Harriet will decide what sort of medicine we should give you. She knows more about these things than I do. But we must get you out of these wet clothes, washed and into bed."

"Thank you. But Aunt Margaret, this is Raphael. He brought me here." Raphael bowed, pressing himself against the closed door.

"Then, Master Raphael, we thank you kindly. I hope you will stay the night here too. We have dry clothes and a bed for you."

"Thank you, ma'am. I would rather stay in the stable."

"No, indeed, we cannot allow it. You've brought my beloved nephew here; you are our guest. Whilst I wash and dress this wound, Harriet will fetch some food for you both."

Margaret whispered to Harriet, who disappeared through a door to the larder, reappearing with a crock filled with soup. Emptying the contents into a pan, she set it on the hotplate and stoked the fire, adding more wood to encourage the flames.

"I want you both to have some bread and soup and then you must sleep. We can talk in the morning," said Aunt Margaret.

Frederick woke beneath fresh, clean sheets and looked around. Morning light streamed in through a lattice window and above him he could see rafters draped with a few vines of dried hops. Looking to his right, he saw Aunt Margaret seated by the bed.

"Good morning, Fred," she said, beaming with pleasure.

Frederick was overwhelmed with happiness to recognise a face he had not seen for over ten years. Her cheeks were ruddy from sunburn, and he noticed the fine lines around her eyes and mouth. He saw that her hair beneath her bonnet was still light brown but streaked with white. She was wearing a plain, rust-coloured dress and a cream shawl around her shoulders.

"How are you feeling, Fred?"

"My head still stings, but I feel better. Thank you for this." He indicated the bandage and closed his eyes. "Where's Raphael?"

"He's in the yard, tending his horse. He insisted on sleeping in the stable rather than the house, but Harriet has given him some breakfast. He wants to know that you're well before he sets off. I'll call him." Margaret went to the window overlooking the yard and opened it, calling Raphael's name.

Frederick tried to push up onto his elbows and then flopped back onto the pillows.

"Don't move. He will come up and see you."

Raphael entered the room, grinning at Frederick, who had managed to sit up. "You look a lot better now, sir."

"I feel much better, Raphael. You saved my life."

"It must have been God's will that I followed that path and was able to help you."

"Perhaps it was," agreed Frederick. "Are you leaving now?"

"Yes, I have business in Winchester."

"How can I repay you?"

"You don't have to. Glad to have helped."

"I do want to, in some way."

"No, it was nothing. I might call by on my return journey?"

"I should like that," said Frederick, holding out his hand, and Raphael shook it.

"Look out for yourself, good sir. Don't let yourself be robbed again."

Frederick heard his steps tramping down the stairs and felt tears pricking at his eyes.

"Now, Fred," said Aunt Margaret, "you won't be surprised to learn that I've had a letter from Mrs Cotesworth. She and all the royal family have been beside themselves with worry. What happened? Did you mean to run away like that?"

Frederick lay back on the pillow, picturing that dreadful dinner and George's revelation. "Aunt Margaret, did you know that the King was my real father?"

Aunt Margaret lowered her eyes before looking directly at him. "Yes, I did."

"Why did no one tell me?"

"Fred, you were not yet four years old when you went to live at Richmond. You couldn't have understood."

"You might have told me in a letter, Aunt Margaret. I've spent ten years not knowing. Yet, others knew. Coaty, Mrs Cotesworth, she knew?"

"Yes, she knew."

"I suppose lots of people knew. Everyone. Oh, I feel such a fool. I kept hearing people say how much I looked like the Prince of Wales. I do. But it never occurred to me that we are actually half-brothers."

"Fred, I have to let Mrs Cotesworth know that you are safe. She needs to know you are here."

Frederick nodded. "I'm not going back."

"I understand how you feel, but you may not be free to decide."

"How can I return? I've no place there. You've no idea what's it's been like, Aunt Margaret. I've had weeks to think about this and now I understand that I was never a proper member of the family. I thought I was William Blomberg's son, the King's best friend, and that's why they adopted me. But I'm not. Turns out I am the King's son but was never treated like his true son."

Frederick's eyes filled with tears, his chest heaved, and he gave way to pent-up grief. He no longer cared that he was crying. Floodgates opened, the stress of the last few weeks pouring out with his tears.

Chewing her thumb, Aunt Margaret nodded her head and patted his arm, waiting until he had calmed down. "Fred, you've been through so much. We don't need to make any decisions at the moment. I'm so glad to see you and happy that you're now safe and well. I know Harriet is eager to talk to you and we both want to hear about the life you've been living and the journey you've just made. Do you realise you've been missing for seven weeks?"

"What date is it?"

"It's September the thirtieth."

"And George's thirteenth birthday party was on August the twelfth. He was cruel to me. I don't understand why he did it."

"And you're fourteen now. You missed your own birthday."

Wiping his eyes, Frederick said, "I feel a lot older now than when I left Kew. Where's Harriet?"

"She's finishing the milking and then she'll be up to see you. I've done my best to clean your clothes. Where did you get these?" Margaret indicated the old green jacket, worn breeches and frayed white shirt. "And I found this in the pocket of your jacket." She drew out the blood-soaked linen package containing the ribbon and lace.

"It's a present for you and Harriet."

"You spent your money on us!" Aunt Margaret patted the package. "Shall I open it?"

"Yes, but now it's covered in blood."

Aunt Margaret undid the string and peeled open the linen

covering, drawing out the lengths of lace and ribbon.

"The lace is for you and the ribbon for Harriet. I thought you'd like them."

"Oh, my dearest boy, you were so kind to think of us. I will wash them carefully and they'll be lovely."

Chapter Fifteen
A New Opportunity
October 1775

From Mrs Cotesworth, Dover Street, London
To Mrs Poulton, Laing Farm, Kent
7th October 1775

My dear Mrs Poulton,

You cannot conceive of the relief I felt on receiving your letter. We are all so pleased to hear that Master Frederick is safe and well and has found his family. Your account of his flight from London filled us with horror. He has endured so much, and we know how unprepared he was for life beyond the palace walls. It appears he has learnt something of the kindness of strangers as well as the evil ways of men. I have often viewed the royal palace as a gilded cage. It does not prepare its young people for the ways of the world.

The Prince of Wales has been particularly anxious to know that Master Frederick is safe. I was not present at the birthday banquet, but I gather, from those who were, that he was most dreadfully rude to the King, the Queen and to Frederick. He has told me that he wants to make amends. The King and the Queen are also anxious for news of Frederick.

The King has commanded that Master Frederick should return to his care. Now, I know from your letter that Frederick has expressed his views on this. However, until he is of age, we, his guardians, must make decisions for him.

In consideration of all that has happened, I would like to make a proposal – to formally adopt Frederick and become his guardian. In the years that he has been in my care, I have come to love him dearly and believe he holds me in his affection too. I have funds, inherited from my family and from other sources. My service as a governess to the royal children has been terminated. However, my pension will be equal to the

salary I formerly received. I would like to welcome Frederick to live with
me in my house in Dover Street where he will continue his education and,
in due course, decide what the future may hold for him.

In view of the separation from Frederick you and Harriet have
endured for the past ten years, I would like invite you both to live with
me. My house is large with three servants. I should like to help Harriet
prepare herself for the future. It may benefit her marriage prospects if
she were to understand the ways of the court and be presented to society.

Their Royal Majesties are anxious that Master Frederick should
continue to enjoy the position in society to which he has become accustomed,
and to which he is entitled.

I will arrive at Laing Farm on 20th October. I expect to take Master
Frederick, but also hope that you and Harriet will return to London with
me. We will make one overnight stop at Rochester.

Yours sincerely,
Mrs Cotesworth (Henrietta)

Frederick was impressed by the confidence with which Harriet tended the gash on his forehead and surprised when she gathered cobwebs from the barn, placing them over the wound, assuring him that this was a trusted country remedy to mend broken skin. She brewed Shepherd's Purse tea to help the healing process, and the treatment worked so well that, within a week, the wound receded to a small red line across his right eyebrow. He was pleased to see her when she came into his room a few days later to check the recovery of the wound and sat down next to his bed.

"Thank you, Harriet. Did you learn all this from Mother Billington?"

"I did. She's very clever. She can't read or write, but she can identify plants and knows exactly which ones to find and how to use them. Everyone in the village trusts her. She's been very kind and has taught me everything."

"I can't say that about my teachers," mumbled Frederick. "My music teacher was kind. The rest were tyrants. All us boys were beaten."

"Mama said she'd seen scars on the backs of your legs. I'm so sorry, Fred. Has it been awful? Not that I expect you to describe ten years living with the royal family in a few words!" Harriet chuckled and Frederick laughed too.

"It wasn't all terrible and I have been happy but, now I'm here, I look back on my time at Richmond and Kew and know that I always felt on edge. I might not have known that George was my half-brother, nor did he, but we were good friends, far closer with each other than with the younger princes. We played together, did things, got into trouble," Frederick added with a snort. "George used to say that we were like tally sticks which fit together or heads and tails on a coin. We were the same but different and we'd laugh about it when we tossed a penny to start a game. How stupid I was."

"Well, we are your true family, Fred. I'm sorry about the beatings and the cruel teachers. Did they read your letters? Were you afraid to write and tell us what was happening?"

"I don't think they read my letters, but I was always scared I might be punished for something."

"But Mrs Cotesworth was kind?'

"Yes, Coaty was kind. But she was busy. There were so many children to look after. Once we boys moved to the Princes' House, she couldn't be there to protect me. Harriet, do you know what a 'whipping boy' is?"

"No, but it doesn't sound good."

"I was George's 'whipping boy'. I had to take the punishment when he was the one who deserved it. It went on like that for years. Of course, he'd always creep up to me later and apologise, but he never suffered like I did."

"I don't like the sound of Prince George."

"That's it. He's not a nice boy. He's a bully, selfish and demanding, but I can't help liking him. I'm glued to him in some strange way and always end up forgiving him. He gets away with things whilst I get hurt. Then I tell him it doesn't matter, that I'm fine, and he goes away happy."

"Well, maybe Mama and I may meet him one day," said Harriet, shivering with anticipation. "I'm so excited that Mama and I have been invited to live in London with you and Mrs Cotesworth. It's so generous of her. I'm tired of being a milkmaid and a servant to my cousins. Sam and Noah are pleasant boys and I'm glad you've been able to meet them at last. Their future is secure. They know they'll be farmers. Well, Sam, being older, will inherit Laing Farm and Noah might have to establish one of his own somewhere else. Mama and I don't count. We're just women. I don't think we ever mattered to Uncle Charles. And now that Grandmother Laing is dead, there's nobody who'll miss us here at the farm."

"I'm sure they'll miss you," said Frederick, "but I'm so pleased we can all live together in London."

"Yes, it's wonderful. Though I'll be sorry to leave Mother Billington. Here, Fred, let me show you the book I've created." Harriet picked up a book from her basket on the floor, opening it on the bed and flicking through the pages. "I've pressed herbs and plants and stuck them in. I write down their names, sometimes make a sketch of them and record all the things you can do with them. Then I write the recipes for how to use them and what they are good for. I'm going to bring it with us."

"Coaty's been very kind," said Frederick, not really listening to Harriet or looking at the book. He was thinking how much he loved his kind governess and how much he missed her. "Coaty suffered when she was a child. I think that's why she wanted to protect me."

"What happened to her?" said Harriet, putting away her book.

"Her mother was a housekeeper to the Cotesworth family who lived somewhere in Newcastle. There were four children. Then, after the first Mrs Cotesworth died, Mr Cotesworth married his housekeeper, and Coaty was born. Her half-brothers and sisters didn't accept that she was legally their sister. They were cruel to her and tried to prove that their father had not married her mother so they could deny her an inheritance. A kind uncle, her father's younger brother, saw what was happening and rescued Coaty, taking her into his own home and making sure she received the inheritance. He invested it so well that she became a rich young woman; that's why she was well educated and able to travel round Europe independently. She's full of stories about her adventures in Italy and Greece and the things she collected."

"I'd like to hear more about that," said Harriet. "Fred, do you remember I wrote to you about the girl I saw giving birth?"

"Yes, what happened to her?"

"It's good news. The father of the baby was a soldier. He returned when the child was a few months old and married the mother. So the baby has her father's name."

"Harriet, do you think that's what happened with my father, William Blomberg? Did he marry my mother just to give me a name and stop me from being Melissa Laing's bastard?"

"Don't use that language, Fred."

"But it's the truth. I have to accept that Melissa, my mother, let the King fuck her – that's the word George uses. He used her and then went away."

"Don't say that, Fred, I don't like it, but I understand that you do need to know what happened. Mama is the only person who knows the full story and she's so sensitive about it. She's still protecting you."

"I will ask her," said Frederick, "and she will tell me. I must know the truth."

Frederick and Harriet discussed all that they knew and tried to piece together the story of Melissa Laing's marriage and sad death. Harriet was cautious about asking her mother to tell them the circumstances of Frederick's birth but, one evening, two days before Coaty was due to arrive, they both sat opposite Aunt Margaret at the kitchen table, after dinner, and pressed her with questions. Resisting at first, protesting that there were chores to attend to, Harriet grasped her mother's hand and Frederick urged her to sit down again. With a deep sigh she agreed to tell them everything.

"You have to understand," she began, smoothing the curtains of hair framing her forehead, "it was in 1760, a year before Prince George became King George III. He was a young man, Fred, twenty-one years old, the same age as your cousin Sam. He had toured the southern counties of England, enjoying his first taste of freedom after spending years cooped up in royal palaces.

"His father, Prince Frederick, who'd been Prince of Wales, died suddenly when George was just twelve years old. Fred, you must have heard what happened."

"The accident with the cricket ball?"

"Yes, it was a huge shock when we read that Prince Frederick, the heir to the throne, had died after being hit in the chest by a cricket ball. We knew he had been a keen sportsman, but to die from a blow to the heart was awful."

"He died at Leicester House," put in Frederick. "But he was not on good terms with his father, George II."

"No. And then King George II became guardian to young George. As a grandfather he was very protective of the prince, keeping the heir to the throne safe. He was never allowed to go abroad like his younger brothers; he had to stay in the royal palaces in London. Young Prince George was desperate to get out into the world. Finally his grandfather relented and allowed him to leave the safety of the royal household as long as he went in the company of his trusted childhood friend, Major William Blomberg."

Aunt Margaret pressed her lips together, raised her chin and, closing her eyes, recalled those distant times. "Prince George and

William Blomberg rode into the farmyard here one day in late August 1760, asking for water. They'd been all over the countryside, staying in coaching inns and the homes of friends in fine houses. George was interested in farming and my father was keen to show him around, flattered at the interest from such an illustrious visitor. The young men came into this kitchen and sat at this very table. And that's when they met us girls."

Aunt Margaret sighed, glancing at the wedding ring on her left hand. "I was twenty-three. Harriet, you were about four months old, but I was in mourning. Your father, my dear Alexander, God rest his soul, had died so suddenly in an accident at the paper mill. We'd only been married a year. But these two fine visitors brightened our lives."

Aunt Margaret paused and breathed in deeply. "For two glorious weeks Prince George and William Blomberg rode over to the farm every day from the inn at Chartham. It was harvest time with warm weather and long days. They helped with the scything, building the hayricks, even ploughing. They rolled up their sleeves and worked like farmhands. George played his flute at the harvest festival, everyone danced, and we forgot that he was the Prince of Wales and heir to the throne. He was just a young man helping on the farm and everyone could see that he and Melissa had fallen in love. He adored her. She was such a pretty girl."

Aunt Margaret took a sip of water. "Where I'm strong and self-sufficient, Melissa was beautiful and delicate, like a doll. Everyone wanted to look after her. She had lovely long fair hair she could never keep tidy under her bonnet. Her face was small with the largest blue eyes, ready to spill tears at the slightest sadness. She gazed at you with such intensity. We were close and loved each other so much." Margaret's own eyes filled with tears.

"Did the Prince of Wales take advantage of my mother?" asked Frederick.

"Fred, it wasn't like that; he loved her, and she loved him back, although we were all concerned, especially our parents. There was so much at risk. We worried for Melissa's reputation and that of our family. Mother and I cautioned her all the time, but Melissa would toss back her head and say that she trusted George. She was smitten, blinded by love. My father was fearful and angry, but he couldn't control her. And it was difficult for him. How can you tell the heir to the throne to leave your daughter alone and get out of your house? He just watched helplessly, like the rest of us."

Frederick and Harriet nodded in partial understanding.

"We all knew that George and Melissa's romance could be nothing more than a brief interlude, but we could tell that their affection was real. George was going to be king; he couldn't marry a farmer's daughter. He might have found a way to make Melissa his mistress, but we were too innocent about these things. Fred, you probably know more about the life of a mistress – we only read about them."

Frederick chewed his thumb. He was aware of Uncle Cumberland's many mistresses and those of the other brothers of the King.

"I counselled Melissa," continued Margaret, "and urged her not to let her feelings run away with her, but she couldn't help herself. Then the day came for Prince George and William to leave, and Melissa was heartbroken."

"The next thing we heard was that George's grandfather, King George II, had died. It happened suddenly at the end of October in 1760 and was a huge shock."

"I heard about that as a child," put in Frederick. "The old king died of a heart attack whilst sitting in his closet. I remember George and I pretending to be him, tumbling out of our water closet, clutching our chests and laughing."

Harriet giggled and Frederick smiled at her in relief at the brief change of mood.

Aunt Margaret took a breath and continued her story. "Yes, the old King George was not a popular man, but his death was a blow to young Prince George. Suddenly he became king at only twenty-two. We assumed we'd never see him again."

"But he did come back?" said Frederick.

"Yes, two months later, in December of 1760, he and William returned. He was going to Canterbury to meet with the Archbishop to discuss his coronation, but really he wanted to see Melissa. They had continued to write to each other all autumn. Melissa and I were sent a royal invitation to meet Prince George and William Blomberg at their hotel in Canterbury. They were staying at The White Hart near the cathedral. The invitation was for dinner, but we were given a room to stay in since we could not come back to the farm on a winter's night. By this time you were six months old, Harriet, and I left you with my mother.

"Melissa was so excited; she spent hours in front of the mirror in her bedroom, brushing her hair and choosing what to wear. Prince George sent his royal carriage here to take us to Canterbury and we rode into town feeling very grand.

"We were delighted to see George, now King George III, and William again, even though they were surrounded by guards and courtiers, who took over the hotel. We had a wonderful dinner, with the best wines, and laughed and talked all evening. And then we retired to our bedrooms.

"Once we were in our nightdresses, there was a knock at the bedroom door. William told us that George, the King, was very anxious to talk to Melissa. She jumped from her bed, pulling a shawl over her nightgown. I pleaded with her not to go. I barred the door, but she pushed past and went with William to George's room. I sat up all night in a chair by the fire and waited until morning."

"Aunt Margaret," exclaimed Frederick, thumping his fist on the table, "I can't believe that you just stood by and let my mother go to his room. You're telling us that the King fucked my mother in a hotel room and then left her."

"Fred, I know you're angry and confused, but that's what

happened. It was genuine love. Melissa couldn't stop herself. I need a glass of porter." Aunt Margaret rubbed her face, rose and poured herself a glass.

"Early in the morning she came back to our room. We both looked out of the window and saw King George and William getting into the carriage to return to London. They waved at us, blowing kisses, and that was the last we ever saw of King George III."

The atmosphere in the room was heavy with imagined visions of an illicit coupling nearly fifteen years ago.

"Mama," began Harriet, "why didn't you ever tell me this? Like Fred, I feel ashamed at not knowing the truth. Do Uncle Charles and the rest of the family know, Sam and Noah?"

"No. It was an absolute secret," Aunt Margaret replied. "Only our mother and father knew the truth, although there were plenty of people on the farm and around the countryside who saw Melissa and Prince George that autumn and it was obvious they were in love."

"And not with William Blomberg, who married her," said Frederick. "What about William? What was he like? We know so little about him."

"William was a sensitive young man and a fiercely loyal friend to George. He was a few years older and an officer. His family are aristocrats. The Blombergs are barons, titled people who came over from Germany with the first King George. William was a man of status and property. You should be proud to bear his name."

"But he's not my father, is he," retorted Frederick. "You've just told us what happened. The new king enjoyed his night with my mother and then went off to marry Queen Charlotte. Do you think he had any idea that she might have been left with child?"

"Fred, listen," said Aunt Margaret sharply. "It was complicated. Prince George was going to be king. He knew that he would have to marry a suitable girl from the right family. Courtiers were sent out all over Germany to select daughters of the German royal families. That's what happens; it's the way they do things. The King had to find a wife before his coronation in September 1761, so there wasn't much time. You've met Queen Charlotte, Fred; you must know that she was a princess, but she was only seventeen when she married King George. She arrived in London one day and was married to him the next. Then she was crowned queen two weeks later. This was just days after you'd been born, Fred. I feel sorry for her. It'll be the same for your young George, the Prince of Wales; he will have to find a suitable wife."

"But Mama," said Harriet, "you told us that William and Melissa married in Rochester in April that year. How did that happen?"

"The family was in turmoil. In March 1761 my father sent an angry letter to the new king, telling him that Melissa was with child. He couldn't accuse him directly, in writing, in case any courtiers reading the letter would know the truth. He suggested that the pregnancy was the result of his visit to Canterbury with William, inferring that William was responsible. And to give King George his due, he wanted to make amends and avoid a scandal. So he asked his good friend William to marry Melissa. It was the obvious solution, and William was so devoted that of course he agreed. My mother and I were at the wedding in Rochester. Father would not attend. Harriet, you were left with Mother Billington at the farm. Melissa cried throughout the service."

"I remember Grandmother Laing telling me that," put in Harriet, "when I talked to her about the baby's birth I'd seen. She said it had been a windy day in April and that apple blossom blew around the couple when they came out of the church."

"It's true, it was windy, and Melissa was distraught. She didn't love him but had to be married before the baby arrived. William found us a house in Rochester, where he was billeted, and Melissa became like any other army wife living in the town, expecting a baby and knowing her husband would be away with his regiment. I left this farmhouse to stay with her. I had you to look after, Harriet, and no husband, so it was a good plan that we sisters should both share a home in Rochester with our babies. Joan was our housekeeper."

"And then I was born," said Frederick.

"Yes, you were born." Aunt Margaret drank her porter. "For such a small and frail girl like your mother, giving birth to you was hard." Margaret paused and closed her eyes. "I felt so desperate seeing her suffer. Having had a baby eighteen months earlier, I knew what was involved and a local midwife attended the birth. My mother came to Rochester to be with us and stayed to look after you, Harriet, whilst I supported Melissa. I sent word to William, who was in Greenwich at the time, that the baby would soon be born. He came as quickly as he could but too late. Our darling Melissa suffered dreadfully, and the midwife could not stop her bleeding. She died in childbirth.

"William arrived when you were three days old, Fred, and Melissa was in her coffin. He was desperately sad to hear what had happened and so moved to see you in your cot. He named you: Frederick William. They are Blomberg family names. He couldn't be with you for long because his regiment would soon sail to the Caribbean. You were baptised in Rochester a few weeks after your birth. I am your godmother, but you've always known that."

"Yes, Aunt Margaret, I'm glad you are."

"We found a wet nurse for you, Fred, but William was concerned that people were asking questions in Rochester. As soon as you were weaned, he moved us all to a cottage he had found in Dorset. I chose to stay and look after you, Fred, with Harriet, and Joan came too."

Margaret took another sip of porter, mopping her eyes with her apron.

"William told me that he wanted to keep his marriage to Melissa and your birth a secret from his family. He didn't even tell his commanding officers in the army. I don't know why. I think it was a promise he'd made to the King. Then he was sent away to the Caribbean to fight the French. As you know, our army was protecting the American colonies. William visited just once when you were two years old before sailing back to Dominica. And soon after that, in 1764, he was killed."

"I remember when he came," put in Harriet. "He gave us both hobbyhorses. I wish we still had them."

Sighing, Frederick ran his fingers through his hair. "Thank you for telling me, Aunt Margaret. I feel calmer now."

"Thank you, Mama," added Harriet, "I wish we'd known this before. Grandmother Laing told me some of the story shortly before she died, but it was muddled and hard to understand."

Afterwards, once Aunt Margaret had gone to bed, Frederick and Harriet picked over the story. They wondered why William had kept his marriage and child a secret from the army and even his family? It didn't seem logical. But if it was true, the question remained: how had the King and Queen known where to find Frederick? And why did they choose to adopt him? Convinced that there was much more to learn, they resolved to coax more details from her another time.

"Well, Fred," said Harriet, throwing back her head and tightening the gifted ribbon in her long brown hair, "thank you for changing my life. I'm ready to experience London and look forward to living with Mrs Cotesworth. I know you've had lots of adventures already, but I've never been anywhere, and I can't wait to see and do new things."

Chapter Sixteen
Frederick Returns to London
Late October 1775

When Coaty arrived at the farm, Frederick greeted her with undisguised joy, embracing her with both arms, overwhelmed with gratitude for her kind offer to adopt his family.

Light rain sprinkled the yard as the family prepared to leave. Mrs Cotesworth and Aunt Margaret sat together in the carriage, whilst Frederick and Harriet sat opposite, with their backs to the driver. Frederick experienced a deep calm and pleasure, feeling cossetted and safe, in the company of the three women he loved the most in the world. His initial worry about returning to London was banished with the knowledge that he would be returning to a life of wealth and comfort with Coaty as his guardian. She had assured him that, once he was at Dover Street, he would have nothing to fear; he would be independent of the royal family and no longer under the aegis of the King, the court, the tutors and the royal children.

The day before departure, Uncle Charles drew Margaret aside in the farmhouse, giving her a pouch filled with guineas representing the capital from the inheritance that her late father's will had stipulated she should receive. She accepted it, reluctantly agreeing to make no further claim to the farm on her, or Harriet's, behalf.

With a creak of wheels, the carriage departed and soon they were cantering through the Kent countryside, arriving at Rochester as daylight faded. Mrs Cotesworth had booked them rooms at The Bull Inn and, as they entered the dining parlour, Frederick spotted Jenny. She hurried towards her new guests and then stopped in her tracks when she recognised Frederick.

"Jenny," cried Frederick, bowing to her, "it's good to see you."

"Fred. 'Pon my soul, what are you doing here?"

He turned to his party and said with pride, "This is Jenny, she is the inn-keeper's wife," adding, "and she runs this place. Jenny helped me when I arrived here with no money and in torn clothes. She asked me to play the violin to earn my living."

The women all smiled and nodded in recognition.

"Jenny, I told you I'd come back and say thank you."

"Indeed, Master Frederick, and I never believed you."

"Now I can pay for the clothes you gave me."

"Oh Lord, I never expected to see those old things again. I can see you've found something much more suitable," she said, reviewing the clothes he had been given by Noah Laing, the younger of his two cousins. "Hold on to your money. We've got the best bedrooms ready for you. It'll make a change from the straw mattress you lay upon last time," she said, chuckling as she led them upstairs.

When the evening meal was over, Jenny approached their table holding the fiddle.

"Master Frederick, I have a suggestion for the repayment you offered to make. Your party might like to hear a tune."

"Oh, no, I don't think I…"

"Yes, yes," they all cried.

Taking the violin, Frederick stroked its polished wood, and holding it to his neck, he ran the bow over the strings, adjusting the tuning. "I like this old fiddle very much," said Frederick. "It's not as fine as the one the princes gave me or the one Mr Crosdill allowed me to practise on during lessons, but I can still coax a fair tune from it."

"Will you play a jig?" urged Jenny.

Frederick laughed, aware he was blushing. "Very well," he said, sitting on a stool and positioning the violin to his chin. He recalled the jig from the wedding all those weeks ago and summoned the tune from the strings. The older women beamed with pride and Harriet tapped her hand on her knee.

"Oh Fred," said Aunt Margaret, "you have such a talent. I had no idea you could play so well." Harriet leant across and gave him a quick hug.

"I always admired Crosdill's teaching," added Coaty, beaming with satisfaction.

Frederick smiled. Teasing those simple jaunty tunes from the instrument solidified a thought in his young mind. Whatever the future might hold for him, he knew that he must always have music in his life. He picked up the violin again and played another jig.

Chapter Seventeen
Arrival at Dover Street
23rd October 1775

Harriet lowered the carriage window, turning her head to the left and right, taking in the sights and sounds of the capital. Frederick did his best to look nonchalant, inwardly sharing her delight in the noise and energy of the city.

"Welcome to Dover Street," cried Coaty as the carriage lurched to a halt outside a tall townhouse in a street running northwards from Piccadilly. "I hope that you'll approve of this house. It is comfortable and in good condition. It was built about forty years ago and I think it has a warm atmosphere."

Stretching their cramped limbs, they stepped down to the pavement.

"Eugh," cried Harriet, bunching up her cloak to avoid the piles of horse manure on the street.

Frederick smiled at her and took her arm, following Coaty towards the house. The smell of burnt coffee, cooked food, tobacco and candlewax were familiar to him, reminding him of the aromas at Richmond and the Princes' House. Coaty led everyone up the few stone steps between the railings and through the door at the front.

Three people were standing sentry in the hallway. A plump middle-aged woman, a tall man with a bent spine and young woman in a mob cap.

"May I introduce Mr and Mrs Sparks," said Coaty. "Mrs Sparks is our most excellent cook. She will prepare supper for us later. Her husband, Mr Sparks, manages matters in the house and drives my carriage when I'm in town. And this is Dorothy, our maid, who has been with me since she was a young girl. She looks after all the fires, fetches the water, empties the pots and generally helps in the kitchen. So, my dears," continued Coaty, "I will now show you where everything is."

After handing their cloaks to Dorothy, the three guests followed Coaty as she pointed out the parlour on the left of the front door, the dining room at the back and the door down to the servants' quarters. Gathering their skirts in one hand, and holding the smooth curved bannister with the other, the women and Frederick climbed the narrow staircase to the first floor.

"This is the drawing room," announced Coaty, ushering them into a large room spanning the width of the house. Bright evening sunshine streamed through three tall windows opening onto a narrow balcony. Horses' hooves and clattering wheels could be heard from the street.

"My study is here, at the back, where it's quieter, and upstairs are the bedrooms," she continued, leading the way up to the next flight. "We have four. This is mine," she said, indicating the large room at the front. "I thought, Margaret, that you might like the quiet room next to me at the back. And if you two go upstairs, you'll find two more. You can choose between you. There's an attic room for Dorothy and Mr and Mrs Sparks live in their own rooms in the basement."

Harriet ran up the stairs with Frederick close behind. The room at the front, overlooking Dover Street, mirrored rows of houses stretching as far as the eye could see. The room at the back overlooked a small yard with further rows of roofs, topped by chimney pots belching out smoke.

"I'd like this one," said Frederick, choosing the room at the back. "You'll enjoy the one at the front."

"It's so elegant," declared Harriet as she explored her room, running her fingers over the polished surface of a mahogany chest of drawers and glancing at herself in the oval mirror on the wall.

Walking into his new room, Frederick closed the door and lay down on the bed.

Stretching his arms and legs and running his fingers over the embroidered cover, he recalled his first night at Richmond as a small boy. This was different and he believed he would now have some control over his life. The wound on his head had healed well and he'd regained most of the weight he'd lost during his weeks of travelling. Sitting up, he looked at his reflection in the mirror on the dressing table. Studying his face properly for the first time since that dreadful birthday dinner, he pushed out his chin, examining his upper lip. Yes, he could see the beginnings of hairs sprouting from his skin. Brown eyes sparkled back at him and his face looked tanned, his cheekbones more defined.

"And so it begins," he said out loud to his reflection. Manhood was fast approaching and life as a boy was ending.

Running his fingers through his light brown hair, a lock flopped across his forehead. Pushing it aside, he resolved to find a barber as soon as possible. Recalling George's views on hair, he remembered their conversation shortly before that dreadful party when they approved the latest fashion to no longer to crop the hair close and wear a wig, but to grow one's own hair and then have it powdered for special occasions.

Standing up, he reviewed his clothing, turning to the left and right in front of the mirror, shaking off the jacket his cousin Noah Laing had given him. The young farmer's clothes were made of sturdy cloth and fitted reasonably well, but the jacket sleeves were too long. Coaty had told him she would arrange a visit to a tailor soon and he would receive two new outfits.

These new clothes represented a welcome start to a new identity, although he missed his treasured box of possessions and his beloved violin and wondered whether they were still under his old bed at Kew.

Although Frederick was relieved that Harriet and Aunt Margaret would be near him at last, he didn't really know them. Ten years of letters provided snippets of news, but each of them had so much history to reveal and they had all lived such different lives.

Sitting up once more, he stared at his face again in the mirror. Did he still look as much like George as everyone said? Yes, his nose with its gentle upward slope, plump pouches of skin below his eyes and full lips did resemble his half-brother. Visualising George, he acknowledged a sensation he had been loath to accept – he missed him. The boy was insufferable, selfish, irritating and thoughtless, yet he loved him. And, to a lesser extent, he missed the younger princes and the other royal children. Frederick had forged a strong bond with the boys and now they too knew the truth. The one thing Prince George had achieved was to remove any doubt about his parentage. His half-siblings now knew that he was of the same blood and should respect him. In reality, they were far more his family than Harriet and Aunt Margaret.

He wondered what it would be like to see the royal family again, and if he did, could their relationship ever be the same? Perhaps, now that the truth was known, he would be in a better position to ask the King and Queen one day about the circumstances of his adoption.

Frederick breathed deeply, tilting his face from right to left, studying his reflection. Was he attractive? he wondered. In recent months he had found himself wondering about girls, noticing their figures, manners and staring at their faces. He'd started thinking about love, wanting to understand the huge emotions powering actions of adults. It seemed astonishing that King George III had been his mother's lover, yet he still knew so little about her and what she had meant to him. Chewing his thumb, he made a decision. If he were to ever see the King again, he would ask him.

Later that evening, at dinner, Coaty picked up the claret jug, filled her own wine glass, and held it over Harriet's glass.

"No, thank you," said Harriet, placing her hand over the brim, "I couldn't drink any more."

"Very well, my dear, but you may develop a taste for it when you are older. I know that Fred has become used to wine and can identify some of the vintages. The royal children often drank wine at mealtimes, albeit diluted with water. Now we are in my house, I would like you all to address me as Henrietta, or Coaty, if you prefer. I was never Mrs Cotesworth anyway."

Fred took a sip of wine and looked up at her with astonishment. "Coaty, sorry, Henrietta, then what is your name?"

"Oh Fred, it is Cotesworth, my maiden name, but not Mrs. I was never married."

"Then why did we assume you were?"

"It's a convention of the royal nursery. All the governesses took the title of Mrs, but they weren't married."

"Mrs Cheveley wasn't married?" asked Fred, shuddering at the mention of her name.

"No, indeed. The only married governess was Mrs Finch, Lady Charlotte, our beloved Lady Cha."

"Then why did she choose to leave her own children to look after the royal ones?" asked Aunt Margaret.

"The Fermors are an old aristocratic family and very close to Their Majesties. Queen Charlotte asked Lady Charlotte to become a governess and help look after her children. One does not say no to a royal summons."

"No," said Aunt Margaret, lowering her eyes. "I remember our summons. We were not able to refuse it."

Frederick noticed the wistful expression on Aunt Margaret's face. "I've always wanted to know, Coaty, how did you meet Lady Cha?" he asked.

"We met at Scampston in the summer of 1762. It's a fine estate near York. I was invited to stay there when she was also a guest, and we became great friends. I was forty years old and she a couple of years younger. I was an educated and extremely well-travelled lady at the time and full of interesting conversation, though I say it myself. She was new to the royal appointment to run the nursery and needed help with Their Majesties' growing family. So she invited me to take the role of Deputy Governess. You, Fred, became my special charge and I am glad of it."

"So am I," said Frederick, raising his glass. "My time in the household might have been very different if you'd not been there."

"And now we can create a happy household for the four of us," said Coaty, pouring more wine from the claret jug. "My dears, I want to say how very delighted I am to fill this house with family, for that is how I regard you. However, there is something very important which we will need to discuss at a later date. Margaret, dear, you remember I took the red Morocco box which Major Blomberg left with you?"

"Of course. I hope you still have it."

"I do. It's in my study upstairs. I have, on occasion, gone through it and established that there is a property in Yorkshire to which, I believe, Fred should be entitled."

"Where is this property?" asked Frederick.

"It's a place I happen to know quite well called Kirby Misperton. It's a fine estate in the countryside, not far from Malton and Pickering. Indeed, it's not far from Scampston and a mere half a day's ride away from York. When I was living at Middleton with my mother and her second husband, a drunkard of a clergyman, I would occasionally visit the place."

"Does someone live there?" said Frederick.

"Yes, members of the Blomberg family have lived there for several generations. It came into their family many years ago through marriage. Baron Charles Blomberg married Elizabeth Dickinson, whose father, Doctor Edmund Dickinson, was a physician. He treated King Charles II and James II and was gifted the estate in gratitude. You, Frederick, are a direct descendent of that family.

"The current occupant is Mrs Ursula Blomberg, widow of the Reverend William Nicholas Blomberg, who took possession of Kirby Misperton in the 1730s. She had a son, called William Frederick, which is confusing, since that is the same name as your father. However, my solicitor has been informed that the young man died last year, aged thirty-eight, and that there were no children. I'm sure you should inherit the estate. However, we will need legal help to establish your claim."

Frederick pondered this silently. He longed to possess a home of his own. He didn't want to be poor or experience a modest life like his aunt and cousin. He'd known poverty and homelessness for a few brief weeks and had no desire to revisit it. He had lived the life of a prince for ten years and now, on the brink of adulthood, he recognised that he still wanted to live like one. The idea of working for money was unappealing. That was not what gentlemen did. And, surely, he was a young gentleman?

Dorothy circled the table collecting dishes before leaving the dining room through a door at the back of the room and disappearing down stone steps to the kitchen.

"So, my family," announced Coaty, beaming at everyone, eyes drooping and headdress askew, "I want you to regard this as your home. I will now retire to my bed. I hope that you will all sleep very well. Dorothy has stoked the fires in each room and put fresh water in the jugs. She will empty your pots in the morning.

"And Fred, in two weeks' time, when your new clothes have arrived, you will be ready to meet the King and Queen."

Chapter Eighteen
A Meeting at Richmond Lodge
18th November 1775

The guards and court servants bowed to Frederick and Coaty whilst pages held open the austere double doors leading to the hallway. After tugging at the cuffs below the sleeves of his smart new jacket, Frederick smoothed the line of his breeches.

"Take my arm, will you, Fred, just for the stairs."

Frederick led Coaty up the carpeted steps to the King and Queen's suite. Seeing their approach, and knocking on the drawing room door, a page ushered them into the royal apartment. Coaty and Frederick entered, and King George and Queen Charlotte rose from the sofa in the centre of the gilded room. Coaty curtsied and Frederick bowed. The Queen took a few steps towards Frederick, clasping him to her breast. He looked up at her face and could see that her eyes were bright with tears. Once released, he turned to the King, who took hold of his right hand, squeezing it with great strength, pulling him closer for a full embrace.

"My dear Master Frederick," said the Queen, "you gave us such a fright."

"I'm sorry for it, Your Majesty. I never intended to frighten you."

"Frederick, you made us very anxious," began the King as he sat down again, rubbing his palms on his knees. "And also angry. You showed little gratitude for all we have done for you by running away. We searched far and wide for you," he continued, "and we asked everyone in Kew and beyond."

Frederick pressed his hands together and felt the itch flaring in his elbow. "Your Majesty, I apologise for causing you distress. I had to leave. When George said… what he did… I couldn't stay at the table."

"Yes, yes, what, what. We remember all he said. We, the

dear queen and I, do understand," said the King, "but it was still irresponsible to run away like that."

"We were very worried about you," said Queen Charlotte. "Mrs Cotesworth, Master Frederick, please do sit down."

Perching on the edge of the sofa opposite the royal couple, Coaty and Frederick could see the King and Queen's concerned faces reflected in the polished table between them.

"However, my dear Master Frederick, we were heartily relieved when Mrs Cotesworth told us that she had heard news of you from your aunt. Now," continued the King, "we must make plans for you, Frederick. Will you be returning to the Princes' House? You are a valued member of the royal family. Your hound, Jupiter, misses you."

Frederick swallowed hard. This was the conversation he had been dreading. He longed to see Jupiter. He wanted to nuzzle his delicate ears and run through the park with him but knew he must resist.

"If you please, sir, I would like to continue my education whilst I am at Coat… Mrs Cotesworth's house, in Dover Street. She has kindly offered to become my guardian and has also opened her home to my aunt Margaret, Mrs Poulton, and her daughter, Harriet, who is a year and a half older than me. I enjoy being close to them once again."

"Ah, Margaret and Melissa of Laing Farm," said the King in a singsong voice. "Frederick, we must speak plainly. I have discussed this with Her Majesty, and she is fully understanding of my youthful indiscretions. Frederick, I accept that you are my son. There, there, it's been said. But this must never be referred to beyond these walls."

"Sir, thank you, sir, and since we are speaking plainly…" began Frederick, his hands trembling as he rubbed his palms together, "I wanted to ask you about my father, my name father, Major William Blomberg."

"William was a very dear friend. I remember telling you about him when you were much younger. We knew each other as boys; he was like my older brother. His grandfather, Baron Blomberg, was a close friend of my grandfather, George II, and the generation before. He and I enjoyed many boyhood games and adventures. I shall never forget how attentive and kind he was when we set forth on the journey which led me to… your mother."

"Yes, I have heard about my mother, Melissa, from my aunt Margaret. Sir, would you do me the honour of telling me what you remember of her?"

King George pressed his lips together and narrowed his eyebrows. "My dear queen, I hope you will forgive me. At the time I knew young Frederick's mother, I was an unformed youth of twenty-one, and she was a maid, just two years younger, so very pretty and charming. We enjoyed each other's company in such simple pleasures. It was a sweet but short-lived experience. You must understand that, so early in my reign, I had to avoid a scandal. William was a loyal friend. I was very sad to hear about the death of your beautiful mother.

"However, I knew I had my duty to perform as king. And George, our young Prince of Wales, must do the same, in time. I admit, I was exceedingly angry with him after the birthday feast. He was rude to you, to me, to Her Majesty and everyone in the room. But, Master Frederick, what this episode has achieved is to remove all doubt about your place within this family.

"Now, hear me. I will not publicly acknowledge you as my son. To do so would cause any number of constitutional issues, set tongues wagging and not be to anyone's advantage. However, within these walls, and court circles, I have let it be known that you are regarded as a much valued, and indeed much loved, member of the family. My dear wife, who first heard of your plight from Lady Charlotte, decided to give you a home. You were adopted by us as an infant and, by circumstance, have enjoyed a life of privilege. This is what happened and we, as a family, will never cast you out. So, Frederick, we will continue to support and embrace you. You may be fourteen now, but in a few years' time, there will be decisions to make regarding your future."

"Master Frederick," added Queen Charlotte, "with this in mind, the King and I have decided to give you a regular allowance to complete your education. We will ensure you receive a stipend of three hundred pounds a year until you are twenty-one years of age. This will pay for tutors, travel or whatever you need. We are, indeed, very grateful that Mrs Cotesworth has kindly offered you a home. Mrs Cotesworth, I shall call on you in Dover Street."

"Of course, ma'am, I would be honoured," said Mrs Cotesworth.

"Thank you, sir," said Frederick, "you are most kind and I don't know how to repay your generosity."

"No need, no need," replied the King with a wave of his hand. "All I ask is that you remain a good friend to our young Prince George and help steer him towards a better course in life. He indulges himself too much, behaves foolishly and has a poor grasp of the truth. We both find him exasperating. The Queen and I will do our best to direct him towards a righteous path but, by some instinct, he seems to go the other way. I fear for his younger brothers too. We look to you, Master Frederick, to exert a better influence."

The Queen nodded in agreement, patting her swollen belly. Coaty recognised the sign.

"I offer you congratulations, ma'am," said Coaty. "Your eleventh child will be a blessing. I'm sure the nursery will be delighted to welcome a new prince or princess. Sir," she added, addressing the King, "you have been very kind to Master Frederick. If I may make so bold, Your Majesty, I do have an idea concerning his future which, I believe, will please you. But first of all, Frederick and I will consider the next stage in his life and the nature of his education. Sir, ma'am, please rest assured that I have his best interests at heart. I am also embarking upon a legal action to obtain the inheritance Major William Blomberg was anxious that he should receive."

"Ah, yes, Blomberg's interests. Frederick, for that reason it is also important not to reveal your true parentage in case it influences your claim. Please keep me informed of your progress with this, Mrs Cotesworth."

"I will, Your Majesty, thank you."

After an uncomfortable minute, whilst the King stared in silence at his hands, he then looked up, clapped his hands together before picking up a tiny bell on a nearby table and tinkling it.

"Thank you for coming. I will let you go."

The two visitors rose, and a page entered to guide them, bowing as they reversed to the door.

Chapter Nineteen
A Royal Visitor
7th December 1775

Dorothy ran to the door in response to the bell's noisy clanging, pulled it open and surveyed a tall, broad-chested young man carrying a cane. Beneath his thick serge coat, he sported a bright blue jacket, lace cuffs, pink breeches and white stockings. The first few swirls of winter snow were drifting from the sky and the street air was very cold. A large four-horse carriage with driver and footman waited outside the house.

"Good afternoon," said the young man, removing his hat. "I have come to see Master Frederick. Is he at home today?"

"Master Frederick is at home. Whom, sir, shall I say is calling?"

"It's the Prince of Wales."

Astonished, Dorothy curtsied several times, ushered him in, taking his coat, hat and cane and placing them on the stand in the hall. Leading him up the staircase to the drawing room, she indicated the chaise longue. Darting to the fireplace, she emptied more coal into the grate, and, after poking the flames to life, she ran out of the room and up two flights of stairs to rap on Frederick's door. Not waiting for an answer, she barged in.

"Dorothy, what's happened?"

"Oh Master Frederick, there's a young man, no, it's a Prince of England, no, Wales. He's in the drawing room. He wants to see you. Shall I fetch tea?"

Frederick rose from his writing desk by the window and went to the wardrobe to find his best jacket.

"Thank you, Dorothy. But he'll prefer a glass of Madeira. Do we have any?"

"We do. Madam always makes sure of it."

Running down to the drawing room, Frederick found George

sitting nervously on the chaise. He leapt up as Frederick entered.

"Fred, my dear Fred, how pleased I am to see you." George flung his arms around Frederick, who responded with restraint, keeping his arms to his side. He was still not sure he could forgive George for what he'd done.

"Sir," said Frederick, now taking a step away and bowing.

"Oh, fie to the etiquette, Fred, we have so much to discuss. I gather you saw Mama and Papa recently."

"I did. They were very kind. I hadn't realised they'd been so concerned about me."

"They were frantic, Fred, believe me."

"I'm sorry for it, George. I was fine, thank you. I met kind people and made my way to my family, my real family, but no thanks to you."

"Oh Fred, how can you say that?" cried George, running his fingers through his thick brown hair and rubbing his chin. "Surely the good thing about my... my little revelation was that it's cleared the air. You knew people were puzzled about you, what with you looking so like me, though less handsome, of course," added George, joshing with Frederick and pushing his shoulder.

Frederick felt cold. He didn't want to forgive George and make light of what had happened.

"George, just because you're taller than me, richer than me and heir to the throne doesn't entitle you to embarrass and humiliate me."

George paused for a moment. Frederick could see he was taken aback by his outburst and couldn't tell whether he'd been rude or joking. Then George threw back his head and laughed.

"Ha, Fred, you comical person. Of course you'll forgive me. You always do."

A knock at the door interrupted their conversation. "Now, ah, I see we have some... no, it's not tea; it's something much more interesting. This is very welcome."

Dorothy appeared holding a tray of drinks, set it down on the table and, bobbing a curtsy, left.

"This is what I need, Fred," said George, filling the two glasses with Madeira wine, taking a large gulp and holding out his glass for Frederick to clink. "You're in the right house for wine consumption," he added.

"George," began Frederick, "sit down. I want to ask you something." They sat down side by side on the chaise. "At the dinner, you said you'd got the true story from Coaty. What did she tell you?"

"I did. It was all from Coaty, and believe me, I hadn't meant to make that announcement using what she'd told me."

"Then why did you?" asked Frederick coldly.

"Earlier in the day I'd had a furious spat with Father. I'd been at Richmond Lodge for another of his tedious services in the chapel and wanted to ride my horse back to Kew. He'd objected, muttering some nonsense about me being a dangerous rider. He made me return in the carriage. All I wanted was a bit of freedom, but he absolutely refused."

George downed the Madeira and helped himself to more. "And then, when I got back to the Princes' House, I spotted Coaty in the garden. Well, she was in her cups, sprawled on that bench she loves by the trees, and was barely awake. Don't know what had been going on in the nursery. I later heard that Mama had dismissed her, but I didn't know that at the time. She had a basket with two bottles of brandy and a glass. So, I sat next to her, and she didn't shoo me away. In fact, she was very civil. I told her I was furious with Father, and she suggested that all fathers have issues with their sons. She then told me that my father had hated his father and so it goes, right up to George I. All fathers hate their sons. It's what we do.

"And then I mentioned, in jest, that must be why he never had any complaint about you, Fred, his adopted son. And that's when Coaty spilled the beans and said, 'Oh, but Master Frederick *is* the King's natural son. He's his firstborn.'"

"She actually told you that?"

"Yes, and that got me going. I quizzed her a bit more. She was so drunk that I could have asked her anything and she'd have told me. And it did answer a few questions. I mean, I'd thought it, my brothers and sisters thought it. Presumably the idea might have flickered through your brain?"

"No. I thought my father was Major William Blomberg."

George wrinkled his nose. "Yes, well, knowing I had to make a speech at the dinner, and that I hadn't prepared anything, I decided I'd share this revelation. I thought it might spice up the evening and be a really good way to get back at my father."

"What!" cried Frederick. "How could you be so selfish? It might have spiced up the evening for you, but it was devastating for me! Didn't you give a moment's thought to what I'd think? How I'd feel? You blurt out to everyone at dinner that I, Frederick Blomberg, am the natural son of the King?"

"Well, no, at the time I didn't think of it that way. And I'm sorry for it, Fred, truly. Once I knew the truth, I thought it had to be said and I knew it would annoy Father."

"You did annoy him, but more than that, you publicly humiliated me and then you think I'm going to be happy about it? No, George, it was cruel, thoughtless."

George pushed his hands between his knees and looked up at Frederick. Wondering how contrite he really was, Frederick felt bubbles of pent-up anger surging through his body; he was ready for the duel they'd talked about when they'd first met as small boys.

George looked up, his mouth turned down, and rubbed his chin. "Sorry, Fred. I truly am sorry. Where did you go, when you left? Tell me about it."

Frederick took a slow sip of Madeira, sitting back and savouring this moment. He realised he could make George jealous; he had experienced freedom, something George craved.

"I was sick first. Then I ran out of the palace, through the park to the river. I hid in the beer barge, which set off whilst I slept, and

I woke up in Southwark. I joined a band of pilgrims on their way to Canterbury. I sold my clothes to a man named Raphael, who'd been a page to your, our, grandmother, Augusta. I stayed at an inn and slept on straw. I was robbed, slept in a woodshed, I earned some money playing the fiddle and picking hops. I was robbed again, beaten over the head and gashed my forehead. See, there's a scar." Frederick lifted his hair to reveal the healed wound.

"I nearly died in a ditch and was rescued by the same man I sold my clothes to. Raphael helped me reach Laing Farm, my mother's family farm. They took me in. They were pleased to see me. I now have my family, George. I have Aunt Margaret, and my cousin Harriet, who is more like a sister. And now Coaty is my guardian."

George blew out his cheeks as he absorbed the story. "That's amazing, so much danger. All that experience makes me envious, Fred."

"It wasn't fun, George. I feared for my life on several occasions. I was cold, wet, hungry and lost."

"Yes, I believe you. But I still envy you. You've done things I could never do. You've been on a quest."

"I needed to find my family."

"Of course. I'm sure there's so much more to tell. I'm jealous, Fred."

"Good. I'm glad you're jealous. I thought you would be."

"Well, up to a point. The idea of sleeping in a woodshed and not eating…" George shuddered. "I'm sure it was far more frightening than you're admitting, but you're safe now. And you look older. Fred, I propose we go out to dinner, and you can tell me more details of your adventure. My carriage is outside, I have money, and I know where we can go."

"George, you're only thirteen. How can you know where to go in town?"

"I know from my uncle Henry, Duke of Cumberland. He takes me places and I remember them. Papa says he's a bad influence, and

I'm glad of it." George pressed his lips together, tapping his nose with his forefinger.

"George, you're impossible." Frederick couldn't help laughing.

"I like to think so. The Duke is quite the man about town, and I do like him. You know how much Papa considers himself an example of goodness and piety? Well, his brother, Uncle Henry Cumberland, is the complete opposite and I'm glad of it. Ha! He knows all the worst places in London. He takes me to them when my parents and tutors think I'm out riding or in chapel."

"George, you need to be careful." Frederick smoothed the fabric of his breeches and shook his head. "You should think about your position, your reputation."

"Oh, listen to yourself, Fred. You sound like my father. I'm young. I have years of waiting to be king. I might have to wear a crown one day, but until then I'm going to please myself. Fred, I am sorry. Do you believe me?"

A tap at the door interrupted Frederick's reply and Coaty entered. She curtsied to the Prince, who stood up and bowed.

"Coaty, how pleased I am to see you."

Turning to the door, Coaty beckoned Aunt Margaret and Harriet to enter. The two women curtsied, receiving gracious bows from George. Everyone sat down on the chairs opposite the chaise longue.

"I'm pleased to see you have offered His Royal Highness hospitality," said Coaty, indicating the Madeira. "Sir," she continued, "it is a pleasure and an honour to welcome you to our home in Dover Street."

"The honour is all mine, ma'am," George replied. "I've been hearing from Fred about his adventures. It sounds as though he was unlucky and lucky in equal measure."

"I discovered the kindness of ordinary people," said Frederick.

"Quite right, quite right," agreed George, looking and sounding very like the King. "Mrs Poulton, Miss Poulton, I am delighted to meet you both at last. Whilst Fred was with us in Richmond and Kew, he used to show me your letters and drawings and told me of your rural lives. Are you enjoying London?"

"We are, thank you," replied Harriet. "We've only been here five weeks, but the city is very noisy and busy in contrast to the countryside in Kent."

"Madam, there are times when I would wish for a quieter life, but the court is always full of people. Everyone is always moving around. One week we are in Richmond, the next in Kew and then the following day we are at St James's Palace or at Buckingham House. Indeed the latest place is Windsor Castle. Sometimes it's hard to know where I am when I wake up!"

The women laughed.

"Mrs Poulton, Miss Poulton, delighted to have met you. Coaty, I hope that you will be happy to see me as a regular visitor."

"Of course, sir," said Coaty, "we would be pleased to welcome you here any time you wish to call."

"Thank you. I have suggested to Fred that we take a tour in my carriage. I would like to introduce him to a place in town where we will have dinner and enjoy a concert. I promise to return him to you in a couple of hours. Indeed, I must be at St James's Palace by seven o'clock for an event."

Frederick followed George to the door of the drawing room and, shrugging an expression of defeat at Harriet, descended the stairs to the hall. Dorothy handed the young men their overcoats, hats and canes and they disappeared into the royal carriage.

"George, I don't like this place," said Frederick, sitting stiffly upon a sofa. The room was hot and over-scented with pomanders and hair powder. A sickly haze of pipe smoke, cigar smoke and snuff hung in the air. The women's attentions irritated Frederick. To his mind, they appeared ill-dressed for a concert and over-attentive in their provision of drink and dainties on silver dishes.

"This place, Fred, is the best bordello in London, so Uncle Cumberland says."

"George, d'you think it's proper we should even be here?"

"My uncle thinks it's acceptable. He's here all the time. I'm surprised we haven't seen him."

"I was thinking of your father and whether he'd approve."

"I'm not going to think about him. Tell me, Fred, has he told you to stop me from enjoying myself?"

"No," Frederick replied, turning away to hide his blushing cheeks and feeling his conscience prick. Having promised the King that he would steer George away from his indulgent life, he'd not started his mission well. Here they both were, perched on a chaise in the 'best bordello in London'.

Two women in brightly coloured dresses swished past them, pausing to curtsy deeply, their breasts nearly tumbling from their low bodices. Their teeth looked yellow against the white powder on their faces.

"There are things you can do with these women," said George, licking his lips as he watched them pass by. "I haven't tried it yet, but Uncle Cumberland says he's going to arrange it for me when I'm fifteen. It's a thing we all need to know about; it's the fucking. When we start doing the fucking with these women, I'd like you to come too, Fred. It's important we do these things together. I'd invite Prince Frederick, but he's too young."

"George, I don't understand how you can have grown up so quickly. I've only been away for three months. You even started shaving before me."

"Yes, Fred, I am a marvel of nature! Everyone I meet comments on it. So well educated and so well bred. You're only a tad behind me, despite your advanced year, ha, ha! Now, let me have a good look at these women. A year ago I didn't care about them, but now, yes, I want to get my hands on…"

"Oh George, stop it."

A crowd of rowdy young gentlemen burst into the room, scraping back chairs around a table to sit with legs outstretched and thumping the surface with their fists. A large, flat, shiny dish, like a mirror, was set in the middle of the table and a young woman climbed onto it. Frederick watched in horror as she pulled up her skirts in full view of the men, hopping around on the dish, flashing her petticoats and rolling her hips whilst the men roared, making lewd comments.

Tugging at George's sleeve, Frederick hissed in his ear, "Let's get out of here."

"No, we are waiting for our dinner and there's always a concert in this room at six o'clock. I want to stay. I'm not due at St James's for another hour."

"We shouldn't be here. We must go."

"Seriously, Fred, calm down. I'm telling you, there's quite an experience waiting for you when one of these women takes you to her private chamber through there," said George, glancing in the direction of the double doors at the far end of the stuffy gilded room. Every so often a woman would saunter out of the doors, gaudily dressed with a freshly powdered face and elaborately dressed hair. And every now and then a man in the room took a woman's arm and they disappeared through the doors together. All Frederick could glimpse through the entrance was a corridor lined with red plush curtains.

"George, you told me we were here for dinner and a concert. You fooled me."

"I didn't fool you. Look, Fred, here is the food. It's roast beef with potatoes, your favourite. And the players are just arriving. Oh, good, and we have the lady who sings bawdy songs too."

"George, I will eat some of this food and listen to the concert, then I insist that we leave."

"Very well, Fred. My carriage will take you home on when I go to St James's. By the way, I think we should give a concert together soon. I've been practising Crosdill's transcripts of the Handel pieces."

Frederick's eyes widened at the prospect. "I'd love to. But I don't have an instrument. I left the violin under my bed at Kew, with everything else."

"Leave it with me, Fred. I'll arrange for all your things to be sent to Dover Street, including your violin and your precious box. And tell you what, I'll ask old Crosdill to find you a cello. Wouldn't you like one of your own? I'm sure my father will pay for it, or I will. I've been given an allowance. It's not much, but it's useful. I can order and buy things. I have sovereigns in my purse." He patted his jacket pocket and coins jingled. "Of course, when I'm eighteen I'll get a more substantial allowance and my own place to live. Then, when I'm twenty-one, oh, the world will open up for me."

"Thank you, George. That's generous. I do so wish to have a cello and I have missed playing my violin. Of course I'd love to give a concert with you."

"So, are you never coming back to Kew?"

"No, never." Frederick shuddered.

"Very well. My valet will bring everything to Dover Street in my carriage."

"Thank you, George." Frederick sighed. "But we can't stay here."

"Oh, very well, Fred. We'll leave soon. Let's finish this food and we'll go. I'm glad we're friends again."

Chapter Twenty
A Revelation
3rd June 1777

Straightening the cravat around his neck and tugging the cuffs below his new green jacket, Frederick prepared for his conversation with Coaty. At dinner a couple of nights ago, she had hinted that she had something important to discuss with him. He thought that, after nearly two years of tutoring at home in Dover Street, she probably had some new educational scheme in mind for him and hoped that it would be further music lessons or perhaps the chance to travel. He had mentioned his desire to experience the Grand Tour and join some of the young aristocrats in George's circle who were planning to explore the Continent. Coaty valued travel and he shivered with excitement at the prospect of this new adventure. Smiling to himself, he stretched his neck and patted his hair before tapping on the door of Coaty's study.

"Enter," came the shrill reply.

Closing the door behind him, he walked towards Coaty, seated behind her large desk in the centre of the room. Her appearance bothered Frederick. She looked drawn and tired, her un-powdered grey hair hung in a limp bun at the back of her neck and her fingerless, lacy gloves were ink-stained and grubby. Squinting at the sun's reflection in the glass-fronted cabinet behind her, he noticed some gaps where the silver plate used to be. And where were the sculptures from Italy? He knew she loved to take them out, handle them carefully and tell the story of their purchase during her youthful continental travels. Why weren't they there?

"Fred, come and sit down. I asked you in here because we have some important matters to discuss. You will be sixteen at the end of August and we must make plans for your future."

Flapping up his coattails, Frederick settled on the padded chair opposite her, leaning back, stretching his legs and anticipating pleasant news.

"Fred, as you know, I am delighted that you and your family have come to live with me. I never thought, in my dotage, that I would be lucky enough to share my life and my good fortune with people whom I love and wish to help. However, you are in a difficult situation."

"Why?" Frederick sat up, concerned that this conversation might not be going in the direction he had anticipated.

"The King and Queen acknowledge your position within their family, but the rest of the world cannot know the connection. Aunt Margaret and I admire your restraint regarding this secret."

"I promised the King I would be discreet, Coaty. I can't help it if people make comments, but I never confirm anything."

"The King and Queen have been generously funding your education and I have contributed what I can. The three hundred pounds per annum will continue to come to you until you are twenty-one, or until you finish your education. I hope you've been pleased with your tutors and the music lessons?"

"Yes, I have, thank you, Coaty. I've learnt far more from them in the last two years than I did at Kew. I'm glad that Harriet has benefitted from them too. And my cello playing is much more confident."

"Good, I'm glad to hear it. And I want to reassure you that you don't need to worry about your expenses. I will continue to look after everything for you."

"Thank you."

"Fred, the subject of this discussion is twofold. Because of your situation, it is important that you acquire a profession. The case concerning your Blomberg inheritance is taking time and we cannot be assured that you will inherit the estate."

"A profession! No, that's not what I'd had in mind. I thought I was going to be a gentleman. And when I inherit the Blomberg estate in Yorkshire, the income will sustain me, and everyone in this household."

"I'm afraid, for the time being, Fred, becoming a gentleman is out of the question. We don't have enough income. You need to follow a profession."

"What! Coaty, no! No, no, no. That is not what I expected. Given my connection to the royal family, the least I would expect is to be regarded as a gentleman. I can't seek employment. No, no. That would be impossible."

"Fred, you may wish to live as a gentleman, but my modest resources are being stretched. I cannot commit everything to you. I have to think about Harriet and your aunt Margaret."

Frederick's shoulders sagged. "Won't the King help me? He did promise to."

"He is helping, but the funds from Their Royal Majesties are for your education, not to support the life of a gentleman. Besides, there are fewer funds available to the Privy Purse following the loss of the American colonies. You must understand that."

Frederick was devastated. For the last two years, whilst living in Dover Street, he believed that he could, in some way, retain his half-princely status and close association with the royal family, at least with Prince George. He liked feeling important and being accepted in society. He enjoyed having access to exclusive places. A profession, no, that wouldn't do at all. How could he consort freely with members of the aristocracy if he had to earn a living? Only gentlemen of leisure or ladies of rank could be accepted and respected.

Standing up, Frederick thumped the top of the chair before pacing to the window and looking out over the yard to the backs of houses in Albemarle Street. "This can't be right. Coaty, surely there's something to be done? Has the King forgotten what he promised? I have to maintain my position; it's important to me. What would the Prince of Wales think? George would laugh at me."

"Frederick, sit down and be quiet for a moment. Listen carefully. This is what will happen."

Frederick sat down on the chair.

"You will study divinity at Cambridge University and then you will be ordained into the Church of England."

Frederick held up his hands, mouth open in horror. "Divinity! Ordained! You mean become a vicar? No, absolutely not."

"Yes, you must enter the church. It's a very sound and sensible solution. I'm sure you'll have no problem with the academic work. You are a studious and sensible young man, so unlike George. Can you imagine him studying divinity?"

Frederick sat back in the chair, snorting with mirth. "George, divinity, ha!"

"Exactly," said Coaty, smiling at the shared vision. "Fred, I have discussed this proposal with Their Majesties."

"What! When? Coaty, how could you?"

"I broached this idea soon after I became your guardian and we discussed it again when I saw them at their drawing room at St James's, two months ago, in April. They agree with my idea and think it's a very good plan. I received a letter from the Keeper of the King's Privy Purse this morning confirming their support and the funds for your university studies."

Leaning forward, Frederick put his hands on Coaty's desk and banged his head on it. "Must I? It feels so humiliating. They can't want me to be… to be a vicar. No, it cannot be true!"

"Fred, listen. The King has personally arranged it. In late September you will go up to St John's College in Cambridge to begin a degree. Then, after four years of study, you will spend another three years preparing for ordination. It is a good plan. The King has kindly offered to fund your studies, and in due course, he will ensure that you are granted a good living, or several livings, in some of the best parishes in the country. This will make you wealthy and you will have somewhere to live."

"No, please no," groaned Frederick, slumping back into the chair.

"Being a clergyman is a very sound profession, Fred, and will bring you respect. You can take your place in society and hold your head up high. And a living within a parish, or even a cathedral, brings financial security. You will have status and be accepted at court. Everyone will look up to you."

"Coaty, don't I have any say in this? I hate the idea. I've never thought of myself as a vicar. Divinity or the church was never something I even liked. At Richmond, Kew or St James's Palace, we were always in and out of chapel; it was boring. I know the King loves religion. He always made us attend, but none of us cared for it. All I liked was the music. What makes you think I'd be a good vicar? If I have to have a profession, can't I do something else, the army, law maybe?"

"The King desires you to have this profession. He is delighted to think that you will be educated in Christianity and become a man of God. It gives him great pleasure and you really have no choice. For a young man who is not quite a gentleman, or a prince, by dint of not possessing money or an estate, there is no option."

"But Coaty, I do have an estate. What about this Blomberg estate, Kirby Misperton in Yorkshire? If I owned it, then I wouldn't have to study and become... a vicar. Can't we establish my claim? What's taking so long?"

"Fred, I'm doing all I can to secure the estate for you, but it is proving difficult. That's the other thing I wanted to talk to you about. As you know, I have examined the contents of the red Morocco box which your father, Major William Blomberg, left you."

"I know about the box, but you've never let me see what's in it."

"My solicitor, Mr Brady, has reviewed everything and agrees that you do have a claim, but there are impediments. Because your father chose not to inform his family or his commanding officers of his marriage and his child, the Blomberg family has no record of you; they have no responsibility for you or expectation of your claim.

We have a case, but it is costing me, and the family, far more than I had anticipated to prove it."

Frederick bit his thumbnail, gazing beyond Coaty at the empty shelves in the display cabinet.

"Is that why so many of your treasures are missing? You've sold them?"

"Yes, Fred, I have sold some of my things. That's all they are, just things. I can live without them. Establishing that you are the rightful inheritor of Kirby Misperton is more important."

Frederick stared at the blank spaces in the cabinet, letting his eyes swim and the image blur. He wished he'd known the full story long ago. He was annoyed at himself for not anticipating this. So many elements of his life did not fit together as he had planned. The thought reminded him of being a child in the nursery at Richmond, struggling to assemble one of Coaty's wooden puzzles.

"Coaty, I do have a question about this. What I don't understand is… in fact, what I've never understood is, if my father, William Blomberg, never told anyone about his marriage and me, then how did the King and Queen hear about me and know where to find me?"

"That, Fred, is the most mysterious part of your story, which I have resisted telling you until now. But you are nearly sixteen years old, and it is time you knew."

Coaty opened the lowest drawer in her desk and drew out the red Morocco box. She opened it and sifted through the documents. Taking out a letter, she handed it to Frederick.

"Here, Fred. You need to read this letter. It was written in 1765, when you were only three and a half years old. It was sent to Lady Cha from Colonel Stewart, William Blomberg's commanding officer. As you know, your father was stationed in the Caribbean with his regiment to fight the French and Spanish in defence of the American colonies. Lady Cha received this letter and then showed it to Their Majesties. I then gave this same letter to Aunt Margaret to read when I first came to your home in Dorset to take you away to be adopted. I discussed this with Aunt Margaret yesterday and she agrees that now is the time that you should know its contents. Before I say any more, you should read it."

Frederick took the letter, unfolded the brittle paper, turning yellow at the edges, and began to read.

From Colonel Stewart, Mayfair, London
To Lady Charlotte Finch, Head Governess,
Richmond Lodge, London
30th June 1765

My dear Lady Charlotte,

I humbly crave your indulgence in writing to you so directly about a matter of the highest sensibility and curiosity. I wish to impart to you a strange story relating to the welfare of an orphan boy named Frederick Blomberg. I hope that you will see fit to relay this tale to Their Royal Majesties, King George III and Queen Charlotte. I understand you are governess to the two royal princes and hope you will receive this information with the sympathy your station commands.

I write to you from London, but I am lately returned from the island of Dominica in the Caribbean where I was stationed with my battalion. My story concerns a fellow officer in the Royal Lincolnshire Regiment, a Major William Blomberg. I believe he shared a childhood friendship with His Majesty and, as young men, they travelled together in England.

One evening, in early March 1764, my colleague, Captain Mountsey, and I were resting in our barrack room. It was late and we had retired to our beds, separated from one another by a curtain. A shadowy figure entered our room and spoke in a quiet but forceful voice that he was Major Blomberg. I was surprised and cried out "Blomberg, are you mad?" He was supposed to be stationed at a nearby island, not appearing in my bedroom.

The figure, claiming to be Major Blomberg, told me that he had been killed that day. Despite his death, the apparition said that he was compelled to come to me from beyond the grave with an urgent message. He was concerned for the welfare of the child of his secret marriage. He wanted the King to know where the child was. He gave me an address in Dorset where, he said, I would find him, now orphaned, since his mother had died at his birth. He also told me that I would find a red Morocco box at the same address containing documents pertaining to the child's inheritance.

In an urgent tone, the apparition bade me go to this place, find the child, confirm that he was alive and to inform the King. Major Blomberg's message suggested that His Majesty would be interested in his welfare, inferring that the orphan child should be brought up with the care and attention that he would wish upon his own son.

The ghostly figure then left the room. I was astonished and asked Captain Mountsey if he had seen and heard this exchange. He confirmed that he recognised Blomberg's voice and had seen the figure enter the room and then leave. We searched the barracks and there was no sign of Blomberg.

The following evening we learnt that Major Blomberg, along with several soldiers, had been killed following an exchange of gunfire with the French on a neighbouring island. His corpse was later brought back to barracks for burial. Mountsey and I found it hard to believe what we had been told by the visitation. It seems we had indeed seen and heard from the ghost of Major Blomberg.

On our return to London, many months after this event, we decided to visit the address given to us by the apparition. There, on the edge of the named village, we found a cottage where a boy of three years old was living with his aunt, the sister of his late mother, another child and a servant. We asked for, and were shown, a red Morocco box, which contained documents that referred to Major Blomberg and his family.

Lady Charlotte, because Major Blomberg kept his marriage a secret from his commanding officers and his family, this child, despite bearing his name, is not entitled to any pension or army support. He appears to have no financial means save the affection of his aunt and her family, who are farmers.

I am therefore writing to you to acquaint you with this situation, as requested by the apparition. I ask you whether it is appropriate for the King and Queen to learn of this story? I have no further information to provide other than that which I have related. I humbly request that you consider this situation. If I can be of any further assistance, please do write to me. I shall be at my address in Mayfair until the end of next month. Thereafter, I must re-join my battalion and return to the Caribbean.

With the greatest respect,
Yours etc. Colonel Stewart

As he absorbed the contents of the letter, Frederick's eyes widened. He folded up the paper, putting it down on the desk next to the box.

"So, Coaty, I'm to believe that my father, William Blomberg, appeared as a ghost after his death? And this apparition told his commanding officer where to find me? It's bizarre."

"I know, Fred, it sounds incredible, but it is the truth."

"Why didn't you or Aunt Margaret tell me sooner? I've been living with you in Dover Street for nearly two years, not to mention all my childhood at Kew, and now you see fit to tell me! And do people in the royal household know the story? For years I thought that the King and Queen must have heard about me from some distant Blomberg relation. Now, I discover that a ghostly version of my father is behind it! It's very hard to believe."

"I know, Fred, it is a very curious tale, and Aunt Margaret and I couldn't tell you when you were young. We wanted to protect you. When Lady Cha received the letter from Colonel Stewart, she didn't know what to think. She met him in London, and he retold his story with such conviction that she had to believe it. It was of no consequence to him, personally. He and Mountsey had played their part out of love for their fallen comrade. They were as surprised as anyone to discover you existed.

"Lady Cha promised the Colonel that she would present the

letter to King George III. The King and Queen read it and that's when they decided to adopt you."

"This is such a strange story. And Aunt Margaret has read this letter too?"

"Yes, when I came to your Dorset home to take you away, I showed it to her. She was bewildered and adamant that you must not be told."

"I don't know what to think," said Fred, sitting back on his chair. "I have a very faint memory of two soldiers coming to the house. So one of those soldiers was…" He picked up the letter to scan it again. "That was Colonel Stewart and Captain Mountsey."

"It is a strange story indeed," said Coaty. "Lady Cha was uncertain whether to show the letter to the King and Queen, but she did. And she told me that, on reading the letter and hearing the story, the Queen said most emphatically, 'We will take this boy.' Those were her very words."

"And the apparition knew about the red Morocco box, that one on your desk?"

"Indeed, and it contains documents relating to your inheritance."

Pointing to the open box, Frederick asked, "Are the details of the estate in there?"

Coaty pulled out a document headed *Kirby Misperton Estate* and handed it to him.

"Yes, that's it, Fred. Kirby Misperton. As you've been told many times, it's a large estate in North Yorkshire in a village also known as Kirby under Carr, not far from Pickering. You can take the map from my shelf over there and look for it. It's not far from Scampston, where I met dear Lady Cha. The Kirby Misperton estate has an elegant mansion house at its heart with excellent stabling, two lakes and several farms which yield a good income."

"So, if I were to inherit this place, I could be a gentleman?"

"Yes, Fred. However, we must prove that you have a stronger claim than the family who are currently in residence. As you know, your great-great-grandfather was a baron. One day you might take that title. I'm sure His Majesty wants you to inherit the estate and the title. I've asked him to help but, I gather, he's not been well of late; he's had a strange debilitating illness, similar to the ones we witnessed when you were little, and I don't want to press him."

Frederick stood up and, smiling wryly, replaced the document in the box. "So I could be a baron? Well, that's something. There's so much to think about."

"Of course. I'm sorry you've been ignorant of this for so long. Aunt Margaret and I were only protecting you."

"Yes, Coaty. Thank you. I know you want to help me. It's a huge thing to take in."

"In families, we do all we can to support each other," said Coaty. "You and I must help Aunt Margaret and Harriet. You will soon be of age and then you'll be the man of the house."

"Yes, I know. And I want to look after you too."

"Fred, please don't worry about me. I became a wealthy woman when I was young. I've been fortunate and many people in my life have helped me. My uncle was kind and managed to double the value of my inheritance. I vowed, in turn, to do what I could for other people, and it pleases my soul to support you and your family. So, Fred, think about my suggestion for your future. Meanwhile, I want you and Harriet to continue your education. Please show this letter to her. I'm sure you'll both have many more questions which Aunt Margaret and I will do our best to answer."

"Coaty, thank you. I apologise for my rudeness before. The idea of entering the church was a shock. It had never entered my mind. However, if I can inherit and become a gentleman, or a baron, then that is what I really want. And I do want to make you proud."

Chapter Twenty-One
University Life
6th May 1779

The summer term of his second year at St John's College would soon be over. Leaning back on his hard chair, Frederick stretched his arms behind his head. Outside in the quad the sound of students laughing and chattering merged with the steady tread of feet tramping along the covered walkway beneath his room.

In recent weeks the weather had improved and at last his study was warm. A fresh breeze wafted through the window, bringing the river's scent. He longed to go for a walk or run across the meadows of The Backs or idle his time along the banks of the River Cam, spotting the blue flash of a kingfisher. But he had exams to prepare for and two essays to write.

Scratching his chin, he yawned and set down his pen. Feeling restless, he opened the folder on his desk containing his correspondence and scanned Harriet's recent letter. She was now consorting with the royal family, and the knowledge made him envious. She had even met the Queen when she visited Coaty at Dover Street. Frederick sucked his teeth as he re-read her news.

1st May 1779

Fred, I have been to Kew! I have seen your old home, the Princes' House, which they now call The Dutch House. How did this happen? Well, the Queen took tea at Dover Street with Coaty, and I joined them, hearing them chatting like old friends.

Then, after enquiring about my interest in plants and medicine, the Queen invited me to Kew to see the rare specimens they have in the gardens and hothouses. She suggested I should meet an elderly friend of the royal family called Mrs Delaney, who is a botanist and an artist. A few days later I went to Mrs Delaney's home in St James's Place, just a step away from Dover Street, and she showed me how she cuts out tiny pieces of coloured paper, like mosaics, to represent plants. I'm to help her with this work.

And yesterday, I visited Kew with Coaty, and the Prince of Wales kindly showed us around your old home, pointing out your former bedrooms on the second floor and your classrooms. He spoke fondly of you, curious to hear how you were faring in Cambridge, and says he misses you. He hopes to arrange a concert when you return to London for the summer.

Fred, did you know that the royal family has moved entirely to Windsor? They've expanded the apartments at the castle for their growing brood – thirteen children! The Prince is eager to show you around his new rooms when you return to London.

I hope your exams go well. Goodness, your second year of university will soon be complete, and we look forward to your return in June with open arms.

Your loving cousin, Harriet

So, Harriet was out in society. At nearly nineteen she was attending balls, making acquaintances, consorting with the royal family and even friends with the Queen's favourite, Mrs Delaney. Most irritating of all was that she was now within the orbit of Prince George. Frederick experienced a mixture of envy and concern for her safety and reputation. Yes, Harriet had two 'lioness guardians' in her mother and Coaty, but Frederick knew how predatory young men of London operated in their pursuit of women, and did not want Harriet to become a victim.

Folding up Harriet's letter, he pushed it into the correspondence folder, glancing at a recent missive from George. Clearly, the young prince was enjoying the pleasures available at the dubious clubs in London. Where once he recounted details of furtive kisses with serving maids or ladies-in-waiting, now at nearly seventeen, his letters were filled with accounts of his desperate passion for this or that lady and his desire to 'know' them.

The knowledge that other people were having fun in London whilst he was devoting his life to study irritated Frederick. He envied George's money, freedom and the company of women. Why couldn't he consort with women too? He was interested in them, enjoying watching the swish of a woman's skirts as she walked down a street in front of him or gazing at the lips of the young girls who served him his dinner in the Great Hall, wondering what it might be like to kiss them.

Where George had ventured through that mysterious door at the bordello, Frederick had still only managed a few furtive kisses with girls in the town after an evening of ale drinking with fellow students. He'd made plenty of friends at Cambridge and shared a love of music with a fellow divinity student, Robert Burt, who'd been studying at Trinity and was just four years older.

Burt spent much of his time at Cambridge in the local hostelries and at card tables. Burt's father was the vicar at Twickenham, an area Frederick remembered from his time at Kew, and he had enjoyed sharing his knowledge of the area with Robert as they chatted over dinner or walked to the nearest alehouse together. Frederick considered pursuing his sister, who had impressed him when she visited her brother in Cambridge. Robert had assured him that she would have welcomed his attention – but still he resisted, citing the demands of his studies as a barrier to flirtation.

He wished he could feel less shy in the company of women and more at ease within his skin. At nearly eighteen, his brown eyes glowed beneath dark lashes. Having shed the pimples of his early teens, the skin over his high cheekbones was now clear and smooth. His voice had dropped to a pleasant tenor, and he shaved daily. He would never be as tall and broad as George and was thankful that he had not inherited the same tendency to overindulge.

Thinking of the portrait by Richard Brompton, and the youthful confidence it conveyed, he pictured himself in that rust-coloured suit, nuzzling Jupiter. Had it been the comfort of living like a prince within the royal family that gave him the confident air the painting suggested? How different his life was now, making do with a meagre allowance and carefully maintaining the few sensible clothes he possessed.

Loosening his cravat, Frederick leant back in his chair. His stomach rumbled, but he knew he must wait an hour until he could go down to the hall for lunch at two o'clock. Sighing loudly and reviewing the text on the paper in front of him, he dipped his pen in the ink and started writing.

An argument on the evidence of angels was the subject of the essay he must write. He thought of William Blomberg's apparition and his ghostly message for the King. Could his dead father have been some kind of angel, perhaps, delivering his message out of love, loyalty or guilt? As a student of divinity, he was familiar with manifestations of this kind; the Bible and religious texts were filled with angelic messengers or strange, inexplicable appearances from people who had died.

Having nearly completed two years at St John's College, to his surprise, he had enjoyed much of the study. What lay ahead was two more years of intensive work, to achieve his B.A. followed by an M.A. and then a further three years of preparation for ordination. He didn't want to let anyone down. Coaty was proud, Aunt Margaret delighted, Harriet astonished whilst George couldn't resist mocking him.

Delving back into his letter folder on his desk, he drew out a saucy print on a card sent by Prince George. It showed a scantily clad woman embracing a vicar. Frederick knew that George was being playful, but it made him feel uneasy.

Enclosed in the folder, beneath the card from George, was a private note of encouragement from King George III, written in the monarch's own hand on thick, deckled paper. The King heaped praise on Frederick, expressing his view that men of the cloth represented the highest form of human existence. Frederick appreciated the message, but oh, he thought, it was such hard work being serious all the time when, in his heart, he craved fine clothes, good food, frivolity and female company.

Chapter Twenty-Two
Frederick is in London for the Summer
15th June 1780

"They've taken everyone away from me," cried George, "except you, of course. Thank goodness you're back from Cambridge."

Frederick took a sip of wine and waited for George to continue his complaint, knowing, from experience, that this was a prelude to the usual rant against his father.

"My parents have sent Prince Frederick to Hanover. I mean, I'm nearly nineteen and he's only sixteen. Yet they make him an officer, a colonel no less, and send him off to Germany like he's some kind of conquering hero. And he's got an awful mistress. Then, just as I was having fun in London with Prince William, he too gets taken away, sent to join the navy. They'll send Prince Edward off somewhere next. It's not fair!"

"I'm sorry to hear it," said Frederick, aware that George had only just begun.

George took a pressed linen handkerchief from his jacket pocket, mopping his brow. The temperature at Brooks' Club was overpowering in the hot June air. Waving his hand to summon a servant, George demanded that a window be opened. The servant bowed and pushed up the window behind them a few inches, letting in the noisy clamour from St James's Street and the aroma of horse dung, rancid meat and pipe smoke. "No, no," cried George, "shut it again. I'm going to remove my jacket. I know it's not civil to do so, but I can't bear this heat."

George peeled off his embroidered jacket, flinging it to the floor, unbuttoned the top of his shirt and loosened the cravat around his neck. "That's so much better. Fred, you should do the same. There are no ladies here to swoon over us and I don't care what anyone thinks."

Frederick removed his plain black jacket, and a manservant

swooped upon the men's clothing, removing everything to a hidden cloakroom. Frederick's white shirt stuck to his skin, and he thought how dull he looked compared to the Prince in his colourful outfit and smart buckled shoes. George's hair was newly coiffed, powdered and scented. However, Frederick noticed that George's stomach strained at the buttons of his shirt and his thighs filled every inch of the bright blue breeches, cutting into his flesh at the knee.

"So you're compelled to stay in London," said Frederick. "Well, I'm glad I'm on hand to entertain you. Why don't we set up a concert at St James's or Buckingham House? I've been practising the Bach duet you like."

"Oh no, I'm too distracted to rehearse, let alone put on a concert. You don't understand. I'm desperately in love."

"You were desperately in love this time last year and the spring before. It was that pretty blonde girl at Kew, then that lady-in-waiting. I seem to remember there were a few ladies from the…"

"No, no, this is nothing like that," interrupted George. "It's Mary Robinson. She's glorious. She's an actress; I saw her on stage at Drury Lane and blew her a kiss from my box. Our eyes met… oh, it was bliss; it was agony. I'm in thrall to her."

"And what are you going to do?"

"Do, do! What? I'm going to devote my life to her adoration; that's what I'm going to do. She is my all, my everything."

"Oh, your everything?"

"Have you no idea what it is like to be so unutterably and agonisingly in love? It takes up every moment of your day. From the minute you wake up, there is her image in your head," said George, thumping his forehead with his palm. "And last thing at night, there she is again, like an angel bending over you with a kiss goodnight."

"And I take it you have *known* her, in every sense?"

"Of course, of course. It annoys me that I'm not the only man who craves her attentions. There are many beaux out there in London who wish to take her home of an evening and fuck her."

"But only one Prince of Wales."

"True, my position does have a certain appeal to the ladies. Miss Mary Robinson is female perfection personified. I'll take you to the theatre and you'll see. She performed the most enchanting Perdita in *The Winter's Tale*. I am now her lover, and I call myself Florizel. Isn't that wonderful? We exchange letters using these secret names and we have assignations. She loves me. She flaunts it. I find it so charming. I have a lock of her hair, see."

Pushing his hand into his breeches pocket, George took out a small velvet pouch. Loosening the drawstring, he carefully lifted out a tiny curl of honey-blonde hair fixed in place with a tight red ribbon. "Ah, bliss," he said, kissing it, "would that she were here now, and you could meet her. I promise you too would be smitten."

"I'll take your word for it."

Frederick shook his head, smiling at George. He would never change. He may appear to be a grown man, but in so many ways he was still a child, thought Frederick, observing George tugging at his clothing, fiddling with his hair and tossing his head like a horse. He watched him paddle his fingers in a bowl of nuts on the table in front of them before grasping a fistful and stuffing them into his mouth. Recognising the signs that George was restless and in need of attention or food, Frederick distracted him by summoning a servant to bring more sherry.

"But Fred, I've been remiss, telling you all my news and not asking about yours. How is Cambridge and life in Dover Street now you're here for the summer?"

"Cambridge has been hard work, thank you for asking. And Coaty no longer lives in Dover Street."

"Gone from Dover Street? What, why?"

"It's my fault. She used to have plenty of money, but it's gone. She's spent a fortune on a lawsuit to prove my inheritance claim. You might remember that my Blomberg father left me an estate in Yorkshire."

"How could I forget the Blomberg ghost story? I even heard a version of it from my mother, so it must be true – the tale of the officer who came back from the dead to let my father know about you. I've dined out on that story many times."

"Have you." Frederick frowned. He disliked being the subject of gossip. He could tell that this story had clearly fuelled many an evening's lively conversation and speculation about his true origins, and it annoyed him. "Well, George, as a result of my desire for my inheritance, poor Coaty has sold her books, silver plate, pictures, sculptures and anything of value. I feel ashamed. If I'd been in London, I would have stopped her, but she's lost everything. I'm still determined to inherit Kirby Misperton and then, George, I can resume my life as a gentleman and not be a vicar."

"Oh, Fred, don't you want to be a vicar?" declared George, his face mocking with a downturned mouth.

"No, but I'm resigned to my fate. Despite my sober appearance, I too would like to have enough money to buy fine clothes like yours and be generous to those I love. But, for the time being, I can't. Coaty has given up Dover Street and taken the lease on a cheaper house in Queen Anne Street in Marylebone."

"Dear, dear. That's not a very fashionable area and so far from St James's. Have you no income yourself?"

"I have a small allowance from your parents, but Coaty was in charge of it. She's spent much of it on the case, and I have barely enough to survive my student life. Aunt Margaret writes letters for money to supplement the small interest from the capital her uncle, Farmer Laing, gave her."

"So you've all moved to the other side of town." George shook his head and pursed his lips.

"It was hard for all of us. Harriet and Aunt Margaret still live with Coaty, and they are down to just our maid, Dorothy."

"One maid, Marylebone. Oh, this is bad news indeed. Old Coaty was always such a generous soul. I'm sorry indeed that she's come down in the world. But she did have a little problem." George mimed the raising of a glass to his lips.

"I know, and it concerns us. We wish she wouldn't drink so much."

"So, will you inherit your estate?"

"I don't know. I have an appointment with the solicitor next week and then I'm going to visit Yorkshire and see the place for myself. I have to because it's almost ruined Coaty and been the cause of so much grief to my family. I may find that it's worthless and I'll tell her to stop the whole process. Then again, it might be valuable and whoever lives there at present might believe my claim and effect the transition to me."

"Does somebody live in this Kirby… whatever?"

"Kirby Misperton. Yes, a member of the Blomberg family, the widow of Reverend William Nicholas Blomberg, who was the vicar at Fulham decades ago. You see, George, if we Blombergs are not soldiers, we are clerics!" Frederick held out his arms and then placed his palms together in mock prayer. "Oh Lord, I wish I could take this religious study more seriously!"

"I'm relieved that you have not become a monk. So you'll meet this woman?"

"The vicar's widow, yes. Apparently she won't give it up and, as far as we can tell, won't accept that I'm the legal heir. Coaty's solicitor confirmed that she had a son, but he died in 1774 and there's no record of any children from his marriage. So, if Mrs Ursula Blomberg won't accept me in life, we have to wait for her death and then I can make my claim. I'm going there in two weeks and Harriet's coming with me."

"More adventures for Master Frederick! I envy you."

"There's not much to envy. It's a long journey to Yorkshire. Anyway, you're usually in a position to have what you want."

George shrugged. "When I'm twenty-one I certainly will."

"George, look at me. Seriously, I was brought up in the same way as you, as a royal prince. I had expectations and I haven't forgotten them. Don't be surprised that I want a title and an estate or, at least, to be a gentleman. Wouldn't you want that for me, rather than see me as a vicar?"

"Yes, I can see your point. Our chaplains can be such dreary folk – don't mean to offend. But, secretly, I rather like the idea of you being appointed chaplain in my household. I would like to keep you close, and it would be like having my own voice of conscience sitting next to me, stopping me if I get too carried away. I know that's what Papa hopes for. Besides, Fred, is being a vicar really work?"

"George, of course it is! I've been studying so hard for this, trying to understand the religion, the history and the spiritual side. Vicars are close to people at such important moments in their lives – birth, marriage and death. And, actually, in many ways, it's been very enlightening and quite enjoyable. If my inheritance does not materialise, then part of me genuinely looks forward to being ordained and beginning my ministry."

"Oh Master Frederick, what have we here? Am I in the company of a good man?"

"Don't mock, I'm working hard to make something of my life and help my family."

"And you think *I* don't have to work at all?" George responded.

"I haven't said that. I understand the responsibilities of being a monarch or Prince of Wales. You have my full support."

"Good, I was worried I might have to behave properly in your presence."

"George, we've been friends, nay brothers, for far too long to start questioning each other's motives or our loyalty. Let's just agree that we both have different paths to follow."

Emerging from Brooks' Club two hours later, Frederick began the two-mile journey from St James's to his new London home. Pulling down his hat to shield his face from the afternoon sun, he kept his jacket on for propriety but longed to drape it over his shoulder like lower-class men did. His feet were swollen in the heat and his black shoes pinched his toes as he walked swiftly towards Marylebone.

He was glad to have seen George again. No matter how much their lives diverged, and how intensely annoying he could be, Frederick knew that their friendship, rooted in childhood, would maintain their bond. Aware that George was giving rein to his passions, he wished he could do more to temper the younger man's appetites. Where the King had exhorted piety and duty in his son, George was becoming dissolute and self-pleasing and Frederick realised he was hardly in a position to control his brother's behaviour. Being in the orbit of someone so self-regarding was in such contrast to the life he was now living. But being a man of the cloth didn't mean he had to lead a completely ascetic and monkish life. He was envious of George and wanted the same freedoms and experiences.

Quickening his step, he lifted his hat in greeting and smiled at a couple of young women who paused in front of him, preparing to cross the road. Their pretty faces and colourful clothes attracted him, and he resolved to quell his natural shyness. He decided that he should speak to Robert Burt's sister the next time she visited Cambridge.

Yes, he thought, it was time he became less burdened with the pressure of religious or clerical expectation. With that happy conviction bubbling in his mind, he completed his walk across town, ran up the steps of the Queen Anne Street house to the front door and rang the bell. Dorothy greeted him and took his hat and jacket.

"Oh Master Frederick, I'm pleased you're home. Madam is not feeling well and would like to see you in her bedroom."

"Oh dear. Thank you, Dorothy, I'll go up straight away."

Knocking on Coaty's bedroom door, Frederick entered and found her propped up in bed, her hair fixed in place with her customary lace headdress. A knitted shawl was draped across her shoulders.

"Goodness, Coaty, aren't you hot?" said Frederick. "It's boiling outside."

"No, I'm quite comfortable, thank you. I can see the sun is shining, but it's cool at the back of house with the drapes closed and I'm sure I can feel a draught coming from somewhere."

"I'm sorry I didn't see you at breakfast. I left early and spent the day walking all over town meeting different people. Can I fetch you anything?"

"No, thank you. Aunt Margaret, Harriet and Dorothy are looking after me. I wanted to talk to you about Harriet."

"What's happened? Isn't she here?"

"She's out. As you know, she's made several friends in London and most of them are suitable, but I feel she needs some guidance."

"She's told me a great deal about Mrs Delaney, the artist."

"It's a shame we are no longer living so close to that gracious lady's home in St James's Place. Harriet was skipping down there almost daily to help with her botanical illustrations."

"Well, that sounds perfectly respectable."

"It is, it is. But I want to talk about her gentleman friend."

"Yes, Mr Tate, the art student. She told me about him the moment I returned last week. I've yet to meet him but hope to sometime during the summer."

"I have met him. He is a pleasant enough young man, but he comes from a provincial family with few society connections. His people live in Northumberland and his father runs an agricultural engineering business. I understand from Harriet that they would like young Mr Tate, Gideon, to take over the business in due course."

"But he wants to be an artist?"

"Precisely, and I, like you, am anxious that Harriet should be sensible and, in time, make a good marriage to give her security."

"I wasn't under the impression they were anything more than friends," replied Frederick. "And I agree that she should make the most of our court connections where marriage is concerned."

"I'm glad you share my view. Harriet needs to be careful. Her mother fears she has inherited your late mother's passionate nature. Should she make a connection with an unsuitable person, society will be quick to judge. She seems unaware of the importance of maintaining a good reputation and consorting with the right class. She's a very independent young woman and I fear she could blight her chances of a good marriage and a comfortable life if she is not careful. And I don't want anything she does to reflect badly on you, either."

"I see. And you'd like me to discuss this with her?"

"Please counsel her, Fred. I know her mother has concerns too, but she is fully aware of Harriet's strong character and reluctance to be directed."

"I will do what I can. I realise that, after you and Aunt Margaret, I might have some sway over her decisions. Though next year, when she is twenty-one, we will not be able to limit her in any way, nor should we."

"Thank you, Fred. I knew you would understand."

"Is Aunt Margaret here?"

"No, Fred. She's at a mansion in Berkeley Square to write some letters for the lady of the house."

"She's always so busy."

"I'm sorry that she has to work so hard, but I see no shame in offering one's skills to be of use to others. She enjoys writing the letters these ladies dictate. Why there should be so many women of class who cannot read or write simply baffles me. But there we are. They choose not to, so that provides useful employment for those who do."

"Did Aunt Margaret tell you my decision? I'm going to visit Kirby Misperton."

"She did. When are you going?"

"Harriet and I discussed it yesterday. She's eager to come too. We are going at the beginning of July. I want to see it and she is keen to travel. We might find that the estate is not worth pursuing."

"I find that hard to believe. Remember, I visited when I was a girl."

"Well, we will prepare for the journey and leave in two weeks. In my last week at Cambridge, I wrote to Mrs Blomberg telling her of my intention to visit but have had no reply."

"You must be sympathetic to the woman. She has lost both her husband and her son."

"Of course I will. I'm not going to march up to the door and claim the estate. I will be polite. But I need to see it before I complete my studies, become a vicar and live in some faraway place."

"Fred, I understand your desire to be a gentleman, but please don't pin your hopes on it. I don't doubt you'll be a huge success as a clergyman and, remember, the King has promised you a good living or several in due course; he is expecting you to do this, and it pleases him to know that you will take holy orders. Tell me, did you meet the Prince of Wales today? Margaret mentioned you were expecting to see him."

"I did. And he's in love, of course."

"That boy is a slave to his passions. I saw it in him when he was a child. Will you give me my drink? It's on the table."

Frederick passed her the glass filled with brandy and water.

"Coaty, you're tired. Would you like me to play the cello for you, or would you rather sleep?"

"I'd love to hear you play."

Frederick went to his room to fetch his cello then sat down beside Coaty's bed. As he drew the bow across the strings, playing a gentle tune by Bach, he could see Coaty's eyes slowly closing.

Chapter Twenty-Three
The Cousins Travel to Kirby Misperton
4th July 1780

The journey north took three days of constant travel. For Frederick, this was a familiar endurance, but for Harriet it was a great adventure. She amused Frederick with her constant chatter, interest in fellow travellers, the countryside they passed through, formations of clouds and the state of the roads. Most of all she talked about Mr Gideon Tate, the young man she had become friends with after an encounter in Piccadilly.

Frederick nodded indulgently each time Harriet repeated the story of their meeting when, rushing from his art school, Gideon had dropped his folder, and a gust of wind sent papers flying. Harriet had helped gather them up only to realise that they were life drawings of male models. She studied the drawings, claiming she showed no embarrassment, before handing them to him. There the friendship had begun. Frederick quickly realised that his cousin's attachment to this young man was strong and that any cautious counsel he might offer would be of little use.

Whilst staying in York overnight, at The City Arms Hotel, they treated themselves to a show at the Theatre Royal and a performance of *The Beggar's Opera*. Harriet was excited to see the production, having attended several performances of the opera in London. Frederick was impressed that she knew all the songs, humming along with the tunes.

The next day, as they continued travelling north, she reprised the songs, almost word perfect, sometimes making up new lyrics to amuse him.

They passed the time by exchanging childhood memories and anything they could recall of the four years spent together in Dorset. Harriet's skill as a natural raconteur brought to life the rural characters she had known there, recounting sayings in their accents and making him laugh at the comical expressions she recalled.

By contrast, Frederick contributed stories of life in the royal household and amusing actions of servants, courtiers, tutors and governesses, but they sounded far more prosaic and ordered in comparison to Harriet's colourful descriptions of rural drama. Only Frederick's accounts of George's and the young princes' antics made his eyes sparkle and face brighten as he recalled tales of bad behaviour and the punishments endured.

Every recollection of his time within the royal family reinforced Frederick's desire to reclaim his privileged life, possess his inheritance and again move easily within royal circles. It excited him to think that they were on the brink of seeing the longed-for property. But anxiety that his true origins might be revealed and his inheritance denied chewed at his conscience. Possessing the Blomberg name was one thing, but there was still a chance that his claim might be regarded as fraudulent.

Climbing out of the carriage at Malton, Frederick and Harriet entered The Royal Oak and watched their luggage being carried in by the driver.

"Tomorrow we'll be there," cried Harriet, settling herself in the window seat of the dining salon and peering out at the view, her face bright with anticipation. "I had no idea Yorkshire was so beautiful," she added, gazing at the rolling hills in the distance, beyond the town. "Gideon talks a lot about Northumberland and says it's majestic. I enjoyed the hills in Kent, but these look much bigger, more imposing."

"Harriet, you have not stopped talking about Gideon since we left London. Will he ever return to his family in Northumberland?" asked Frederick.

"No, he can't. It's too far away and he's always busy with his studies and his extra work in London painting scenery for theatres," replied Harriet before adding, "You must meet Gideon when we are back; you'll like him, Fred."

"I dare say I will. I don't think there's any question that you are in love with him."

"Ha, Fred, you're right. You make me blush. But yes, if always thinking about someone means you are in love… Yes, I must be."

"That's what George said about Mary Robinson. He thinks about her from dawn until dusk. I've not had that experience."

"Oh Fred. Are there really no pretty maids in Cambridge?"

"Of course there are, but I rarely have the opportunity to speak to them. And with four more years of study and training to get through, it's all I can concentrate on."

"I hope you meet someone. Are there no sisters of your fellow students you could meet?"

"There are, and there's one young lady I would like to know better, but she's not likely to be in Cambridge again since her brother has been ordained. I might visit her family in Twickenham when we're back, if there's time."

"I hope you do. Gideon has another year of study then he wants to establish himself as a portrait painter."

"A sound enough profession. You know your mama and Coaty are anxious for you to make a good marriage, find a wealthy husband, with property and maybe even a title."

"They don't think that Gideon has good prospects, but I know they like him. He's been to tea and dinner at Queen Anne Street."

"Nobody doubts your strong feelings for Gideon but, I repeat, you must think carefully about this. We would all like you to make a good marriage."

"I will make a good marriage. I'll only marry for love, not money."

Frederick nodded, realising that Harriet's mind was made up. So, he thought, Harriet loved Gideon and George loved Mary Robinson; both of them were unconcerned about the consequences. He envied their conviction.

The following day, after instructing the carriage driver to wait in the village, Frederick and Harriet pushed open the iron gates to Kirby Misperton Hall and walked down the gravel driveway towards the square mansion.

Harriet skipped the last few steps as they approached the front door, hugging Frederick's arm closer to hers as he rang the bell.

A young woman wearing an apron and a servant's bonnet opened the door.

Frederick removed his hat, standing up as tall as he could. "Good morning. I am Frederick Blomberg, and this is my cousin Harriet Poulton. We are here to see Mrs Blomberg."

"Does she know you're coming?"

"She should do. I wrote her a letter."

"Come in and wait in the hall."

Frederick and Harriet paced around the broad hallway, looking at the dreary pictures on the walls. All the doors were closed and a staircase in front of them rose toward the first floor. The flagstone floor was muddy and long-dead flowers drooped from a vase on the hall table.

After several minutes the servant reappeared and beckoned them to follow her. Opening a door on the right, she showed them into a large room with tall windows. Sitting close to the fireplace was an elderly woman dressed in black. She remained in her chair, staring at them as they approached.

"Good morning, Mrs Blomberg, I presume," said Frederick, bowing. "I hope you received my letter."

"Hah," grunted the woman. "I did. But I didn't expect you to come. Well, you're here now; sit down." She waved a crabbed hand at two chairs opposite her own. "What are your names?"

"Frederick Blomberg and my cousin Harriet Poulton."

"Tell me, Master Blomberg, who, exactly, is your father?"

Frederick swallowed hard, nervous that this woman might somehow know the truth of his parentage. "My father was Major

William Frederick Blomberg, late of the Royal Lincolnshire Regiment. He was killed in action in the Caribbean in March 1764. He was the nephew of your late husband, Reverend Blomberg."

"My son is also called William," said Ursula Blomberg.

"Yes, I am too. It's my middle name. My condolences regarding your son."

"My son is away."

Frederick sat up straight, puzzled at her response, knowing that Ursula Blomberg's son had died four years ago.

"I was informed that he is deceased."

"Whatever do you mean?" she retorted. "He will come back. He always returns to his mother."

"Mrs Blomberg. I must speak plainly," began Frederick. "I am presenting myself to you as the legal inheritor of Kirby Misperton."

"You can't be," Ursula Blomberg retorted, her steely eyes glittering and her body quaking. "My son William is the inheritor."

"Mrs Blomberg, my solicitor informs me that your son has died. I'm sorry to respond so candidly, but I have also been informed that his widow, Anne, has remarried and there were no Blomberg children."

"How dare you make such a suggestion!"

"So are you telling us that he is alive?"

"He will return to me."

Frederick was troubled. "Mrs Blomberg, I do not mean to offend, but it is our understanding that your son, William has, sadly, died. And we believe there are no heirs."

"This place belongs to the Blomberg family. My husband is a direct descendant of the first Baron Blomberg."

"And I repeat, madam, I too am a direct descendant of the same Baron Edmond Blomberg. My father was your husband's younger brother's son. He was an officer who died in action defending the American colonies."

"My late husband, Reverend William Nicholas Blomberg, was

a clergyman. He was the only surviving direct descendant and his claim is undisputed."

"Mrs Blomberg, there is no argument about our family forebears. I wanted to establish that, with no other heirs to claim this estate, I, Frederick Blomberg, am the rightful inheritor."

"No, I have a son. It will be his."

"You have another son?"

"No, my son, William."

Frederick pressed his nails into his palms. This woman could not be sane. "And your son, I ask again, is it possible to contact him?"

"Not at present. It is my wish that he should inherit. As long as I am alive, I will keep this place for him."

"Mrs Blomberg, this is very difficult. I have documents, given to me by my late father, which prove that his heir, that is myself, should inherit this estate. Our solicitor is pursuing the case through Chancery. He has established that you have no heirs and that the property, in due course, should come to me or it will be returned to the reigning monarch, who can do whatever he wants with it. As you know, it came into the Blomberg family by marriage, having originally been gifted by King Charles II a century ago. We came here to establish whether you accept that I am indeed the inheritor and that you agree to the natural direction of the inheritance."

"I know all about your case, Master Blomberg. And I have my suspicions about your claim. I cannot be convinced that you are truly a Blomberg."

"Mrs Blomberg," interrupted Harriet, "madam, it's been a long journey. May I avail myself of the closet?"

"Yes, very well," Mrs Blomberg replied, ringing a bell by the fireplace, and the servant entered. "Mrs Troughton is my housekeeper. Florence, please show this young lady to the bedroom at the top of the stairs where there is a closet and a chaise."

"Thank you." Harriet followed Mrs Troughton out of the room.

"Madam," continued Frederick, "the purpose of this visit is

to confirm my claim, and I shall contest your will, in due course, whatever it says." Endeavouring to soften his tone and change the subject, he added, "Mrs Blomberg, how long have you lived here?"

"My husband and I took possession of Kirby Misperton over forty-five years ago. But we rarely lived here whilst he was alive. Having begun our married life in Fulham, where he was vicar, my husband was the Rector of Cliffe at Bath for eleven years until his death in 1750. That's when I moved here with William, my son."

"And you enjoyed Bath?"

"I did. That is where my son William was born."

"I have never been to Bath," replied Frederick. "I hear that the Season is very lively, and visitors come from all over the country to enjoy the parties and entertainments."

"It is a beautiful place, and the Season is, indeed, a very busy and sociable time. We enjoyed the music and the parties. But I have lived here, with William, for over thirty years. Master Frederick, I gathered from your letter that you are soon to be ordained and offer you my congratulations. However, you will discover that a man of the cloth has no home of his own. You may live in a vicarage, parsonage or rectory, depending on the parish, but you will own no property. Kirby Misperton was the only real home we ever possessed. You must understand how attached I am to it."

"Of course. But for that reason, do you not think it right that a member of the Blomberg family, and a future cleric, should continue living here?" said Frederick.

"I understand what you are after, and I make myself clear. I will not be moved."

Harriet returned to the room and Frederick stood up and bowed. "Mrs Blomberg, we will take our leave. One final thing, would you object if we walked around the estate? We have come a great distance and would like to take the air and admire it."

"I cannot stop you viewing the estate. Goodbye."

Frederick bowed again and Harriet curtsied. They both left the room, closing the door, and encountered Mrs Troughton waiting in the hall. She ushered them out of the house and onto the gravelled driveway.

"I'm sorry you had a wasted visit," she said, walking with them towards the lake. "I know you've travelled a great distance."

"Mrs Troughton, why does she say her son will return?" asked Frederick.

"She's deluded. He died over four years ago."

"Thank you for confirming what our solicitor told me. And there were no heirs?"

"No, none."

"But he was married?"

"Yes, young William married a woman called Anne. She was a pleasant enough girl but totally unsuited to life here in Yorkshire. She was born and brought up on an island in the Caribbean."

Frederick and Harriet glanced at each other – yet another connection with the Caribbean.

"Her father owned a plantation in St Kitts. She came over to England with him to find a husband. He wanted her to make a good marriage because he needed funds to sustain his business."

"Was it a happy marriage?"

"No, I cannot say that it was. She disliked Yorkshire. She missed the warm weather and couldn't abide the cold and rain. She pleaded with William to take her to London but, really, she wanted to meet her childhood sweetheart, a Mr Nesbitt, the son of another plantation owner, who had also come to London for marriage. Anne caused a scandal when she ran away with this man. Our poor William was distraught. He'd loved the girl, and he'd hoped they'd have children."

"And then he died," said Frederick.

"Yes, he took ill in London after she'd abandoned him. When his mother heard what had happened, she insisted that he must be brought back here, even though he was so sick. The journey was too much for him and he died. She's never got over it. There's a memorial to him in the church."

"We will have a look," said Harriet.

"And did his wife, Anne, inherit the estate?"

"I shouldn't really be telling you this," said Mrs Troughton, "but you'd find out from others in the village if you asked. No, Anne signed away all claim on this estate in exchange for six thousand pounds in cash, which she gave to her father. She married Mr Nesbitt and set up home in London. The last I heard, she had died, and he went on to marry a society wife."

"So, there are no other heirs or claimants?"

"Not to my knowledge," said Mrs Troughton, pausing to watch a heron skimming across the surface of the lake. "But I dare say your claim is as strong as anyone's, if you are truly a Blomberg."

Frederick nodded in thanks. Placing his hat on his head, he and Harriet bade farewell to the housekeeper, who walked back to the house.

"What an impossible woman Ursula Blomberg is," exclaimed Frederick. "Come on, Harriet, we're going to have a good look round."

Following a path to the side of the house, they pushed open the wooden door set in a high wall and saw an overgrown kitchen garden. They peered into outhouses, stables and assorted buildings at the back of the mansion. Walking along gravel paths flanked by tall grass and the white bloom of cow parsley, they pushed through a gate and into overgrown parkland before turning down a path towards the lower lake.

"She's a sad woman, Fred," said Harriet, picking up a stick and swishing at the long grass.

"What makes you say that?"

"Whilst I was upstairs, I had a look round. I discovered a bedroom laid out like a shrine to her dead son. It's a nursery with a rocking horse, a made-up bed and toy soldiers arranged on a table.

His clothes hang in the wardrobe, including an army uniform, and there are riding trophies and rosettes. I saw books with their markers still in place and fresh ink in the bottle on his desk and blank writing paper. There's a portrait of him on the wall. It's as though she's waiting for him to come back."

"Poor woman indeed," said Frederick. "This visit has settled two things in my mind. Kirby Misperton is a very good estate. However, I'm never going to take possession of it whilst Mrs Blomberg is still alive."

"Fred, apart from her son's room, I explored more of the house. There are many bedrooms and the views from the windows are beautiful. Mrs Blomberg has let the estate grow wild and it's going to need a lot of work and money to make it comfortable. But, I agree, it would be a wonderful home to own. I can understand why you want it."

"I do, Harriet. I want to live in a home fit for a gentleman. I know that vicars live in a vicarage or rectory with few of their own possessions. Bishops might have a palace next to a cathedral and that's something to aspire to. I would like to be wealthy enough to buy silver plate, paintings and invite people to dinner. I want a music room where I can play my cello and violin."

"Fred, I think you're envious of George and the royal brothers. You want the life they lead. I'm sure you will inherit this place one day," replied Harriet, quickening her pace as they walked along the path back to the house and then down the drive towards the gates.

"Don't you wish to own property, Harriet?"

"Yes, but my ambition is different. I want to earn money using my skills and then buy what I can afford."

"That's a very naïve thought, Harriet, especially for a woman. You need a good husband who can provide security."

"I want to have a home and a husband one day, but I want independence too and control over my life. But, for the time being, as long as I am with Mama, Coaty and you, I have a home. And when I'm older, I will create a home of my own. Really, Fred, I don't think bricks and mortar or even the location of your home matters. It's the people you live with that matter."

Chapter Twenty-Four
Frederick is Summoned Home
15th April 1781

Coaty was not well, and Harriet's letter urged him to come home immediately.

Explaining the situation to his tutor, Frederick was granted compassionate leave from St John's to return to London for a few days on condition that he returned in time to take his finals in May.

Choosing an outside seat to save money, and enduring the occasional shower, Frederick pulled down his hat above his head as the carriage bounced and creaked its way to London.

It was after seven o'clock and dusk was falling when the coach clattered into the cobbled courtyard of *La Belle Sauvage* in Ludgate. Aware of the urgency of his arrival, Frederick paid for a Hackney carriage to carry him west towards Marylebone. Running up the steps of the Queen Anne Street house, he rang the bell. Harriet, who'd been watching impatiently for him at the window, answered within seconds.

"Oh, Fred, thank heavens you're here."

Leading him into the cluttered drawing room crammed full of Coaty's remaining Dover Street furniture, Harriet plumped up the cushions on the chair by the fire and Frederick sat down. Dorothy brought in a tray with a bowl of soup and some bread.

"Coaty knows you're coming, but she's not always aware of what's going on."

"Did the drinking cause this illness?"

"Probably. We called a doctor, who said that her liver could no longer cope with the level of alcohol she consumes. Coaty had bidden Dorothy to bring her drinks for more years than we knew. If madam wants brandy, Dorothy fetches it."

Aunt Margaret entered the drawing room and advanced toward

Frederick, wrapping her arms around him. "It's always a joy to see you, Fred, but I fear that this visit will be a sad one. Coaty is weak and the doctor believes she won't live for long."

Fred tried to control his emotions, but his eyes still welled with tears.

"Fred, I realise this is a shock," said Aunt Margaret, seeing his reaction to her words, "but you must be brave and your usual charming self when we go into her room. She wants to see you."

The three crept into Coaty's bedroom, Fred sitting down at the chair near her head with Harriet and Margaret on the other side.

"My dear Master Frederick," whispered Coaty, "how was the journey?"

"Not too bad, dearest Coaty. I hear you've been unwell."

"Dear boy, I'm dying. I am glad of it. My fifty-eight years of life have been full of adventure and joy, but the best of it has been having you all as my family."

"Coaty, you've done so much for us. This week we students debated the definition of kindness in our lecture, and I thought of all you have done for us."

"You are going to be an exemplary clergyman."

"I'm studying hard, being careful with my allowance. But I've been very happy at Cambridge, especially since joining a string quartet too and playing my cello."

"Good." Coaty moved her thin hands over her silk bedspread, smoothing the fabric. "When one knows the end is near, the happiness of those you love is important. Do not weep for me. I feel no fear or discomfort."

Harriet buried her face in her handkerchief.

"I want to be practical," continued Coaty, her voice growing hoarse. "There is very little of my estate to leave to you. Aunt Margaret has my will. I would like her to continue living here for as long as she wishes. If there are not enough funds, then I charge you, Fred, to support the family and Dorothy."

"Coaty, of course I will."

Coaty closed her eyes and sighed. Frederick looked across the bed at Aunt Margaret and Harriet.

"She's tired," said Aunt Margaret. "We should just stay with her."

Coaty breathed in and out, a rattle sounding in her chest.

Frederick took her left hand and kissed it. The three sat around her bed, watching the gradual slowing of her breath. Without uttering a word, Aunt Margaret rose to light more candles whilst Frederick and Harriet continued their vigil.

A few hours later, Coaty gave a deep, guttural sigh. Her eyes flickered briefly then closed again.

Frederick took her hand. It felt limp and there was no response.

Moving close to Coaty's face, Aunt Margaret looked up, shaking her head. "Oh dearest Coaty, how we will miss you."

Harriet gave a sob, pressing her head into the bedcover next to Coaty's hands. Frederick mouthed the last rites, making the sign of the cross and kissing her on the forehead. "The best of women," he murmured, biting his tongue but failing to stem the tears.

Chapter Twenty-Five
Coaty's Funeral at Kew
26th April 1781

Mourners, including members of the royal household, filled St
Anne's Church in Kew to bid farewell to Coaty. Lady Charlotte
Finch gave an elegant eulogy, speaking tenderly of her friend and
confederate, recalling their meeting in Yorkshire and her conviction
that Henrietta would make an inspiring teacher. She described their
time running the royal nursery, their shared creativity in educating
the princes and princesses and included a few stories of their young
charges' antics, which allowed the mourners to laugh, blow their
noses and wipe their eyes.

Queen Charlotte invited everyone to gather for tea afterwards
at Kew Palace, no longer the Princes' House but referred to as the
Dutch House. As he entered his old home, Frederick experienced a
mixture of anxiety and regret. Whilst tea was served in the dining
room, he withdrew from the reception and wandered around the
mansion, smiling at the marks on the woodwork of the stairs
caused all those years ago by George's reckless ride on his horse
and recognising many of the same paintings still in place. He stood
within the old schoolroom, picturing bookcases, tables and chairs
in spaces where other furniture now stood. Venturing upstairs, he
viewed his childhood bedroom and the space where his bed once
stood.

Though referred to as a palace, the fine redbrick mansion seemed
much smaller than Frederick remembered. He had not grown many
inches in six years, but the building no longer overwhelmed him.
He was a man now.

Conversation in the dining room rose in volume as the assembled
guests began to enjoy sharing their memories of Henrietta
Cotesworth and taking pleasure in greeting people they had not seen

for years. Frederick bowed to his former governess, Lady Charlotte Finch, kissing her hand when they had time to talk afterwards.

"Lady Cha," said Frederick, "I am so pleased to see you again."

"And I you, Master Frederick. I hear you are studying well at Cambridge."

"I'm enjoying divinity more than I thought I would."

"I'm pleased to hear it. You were always a naturally studious boy. You've put your education to good use. We all look forward to seeing you at Windsor Castle when you are ordained. The King has been following your progress and is very proud. I gather he is keen to appoint you as chaplain when the time comes."

"Thank you, Lady Cha, I am heartened to hear that. I hope that Their Majesties are well and enjoying living at Windsor?"

"They are well, thank you. The usual coughs and colds irritate us. The passages at the castle can be very chilly even at this time of year, but we soldier on. You may have heard that the King has had the occasional 'turn' but nothing out of the ordinary. Perhaps you remember the moments you witnessed as a child when he was not himself, but he always recovers."

"I do. Prince George and I often wondered if it was our bad behaviour which caused him to behave strangely."

"I'm sure it was not your actions, and we are alert to any alteration in his demeanour."

"I'm pleased to hear it. Lady Cha, I have a question, and I don't wish to be impertinent. Why was it that Coaty, I mean Mrs Cotesworth, left the royal nursery so abruptly?"

"Frederick, it has bothered me for years too. It was a misunderstanding caused by a sub-governess who was ambitious and manipulative."

"What happened? Coaty would never tell us."

"Do you remember a Mrs Cheveley?"

"I do, but not kindly. She beat me for crimes I did not commit."

"Ah, I've heard many of these stories from the younger princes and princesses and I am sorry I was not alert to her deceptions. She accused Mrs Cotesworth of neglect, and this caused Henrietta's dismissal."

"What!"

"Indeed. It was back in August '75. Mrs Cheveley discovered the young prince, Adolphus, in the nursery in a state of distress in his highchair. Henrietta was in the room with the child, but she was asleep in an armchair by the fire and had not been roused by his cries. We all knew of Henrietta's weakness for drink and Mrs Cheveley knew that she had taken some brandy in her afternoon coffee. Rather than waking Henrietta, Mrs Cheveley went straight to the Queen, telling her about the neglect of the child. Her Majesty was horrified and dismissed Henrietta."

"Coaty may have taken too much to drink and fallen asleep, but she would never wittingly harm a child," said Frederick.

"I know and it was a difficult time. Henrietta was inconsolable."

"Poor Coaty. No wonder she was distraught. And her dismissal took place on the day of George's thirteenth birthday feast?"

"It did. And Mrs Cheveley took Henrietta's place in the royal nursery. However, Her Majesty felt very guilty for dismissing Henrietta. She had been with me in the royal nursery for fifteen years. But, in truth, Henrietta was tired. She'd given long service to the royal family, and it was time for her to retire, as it was for me soon after."

"I wish Coaty had told us. It was always a mystery that she left the nursery so suddenly and moved to her house in Dover Street."

"It was distressing for everyone. The Queen resolved to stay in touch with her old friend. I gather she often visited Dover Street."

"Yes, she did, and also at Queen Anne Street, despite it being a humbler home."

"Frederick, this is a sad day indeed, but I am glad to have had the opportunity to speak to you. It gives me great pleasure to know that my dear friend, who never had family of her own, became an official guardian to you. I'm pleased that you are living a happy life away from the royal family, but I do hope that you'll stay in touch with us and come to Windsor and St James's Palace. We look forward to your visit."

Chapter Twenty-Six
Prince George Takes Frederick to London

George patted Frederick on the knee before sitting back on the bench opposite, his ample thighs splayed across the padded seat of his carriage. The Prince had not attended Coaty's funeral but had hastened from Windsor to catch his old friend after the mourners' tea at Kew Palace with the promise of an evening in London to try out rare string instruments.

Frederick felt tired and on edge. So many encounters from his youth had caused the anxiety of his years at Richmond to flood back. Meeting some of the younger princes and princesses, governesses and even a few of his old tutors churned up many memories. Greeting some of the maids, valets and pages from his years at Kew made him feel nervous.

George had sent Frederick a note demanding him to wait for his arrival in Kew after the funeral, and then to accompany him to an instrument shop in Mayfair which had lately received a delivery of cellos and violins from Italy. Frederick could not resist the chance to try a rare Stradivarius violin. And he wanted to spend time with George, too.

As the coach rattled along the roads to the capital, Frederick peered from the carriage window at the darkening sky, noting the glow of lamplight in the windows of buildings they passed. He knew he should have returned home to Marylebone with Aunt Margaret, Harriet and Dorothy after the funeral, but he couldn't resist this surprise journey with George. If George summoned him, he would obey. That was simply the way things were.

"Fred, don't be sad," said George. "I understand you've had a difficult day, but we'll be there soon and I know that sampling these instruments will cheer you up. Oh, did I tell you they're giving me Carlton House? It'll be ready next year. There's still a lot to do to it though."

"You did. How are the renovations coming along?"

"Very slowly. That's why I'm stuck out at Windsor so much of the time, or else at St James's or Buckingham House. But the palaces are all filled with my father's spies. The only good thing about Buckingham House is that it's close to Hyde Park and I can ride my horse like a demon if I choose. I like to be near all the interesting places in the capital. Ever been to Vauxhall or the Ranelagh Gardens?"

"No."

"Oh Fred, you're missing out. In the summer those pleasure gardens are full of fun and opportunity. There's a great deal of music too. But spies follow me even there and inform the King. Everywhere I go I see faces peeping around the corner or from behind a tree or the corner of a building. But I'm beyond caring now. I'm going to please myself. Having my own household is the start of it. It's costing a lot of money, but I have to reside in a palace fit for a king in waiting."

"Indeed," said Frederick with a smile. "And how is the great romance?"

"Ah, which one?"

Frederick raised his eyebrows. "I'd assumed you were still pursuing Mrs Robinson, the actress. Do you still have a lock of her hair in your pocket?"

"Mary is a delight, but I've tired of her. She became very difficult, demanding money. My father had to pay her off to stop her publishing my passionate letters to her. But London is full of beautiful women. It's very hard to resist their attentions."

"Does the King follow your exploits with them too?"

"Of course. And he reads all the scurrilous papers. He's very quick to judge. It's as if he never had any fun himself. Well," added George, looking sideways at Frederick, "we know he did when he was young. And just look how productive it was!"

Frederick scowled. He disliked hearing George remind him of the circumstances of his birth. The secret of his origins was so hidden in his current life that he was careful to only refer to the King as his patron.

"So, Fred, my plan is that we look at these violins, see what they are made of and try out a few tunes. I doubt I'll be able to buy one because the cost is beyond my purse at present, but I have a different treat in store for you."

"Oh," said Frederick, immediately suspicious.

"Just you wait; you'll enjoy it. You've had a distressing day, and you deserve a distraction. It's all very well being a walking paragon of virtue, but you're too young not to have experienced the joys of life, Fred. You'll be twenty soon. And in two years' time, when I'm twenty-one, my life will change. I'll be able to invite you to dine in *my* dining room at Carlton House, *my* palace. I shall choose whatever food and wine I like and eat and drink as much as I care to."

After an hour in the instrument shop, taking turns to play the rare violins and cellos, Frederick was in thrall to the beautiful sounds they could draw from the strings. Afterwards, and for the next two hours, at Brooks' Club in St James's, Frederick did his best to match George in their consumption of wine, sherry, Madeira and port. Sitting next to each other on a chaise, they took turns to recall a fragment of melody, pretending to play the glorious instruments, stroking their shoulders to mimic the bow's movements and waggling fingers as if pressing the fret. And each recollection was rewarded with a refilled glass.

In this state of intoxication, they left the club and headed to Maiden Lane in Covent Garden, tumbling out of the royal carriage onto the pavement. Linkboys, holding flaming torches, ran towards them with offers to guide them to clubs and bordellos, but George knew exactly where he was going.

"Fred," he roared, loudly enough to be heard over the sound of horses trotting past the carriage. "We're visiting the best house in London. Come along. Mrs Hayes has beautiful girls. They're always new, accommodating and irresistible."

"George, I don't want to," mumbled Frederick drunkenly as he was led into the tall townhouse. "I just want to play that violin. Oh, that Stradivarius, how I want it."

Holding on to George, he staggered through the front door of a large townhouse, a heavy brocade curtain pulled back in greeting then closed against the chill of the night.

Mrs Hayes, resplendent in a huge headdress, wide skirts and low-cut, beribboned bodice, curtsied to the two gentlemen as their hats, coats and canes were put away. George kissed her hand in an over-familiar way, swaying in the hallway, allowing her to steady him. "Mrs Hayes," he bellowed, "we need your best champagne and roast beef upon fresh bread with strong mustard. And we require a special entertainment for my guest. You remember the arrangement?" George winked at her.

Frederick and George followed a servant through the candlelit spaces to a small anteroom where a fire burnt brightly in the grate. Crashing down upon the sofa and spreading his legs, George kicked his feet onto the low table in front of him and bade Frederick join him. Frederick sank into the cushioned chaise, feeling unbearably tired and dizzy as the room span around. A tray was placed in front of them bearing beef sandwiches, an open champagne bottle and two crystal glasses. The young men ate and drank, and Frederick was about to fall into a doze on the chaise when he was roused by the sound of a violin being played.

"Fred, Fred." George was shaking him. "Open your eyes. Look, listen, here is the beauteous Emily."

Opening his eyes, Frederick gazed at a lovely girl standing in front of him, playing an unfamiliar melody on a violin. He drank in the perfection of her figure whilst admiring her musical technique and enjoying the sound. The girl set down her violin, putting it away in its case upon the low table in front of them. Clicking the case shut, she leant so far forward that Frederick could see her breasts almost spill from her bodice.

"Fred, this is Emily. She's all yours," said George, nudging him. "My present to you to cheer you up."

George helped Frederick onto his feet, firmly holding one of his arms, whilst Emily clasped the other to lead him away from the anteroom up a short flight of stairs, away from George, who closed the door. Emily directed Frederick through a corridor and into a large bedroom. Gently pushing his shoulders, Emily bade him sit down upon the bed covered with embroidered drapes before she disappeared behind a screen. The room was warm and softly lit with candles. Frederick could see his reflection in the oval mirror on the wall. He had lost all sense of where he was and what he was doing. How could he be sitting on a bed in a woman's chamber?

Emily emerged from behind the screen and stood before him. Indicating a ribbon on her bodice, she whispered in his ear, "Pull it." He pulled the ribbon, and her bodice immediately fell apart, revealing her full, round breasts. Picking up his hands, she placed them over her breasts. He shuddered at the experience, his fingers feeling the soft flesh and pert tips of her nipples. He felt the strain of his excitement in his breeches. She pulled another ribbon and her skirts fell away. Shaking off the bodice, she now stood naked in front of him. Frederick breathed heavily, admiring her beautiful body but unsure what he should be doing. Emily bent forwards to undo the buttons of his breeches. In seconds, she had removed them, and he was wearing only his long white linen shirt. Pushing him down onto the bed, Emily straddled him. He felt the pressure of her small hand upon his penis and then the extraordinary sensation as she pushed down onto him, sliding it inside her.

Frederick was consumed by the experience. A cascade of images from the day tumbled before his eyes. He kept pushing and pushing and the few seconds of oblivion were overwhelming. And then it was over.

Removing herself from him, Emily disappeared behind the screen. He could hear the slop, slop of water and presumed she was washing him away from her body. He lay back upon the bed, noticing that his penis was becoming flaccid again. Immediately he regretted what had happened, realising that he had lost his virginity to a prostitute. As the alcoholic fog lifted, he felt sick with disgust.

Emily reappeared from behind the screen, looking composed and perfectly dressed, her hair back in place and her face showing no evidence that anything momentous had just taken place.

"Sir," she said, "your breeches – would you like me to put them on you?"

Grabbing them from her, Frederick pulled them on and finished dressing. He needed water and was desperate to leave this place. Without touching him, Emily led him back through the corridor, down the carpeted stairs and back to the small anteroom. There was no sign of George.

"Where is the Prince of Wales?" asked Frederick.

"His Royal Highness is detained in another room," Emily replied.

"Madam, I need water."

Emily turned to a sideboard in the room, filling up a glass with water from a jug and handing it to him. Frederick gulped down the contents before bowing awkwardly to the girl and mumbling a few words about needing to leave immediately.

Collecting his coat, hat and cane from the cloakroom at the front door, Frederick headed out into the night. His head felt thick, and he could hardly breathe. What a day. How could he have let this happen? George might have considered this a gift, but it seemed like a torment and now he questioned his own morality. At the same time it had been a release, distracting him from the sadness of the day. He decided to conceal this shameful experience from all those he knew.

Weaving his way along the deserted streets back to Marylebone, he resolved never to allow himself to be duped by George again.

Chapter Twenty-Seven
Frederick Returns to London as a Clergyman
12ᵗʰ June 1784

Travelling to London as a newly ordained priest, on a fine June
day, Frederick smiled to himself with satisfaction. Fellow passengers
nodded at him with respect, noting the smart black frock coat, broad
black hat and the white collar with two tongues indicating his status.
For this was now his new life with a future mapped out for him. The
King had granted him his first living, as Rector of St Peter and St
Paul in Shepton Mallet, Somerset.

Enjoying the King's patronage had raised a few eyebrows within
the clerical community. Despite keeping a low profile at Cambridge,
whispers about his royal connection had pursued him throughout
his time at St John's College. He was aware of the muttered surprise
amongst seasoned clergymen that a newly ordained priest should be
granted such a lucrative living. Frederick shrugged off the gossips,
citing his good fortune as an example of the monarch's great
generosity and faith in the Church of England.

During the ordination service at Ely Cathedral, his body shook
as the bishop and all the clerics at the altar blessed him and heard
him pledge to live a priestly life, in the service of God, the King and
the congregation within his new parish. The official documents were
signed, and he was fitted for his cassock, surplice and stole, which
were now carefully folded up in his luggage.

Journeying in sober clothing made him a safe traveller and fellow
passengers bowed their heads before making polite conversation.
Strangers might air their problems or engage him in some spiritual
argument when all he wanted to do was gaze out of the carriage
window.

He looked forward to being reunited with Aunt Margaret and
Harriet again. Opening the document case on his lap, he took out

Harriet's latest letter. Reading her news a few weeks ago, his initial reaction had been one of shock and dismay. Gideon, the artist, had proposed and Harriet sounded delighted.

Apart from her nuptial plans, she had also told him about her new life as a theatre performer. He was astonished to read that she had made the leap from a role in the chorus in a production of *The Beggar's Opera* to playing Polly Peachum, the lead! Only a few months ago, she had been working in the same studio as Gideon, helping paint the backdrops and flats and happened to have met the producer of a show who heard her singing as she worked. Now she was a professional singer. Yes, she had a good voice, and he felt sure she would be an attractive and able performer, but how had she achieved such success in so short a time?

Watching the countryside rumble past the carriage window, Frederick fretted about his meeting with her and whether he would be able to express pleasure at the changes she intended to make to her life, the people she was consorting with and her choice of husband.

Taking a Hackney carriage from Ludgate to Queen Anne Street, he arrived at his family's house, darting up the steps to present himself to Dorothy with a broad grin. She stood at the door, staring at him blankly before realising that the serious-looking young man in the wide-brimmed black hat and clerical collar was Frederick. With a flurry of bobbing curtsies and exclamations, she ushered him inside whilst the driver brought in all his bags, depositing them in the hallway.

Aunt Margaret ran to greet him. Flinging her arms around him, she then stepped back to admire this grown man of nearly twenty-three.

"Oh Fred, you look so important."

"Ha!" he cried. "I hope you won't think that for long. I'm home and it's wonderful to see you. Is Harriet here?"

"Not yet. She had a matinee performance, but she knows you'll be home and will come straight here from the theatre. We'll talk properly over dinner."

"Aunt Margaret, do you approve of what Harriet is doing, marrying Gideon and working in the theatre?"

"Approval is neither here nor there, Fred. She loves Gideon and wants to be married. And as for the theatre, well, believe me, she's very good. You should read the reviews and see how much audiences love her. She plays to packed houses and earns a very good living."

"Hmm," replied Frederick.

"Please, Fred, don't be anxious about her. She's a sensible young woman. I know it worries you, but she is a good performer. Let's get these bags of yours into your room," said Aunt Margaret. "How long will you be staying?"

"Not long, I fear. I'm starting my role as a private secretary for the Prince of Wales immediately and then, in September, I'll move to my parish in Somerset. I told you in my last letter that the King has granted me the living at Shepton Mallet. I'm looking forward to seeing it."

"I'm sure it will be a wonderful place to start your career. All that hard work was worth it," chattered his aunt as she helped carry everything up to his room. "Oh, by the way, Fred, Harriet's now in Coaty's old bedroom at the front and we moved the big desk from your room in there too. So there's now plenty of room for your things. I see you've brought your cello and violin. We look forward to hearing you play."

After setting down his bags onto the bed, Frederick opened the window of his room fully to encourage a breeze. Peering out at the enclosed space, surrounded by other houses, he wrinkled his nose at the smell of sewage and rubbish rising from the ground and the sight of washing lines between the windows of upper storeys.

"Aunt Margaret, you don't have to stay here at Queen Anne Street. If Harriet is marrying Gideon, then presumably she'll want her own home. If you like, you could come with me to Somerset. I gather the rectory is spacious and I'd love you to be there."

"And I dare say you'd like a housekeeper?"

"Yes, a housekeeper role would be paid, of course. But I think you might like it. Perhaps a change from London would be good for you? I would like to have you near me."

"Thank you, Fred, I'll think about it. We need to know what Harriet has planned for her future first. Although she's a successful performer, she still needs a safe home and her mother to return to."

"Have they set a date for their marriage?"

"No, but I'm sure they will. Gideon is not yet in a position to support her. It's the other way round."

"Aunt Margaret, doesn't this concern you? Coaty was worried that, by consorting with artists and actors, she might affect this family's standing and reputation."

"Fred, Harriet doesn't see things the same way as you. You should talk to her. She has interesting opinions. Unlike Cambridge, London is full of people with new ideas. She reads books and pamphlets with opinions which you might find radical and attends talks by social reformers. I'm inclined to agree with many of her views, especially the ones about equality and ways in which we should change a woman's place in the world.

"Oh Fred, she amused me the other day when she observed that you and she are both engaged in performance, pointing out that you will have a congregation in church to look up to you in the pulpit and she has an audience at the theatre. I can see how true this is. You shouldn't be critical of her choices."

"I don't mean to be. I'm just concerned and also I must protect my status. Reputations take years to build yet can be so easily destroyed, especially by the behaviour of someone in the family."

"Yes, I understand. However, come downstairs to the drawing room and we'll have tea. I want to hear all about your ordination."

At six o'clock Harriet arrived home by carriage, running into the house still wearing some greasepaint from her performance and wafting scent. Leaping up from the chair by the window where he'd been watching for her arrival, Frederick ran to the door to embrace his cousin.

"What a diva you are, Harriet."

"I could say the same to you," she replied, touching his collar with the two tongues. "Does wearing this make you hold your head up higher?"

"I'm as humble as I ever was," he replied, watching her take off her broad-brimmed hat trimmed with paper flowers, placing it on the Pembroke table.

"I'd love to see you perform, Harriet."

"Then so you shall," she replied and trilled a few notes from one of her songs.

"I'm pleased you've done so well with your theatre career, Harriet."

"Good, so you should be. I've worked hard, just as you have."

"Aunt Margaret was telling me about your reviews and how popular you are. Do you have many admirers? It's always expected that women on the stage will have men falling at their feet for their charms. Prince George has always been especially attracted to actresses."

"I know exactly what is said about actresses," replied Harriet, patting a pile of music scores into order on the card table next to the window. "I accept a few gifts and there are invitations to dinner, which I refuse. There are always flowers left for me at the stage door and I bring them home for Mama. Look at those beautiful lilies! We're not allowed real flowers on stage because theatre people believe they bring bad luck. So I make paper flowers to trim my hat, and I always appear on stage with a bouquet of my own paper blooms and sometimes throw them to the audience. People love to catch them."

"And you never accept the invitations to dinner?"

Harriet cocked her head to one side. "No. The men who invite me don't interest me."

"Congratulations on your engagement. When do you and Gideon expect to marry?"

"We are discussing it but have no date yet. Since graduating he's been looking for a place in a portrait painter's studio, but is carrying on with the scenery painting. He's determined to be a successful artist and he's so talented."

"Yet his family still want him to return to Northumberland?"

"They'd like him to. I've met his parents, John and Ivy Tate. They came to visit family in London – his uncle and aunt live in Charlotte Street – and they are delightful. Gideon's their only son, and yes, they'd like him to return to Hexham and run the engineering business. But they can't force him to do something he has no interest in."

"No," replied Frederick, thinking of the conversation he'd had with Coaty seven years ago when she mapped out his future and gave him no choice.

Harriet glanced at her reflection in a gilded mirror on the wall, checked her hair and smoothed her eyebrows. "Fred, we must drink champagne."

"Champagne! Do you do this every evening?"

"No, but I am often sent bottles and having you home is very special. I'll ring the bell and ask Dorothy to bring in champagne and three glasses. We'll all toast your ordination and return to the family. It's important that we celebrate everything we've achieved."

Chapter Twenty-Eight
Frederick Accepts a Role from Prince George
Late June 1784

"Look, isn't it magnificent?" cried George with delight, pointing up at the high-vaulted fans of the Gothic conservatory at Carlton House.

"It's astounding," said Frederick, straining his neck to view the ornate ceiling and then down at the black and white checked marble floor. "But why do you need such an elaborate space?"

"To show off, of course," replied George, tilting back on his heels and patting his corpulent tummy. He marched up and down, pointing out hanging lanterns, fine planters and carved furniture. "Come and look at the dining room; it's even more stunning. It's been designed by my architects in the most fashionable French style and is very exotic, with the best Chinese and Indian furniture."

Frederick circled the dining table, laid ready for a banquet with sparkling glass, fine china, gleaming silver candelabras set upon crisp, white linen. Shields shone in alcoves, armour adorned the walls and ornaments were clustered on polished wooden dressers. Drapes of delicate white muslin upon the tall windows diffused the bright sunshine flooding the room.

"And Fred," continued George, marching around the space, "come upstairs. There are plenty of rooms to choose from. You can have a suite to stay in whenever you're in London. You won't have to live so far away in unfashionable Marylebone any more."

"Thank you, George, you are very kind. Though I actually like my home in Marylebone because Harriet and Aunt Margaret are there. Thank you for your faith in me, but I must remind you that I can't be here all the time. I am committed to my new life in Somerset and must move to Shepton Mallet in early September. The King has arranged it. There's a pleasant rectory to live in, I'm told."

"Quite, quite. I understand your commitment to your parish, but I do wish you to be here, close to me. And you can take divine service at the chapel when it's built. Fred, I may have many private secretaries, but I trust you above all of them."

Frederick smiled and followed the Prince as he continued the tour of his palace. Shortly before his ordination into the priesthood, George had written, inviting him to take on the role of a private secretary. Whilst he was keen to serve the Prince, Frederick had also been given his parish in Somerset and was concerned that dividing his time between these two positions was going to be complicated.

The role of Private Secretary to the Prince of Wales would not only involve attending to the Prince's personal correspondence and diary and the management of these illustrious events but also the completion and decoration of Carlton House. Who was paying for the opulent renovation of the palace? he wondered. The Prince of Wales had an allowance, but surely it wasn't enough to fund this level of indulgence? He feared that his new position would involve as much fielding of creditors as the entertainment of grandees from the great royal and aristocratic houses of Europe. He could have refused the role but, yet again, he chose to be close to George.

Pausing by the windows on the second floor of the palace and pointing to the south across the gardens to a glimpse of the lake in St James's Park, George confessed his 'Great Plan'.

"I am passionately in love."

"With Mary Robinson?"

"No, no, no. She's gone. It's Mrs Fitzherbert. She is the most sublime, beautiful, perfect woman in the world."

"Mrs Fitzherbert. I've read about her in the papers."

"She's been twice widowed and lives in Park Street, Mayfair. I adore her. Maria is my soul-mate, my alter ego, my perfect partner."

"Isn't she a Catholic?" queried Frederick.

"Pooh, she may be, but I don't care. I'm determined to marry her."

"Marry her! But George, you know the rules. You can't marry

a Catholic. The King won't allow it, Parliament won't, nor will the people."

"I don't care. She is my everything! Separation from her is agony."

"Where is she?"

"She's gone away. I'm desperate. I hear that she's travelling on the Continent. Lately I've tracked her to Belgium. I asked Papa if I could visit Prince William in Hanover. I thought the trip to see him would be a way to seek out my Maria, but Father got wind of my plan and banned me from leaving England. Again! I'm a prisoner here. My heart is straining with agony. Look, I even attempted to end my life; I was so desperate without her." Lifting the layers of his jacket and shirt, George revealed a puncture mark in his belly and Frederick gasped in horror at the scar.

"I did it with a knife!" said George. "Then I sent word of my deed to darling Maria, saying that I would die for her. She came, tended me and then she ran away."

Frederick rubbed his chin and shook his head. This was a different situation. He was impressed by George's commitment to this woman. Clearly he was consumed by love rather than lust and, that, thought Frederick, was a good thing. But Mrs Fitzherbert was wholly unsuited to the role of wife or even queen and potential mother to an heir.

"You must join me for the banquet tonight, Fred. We are welcoming the Duke of Orleans to London, and I promised him a feast. It's a small party of one hundred. I'm sure you'll find it amusing."

"Thank you for the invitation tonight, George. I look forward to the banquet. And I am pleased to become your private secretary. Will there be music this evening?"

"Of course there will be music! What a question! I have my own orchestra."

"I'm delighted to hear it. But most of all I look forward to a time when we can play our cellos again, or even a violin duet."

"Indeed, Reverend Fred, we shall!"

Frederick arrived back at Queen Anne Street after midnight. Drunk and overfed with the variety of delicious dishes from the Carlton House kitchen, he stumbled into the drawing room, flopping into a chair by the fire, too alert to go to bed. The Prince of Wales knew how to entertain, he thought, and the new palace of Carlton House would impress any important visitor. Its modern style and amenities made all the other royal residences look shabby and old-fashioned.

Frederick rose from his chair and, walking round the cluttered room, spotted a pile of Harriet's music and song lyrics on the card table by the window. Riffling through them, he picked one up and hummed the cheerful tune. It was merry, but the words were rather saucy. He gave himself a metaphorical rap on the knuckles for thinking as a cleric. There was nothing wrong with it. People needed amusement and gaiety. He did too, and considered how he might bring music into his church services in Shepton Mallet. Perhaps he might play his cello or violin to his parishioners? Did vicars do that sort of thing? He was still humming, whilst contemplating this happy thought, when Harriet crept into the room in her dressing gown. Recognising the tune, she hummed along with him then also sang the words.

"Did I disturb you?" asked Frederick. "It is rather late. Oh dear, gone two o'clock."

"I'm often awake late," she replied, poking the embers in the grate, then adding some coal. Frederick sat back down in the chair by the fire, and she bent down to kiss his forehead before sitting opposite him.

"Was it a good party?"

"Astounding. George is so generous to his guests. We were served twenty courses and wine to go with each one. I'm not used to such excess." He patted his stomach and burped.

"Ha, I see. And whose money was the great Prince of Wales spending tonight?"

"I suspect it all comes from the public purse. If he wants to put on a show, then he will find a way to do it."

"Do you approve of the way he behaves?"

"He has a position to maintain."

"Fred, why are you his private secretary? I thought you were going to be the Rector of Shepton Mallet. Won't your parishioners in Somerset keep you busy?"

"They will. Being private secretary to Prince George won't be that onerous. I've told him I only have a few weeks at Carlton House before I take up my new role."

"I'm sorry you'll only be at home for a short time, Fred. We will miss you, but I'm sure you're going to be a good rector."

"Well, thank you, Harriet. I may be ordained, but being a rector, and all the responsibility it brings, is new to me. Earlier this year, as a deacon and then a curate, I was attached to a rural parish church in Cambridgeshire. I baptised babies and even conducted a marriage ceremony. I enjoyed meeting different people, but there's so much to learn and it's unusual for someone as young as me to be given one of the best livings in the country."

"You have the King to thank for that, I presume," said Harriet.

"Of course. He instructed the Bishop of Bath and Wells to appoint me. I'm nervous about standing up in front of my congregation and speaking from the pulpit. I know you think nothing of being on stage now and singing in front of a huge audience. I do envy that."

"I was nervous about singing in public at first," replied Harriet, "but I became used to it and now really enjoy it. As I told you in my last letter, when stepping on stage, I am quite transformed into another person. It's invigorating. Tell me, Fred, when you were ordained at Ely Cathedral, did you quake in the presence of God?"

"A little. I felt the importance of it, but it was a procedure, a formal event," replied Frederick. "A bit like a coronation, I suppose, or aspects of it. But I do feel changed."

"Good, I'm glad you felt something. I've thought about this quite a lot. The Bible tells us about transfiguration and all manner of strange, miraculous events. I just wondered whether you felt the spirit descending from heaven and entering you when the Bishop laid his hand upon your head."

"No, I trembled a little but remained calm."

"When I go on stage, I feel changed. I leave Harriet Poulton in the wings and assume the role of Henrietta Laing, the performer."

"Yes, Aunt Margaret told me you'd changed your name. Was this in response to my concerns?"

"Partly. Many performers have stage names. I was offended when one of your letters to me suggested that my work might be indecent. It's not at all."

"I'm sorry if I upset you, Harriet. That was wrong of me. I can see that you are good at what you do, and successful. By the way, did your mama mention that I've invited her to come and live with me in Shepton Mallet?"

"Yes, she did, but she doesn't want to leave me."

"Of course. But when you are married you might live elsewhere."

"I'd still like to keep her near me."

"I wasn't trying to take her away from you."

"No, of course. She's free to make her own decision. But Fred, I wonder if you value your profession above mine and believe my mother would be more respected if she were with you, rather than me?"

"How can you say that? You've chosen your own path, and she doesn't disapprove."

"I know you disapprove."

"Harriet, my approval is neither here nor there. If you are behaving in a moral and acceptable way, then I have nothing against your calling."

"But you don't think it's conventional, do you? I see the way you frown when I talk about my work. I'm not searching for a wealthy husband like most women. No, Fred, I'm engaged in creativity and performance, and I think this is something the church finds threatening. It gives people ideas, doesn't it? People might start questioning the way society works. For example, the Prince of Wales's banquet you've just attended; he didn't earn the money to pay for it, did he? He expects the taxpayers of this country to fund everything. He doesn't thank his subjects for their hard-earned money. He and the royal family sit in their castles and palaces and expect to be treated in this special way. And those who serve them never question the orders they're given."

"Harriet, how can you say that? It's a matter of respect. People need to know their place."

"No, that's wrong because it's like a kind of prison for people. Fred, just because you're born into a poor family shouldn't mean you have to remain poor. That's not right. A person might not be educated because their parents weren't, but that should change. This idea of keeping people in their place, no, no, it's dreadful."

"I can tell you've thought about this very deeply."

"Yes, I enjoy reading about new ideas and radical thinking. Have you heard of Mary Wollstonecraft?"

"No, I haven't."

"I will gladly lend you her pamphlets. She has some very interesting thoughts on education and the way women should be treated. Fred, I would rather spend my life thinking freely about matters than conforming to the status quo without considering alternatives. I don't think it's right to follow rules from another age without wondering if they're actually right. Weren't you doing that at Cambridge? Didn't you question everything?"

"We questioned everything, of course. Harriet, do you not believe in God?"

"Of course I do, but I'm not dictated to by Him. I believe I have free will and can make my own decisions and choose my own direction. I completely understand that you may believe you have a direct communication to God because of your position and we all respect you for this."

"Thank you. I've spent seven hard years absorbing and studying divinity before being accepted into the Church of England."

"Yes, and we're proud of that. But don't you think that everyone, whatever their class or background, should have the chance to better their life?"

"The church teaches us that everyone should accept their place."

"But it's not necessarily right. Did you know that Mama has taught Dorothy to read? She now has her own ideas; she reads the newspapers and comments on events."

"You amaze me."

"I realise Dorothy's never going to work for a king or preach in a pulpit. Nor is she going to sing on stage or do anything of any consequence, but her very existence is every bit as important as ours and we should encourage her to do more with her life."

"So you believe in universal education?"

"Absolutely. At the theatre, I meet people who come from poor backgrounds, cities far away from London and foreign countries. They've all had to find their own way and it's not been easy. They haven't had the advantages of education, a wealthy background or rich patrons. They've made choices, come to their own decisions through their own hard work, circumstances and experiences."

Harriet pressed her fingers to her mouth and looked up at Frederick. "The people I live and work amongst have not been told what to think by listening to a preacher in church every Sunday. They don't accept the narrow teaching which places the rich man in his castle and the poor man at his gate. We - and I count myself amongst these people - do not think like that. We believe in self-determination."

Frederick sighed, unwrapping his clerical collar and casting it onto the arm of his chair. "And do you not see merit in my entering the church?"

"Fred, of course I do. I know how hard you've worked, and I accept that you had this profession thrust upon you by the King, Coaty and others. You're a man of the cloth now and have been given a living for life, with income and a home. That is remarkable. Are you content with the choice that was made for you?"

"I am now. As you know, I wanted to inherit Kirby Misperton and be a gentleman, but things have worked out differently. I've accepted that it may never be mine and I'm going to make the best of my calling. So, I'm going to Somerset, and you will soon be married. Our lives are very different."

"They are."

"But Harriet, as I've said before, you don't have to marry Gideon. I have contacts at court and could introduce you to men with money, titles and a position in society."

"I earn and save my own money, Fred. I've told you before, I'll only marry for love. I am content with my position in society and Gideon comes from a good family. You cling to conventional beliefs without questioning them. I'm not influenced by established rules or expectations in the same way."

Harriet stood up. "Fred, it's late and time to sleep. I'm glad we've talked. Even though we disagree, we will always love each other, but we have chosen different paths. And I will marry Gideon."

Chapter Twenty-Nine
Frederick Arrives in Shepton Mallet
September 1784

Frederick sniffed the interior air of the ancient church of St Peter and St Paul, absorbing the scent of old incense and dust mingled with the pungent smell of livestock and pipe smoke. Shepton Mallet was a handsome old town. He'd enjoyed his coach ride through the streets of his new parish, twisting his neck to view the honey-coloured buildings. Halting outside the gate of the rectory, he spotted a young man in clerical clothes waiting for him, his curate, Reverend James Rudge.

The promise of a young rector in the town had caused a flutter amongst the women. They flocked to the church offering support with flowers, cleaning, embroidery of hassocks and invitations to tea. The men were more circumspect; gentry, professionals, landowners and farmers shook Frederick's hand in guarded greeting. Rocking back and forth on their heels, they pointed to their family names painted on the best pews at the front of the nave. Some engaged him in conversation about his plans for his ministry, making it clear that, even though he had been appointed by the King, his living within the parish was paid by farmers renting church land or generous contributions from local estate owners' wealth.

Daunted by this intense interest, Frederick had little idea how best to respond. He was aware that every person he talked to, and views offered in response, would be scrutinised and judged.

On a damp September morning, his first appearance in the church attracted a packed congregation eager to hear the new rector preach. Putting on his cassock and stole in the vestry, he breathed deeply to quell the butterflies in his stomach. His heart boomed within his chest when he climbed the steps of the pulpit. Standing up straight, straining to make his voice loud enough to reach the farthest pew, he knew his delivery lacked drama or impact. He envied Harriet's confidence or Prince George's authority and ability to speak easily to a room full of strangers. He dreaded the moment when he had to lead the singing, start the psalms and utter the prayers.

He had crafted a sermon on the kindness of strangers, based on the story of the Good Samaritan, including fragments of his personal experience, describing how Raphael had helped him. But the spoken words didn't resemble the text he'd written. He stumbled over sentences, mumbling his description of the hop gardens where he'd worked. He could see older men cupping their ears, straining to hear him, children fidgeting and elderly ladies coughing into their gloves.

Gazing down on a sea of faces, he felt tense and hot, his throat contracting and his voice dwindling to a squeak. He laboured towards the end of the service, mopping his brow in relief. The people of Shepton Mallet might be forgiving this first appearance, understanding his nerves, but if they were to take him seriously, he would have to work hard to improve his delivery.

In the centre of the town, close to his church, stood the draughty, century-old rectory. That night, after his first Sunday service in Shepton Mallet, Frederick knelt and prayed for acceptance. Then, creeping under the chilly covers of his bed, he vowed to make the best of this clerical life. The knowledge that he would soon be called away from his parish by the demands of the Prince was both a relief and a fear. Absentee vicars were regarded as neglectful by their parishioners; and long spells away from a parish never courted favour with a congregation. But he had no choice. Prince George insisted that Frederick's role at Carlton House was far more important than his pursuit of a ministry and he had agreed to the Prince's demands. He knew he would be returning to London soon.

To salve his conscience, he offered a generous salary to the young curate, Rudge, anticipating that he would have to take on the lion's share of his work. On the surface, James Rudge appeared to be a timid man with darting eyes flashing beneath bushy eyebrows. Habitually scanning his surroundings, he carried a small notebook in his pocket, constantly jotting things down. In the rectory rooms, his fingers smoothed the fabric on furniture, adjusted paintings on the wall and shifted cups on the table into order. Having been curate to the previous rector, Rudge was proud of his knowledge of the town and his good memory for parishioners' names and family details. He could recite entire psalms without checking the text and remember Bible stories to recite from the pulpit. Frederick realised that Rudge would, once fully ordained, become a much better clergyman than him.

During plain dinners in the dining room, Frederick enjoyed talking to his curate and, after a few too many glasses of wine, told him something of his story. Rudge listened attentively to the tale of Major Blomberg's apparition and how Frederick came to be adopted into the royal family. Curious about Frederick's life within the royal palaces, Rudge probed him further for stories about the princes and princesses, questioning every detail. When the bottle was empty, Frederick realised that he should not have spoken so freely and implored his curate not to repeat the story for fear of being mocked or becoming a curiosity.

From Mrs Margaret Poulton, Queen Anne Street, London
To Reverend Blomberg, The Rectory, St Peter and St Paul, Shepton Mallet, Somerset
5th October 1784

My dear Fred,

Harriet and Gideon have eloped! I returned home on Friday last week to discover a note from Harriet apologising for the hasty departure. Apparently Gideon had been offered work at a theatre in Paris He was required to leave London immediately with the company catching the night tide from the Pool of London to sail to France. She decided to go with him, insisting that she and Gideon will marry as soon as they have the opportunity and that she anticipates being away for many months. I feel very hurt that they departed so hastily and without proper explanation. She promises to write again as soon as they are settled.

Though I am disappointed at her actions, I know Gideon will protect her. He is, at heart, a good and thoughtful person who loves Harriet and she adores him.

Harriet's departure has precipitated a decision I had been considering for some time. The lease on the Queen Anne Street house ends on the last day of October. Without Harriet's contribution I don't have the funds to renew it and since neither she nor you are here, we have no need for so large a home.

So I will sell all that remains of Coaty's furniture and possessions. I have a few trinkets of my own – clothes, books, and a few pictures – which my friends will keep. Dorothy has found employment with a family in Marylebone.

When Harriet and Gideon return from France, Gideon has finally agreed to join the family business and will move to Hexham. So, my plan is to travel north. I have exchanged letters with Mr and Mrs Tate, Gideon's parents (whom I met when they visited London), and they have kindly offered me hospitality in Hexham, so that will be my destination.

And, Fred, on my journey north, I have determined to visit Kirby Misperton. I feel a strong desire to see this place.

When you next come to London, I assume you'll stay at Carlton House with the Prince of Wales? It is a very splendid-looking palace, and the façade of great columns makes it an imposing royal residence.

So, in a short space of time, everything has changed. The landlord will forward any letters arriving here to your office at Carlton House. I leave on November 7th and am looking forward to the adventure of travel. Having enjoyed dear Coaty's descriptions of her experiences abroad, I wish to see a little of the world before I get too old.

I hope that you feel secure in your finances now. With an income from

*your living and a salary from the Prince of Wales too, you are now a man
of means! I am so very proud of all you have achieved.*

*I am pleased to hear you are such a popular guest within your
parishioners' homes. Three teas in one day, well, well! You must be careful
not to overdo your consumption and become plump like the Prince of Wales,
who is now referred to in the papers as the Prince of Whales.*

I will write to you as my travels progress.

Your loving aunt, Margaret

Frederick sat at his desk absorbing the contents of Aunt Margaret's
latest letter. An elopement was one thing, but doubt about whether
they had married worried him. Concern for Harriet dominated his
thoughts, fearing that her action might cause her to be ostracised by
society. If, it transpired, she and Gideon had not married, then he
resolved to conduct the service himself and give them a substantial
wedding gift.

For the first time in his life, he had funds and could live
comfortably. The King had kindly granted him a second living at
Bradford on Avon, also in Somerset, which, combined with Shepton
Mallet, would yield an annual salary of one thousand pounds.
Together with the more meagre one-hundred-pound stipend from
the Prince of Wales, Frederick was now wealthy. But what was the
pleasure in having money if he was unable to share it with people
he loved?

Pushing Aunt Margaret's letter into an empty desk drawer, he
gazed around the dreary study in the soulless rectory. The effects and
memorabilia of his late predecessor's life surrounded him. Frederick
longed for the cosy, comfortable homes he had known in London.
Even his austere room at Cambridge now seemed attractive.

Yet, he settled into his new life, preaching twice every Sunday,
conducting weddings, funerals and baptisms. He enjoyed meeting
and making friends with the people of his parish, accepting invitations

to dinners, teas and glasses of sherry in homes after Sunday services. Life in Shepton Mallet continued in a comforting rhythm of empty weeks followed by hectic Sundays. And all the time, he wondered about Prince George, Aunt Margaret and Harriet.

*

In September 1785, the one-year anniversary of Frederick's arrival in Shepton Mallet coincided with the harvest festival service at St Peter and St Paul's. To mark the occasion, he decided to spice up the celebration and bring his music into the church. Rather than preach a sermon, he took his violin with him into the pulpit and played 'Autumn' from Vivaldi's *Four Seasons* suite. The reaction was so enthusiastic that some of the congregation spontaneously applauded, demanding an encore. Frederick obliged, working through a repertoire of pieces he knew by heart. It became clear that his congregation appreciated his musicality much more than his divinity.

Emboldened by the positive response, he started to play a different piece of music at each Sunday service. Hearing about the fiddle-playing Rector of Shepton Mallet, people from neighbouring villages and towns deserted their own churches to come to services and hear him play. Attendance at St Peter and St Paul's church doubled in size.

Despite the comforting response to his music, and enjoyment he derived from the chance to perform, Frederick missed the chaotic company of Prince George, the luxury of Carlton House and the relaxed comforts of his old home in Queen Anne Street with the people he loved.

In early December, when a messenger wearing the Prince of Wales's livery galloped into town with a letter for the rector, Frederick was delighted. The urgent message read:

My dear Master Frederick. I need your presence urgently. Come at once to Carlton House. I will explain on your arrival. George, Prince of Wales.

Chapter Thirty

Prince George has an Audacious Plan
Early December 1785

"Fred, you must marry us."

"What!"

Pacing around the drawing room of his private apartment in Carlton House, Prince George sighed loudly before collapsing onto a sofa. "I'm serious. I need to marry Mrs Maria Fitzherbert. I promised her I would and I'm going to. I'm desperate to. I have to. Will you do it?"

"George, how can you ask me such a thing? Of course I want to help you, but my answer is no. Absolutely not! How could you possibly expect me to officiate at a marriage like this? Does the King even know what you are planning?"

"Of course not."

"Because he'd stop you. He'd never approve, nor would Parliament. Mrs Fitzherbert is a Catholic and twice widowed. No, it's not possible. Besides, your father changed the law after your uncle Cumberland married his mistress without permission. As Prince of Wales you can only marry with the King's agreement. Besides, she's six years older than you. You need an heir, a legal heir."

"I don't care. I love and adore my glorious Maria, and she has agreed to be my wife. There is nothing else I desire more in the world. It has to be done. Please, you must do it. For me."

"No, George. I cannot."

"I thought you'd say that," said George, leaning forward, elbows on knees, cupping his chin into his palms. "I did have a clergyman who agreed to do it, but he took fright at the last minute and refused. If you won't do it, Fred, then who will? There must be a cleric in London prepared to do it. I will reward them with money and a role as chaplain at Windsor."

"I'm sure you will, George, but it's not going to make it right or even legal. Does Mrs Fitzherbert know that any informal marriage like this is not going to be recognised? And surely she'll want a Catholic priest to officiate?"

"She's prepared to let a Church of England clergyman marry us. Find me one, Fred. I'm asking you as my private secretary, my closest confederate and my brother. Please, arrange it."

Frederick left the Prince's suite, walking through the gilded staterooms of Carlton House, climbing the stairs to his first-floor apartment. He was conflicted. Loyalty to the Prince and gratitude for his role as private secretary was important. But so was his loyalty to King George III, his patron. He daren't offend the King no matter how loyal he felt towards George.

Thinking hard about the problem, a solution occurred to him. Remembering his Cambridge friend, Robert Burt Junior, a divinity student at Trinity College, Frederick recalled that the young clergyman was now a vicar, with his father, Rev Robert Burt Senior, at the parish church in Twickenham.

Remembering Robert's enthusiasm for gambling at card tables, and how his father had to pay off his debts, Frederick thought he might agree to conduct the ceremony, attracted by the Prince's promise of ample reward. He sent Reverend Burt Junior an urgent note requesting a meeting the following evening at St James's Church in Piccadilly.

Frederick walked the short distance from Carlton House to Piccadilly, waiting at the back of the gloomy church, close to a wall sconce, too anxious to read his prayer book in the poor candlelight. Two men entered and Frederick greeted his friend Reverend Robert Burt, who was accompanied by his father. The two vicars listened to Frederick's request. Initially, they demurred. Frederick then told them about the reward of a valuable chaplaincy at Windsor plus a handsome fee. Robert Burt Junior was fearful that some unpaid gambling debts might lead to imprisonment in The Fleet. Robert Burt Senior wanted those debts settled. The Prince's offer of money and the prospect of a position at court appealed to his vanity. Reverend Burt Senior agreed to perform the ceremony.

On 15th December 1785, Frederick escorted the two vicars to Mrs Fitzherbert's house in Park Street to meet the Prince of Wales, waiting anxiously for his bride. Frederick refused to go into the house with the clergymen and the handful of trusted guests, choosing to walk the streets of Mayfair wracked with guilt and regretting his involvement. He then retreated to his rooms at Carlton House.

Two days later Frederick sent out messengers to gather the latest newspapers and pamphlets. Sure enough, news had seeped out and the satirical cartoonists were quick to mock the clandestine marriage. The St James's Palace gossips had heard of the union and marvelled at the audacity of the deed. How could the Prince of Wales marry a Catholic woman without seeking permission from his father and ever consider her becoming his queen?

On 19th December, Frederick began his journey back to Shepton Mallet, fearing that his role would be found out and his coach stopped by the local militia. Returning in time for the last Sunday in advent, he scrambled to prepare for the Christmas festivities and to join in with the town's celebrations.

He felt sorry for Maria Fitzherbert. Not doubting her love for the Prince of Wales, she had been deceived by him and embarked upon an illegal marriage bringing her no more status than that of named mistress. George's will had prevailed yet again.

*

Winter of 1785 gave way to spring 1786, and Frederick received another summons to meet the Prince of Wales at Windsor Castle. Briefing James Rudge about parish business, he packed up his things, including his cello and violin, and departed Somerset for Windsor. According to George, Mrs Fitzherbert was still living at her own house in Park Street, and he was with the royal family at Windsor. What kind of marriage had this been? Frederick wondered.

As Frederick's carriage approached the castle, he recalled the occasion, fifteen years earlier, when King George III had gathered up all the royal children, from the palace at Richmond, filled a fleet of carriages, and taken them all to see the place. At the time the castle had been a cold and crumbling ruin with rooms open to the sky, water trickling down walls and surrounded by overgrown gardens. Now, the building had been turned into a spacious home for his large family and extensive household.

A guard saluted Frederick as his carriage rumbled through the huge wooden gates at the base of the hill leading to the mound. He was directed along passages, up and down stairs, through a maze of rooms until he found the Prince of Wales's suite. Not far away, down yet another corridor and up a small stone staircase, were the rooms he had been allocated: a bedroom and a study with windows overlooking the castle's south-facing terrace.

Frederick was excited and nervous to see the King again after such a long absence. The monarch would formally present him with the new Bradford on Avon living to add to Shepton Mallet and the prospect made him shiver with anticipation. The following day, putting on his new black suit beneath his clerical robes, Frederick walked over the soft rugs of the corridor towards the King's drawing room. A page bade him wait whilst he knocked on the door. Another page on the inside opened the door before bowing and ushering Frederick in.

King George III rose from his gilded chair, holding out his arms in greeting. Frederick bowed, close to tears as he felt the monarch's embrace. This was his father. He felt more than filial respect; he loved this man. He was overwhelmed with gratitude that the King had written personally to the Bishop of Bath and Wells to secure

Frederick's second living.

George III touched Frederick's cheek with a forefinger, patting the white collar around his neck and nodding in approval. Frederick noticed that the King's face was strangely florid and his eyes, within their fleshy pouches, seemed to bulge more than ever. Wisps of greying hair stuck out from beneath his unkempt wig.

"Master Frederick, I am so proud to see you become a man of the cloth; it's a most excellent calling. And coming from Cambridge with such high recommendations by the bishops."

"Thank you, sir," said Frederick with a solemn bow. "I shall always be very grateful to you for your support and interest in my career. I look forward to taking up my position at Bradford on Avon in addition to Shepton Mallet. Somerset is a beautiful county."

"Yes, Somerset, beautiful indeed. The Queen and I very much enjoy our visits, Bath especially."

"Sir, if I am free to leave Windsor and my parishes, my plan is to visit Bath during the Season this summer. I intend to take rooms in the city."

"Ah yes, Master Frederick, that is a good plan. It is important for a young man to be out in society. You are very much a clergyman and gentleman now. And have you seen much of the Prince of Wales?"

"Not since before Christmas," replied Frederick, anxious whether his involvement with the illegal marriage was known. "But I look forward to seeing him here at Windsor and am very pleased to be his chaplain and private secretary. I gather he has closed Carlton House and resides here permanently."

"Humph," the King grunted. "He overspent his funds for Carlton House and was compelled to return to us here. Would that the Prince of Wales were as dedicated to duty as you."

Frederick nodded. Glancing out of the window, he bit his lower lip and, changing the subject, enquired after the health of the Queen and the children.

"Her Majesty is very well," replied the King. "Our youngest

daughter, Amelia, brings us such joy. I'm sure you'll see her when we walk upon the terrace this evening, enchanting everyone who meets her. She likes to wear her best dress and leads us all out for the airing every day, demanding that I take her hand. Delightful child. And of course you'll see the other princesses and the younger princes too."

"It will be a pleasure. And sir, I look forward to playing some violin or cello duets with the Prince of Wales. He mentioned that we hope to arrange a soirée in your drawing room. I will discuss it with him when I see him later today."

"Excellent idea. So, Master Frederick, nay Reverend Blomberg, I am pleased to have you back in the bosom of the family. I look forward to hearing you play and also taking divine service in St George's Chapel whilst you are here. Now, I will let you go."

Frederick bowed, walking backwards away from the King. A page indicated that the door was open, and he emerged into the corridor, letting out a sigh of relief. The idea that the King might discover his role in the Prince's wedding was too awful to contemplate. He dare not confess his involvement to any of the other Windsor chaplains. He would have to bear the guilty secret alone.

On meeting the Prince of Wales in his apartment, Frederick was relieved to discover that George was still blissfully happy with his 'wife', Maria, and there had not been a schism. She was simply not accepted at Windsor, despite the ring on her finger, and was still referred to at court as Mrs Fitzherbert. Indeed, lack of funds had caused the closure of Carlton House. So, George explained, the couple spent their time together at her home in Park Street, St James's Palace or at the royal holiday destination of Weymouth in Dorset. More recently they had taken a liking to a small seaside village called Brighthelmstone in Sussex.

"I have some bold plans for Brighthelmstone," said George as he and Frederick sauntered around the terrace of Windsor Castle, catching the evening rays of the autumn sun. "I need a country retreat, and I've bought land within the town. The architects are creating designs based on my ideas."

"I commend your vision, George. Does Mrs Fitzherbert like the place as much as you do?"

"She does. She enjoys seeing me happy. And being near the sea makes me unconscionably happy. I bathe every morning and ride out on the Downs; there are race meetings to enjoy, and we go for walks. There's very gracious society down in Brighton, as I now call it. You'll see, Fred, my vision for a country house is going to eclipse anything I achieved at Carlton House."

"And you have the funds for this?"

"Yes, of course I have the funds. Parliament will grant it. They have to. How can they resent me having a country property to escape to? As future monarch I will need it."

Chapter Thirty-One
Frederick Enjoys the Season at Bath
Late July 1786

There was a festive atmosphere to Bath. Bunting hung between buildings, stirring in a light breeze, flowers festooned window boxes and flags flapped above towers and spires. Sauntering around the city with a spring in his step, Frederick enjoyed nodding at acquaintances and exchanging pleasantries. He had taken a suite at a hotel for three weeks and the mantelpiece in his drawing room sported stiff white cards inviting him to parties, dinners and soirées. An eligible young clergyman, with a good income, was always a welcome guest.

Frederick enjoyed the attention. Since returning to Somerset from Windsor, he poured his energy into his two parishes. He gradually added comforts to the rectory at Shepton Mallet – thicker blankets for his bed and two wing chairs set by the fire in the parlour. He enjoyed regular visits to Bradford on Avon where he had installed Reverend Gwynne to manage the parish in his absence. He was a generous employer, setting aside a large proportion of his income to pay the curates' salaries and to fund the maintenance of the rectory and vicarage in each town. Safe in the knowledge that his parishes were in good hands, he was free to accept invitations in Bath and attend the best parties.

Palace education had ensured that Frederick was an able dancer. He knew how to take the gloved hand of a lady and swirl her around the room in a lively gavotte, a more orderly quadrille or an energetic country dance. He knew how to make polite conversation, careful to avoid reference to the weather or the heat of the room.

In early August, shocking news of an attempt upon the King's life arrived in Bath. Newspaper reports described in lurid detail how the King had been greeting his public at St James's Palace when a woman drew a knife from a scroll of paper she was holding and pointed it towards his heart. The King was unscathed, but everyone at court was in a state of shock.

Known for his close association with the royal family, Frederick found himself in even greater demand. Men questioned him over port at dinner parties, women delivered invitations in even greater quantity. Young girls gathered in the Pump Room, hands to their mouths and eyes flickering in his direction. For the first time in his life, he understood how the Prince of Wales must be regarded. Women jostled to be the one to catch his eye, claim him for a dance or engage him in conversation.

As the Season drew to a close, he felt relief at having avoided any connection with the eager, eligible young women in Bath. Although he was attracted to some of the ladies he'd been introduced to, he found their conversation too shallow and their education too limited. Comparing their company with Aunt Margaret and Cousin Harriet, he realised that his two closest relatives were exceptional in their broadmindedness and knowledge of the world. Too many of the women he met in Bath gleaned their news and views from the pages of the *Gentleman's Magazine* and the *Bath Chronicle*, often limiting their reading to the society pages and lists of guests who had attended the various parties and soirées. Frederick craved more depth to conversation. Whilst he witnessed many young men and women pairing off during the summer weeks, he had not met a woman who interested him. That didn't mean he wasn't attracted to the women or had not enjoyed their attentions. He had not yet met the right one.

*

By November 1786, Frederick was back at Windsor, pleased to be joining the royal family for Christmas and the promise of entertaining the household at musical soirées where he and Prince George would play their violin and cello duets.

Sitting at his desk in his rooms at the castle, he opened his box of correspondence and reviewed the latest letter from Aunt Margaret. He was pleased to know that she was now safely installed in Hexham at the home of Gideon's parents, Ivy and John Tate, contributing to the household by once again writing letters for other people. Refusing his written offer of financial support, Aunt Margaret thanked him for his concern, assuring him that she was comfortably off and enjoying residing with the Tates in Northumberland.

He was also relieved to learn that his aunt was in regular touch with Harriet. The couple were, indeed, living in Paris where new theatres were opening every week, she said. They had plenty of work. Gideon was still painting backcloths, and Harriet had developed a career singing her own songs in French. Aunt Margaret remembered Coaty's wise investment in his and Harriet's education at Dover Street, including tutors in the French language. However, Frederick was alarmed to read of the revolutionary atmosphere influencing French theatre and how the producers encouraged her to change the words of her songs to criticise the French royal family and aristocracy. Harriet confirmed that they were happy living in Paris and had no intention of returning. Gideon wished to pursue his art in the city for as long as possible, postponing the promised return to Hexham, a role within the family business.

The other important news from Aunt Margaret's letter was that Ursula Blomberg had died. Mrs Troughton, whom she had befriended when she visited Kirby Misperton, corresponded with her. Mrs Troughton informed her that an elaborate memorial plaque to her had been placed on the wall of St Lawrence's Church, next to the one of her son, William.

Well, thought Frederick, as he contemplated the release of Kirby Misperton, perhaps there was now a chance for him to possess it. But, he realised, he was far too busy working with the Prince of Wales at Windsor, or dashing back to Somerset every few months, to even think about renewing the claim. Also, despite his wealth as a clergyman, he was not sure he had enough spare funds to pursue the case through Chancery.

Enjoying his time at Windsor, Frederick was a familiar figure in the drawing rooms, making up numbers at formal dinners and taking divine service for the royal family in St George's Chapel. He took tea with Fanny Burney, the author whose novels Aunt Margaret so admired, and enjoyed lively conversations with Mrs Delaney, the artist Harriet had become so fond of. The old lady had been given an apartment within Windsor where she remained a favourite of the Queen and continued to produce her detailed paper mosaics of interesting plants. Frederick even bought one of her artworks at a private exhibition, hoping that, one day, he would be able to give it to Harriet.

On days when he was not busy in his rooms handling correspondence for the Prince and dealing with his plans for building the elaborate pavilion at Brighton, Frederick liked to take his horse out into Windsor Great Park, gallop across the open parkland and into the woods. His confederate in this reviving activity was his new friend Peniston Portlock Powney, a local landowner and Member of Parliament for Maidenhead, who revelled in his royal appointment as Park Ranger for Windsor Great Park. Powney was a forthright and amusing character, indifferent to the constraints of social etiquette. He thought nothing of holding forth in his booming voice in hushed drawing rooms, commenting loudly about people, unconcerned that he might cause offence.

On one occasion, when Prince George was within earshot in the drawing room, Peniston announced loudly that he would never lend a royal personage any money, for it will 'never be seen again'. Such was the experience of his father, of the same name, who had lent the King's father, Prince Frederick, a large amount of money – and had 'never seen it again'. Wincing at the insensitivity of Peniston's statement, Frederick bundled his friend out of the room before Prince George could react, saving him from royal chastisement.

Chapter Thirty-Two
A Second Season in Bath and an Introduction
April 1787

Tingles ran up and down his spine and, in order to speak properly, Frederick swallowed to moisten his throat. Miss Maria Floyer possessed a confidence that reminded him of Harriet. Small of build, poised and calm, her pale grey eyes held his gaze with a directness he had not seen in a woman before. Most females he was introduced to fluttered their lashes and hid behind a fan. A small dimple appeared in Maria's cheek when she smiled. She sat calmly in front of him, hands crossed on her lap, seated on a sofa like a comfortable cat.

Frederick already knew something of her family from Peniston, his friend from Windsor. Peniston Portlock Powney was married to Elizabeth Floyer, the eldest of the four daughters of the late Sir Peter Floyer, a renowned goldsmith. As Peniston had pointed out, with a tap to his nose, there were still two unmarried daughters living within his wife's family home in Bath, inferring that one of them, perhaps, might be of interest to Frederick.

On this mild, sunny afternoon in April, at their home in the city, all four sisters were present for the tea party, brokered by Peniston, their brother-in-law, and arranged by their mother.

Mrs Dorothy Floyer invited Frederick to her home with enthusiasm. Any friend of her esteemed son-in-law was welcome, she insisted, placing Frederick on a chair next to her, opposite her two younger daughters, Maria and Letitia, seated on the blue silk sofa.

The older married sisters, Elizabeth Powney and Barbara Bennet, seated on the other side of their mother, chattered with confidence, drawing Frederick into the conversation whenever possible. All four young women spoke charmingly to their mother, feeding her lines to embellish familiar stories designed to amuse Frederick, who obligingly smiled and occasionally laughed. Maria contributed comments, keeping the conversation flowing, whilst Letitia fidgeted and looked towards the French doors in the drawing room.

Dominating the conversation in his loud voice over tea, Peniston recounted events at Windsor, praising the hunting prowess of the King and the musical excellence of the Prince of Wales. He would not stop talking. Familiar stories of his encounters with members of the royal family were of no interest to the polite but bored Floyer girls.

Frederick smiled indulgently and, during a break in Peniston's anecdotes, invited Mrs Floyer to outline further her daughters' talents. He was used to the ways of mothers with daughters of marriageable age. Nodding in assent as each skill was recounted, he could not help staring at Maria, the third daughter, who sat calmly returning his gaze.

Aware that Peniston was about to interrupt the conversation with more comments, Elizabeth, his wife, intervened, suggesting that he, and her sister Barbara, should leave the room and go upstairs to check that the Powney children in the nursery were behaving.

Appreciating the reason for departing the room, Peniston rose, setting down his cup and saucer and winking at Frederick as they all left the room.

"So, Reverend Doctor Blomberg," began Dorothy Floyer, "we hear you survived the Season here in Bath last year."

Frederick smiled, understanding her meaning that he had not left the matchmaking market with a fiancée. A breeze in the garden scented with cherry blossom and bluebells blew into the room. He glanced again at Maria, who returned his gaze.

"There was much to enjoy during the Season, Mrs Floyer," said Frederick, "and I've never done so much dancing. But yes, I survived, as you say. It was a regret that I did not know your daughters last year. I'm sure their company would have enhanced my time here."

"Growing up in Bath, all my girls were familiar with events of the Season."

"I'm very grateful to Peniston for introducing me to your family," said Frederick, nodding to Mrs Floyer over his teacup and saucer. "He's an entertaining character to know and a popular man in Windsor."

"I'm sure he is. We are very pleased that Elizabeth has the chance to live at Windsor some of the time and is often presented at court, which is a great honour. As I'm sure you know, Peniston comes from a very old county family in Berkshire with an estate at Maidenhead."

"Yes, I often hear about it," replied Frederick, glancing again at the women on the sofa. Letitia was staring out of the window. Maria was still gazing at him.

"Girls, it's a beautiful day. Why don't you both take Reverend Doctor Blomberg out into the garden and down to the woods by the field? The bluebells are looking wonderful."

Maria and Letitia assented, rising from the sofa and leading the way to the French doors and onto the terrace overlooking the garden. They walked a few yards across the lawn towards a wooded area bordered by a field when Letitia gathered speed and strode ahead of them. "Maria, I am going to meet Edward. He said he'd be by the field-gate at five o'clock and I'm late."

"Very well," said Maria, "but don't spend too long with him or Mama will worry."

Letitia hurried away towards a gate leading into a wheat field and Frederick watched her rush up to a young man leaning against a tree.

"That's Edward," said Maria, pointing at the tryst. "Letitia's been in love with him for years. They're betrothed and will be married in June."

"Your mother didn't mention her betrothal," said Frederick.

"Mother's not altogether approving of Edward. He's a decent young man, but not from a Bath family. In fact, his home is in Hampshire, and he's been in Bath working as a teacher."

"That's a worthy profession."

"Yes, but not as impressive as Peniston's estate and Windsor connection, or Robert Bennet's position as a partner in a Bath law firm, or as a clergyman with two Somerset livings who is Chaplain to the Prince of Wales."

Frederick smiled and they continued walking through the woods until Maria indicated a felled log to sit on.

"So, Miss Floyer, what do you like to do with your time?"

"I read, write letters, play the piano. I help my mother with the management of the house and run errands. She needs support, especially in the last four years, since Papa died."

"Tell me, Miss Floyer, what do you read?"

"Many different things – newspapers, pamphlets and society magazines. But I am also very fond of novels. Did I hear from Peniston that you've met Miss Fanny Burney at Windsor?"

"Yes, I have, only a couple of times. I don't think she was very impressed with me. I interrupted her free time with demands for tea. It was the result of a prank by her servant. On the second occasion, whilst walking in the gardens at Windsor, she was more friendly and relaxed, but she is a shy person. I understand her reluctance to talk to strangers and I don't think she found me very interesting."

"Then she was mistaken," Maria replied. "I find our conversation very interesting."

Frederick turned and looked at her. He watched the way her lips closed in a delicate curve when she ceased talking. He wondered what it might be like to kiss them.

Continuing their conversation, Frederick agreed with much of what she said but challenged her on some aspects too. Maria was not afraid to review or counter his argument. Here was a woman who would stimulate his mind, he thought. He gazed at her fresh face, glowing as they conversed, calculating that she must be older than his twenty-five years, but still youthful. They continued their conversation until a chilly wind blew through the trees and Letitia joined them, waving at Edward, who walked away.

"Ladies," began Frederick, "I keep a carriage here in Bath. With your mother's permission, would you both do me the honour of accompanying me to a concert tomorrow evening? We could dine at the Pump Room afterwards. I will assure your mother that you will both be home at a reasonable hour."

"Thank you, yes, I would like that," replied Maria. Letitia nodded in agreement. "What is being played?"

"It's Haydn's First Symphony at the Theatre Royal. Are you familiar with the piece?"

"I'm familiar with several of Haydn's chamber pieces," said Maria, "but generally it's rare for us to hear a full orchestra. This is very kind of you, Reverend Doctor Blomberg, thank you. We look forward to it."

"Excellent. I will call at six o'clock tomorrow evening."

Frederick bowed and they walked back to the house.

Well, well, thought Frederick. Could Maria be the person he had been waiting to meet? She was so unlike the pretty but simpering girls he met at dances; she was mature, liked music and was well read. He took stock of the family. Elizabeth, the eldest, was matronly, surrounded by children and tolerant of her noisy husband; the newly married Barbara spoke of household furnishing, servants and plans for her new home; Letitia appeared to be a good five years younger than Maria, yet she was betrothed to marry her sweetheart, Edward. So, thought Frederick, they were all spoken for except for Maria. Not only was she very attractive but she was also intelligent. She questioned views, enjoyed discussions and offered opinions, not homilies or easy agreement. Why was she not married? His heart boomed loudly in his chest and his imagination ran riot as he considered the implications of this meeting.

He took his leave from the Floyer household, counting the minutes until he would return the next day to take Maria and Letitia to the concert.

From Reverend Doctor Blomberg of the Rectory, Shepton Mallet
To Mrs Margaret Poulton, care of Mr and Mrs Tate, Hexham
1st May 1787

My dear Aunt Margaret,

I have news. I am betrothed! Yes, I can hardly believe I am writing these words, but at twenty-five years of age, I am marrying the best of women. Her name is Miss Maria Floyer, daughter of a gentleman, Sir Peter Floyer, who died four years ago. She is thirty years old, the third of four daughters.

Maria is beautiful, educated in music and literature and holds interesting views. As the remaining unmarried daughter, she had resigned herself to staying at home to look after her mother and managing the home. I believe she will make a splendid rector's wife and cope with the demands and duties of the role with great consideration and kindness. I feel such love and respect for her. My fingers are trembling as I write!

Mrs Floyer is very pleased that all four daughters have now found husbands. Her youngest, Letitia, will marry her sweetheart, Edward Woolls, later in the summer.

Maria's marriage portion is a thousand pounds. Such is the generosity of her family. I cannot believe my good fortune.

Dear Aunt Margaret, please come to our wedding on 24th May at one o'clock at Queen Square Chapel, Bath, and afterwards at Maria's home. I realise there is not much time for you to make arrangements and that it is a long journey from Hexham, but it would delight me if you could attend. I will book you a hotel. Then, after the festivities, my future wife and I, would be delighted to welcome you as our guest to our home at the rectory in Shepton Mallet for as long as you might wish to stay.

I still maintain my connections with Windsor and the royal family. From what I hear, Prince George spends most of his time in Brighton with his Mrs Fitzherbert in a state of wedded bliss. I have told George my splendid news. He promises to come to Shepton Mallet soon to meet my new wife, though he will not attend the wedding.

Of course, I have sent an invitation to Harriet and Gideon to their address in Paris, but do not know whether it will reach them in time and think it unlikely they could make the journey to attend.

I am very excited about this momentous change in my life. I send you my best love and regards.

Your loving nephew, Fred

Chapter Thirty-Three
Frederick and Maria's Wedding in Bath
May 1787

The night before his wedding to Maria, Frederick met Aunt Margaret at her hotel for dinner. He felt such pride and gratitude that she had made the huge journey from Northumberland for this occasion, and he looked forward to welcoming her to his home in Shepton Mallet.

His aunt appeared a little stouter than when he had last seen her three years ago, and deep lines now reached from the edges of her mouth to her chin. Frederick noticed, with pleasure, that she had trimmed the bodice of her dress with the lace he had given her all those years ago. Despite the regular letters between their homes in Hexham and Shepton Mallet, there was much to discuss.

Speculating on Harriet's description of her marriage to Gideon, conducted by the ship's captain during their journey to France, Frederick assured his aunt that such ceremonies, though unorthodox, were still accepted as legal. Aunt Margaret shook her head with concern for her daughter and expressed her longing for the day when she and Gideon would return to England.

Towards the end of their celebratory supper, Frederick was delighted when Aunt Margaret agreed to come and stay at the rectory in Shepton Mallet for a few weeks; but only after the newlyweds had enjoyed a week alone, establishing themselves in their marital home.

After the marriage, emerging from the chapel beneath a shower of rice and rose petals, Frederick introduced his new wife to Aunt Margaret, and was filled with happiness as he watched them embrace.

Every window and doorway in the Floyer home was garlanded with flowers for the wedding breakfast. Folding doors were opened to create space for tables and chairs. Pretty posies of flowers in china jugs adorned the table settings, and guests admired a huge four-tiered cake decorated with fresh peonies and rosebuds.

Peniston Portlock Powney, Frederick's best man, read out a message of congratulation sent by the Prince of Wales and gave an amusing speech referencing Frederick's youthful experience as a fiddler at weddings at an inn in Rochester. Acknowledging the cue, Frederick stood up, positioned his violin below his chin and played a series of cheerful jigs. Delighted guests clapped their hands in time to the tunes, patted their thighs and some of them danced.

After the reception, Frederick escorted the new Mrs Blomberg to the waiting carriage outside the front door and helped her in. Guests waved, blessing their union with cheers and blown kisses as the new husband and wife left Bath and returned to Shepton Mallet.

At the rectory, Maria was introduced to Reverend Rudge, the housekeeper and the maids. Showing her around the old, austere rectory, Frederick told her that he would agree to any changes she desired – a new range for the kitchen, drapes at the window, linen for the beds.

Later that evening, sitting at the dining table opposite Maria, he could barely eat the simple supper placed before them. All he could think about was the night ahead, hoping that he would know how to love Maria. He wondered what she expected and whether he would do the right thing to express the depth of his feelings for her.

After the encounter with Emily at Mrs Hayes' house all those years ago, his experience of women was limited to fumbled couplings paid for at a bawdy house in Cambridge, and a few furtive kisses with women in the town. He knew his feelings for Maria transcended all the encounters or imagined passions of his past.

Though suspecting that Maria would be equally anxious about the physical side of marriage, he was impressed that she showed no nerves, chatting calmly to him throughout supper, re-living their wedding day as she cut up her orange with a knife and fork. She ate the segments with such neatness and composure that he wondered if anything would ever disturb her. The moment came. He picked up the candle and, taking her arm, led her upstairs to their bedroom, closing the door.

*

It was late September 1788. Frederick and Maria had been married for sixteen months and living contentedly in the Shepton Mallet Rectory with Aunt Margaret, who had agreed to stay on and help with improvements to the Blomberg home.

Maria and Aunt Margaret swiftly became confederates in household management, discussing the quality of fabric required for drapes in Frederick's study, new rugs for the parlour and attractive paintings for the wall. After a year of constant building work, decoration and the introduction of new furniture, the old rectory had been transformed into a comfortable and welcoming home.

Now, on this warm, autumnal day, Shepton Mallet was preparing for a party. The people of the town were excited to welcome a royal visitor. George had promised Frederick that he would visit, but a year and half had passed since the wedding and Frederick had grown weary of enquiries about the proposed visit. Now it would finally happen. The Prince of Wales was to visit Shepton Mallet. Paths were swept, flowers deadheaded, hedges trimmed, flags raised, and bunting fluttered across the streets.

Billowing cloths were laid upon tables and dishes laden with food were set in place. Glasses and tankards were arranged in neat rows next to bottles of wine, beer and cider. Specially baked buns were piled high in the town's bakery, ready for distribution to every resident. A canopy and platform set up in the market square provided cover for the town's musicians, who had been practising their pieces for several weeks, and a rostrum was in place for the Prince of Wales to stand when addressing the people of the town.

Frederick was nervous and excited. A few weeks earlier, at the matins service one Sunday, he had announced that the Prince of Wales would be coming to Shepton Mallet. A frenzy of speculation and preparation erupted. What an honour for the town; how did the rector have such close connections with the heir to the throne? What should everyone wear?

The Prince had assured him that he would arrive by one o'clock at the latest and it was now gone two o'clock with no sign of him or his party. Frederick looked up at the clear blue sky, praying for news. Though he had never trumpeted his royal connections, he knew his ability to attract a royal visit enhanced his reputation. So much depended on George actually arriving.

As the day wore on, fresh flowers in vases drooped in the sunshine and banners hung limply in the humid air. Frederick was concerned. Surely the Prince of Wales would not let him down? In a recent letter to George, Frederick had expressed his joy at becoming a married man, confessing that he now understood the Prince's enduring passion for Mrs Fitzherbert. He agreed that it was important to make a promise before God to protect and love one woman. Matching Frederick's enthusiasm in his reply, George named the date and time of his arrival in Shepton Mallet.

By three o'clock Frederick was desperate. The parishioners' mood in the town had darkened. Grumbling about being taken for a ride, doing all this work for nothing, no reward, no visit, the people were becoming impatient. When were they going to eat the food and drink the beer?

At ten past three, a mounted messenger wearing the Prince of Wales's crest thundered into the town, halting at the square, asking directions to the rectory. The rider dismounted and delivered a note to Frederick. Relief, news at last! Frederick took the note into his study to read it. As he suspected, George would not be coming, but the message carried further news. The King was seriously ill. Doctors attending him had been unable to restore composure to his addled mind and the King's condition was so serious that he might die. The Prince of Wales had been summoned to Windsor.

Immediately understanding the significance of this situation, Frederick now knew why the Prince had not appeared. Maria, standing at the door to his study, waited for news. Taking her hand, he led her through the garden to the street outside the rectory where he made the announcement to the townspeople. "The Prince of Wales regrets that he will not be able to visit today but demands that the Shepton Mallet party should go ahead."

Everyone roared approval, falling upon the tables to devour the food they had stared at all day. Kegs were hammered open, and beer poured into tankards for all to enjoy.

Later in the evening, before the moon rose, Frederick joined the town's musicians in the square, playing jaunty tunes and jigs, encouraging everyone to dance. Women grabbed their skirts, kicking their knees high, and men leapt about the marketplace in rhythm to the music. By midnight, after every scrap of food had been consumed and the empty kegs rolled back to the brewery, the people of Shepton Mallet no longer cared that the royal visitor had failed to arrive. The day was declared a huge success. Frederick heaved a sigh of relief as he and Maria finally climbed into bed in the early hours of the morning.

It was then that he had to tell Maria that the letter from George had also included a summons to Windsor Castle. As Chaplain to the Royal Family, and someone who was familiar to the King, he was needed.

"My darling, I'm so sorry, but I'm going to have to leave immediately," said Frederick. "If indeed the King is dying, then George will need me."

Maria listened with grave acceptance. "I know. I understand. I'm sorry our happy life here must be interrupted. But I will be fine, Fred. You mustn't worry. Aunt Margaret is here. She and I make fine company."

Frederick kissed his wife, sinking into her embrace. Each night he looked forward to the moment when he and Maria retired to their bedroom, taking pleasure in whispered conversations and the privacy of lovemaking.

The following morning, with a heavy heart, Frederick ordered his coach and collected a few of his belongings. A small crowd of parishioners watched him embrace his wife and aunt then, waving before the carriage set off, Frederick leant out of the window until he rounded a corner and his little family disappeared from view. He sat back in the coach, secure in the knowledge that he had a home to return to with people he loved waiting for him.

Chapter Thirty-Four
Maria Blomberg Receives a Visitor
15ᵗʰ November 1788

A loud clanging at the front door disturbed Maria's peaceful evening, alarming her. Apart from the cook and the maids, she was alone in the rectory. Rudge had gone to Wells, Aunt Margaret was visiting friends in the town who shared her interest in books, and it was too soon for her to be home; besides, Aunt Margaret would use the back door, like everyone who lived there.

Maria picked up the candle on the table next to her chair, making her way to the front door.

"Who's there?"

Through the stained glass window in the door, she could see snow falling outside, blanketing the bare branches and trimmed hedges around the rectory garden. On the street, she saw the light of a carriage as it disappeared away from the gate, and a figure in the porch.

"Are you Mrs Blomberg?" a woman's voice called.

"Yes, who is it?"

Maria was used to receiving visitors in need of alms, women wanting food for their children and men wishing to borrow tools. But nobody would call at seven o'clock at night.

"I'm his cousin," came the quiet reply.

Maria pulled back the bolt and opened the door carefully. The night lantern illuminated a woman in a dark cloak clutching a large leather bag.

"Harriet? What a surprise. Come in. We've been expecting you for weeks," cried Maria, pulling back the door and ushering the woman into the hallway. "Come to the fire. It's such a cold night."

"Thank you, Maria, it's lovely to meet you at last."

Covering the flickering flame of the candle against the draught,

Maria took Harriet's cloak and hung it on the stand in the hall. She led Harriet into the parlour, indicating a chair by the fire.

Watching her ease herself into the seat, hugging her belly, Maria could see that Harriet was with child.

"Congratulations to you and Fred on your marriage," said Harriet, wearily. "I'm sorry Gideon and I were not able to attend. We were in France until the end of last year."

"Yes, we knew and understood. I'm so pleased you are here. Fred talks about you so much, and so does your mother, of course. We understood you were travelling and would arrive here in the autumn. Your mother has been very concerned about you."

"Is my mother here?"

"She's at a friend's house in the town. I'll send the stable boy to fetch her back. Please, Harriet, stay by the fire and I'll bring you some food."

Maria ran to the servants' quarters to send Robert the stable lad out and then prepared some food on a tray, returning to the parlour with tea, bread, some pâté and cheese.

"Thank you, Maria, this is very kind. I'm sorry to alarm you on this cold night."

"We have visitors at the rectory all the time, but not often after dark."

"Where is Fred?"

"He's at Windsor Castle with the Prince of Wales. He's been there since the end of September. The King is unwell, and they need him."

"They always need him," said Harriet quietly, taking a bite of bread and butter and a piece of cheese.

Margaret shrieked when she saw her daughter sitting in the chair, dashing to embrace her.

"Oh, Harriet, my dearest child, you're here. I wish you'd let us know you were arriving tonight, and I would not have gone out.

We've been so anxious for news."

Lowering her head, Harriet covered her eyes, weeping.

Margaret drew a handkerchief from her pocket, handed it to her daughter and waited for Harriet to compose herself.

"Darling girl," said Margaret, "why didn't you write and tell us about your condition? When is your baby due? Where have you been? What's happened to Gideon?"

"I'm so sorry, Mama. I couldn't tell you in a letter. So much has happened."

"Six months ago you wrote that Gideon was gravely ill after an accident in Richmond. His mother wrote to me with more details but said you had left Yorkshire, and she had no idea where you'd gone."

"I couldn't stay there any longer. It had all become too difficult. Then Gideon fell from the gantry at the theatre in Richmond and landed on boxes on the stage. He was so injured. It's a miracle he survived," said Harriet, wiping her eyes.

"But you left him. How could you do that, especially when he was badly hurt? Where have you been?"

"I can't tell you about it now. I'm too exhausted."

"Very well, Harriet, you must rest. Stay here and Maria and I will prepare the spare room. Cook will bring up hot water and I'll bring you some nightclothes. We'll talk tomorrow."

The following morning Margaret entered Harriet's room with a tray of breakfast things, setting them on a table. Harriet sat up and embraced her mother.

"How are you feeling?"

"Much better, thank you. I'm so relieved to be here."

Margaret poured out tea and handed her daughter a cup. "Are you ready to tell me what happened?"

Harriet sipped the tea. "Gideon wronged me. It all began whilst we were in France. He met other artists and started staying out late, drinking. I was working so hard, performing at theatres in Paris, earning a good living, but he would take the money and spend it on his friends in local bars. I became so angry and fed up with him. He was still painting scenery but not gaining any portrait commissions. Then his father issued an ultimatum. He would no longer send Gideon funds when he asked for them unless he returned immediately and joined the family business, as he'd promised. Honestly, it seemed the best option for Gideon, but he was resentful."

"So that's why you left France?" Margaret enquired.

"Yes, but things were becoming quite dangerous in Paris at the time. Gideon was swept up in revolutionary ideas and attending meetings with activists. But mostly he was drunk all the time. He became unreliable and never finished the scenery he had been commissioned to paint. When a theatre manager sacked him, it was time to leave.

"We arrived back in London in January. I wanted to check with the port authorities about our marriage certificate. We discovered that the ship we'd taken to France had been wrecked and all the paperwork lost. We are legally married, but don't have proof.

"We stayed with Gideon's uncle and his family in Charlotte Street in London for a few weeks and then joined a travelling theatre company preparing to head north, performing at theatres all over England. We reached Richmond in North Yorkshire and were helping establish a new theatre in the town.

"I was performing two or three times a day. It was tiring, but I was enjoying the work. Gideon was scene painting as usual, but still drinking. He never stopped drinking.

"Then, one evening, we were in the dressing room when he announced that a local landowner had commissioned him to make portraits of his family. This was wonderful news and Gideon was delighted. He showed me the money the man had given him as a deposit and then said he wanted to go out with the theatre manager to discuss a new backdrop design. I feared for that money.

"Because he was staying on at the theatre, he told me that the patron who'd commissioned the portraits would give me a lift home in his carriage. I normally go home with Gideon, but it seemed a perfectly reasonable suggestion.

"I joined the landowner in the carriage. He was a large man with a florid face. After saying how much he'd enjoyed watching my performance, he came over to my side of the carriage and tried to kiss and fondle me. I resisted, batting him away as much as I could. Realising he was getting carried away and that he might use greater force upon me, I shouted very loudly and thumped on the roof so the driver would hear me and stop the carriage. The patron was annoyed and pushed me out of the carriage, slamming the door. He'd taken me far from the town. I had to walk a long way back to our rooms.

"I was so angry with Gideon. He had behaved so selfishly and hadn't given a thought to my safety.

"Gideon came back to our rooms later that night blind drunk, climbed into bed next to me and immediately started snoring. All night I lay awake, feeling furious. He no longer thought about his art, career, or our life together. I'd had enough and decided it was time to leave Gideon.

"Whilst he was still asleep, I got up, walked to the market, enquired at the post about coaches travelling south and booked a seat. After buying some new shoes and travel clothes, I returned to our rooms at noon to pack my things, knowing that he would have left to go to the theatre.

"When I arrived at the theatre for the afternoon performance, the place was in turmoil. The manager grabbed my arm and took me to the dressing room where Gideon was lying on a stretcher on the floor, howling in terrible pain. Apparently, he'd been supervising the hanging of the new backcloth and it had snagged. He'd insisted on climbing up to the gantry to unhitch it but lost his grip, falling onto some boxes and props on the stage.

"He'd obviously broken several bones. There was a really bad break to his right leg, and he must have injured his pelvis and ribs too. The manager called for a doctor, who came quickly and together we removed him to a room in his surgery where he did his best to bandage the broken limbs.

"I sent an urgent message to Gideon's parents, telling them what had happened. They arrived three days later and were so shocked at his condition. They decided to take Gideon to a specialist surgeon they knew in Newcastle. Rather than go with them, I said I'd stay in Richmond, making up some story about being committed to finishing my run at the theatre and clearing our rooms and would join them in Hexham later. Then they took him away.

"The theatre manager assumed I'd want to follow Gideon and paid my fees. The following morning I began my journey south."

"Harriet," said Margaret, "the Tates have been desperate to know where you are. They've sent so many letters asking about you. You should have told us what happened."

"It was too difficult to express in a letter, besides, I needed time on my own to think and come to terms with my situation. My friends in the various theatres along the way helped. Many of them are single women who earn their living on the stage and seeing their independence strengthened my resolve that I'd done the right thing to leave Gideon and our marriage.

"However, a few months later, in June, to my surprise, I realised I was with child. After four years of marriage I thought it might never happen. I'm twenty-eight and always wanted to be a mother, but the situation was difficult. The more obvious my condition became, the more I worried about my future with a baby. I did think about going back north to Gideon and the marriage but decided to continue travelling south.

"I stayed with friends in York, Leeds and Derby. By the summer I'd reached Nottingham and could no longer perform. An actress friend living near the Theatre Royal introduced me to her neighbour, an elderly woman who wanted a companion to help her move to her son's home in Oxford. The lady and I travelled together and I stayed with her in Oxford until the end of October. I found work at the Sheldonian Theatre, teasing wigs, mending costumes and other backstage chores.

"It was hard to estimate how long it would take to travel to Shepton Mallet from Oxford and I'm sorry my recent letter did not give you a date. The last few days of the journey have been very tiring. The baby must be coming soon."

"Harriet, I'm so relieved you are here. Have you told the Tate family about the baby?"

"No, I couldn't, but I will now I'm here. Gideon is the father of this child, of course he should know. Marrying Gideon in that careless way and travelling with him to France was such a mistake."

"Harriet, you have not made a mistake. You followed your heart," said Margaret. "You are a talented and resourceful woman. You will be a wonderful mother when the time comes. We must let Fred know you are here, but I won't mention the baby yet. He's staying at Windsor with the Prince of Wales. We all hope that the King's health will soon be restored and that Fred can come home."

Chapter Thirty-Five
The King's Madness
23rd November 1788

Since the summons from the Prince of Wales at the end of
September, Frederick had now spent nearly two months at Windsor
Castle offering comfort to George and the rest of the royal family.

Meanwhile, the King had been removed to secure rooms at Kew
Palace, tended by doctors attempting to contain his mania.

Prince George and Frederick visited the King at Kew and
stood nervously outside his rooms on the ground floor of their old
childhood home.

"Are you sure you want go in there, Fred?" said George. "The
doctors say he's violent and might hurt you. They've had to restrain
him."

Frederick could hear a commotion inside the room. The King's
voice was hoarse and ugly. He was shouting, snarling, hissing and
would not stop talking. Then after a pause came a deep, animal cry
of pain.

"They're cupping him now," said George. "They tried a cold bath,
bled him then made blisters on his legs. He was still raving. So they
strapped him to a chair. I can't bear it."

Frederick rubbed his chin, wondering what to do. He had no
medical knowledge, but he believed he might be able to soothe the
King by seeing him once more and offering some spiritual comfort.

On the other side of the door, he heard further howls of pain
and indignation. Then the King cried out loudly, "I want my dear
son Frederick. Frederick is my friend."

George shook his head. "He doesn't mean Prince Frederick the
Duke of York; he wants you. He hates Prince Frederick as much as
he hates me," said George. "Fred, you're his favourite son. If you go
in there, I'll stay here outside. Seeing me only inflames him more

and I'm frightened of him."

Frederick ran a finger around his collar, smoothing the two tongues upon his chest. He knocked on the door and one of the physicians shouted as he opened it. "We said no visitors. Oh, it's you. He will see you."

The room was dark, smelling of blood and burnt flesh. The King was secured in a wooden chair with tight leather cuffs wrapped around his wrists. His fists were clenched, and his shaved head showed great welts on the skin of his skull where hot cups had been applied. The raised flesh had been sliced open to allow the steam to emerge. His arms were bandaged below the elbows where he had been bled and a large dish of dark blood sat upon the floor nearby. A doctor picked up the dish, sniffing it with distaste before removing it from the room.

Frederick approached King George. It was terrible to see this man looking so pathetic and hurt. The King gazed up at Frederick with querying eyes, glittering in a pool of inky black. "Is that you, Master Frederick?"

"It is, Your Majesty. Sir, I have come to see you again. I'm sorry you are not well."

"I'm not ill, Frederick; I'm anxious, very, very anxious."

As he spoke, froth appeared at his mouth and the words came spitting forth. Frederick drew a chair closer to the King but far enough away should the man break his bounds and lunge at him.

"Her Majesty the Queen is very anxious about you, sir. I saw her earlier and she, too, is concerned for your swift recovery."

The King threw back his head and growled. "I need to see the Queen. They keep her from me." He strained at the straps at his wrists, twisting them as far as he could, but unable to free his hands. "Look, Frederick, look what these demons have done to me. I detest the doctors. I only trust you and men of the cloth. I want to see my archbishops. I want confession, absolution. Why have I been afflicted with this agony, this purgatory? I wish to converse with

God. Please, Frederick, arrange it?"

"Sir, would that I could arrange a conversation with God. We know, from the Bible, that God is around us, within and without. Whatever happens, to anyone, is also known to the great creator."

"Then why does he treat me so cruelly? I've only wanted to be good. I am a good husband and father. I have been granted many children. But you, Master Frederick, are my firstborn. Can this be retribution for my earlier sins? I have been kind to you, have I not? You have been happy?"

"Sir, you have been kind to me. I have been happy, and I am very happy. You may not have heard, but I am married."

"Indeed, what, what, that is good. I am pleased. A man should marry. And where is your wife?"

"She is at our rectory in Shepton Mallet in Somerset. We were married in Bath over a year ago. Her father's name was Floyer, Sir Peter Floyer. He was a goldsmith. You granted him a knighthood. You met him at St James's Palace."

"Floyer, Floyer…" The King shook his head. Frederick realised that asking him to remember names was hopeless.

"Sir, would it help you if we were to pray together for a few minutes? It might calm you."

"Yes, yes, it will calm me, Frederick. Say the Lord's Prayer with me; I fear I will forget the words. And tell me the parable of when Christ casts out the devil from the man. I need to hear that this demon inside me can be cast out. Can you do this for me?"

"Sir, I doubt I can cast out any demons, but I will pray for you and will ask everyone at Windsor to do likewise."

"Thank you, thank you. I am anxious, so anxious and very tired."

The doctors approached and examined the King, who had closed his eyes and appeared to have fallen asleep. Undoing his cuffs, they carried him to his bed across the room before clipping the cuffs to chains at the bedposts to prevent him from getting up.

Frederick rose from his chair, leaving the room.

"Fred, once again, you've worked a miracle," cried George, patting him on the back as Frederick came out of the room.

"No, I haven't. I don't know what's wrong with him, but he's afflicted by some strange madness. I've no idea what the best treatment would be. He looks so thin, weak and vulnerable. If my presence helps, then I'm glad of it, but the doctors should be less cruel to him. His head is very injured. They've caused him such pain."

"You should have seen him when it all began," said George. "This latest episode was worse than anything we'd seen before. I told you; we were at dinner, and he wouldn't stop talking, got up and walked round and round the table, talking nonsense in a loud voice. The Queen was shocked, and all the princesses started weeping. Then he grabbed me by the collar, pushing me against the wall, causing my cheek to be hit. Look, there's still a mark." The Prince pointed to a faint bruise below his left eye. "I was so shocked. The doctors took hold of him, bundling him into his room. I had to lie down and called to be bled. It was all I could think of to make myself feel better."

Frederick shook his head. The situation at Windsor was out of control and now the King was separated from his family at Kew. Frederick recalled Coaty telling him that the King had first been ill long ago in 1765, shortly before he was adopted into the household at Richmond, and she had witnessed moments when, for no reason, he would turn and snarl at everyone. He would be abusive and rude but then would recover. The King's fits of madness had not lasted long, and everyone glossed over the episodes, and they were forgotten. The Queen had insisted that the world beyond the castle should never know of his crazed state.

This was different. His mania was lasting for days and difficult to treat. He would recover briefly, and everyone held their breath, hoping that he would be normal again, then, without any notice, he would plunge back into a state of anxiety, constantly walking, talking and making no sense. Doctors described his condition in many ways but, when he was manic, the King was not capable of managing affairs of state. Frederick felt deep distress at the situation and his own inability to help. The monarch, and the country, was in crisis.

In the carriage back to Windsor Castle, George spent the journey muttering that it must soon be time for him to take over the King's position and be appointed regent. Politicians were preparing for the change. If the King showed no sign of recovery, then his heir could rule in his place.

Frederick saw the delight in George's face as he considered the prospect of real power at last. He also knew that there would be courtiers, politicians and clerks huddled in palace rooms and Parliament plotting solutions. Many of them would be looking for ways to work this sad situation to their advantage.

For the worried occupants of Windsor Castle, Kew and the other royal residences, there was only one subject of conversation – the King's madness. In early December, the mania subsided, and the King was restored enough to resume his role.

It was time for Frederick to return to the tranquillity of his Somerset home.

Chapter Thirty-Six
Frederick Returns to Shepton Mallet
11ᵗʰ December 1788

Climbing out of his carriage outside the rectory, late at night after three days' travel from Windsor, Frederick was surprised to see every window ablaze with candlelight. Pushing through the back door into the kitchen, he saw pots of water bubbling on the range, filling the room with steam, and great mounds of linen piled upon the table.

During his journey home, he'd imagined returning to a scene of domestic calm, Maria greeting him with kisses, Aunt Margaret sitting at her chair by the fire in the parlour and Harriet pleased to see him after a four-year absence. He envisaged warm fires, a welcome glass of wine and dinner on the table in the dining room.

No one was there to greet him. But from upstairs he could hear voices and loud yells coming from one of the bedrooms. What on earth was going on?

Still in his overcoat, he climbed the stairs calling out. Maria emerged from the spare room, closing the door behind her, and embraced him. "Oh Fred, how wonderful you're back. There's a lot going on in this house."

"Yes, I'm aware of that. What's all the noise about?"

Another loud shriek emanated beyond the closed door and Frederick took a step towards it, but Maria darted in front of him to prevent him entering. "It's Harriet. She's in there. She's giving birth to her child. Aunt Margaret is with her and Mrs Codling, the midwife. It's all going well, but these things take time."

"Giving birth! Why didn't you tell me she was expecting a baby? This is a surprise!"

"We didn't know when you'd return or when the baby would arrive. But how fortuitous that you've come home on the night your new niece or nephew will be born."

"Yes," replied Fred, scratching his chin. He and Maria came back downstairs and into the dining room where Frederick sat at the empty table.

Maria kissed her husband, taking his coat, poured him a glass of Madeira, bade him stay where he was and ran to the kitchen, returning swiftly with a plate of cold ham, cheese and bread.

Having eaten at last, and feeling restored, Frederick sat back in his chair and patted Maria's hand.

"When will the baby be born?"

"Soon. Aunt Margaret says it's close but could still be an hour or two. It's nearly midnight, Fred, and you must be tired."

"I am. It's been awful at Windsor and Kew. And this," he added, nodding his head in the direction of the stairs, "is not quite the homecoming I'd anticipated."

"I know," said Maria, smiling, "I'm sure you were hoping for a peaceful household, but babies keep their own time. Cook has put hot water in our room. Go and rest. I'll let you know when we have news. I can see you're exhausted. Is the King any better?"

"Not really. Two weeks ago he started showing signs of recovery, then he relapsed and started raving again. He was slightly better a few days ago, when I left Windsor. I'll tell you about it tomorrow."

Frederick left the dining room and climbed the stairs, pausing briefly outside the spare room at the sound of shouts and quickly sought refuge in his bedroom.

In the spare room, Harriet writhed on the bed, panting and yelling whilst gripping Margaret's hand. Mrs Codling, whispering encouragement in a soft and confident voice, instructed Harriet to give one final push. After a long yell from Harriet, the baby slid from her body and Mrs Codling swaddled the infant, holding it tight and tickling its nose with a feather. The baby sneezed, spat and roared noisily before subsiding into quiet squawks. Harriet immediately took her baby in her arms, opening the wrappers to view her newborn child.

"A boy, it's a boy," she whispered. Her hair hung over her eyes and tears rolled down her face. "I did all this for you." She nuzzled the baby's head, beaming at her mother, who was wiping tears from her own eyes.

"Well done, Harriet. You have a beautiful son. How lucky you are. It's just after midnight, so his birthday is the twelfth of December."

"Yes, I am lucky. I have a son."

"What will you call him?" asked Margaret.

"I'll name him Tom. Would you like to hold your grandson?"

"Little Tom," murmured Margaret, taking the baby from Harriet. "You are welcome here. I greeted your mother and cousin Fred in the same way when they were babies. You look just like them."

Margaret drifted around the room, cooing at her grandson before handing him back to Harriet.

Hearing the sound of a baby crying, Frederick pulled on his dressing gown, left his room, walked along the corridor and stood, hesitating, at the door to Harriet's room. He knocked and was admitted. The scene of new life and female tenderness was almost too much to bear. Seeing Frederick, Harriet beckoned him towards her. He approached the bed and embraced her.

"Congratulations, Harriet, I'm happy for you. What an eventful night!"

"Yes, I'm sorry your return coincided with the arrival of your nephew. Meet Little Tom," said Harriet. "I'd like to give him your name too, as well as my father's, Thomas Frederick Alexander Tate."

"Of course, I'd be honoured. What a fine boy, Master Thomas Tate, you are a surprising arrival. Welcome back to the family, Harriet," said Frederick. "There's much to discuss, but we must all rest and will talk in the morning."

Early the next morning, Fred and Maria sat quietly drinking tea in the parlour. Upstairs they could hear the baby's cries and the sounds of female chatter and laughter each time the bedroom door opened and then shut.

"I will baptise Little Tom and add him to the parish register," said Frederick, "and give him his father's name. Maria, you told me in your letter that Harriet was concerned that her marriage papers were lost at sea and she doesn't have a certificate."

Maria outlined Harriet's story and agreed with Frederick that Gideon should be told about the birth. Aunt Margaret was determined to write to Ivy and John Tate with the news. Then Maria asked Frederick about his time at Windsor and the condition of the King.

"It's so difficult," said Frederick with a sigh. "The view at Windsor and in Westminster is that the Prince of Wales is not suited to the role of king, but, of course, he's going to be monarch one day. They know his weaknesses; he's a spendthrift and lazy too. I saw the condition he was in after a few days of dealing with the politicians and affairs of state in his father's place. He was exhausted and took to his bed. Yet, Parliament agrees that he will have to be appointed regent if the King does not recover."

"Poor King George and Queen Charlotte, and Prince George. Fred, is the Prince still happy with his Maria, Mrs Fitzherbert? Can she give him the support he needs?"

"He's very happy with her. They love being in Brighton and he's building the most ostentatious of country retreats there. I laughed out loud when he showed me the plans. He envisages a fantasy building based on Indian and Chinese designs, like a mogul's palace. It looks very opulent and is going to cost a fortune, of course. I pointed out that the Privy Purse can't give him more money, but he simply waves his hand, claims that it must be done and announces: 'I am the Prince of Wales, don't you know.'"

Maria laughed. "You and George sound complete opposites. It's hard to believe you are related. You're good for him, a counterbalance to his extravagance."

"I don't want to be cast as a miser or nay-sayer, Maria. Everyone comes to me if they feel George needs restraining or has to be told something sensitive. It makes me look and feel very dull and dour and I'm not. Do people think I don't know how to have fun?"

"Of course you know how to have fun, Fred, but it's a relief for everyone that you are so level-headed. Did you have a chance to play your fiddle whilst you were in Windsor?"

"Yes, and thank heavens for it. George and I gave a concert, and it was wonderful. We played some very vigorous Vivaldi; it was a good performance, though it wasn't perfect. We made several mistakes, but we know each well enough to cover the missed notes or scrambled passages."

"Fred, I've been thinking about your fiddle playing."

"Indeed, thank you, Maria. I appreciate that you think about me at all." He smiled and took her hand, kissing it.

Maria laughed. "I have an idea. This sounds unorthodox, but I think you should play your violin, or even your cello, regularly in church. You are so talented, and people love to hear you. I know you like to play for special occasions, like harvest festival, Easter or Christmas, but I think you should play every Sunday. Your congregation have missed you dreadfully this autumn and I'm always asked when you will return and when you will play your violin again."

"Won't people think I'm indulging myself and being neglectful of my pastoral duties if I play my violin at every church service?"

"No, quite the opposite! I think people will appreciate it. They've missed you whilst you've been at Windsor. Reverend Rudge is perfectly fine in the pulpit and excellent at managing pastoral affairs, but he can't play the fiddle. No, Fred, it's right that you should play for your congregation. The choir sings anthems and the organist shows off when he has the chance. You don't like giving sermons and become anxious when you're preaching. You should give your parishioners a regular treat and play your violin or cello every Sunday. We know people come from far and wide hoping to hear you."

"Hmm, well, yes, it's an idea. I do like nothing better than playing my fiddle or cello, but I need time to practise. Actually, there may be a way to do this. Whilst at Windsor, the Prince and I spent time together, uninterrupted by courtiers, taking a carriage and driver from the stables and arranging music stands between us. We trotted around the park playing our pieces undisturbed except for the occasional bellowing deer and squawking rooks in the trees. It was a marvellous way to rehearse and converse privately."

"That's a wonderful idea," cried Maria, clapping her hands together. "You must adapt your Shepton carriage. Robert could drive you; he's eager to be a driver and not just a stable boy."

"Do you really think I should tour the town in a carriage playing my fiddle as I make my visits?"

"Yes, Fred. Everyone would love it."

"Well, it might amuse my parishioners to hear me practising pieces they will later hear in church."

"It will bring pleasure to you and everyone who hears you."

"Thank you, perhaps I'll talk to Robert tomorrow. However, despite my pleasure at being home at last, there is work to do. Rudge is waiting for me in my study."

"I will bring you coffee at noon."

"Thank you, Maria. I will work hard today but look forward to tonight when we slip beneath the covers and I can hold you in my arms again. Having met Little Tom, I would like us to have babies of our own."

Maria smiled at him. "And so we shall, Fred."

Chapter Thirty-Seven

George and Frederick are in Weymouth
10th July 1794, six years later

For the last six years, Frederick, Maria and Aunt Margaret had been enjoying life in Shepton Mallet, in the company of Harriet and Little Tom, turning the rectory into a family home.

The King had recovered from his attacks of mania, and Frederick was only occasionally summoned to London to deal with the Prince of Wales's office and to take divine service at St George's Chapel. However, each summer, Frederick's main task was to arrange accommodation and entertainment for Prince George and the royal family during their month-long holiday in Weymouth.

The weather in Weymouth was warm and the sea inviting. George and Frederick challenged each other to an early dip on this bright July morning and there were few people on the shore to observe them. They had not seen each other for several months and this was the brothers' first opportunity to relax and speak without any witnesses from the royal household eavesdropping on their conversation.

"It pains me to say it," said George, "but it's all over with Mrs F."

Dipping his head under the water, he emerged from the waves with a great shake of his wet hair, resembling a fleshy Neptune. His enormous stomach could be seen straining through the fine shirt he wore above loose breeches for his swim. Frederick, also wearing a long linen shirt over his slighter figure, dived into the waves, bobbing up again beside George.

"I'm compelled to make an official marriage. It has to be done," continued George.

"I'm aware that you have to find a suitable wife and produce an heir," said Frederick. "It is your duty, George, but I'm sorry you are separating from Mrs Fitzherbert. I know you enjoy each other's company. And despite my early misgivings about the connection, she's such an intelligent, interesting woman and still good-looking."

"Indeed, she is all those things, but she's weary of my wandering eye. I've been spending too much time with Lady Jersey, who entices me in new ways. Maria and I argue too much and, after ten years, romances do come to an end."

"I'm sorry for it," said Frederick. "I liked her. She's one of the few people, apart from myself, who understands how to manage you."

"True, but we are parting," said George, shaking his head.

"Have you told the King and Queen of your great decision to renounce her?"

"I will do later today, teatime at Gloucester House." George waved an arm in the direction of a row of large houses on the sea front. "I've made up my mind. Mrs F was truly only ever my mistress and feelings fade. It's time to be pragmatic and produce a legal heir to the throne. In truth, my wedding all those years ago was unconstitutional, but at the time it was vital. My God, I loved that woman."

"Where's Mrs Fitzherbert living now?"

"She's gone abroad. I've granted her an annuity. She was wealthy anyway from the two late husbands. She'll be well looked after wherever she goes."

"You are a generous soul at heart, George."

"I'm glad you think so, Fred. I agree. I am generous, aren't I? I do care." George swam closer to the shore and into his depth. He stood up, puffing out his chest, patting his corpulent stomach as the waves slapped into it and the linen shirt flowed out in the water before clinging to his body.

"And agreeing to a legal marriage wouldn't have anything to do with the half a million pounds of debt which you have to pay?" asked Frederick, wryly.

"Well, I do need to live like a prince, don't I?" George floated back onto the water, thrashing his arms. "It's not possible to keep a tally on the funds. A prince must look the part, entertain and be kind to people. Money must be granted for me to fulfil my role properly."

"And by being suitably married you'll receive more of an allowance."

"Exactly, Fred. It has to be done. I'm thirty-two; it's the right age for marriage. They've found me someone already."

"Who?" asked Frederick, kicking up his legs and floating on his back on a cresting wave.

"Caroline of Brunswick."

"Your first cousin! Have you ever met her?"

"They've sent me a portrait of Caroline. She's no beauty but looks attractive enough. We've been marrying members of our family for centuries, Fred. It's what the royal family does. My father married my mother without ever meeting her before the wedding and the marriage has been a success. They've had fifteen children! Princess Caroline is an entirely suitable bride. This marriage is the answer to all my problems, and I look forward to a comfortable life as a new husband."

Frederick shook his head and pointed across the beach. "Look, George, there's the King. He's about to bathe," They both gazed across the waves to the King's bathing machine, which was being dragged into the water and watched him standing at the front of the wooden hut, mounted on wheels, before inching his way down the steps to plunge into the waves. They heard loud shouts about the chill of the water and George laughed loudly as he saw the King turn, grasp the rail above the steps and swiftly haul himself back into the hut.

"Shall we swim over and greet him?" suggested Frederick.

"No, not this morning," said George. "I know he'll have questions for me which I don't feel inclined to answer. And, as I said, I'm going to tell him and mother this afternoon that my so-called marriage to Maria is over. They will be happy with my decision."

Nodding towards the bathing machine, he added, "When I see

them later, I want to savour the moment. My tailor has made me some new clothes especially for this conversation."

George and Frederick swam about in the shallows before emerging from the waves, heading for the beach where a valet was waiting with towels and dry clothes.

Frederick bit his lip thinking about George's decision. Of course he had to find a suitable wife. Marrying for land, status, money and the legal production of an heir was normal within royal circles and European aristocrats. The arrangement, generally, had little to do with love. Since Prince George was always falling in love, Frederick couldn't help feeling anxious about the success of this latest plan.

Thank heavens he'd had the good fortune to be introduced to a woman who turned out to be perfect for him, he thought. He loved his Maria very much and wished she'd been able to come to Weymouth with him, but she had declined because she suspected she might be with child and wanted to avoid a lengthy coach ride. Frederick shivered with delight at the possibility of fatherhood.

The arrival of Harriet and Little Tom had shattered the former peace and quiet of the rectory and their home was now riven with a five-year-old child's shrill voice, female laughter, the clatter of pans and the constant opening and shutting of doors. He realised how much he enjoyed being surrounded by his extended family. He also acknowledged that, like George, at thirty-three, he too desired a child. But rather than producing a child to inherit a throne and maintain a family's status, he wanted one to be the natural outcome of a loving marriage. Maria was now thirty-seven years old. Frederick was constantly at the beck and call of the Prince and so often absent from the marriage bed that the chances of conceiving were dwindling. He mouthed a silent prayer that maybe this time they would be blessed.

Chapter Thirty-Eight
Prince George Marries
Princess Caroline of Brunswick
7th April 1795

Frederick was nervous about this marriage, knowing that, just two days earlier, the groom had met his future bride for the first time and had taken an instant dislike to her.

On the night before the wedding, in the dining room at St James's Palace, Frederick sat at the far end of the chamber observing the top table and could almost feel the crackle of animosity between the newly betrothed couple. He watched Lady Jersey, George's current mistress, seated next to the Prince, fawning upon the unfortunate groom and baiting the future bride. Stepping into the role vacated by Maria Fitzherbert, Lady Jersey clearly enjoyed causing mischief and, in her role as Lady-in-Waiting to the Princess, had given cruel and unsuitable advice to the girl.

Frederick heard from other ladies-in-waiting that Lady Jersey had encouraged Caroline to wear rouge on her already florid cheeks and recommended that she put an evil-smelling oil on her hair and chew garlic at all times. However, the young Princess Caroline had quickly understood her rival's motives and was vengeful. Seated next to her future husband, she blew smoke from a long-stemmed pipe across his face towards the English lady on his left and threw grapes and cherries at her. Frederick caught the eye of the unfortunate prince, sitting miserably between these warring women, and nodded at him, understanding how uncomfortable he must be feeling.

"She dresses like a milkmaid," spat George, lumbering away from the dining room with Frederick towards the closet. Relieving themselves, side by side, George shook his head in despair. "She eats and drinks too much and smells dreadful. Her lady attendants have told her that she must wash. Oh, she's ghastly. She can barely speak

English, yet she knows all the worst words. She is rude to my closest friends and over-familiar to strangers. She is not a wife I could ever desire. Oh Fred, I have made a terrible mistake."

Frederick shook his head, patting George on his shoulder. There was nothing to be done. The Prince had to go through with the ceremony. Caroline of Brunswick would be his wife tomorrow evening. George had agreed to this marriage, and it was the only way to clear his debts. As Frederick pointed out, George would have to brace himself and behave like a husband because he needed an heir. Any notion of attraction, or even love, had nothing to do with the arrangement. He must ensure that she produces a child.

"Fred, not only have I made a terrible mistake, but I have wronged the only woman I ever loved. I want to reunite with my Maria. I miss her and my life is intolerable. I must go through with this marriage as if I were having a tooth pulled or being bled by a surgeon. Caroline disgusts me. I can never love that woman, yet I am compelled to be intimate with her. Let us return to the dinner, Fred. I need more champagne."

The following evening, on 8th April 1795, Frederick stood with the archbishops, bishops and all the other highest clerics in the land in the Chapel Royal in St James's Palace. Smoothing the stole above his cassock and running his finger inside his collar, Frederick was fearful for his brother as he watched him stand, swaying at the altar. George was still drunk and slurred his way through the vows, weeping as he promised his fidelity to Caroline.

After the ceremony, Frederick left the chapel, returning to his rooms at Carlton House. The palace smelled of fresh paint and polished wood in readiness for the newly married couple's arrival after their wedding night at St James's Palace. The following morning the royal residence was buzzing with gossip. Servants attending the marital suite recounted with glee how they had seen Prince George stumble up to the bedroom after midnight. The door was shut, but noises were heard. According to Princess Caroline's maid, George had fallen over in the bedroom, passed out and slept in the fireplace. Then, in the morning, he crawled into bed with his bride, fulfilling his conjugal duty.

*

From Rev Dr Frederick Blomberg, Carlton House, London
To Maria Blomberg, The Rectory, Shepton Mallet
8th January 1796

My darling Maria,

We were all very tense last night waiting for news, but Caroline, Princess of Wales, has given birth to a daughter. The King and Queen have sent their congratulations. George is extremely relieved and pleased with himself. Of course, he wanted the child to be a boy, but his new daughter is healthy and very large.

George was adamant that I should be with him for the birth, and you know how difficult it is for me to resist his commands. However, we may now feel relieved that succession, for the time being, is secure.

It has been exceedingly cold in London. When I woke this morning, there was a layer of ice at the top of the glass of water beside my bed. The fires are burning all the time at Carlton House, and everyone struggles to stay warm in this draughty palace. I hope to journey westward whilst the roads are still frozen. There's nothing worse than travelling through soft mud and seeing the horses knee-deep in mire.

I shall now be able to spend more time in Somerset. George has agreed that I may give up my position as his chaplain. The King has appointed me a prebend at Bristol Cathedral and also granted me a further living at St Andrew's in Banwell, to the west of Bath and not far from the sea. It will be a pleasant place to reside during the summer. I am sure that Tom will enjoy all the pleasures that the beaches afford.

My dear, we will always regret that the child we had longed for did not manage to join us in the end. I feel a great sadness at the loss. But we must take pleasure in the family we have around us and make the most of this new home.

We are very comfortable at Shepton, and I will regret leaving the parish. But, as we know, a cleric's life is not his own and we must move to this new living.

However, I was peeved to learn from George that he had recommended me to be the Bishop of Hereford, but the King refused to approve the appointment. When confronted by George, apparently he tut-tutted in his usual way and exclaimed: "What, make a bishop of a fiddler! Never do, never do." So, my fate is sealed and a parish priest I shall remain. The King knows my character well, and I always believed he approved my skills on the violin. However, it seems that my fiddling has proved a bar to taking high office. I shall never wear the mitre, but I remain grateful for his generosity to me.

I will send word when I begin my departure and hope to see you all in a week.

Your loving husband,
Fred

Chapter Thirty-Nine
Visitors Arrive in Shepton Mallet
6th May 1796

On a bright Saturday morning in May, Harriet was in the kitchen boiling up some meadowsweet in a large pan to make a tincture for complexions, a tonic popular with the girls in the town and surrounding villages.

Shortly before noon, a carriage drew up outside the rectory. Little Tom and Grandmother Margaret were the first to see its arrival from Uncle Frederick's study, overlooking the street. Running to the kitchen, he alerted his mother, pulling her towards the front door to greet three visitors walking up the path. Wiping her hands on her apron, Harriet opened the door, gasping in surprise. A man leaning on a stick stood in the porch and behind him were an older man and woman.

"Gideon!" cried Harriet.

"Harriet," said Gideon, gripping his stick with both hands. "It's good to see you."

"You're walking!" Harriet held open the door. "And Mr and Mrs Tate. We were expecting you to arrive tomorrow, but you are welcome. Come in, please."

Mr Tate doffed his hat and ushered his wife and son into the rectory.

"We allowed a fortnight for the journey," said Ivy, pausing in the hall to remove her bonnet. "We stayed in London for a few days, but the journey west was swifter than we had anticipated. I apologise for surprising you."

"Come into the parlour. Mama, look, they are here."

Margaret came to greet the arrivals, embracing Ivy and John. She placed their cloaks on the stand in the hall before ushering them into the parlour to sit down.

"And this is Tom," said Harriet, taking her son's hand and drawing him in front of her. "We used to call him Little Tom, but he's grown so much we had to stop. He's seven and a half years old."

Gideon held out a hand towards Tom for him to shake, but the little boy recoiled, hiding behind his mother's skirts.

"My dears, I'm so pleased to see you again," said Margaret, once everyone was seated in the parlour. "The time has flown by. I'm sorry that my nephew, Frederick, and his wife, Maria, are not here at the moment. They're visiting his new parish in Banwell. They'd like to meet you. Have you made arrangements? I'm sure we have room here for you."

"We've booked rooms at The Crown Inn, thank you, Margaret," said John Tate. "We didn't want to impose."

"No," added Ivy Tate. "We were grateful for your invitation, Harriet. We've wanted to come for some time. Now that John has sold the business, we are able to leave Hexham, and Gideon, as you see, is well enough to travel."

Harriet stared at Gideon, noticing his dulled eyes set within a thin face and sunken cheeks. His whole body was bent over. He leant forward in his chair, clasping his stick to his chest.

"Gideon," she said, "you were so injured. But you can walk now."

Before Gideon could answer, his mother described the lengthy treatment her son had endured; there was the surgeon from Newcastle who set the broken bones, the firm leather corset, specially made by a saddler, and the great tub of water in the laundry room where he would be immersed and exercise his muscles.

"The bones in his spine and pelvis have mended over time," Ivy explained. "And finally he could stand up, but he needs a stick for support. The broken ribs punctured his lungs, giving him trouble breathing."

Harriet waited patiently until her mother-in-law had finished describing Gideon's ailments. She looked directly at her husband. "And are you painting, Gideon?"

Gideon smiled up at Harriet. "Yes, that's the one thing I can still do. I have a studio at home so I can paint whilst seated. I now make a modest living from painting portraits."

"I'm pleased to hear it."

An uneasy silence followed as Cook stood in the room bearing a tray of tea things. Margaret took the tray, suggesting that Ivy might like to follow her to the drawing room. John Tate declared he would take a stroll around the town.

Harriet sat down opposite Gideon.

"Tom, dear, you go with Grandmama and help with tea. Look, you have two grandmamas to talk to. You must show them your writing."

Tom obediently left the room with the older women.

Harriet looked directly at Gideon. "You were so injured all those years ago I feared you might not survive."

"It's taken a long time for me to recover, but now I'm strong enough to travel. I wanted to meet my son. Your mother's letters tell us all about him and how he's growing."

"Why didn't you write to me?"

Gideon sighed. "I didn't think you would want to hear from me."

"That's not much of an excuse."

"I'm ashamed about my behaviour in France and Richmond, being drunk and irresponsible so much of the time. This is my punishment, seven years of pain," he added, pointing to his stick.

"Maybe that is too harsh a view," replied Harriet. "But yes, you did not behave well. Not like a husband when you drunkenly suggested I get into the carriage with a strange man who rode off with me into the countryside. Had I not been strong enough to fight him off, he might have forced himself upon me."

"I'm sorry, Harriet, I put you at risk. I was drunk and it never occurred to me that he would behave badly. I know what happened because your mother has written to mine about this."

"Gideon, I cannot forget your drunkenness and bad behaviour, but I am going to accept that you are sorry," said Harriet.

"And it distresses me not to have known about the baby, my son."

"I didn't know I was with child when I left. I'm lucky that I have a family who took care of us both."

"And I'm lucky that mine cared for me too," replied Gideon. "We started our life together so full of hope," replied Gideon, "and I squandered our love."

Harriet rose. "Would you like something to drink, Gideon? I can offer you tea, coffee, ale. I make a very good tansy tea. We have wine, if you prefer."

"I no longer drink alcohol. My recovery was not just from the injuries but also an excess of drink. I did crave it but wasn't allowed any. The doctors gave me laudanum for the pain. I would like to try your tansy tea later."

Harriet and Gideon sat in silence for a moment.

"Tom looks a fine boy," said Gideon.

"He is. I often see your face in his features. He's an interesting mix of both of us. He's full of fun and mischief and keeps everyone on their toes. He wears my mother out, but she adores him too and is a wonderful teacher. It's like she's started looking after other people's children all over again after a thirty-five-year gap. But she's getting tired, and I have to be careful he doesn't exhaust her. He goes to the church school here in Shepton."

"I would like to know him."

"But you live in Hexham."

"I should still like to know him."

"Are you planning to stay in Shepton for long?"

"For a while, if you are agreeable. What were you making when we arrived?"

"Oh, it was a herbal medicine. I've returned to my first love, creating treatments. It's rather more suitable employment for the cousin of a clergyman than singing and dancing on stage," she said, smiling.

"What did Fred say when you finally arrived here?"

"He returned home from Windsor on the night Tom was born and had no idea that there would be a baby to meet too. It was a surprise. But he loves Tom. Everyone does. I can't imagine we ever had a life without him."

"And Fred and his wife have no children?"

"No, Maria has not been blessed, I'm sorry to say. We had hoped… but no, it was not to be. She loves having Tom around the house. She's a natural mother and Fred loves him like a son."

"I'm pleased to hear it." Gideon sighed, sitting up as straight as his back would let him.

"Gideon, I will fetch you some tansy tea. You look tired. Would you like to rest? You can lie on the chaise in Fred's study. It's comfortable and quiet. I hope you'll all come here for dinner tonight? I was expecting you tomorrow, but I'll talk to Cook."

"That's kind, thank you. I don't want to make free with Fred's home when he's not here."

"He'd be the first person to invite you to dinner, and so would Maria. She loves having people in the house. She's such a good wife and so kind to everyone in the parish."

"Sounds as though Fred has fared well. And he's still close to the royal family?"

"Of course. He's with them all the time, always rushing from one royal palace or another to be with them. They ask him to take divine service at the royal chapels and he is a regular dinner guest at events. Most of all he loves the chance to play his violin or cello with the Prince of Wales. They always create opportunities to play together."

"I'm pleased he still enjoys his music."

"He does. It brings him such pleasure. Fred was in London a great deal at the end of last year because Princess Caroline was expecting a child. But George, I mean, the Prince of Wales, can't stand his wife and they lead separate lives."

"It must be interesting being so close to the royal family, having some influence."

"Yes, in a way. Fred adores them all, even though I don't think his childhood was very happy. As you know, they sent for him when he was young, and he can't escape their grasp. It's very demanding. All my dear cousin wants is to live here with his family and play his violin or cello. He's quite the eccentric clergyman now. Since he discovered the King would never appoint him as a bishop, he is happy to let music play an even greater part in his life and he entertains his congregation in church every week with a concert."

"I'm glad he's so happy and is using his talent so well."

"He is happy, Gideon. Ha, this will make you laugh. Fred's adapted the carriage he uses to drive around the town and turned it into a kind of moving music room. In this weather it's an open carriage with a music stand fixed in it. He rides around the streets and lanes of Shepton, playing his fiddle. People love seeing and hearing him. They stop on the road, doff their hats or wave, and he plays with even more of a flourish when he sees them. He's got a reputation as the 'fiddle-playing rector' of Shepton Mallet. I don't know what they'll make of him in his new parish of Banwell. I imagine he'll want to ride his carriage around there too. He's an excellent musician."

"It sounds as though he has a sense of theatre. Just like you." Gideon's eyes twinkled and Harriet smiled.

"He does. People come from miles around to attend the church here. They don't want to hear him preach. To be honest, he's not a great preacher, but everyone loves hearing him play. He's now connected with Bristol Cathedral and even they ask him to play there. You're right; performance is a family trait."

"It's good to see you settled here, Harriet. I am glad we can talk like this. I was afraid you'd turn me away. I am sorry about what happened in Richmond."

"I know, Gideon. I believe you. Forgiveness is hard, but I accept your apology, and it is good to see you. Thank you for coming."

Hearing that the Tate family had arrived at Shepton Mallet, and eager to meet them, Frederick and Maria suggested that, if they had no pressing need to return to Hexham, they might extend their stay in Somerset, dividing their time between the rectory and the newly acquired vicarage at Banwell. They also suggested that their guests should visit Bath for a few weeks of the Season, staying in a hotel close to the Floyer family home. Maria's mother was expecting visits from her other daughters – Elizabeth, Barbara and Letitia – with their families, and Maria busied herself with plans for entertainments to amuse everyone.

Although still weak from his injuries, Gideon began touring the countryside around Shepton Mallet in Frederick's music carriage, pausing to paint watercolour landscapes. By late July 1796 he had created enough work to hold a small exhibition in a gallery in Bath. The extended family moved to Bath for the two-week show, accommodating themselves near the Floyer home, taking pleasure in each other's company, attending concerts, dances and plays.

Back in Shepton Mallet, in August, Tom now felt close enough to his father to take him by the hand and, walking slowly, show him around his favourite places in the town and the surrounding countryside, pointing out fairy rings of toadstools, ponds with newts and trees he enjoyed climbing. A pleasurable pattern of family life prevailed and, by the end of August, it was clear to everyone that Gideon and Harriet had reconciled.

*

Three weeks of banns, read from the pulpit of St Peter and St Paul's church, heralded the marriage of Gideon and Harriet Tate, due to take place on 30th September 1796. Shuffling the papers on the desk in his rectory study, Frederick asked Harriet if she was absolutely sure she wanted to go through with the ceremony.

"Yes, I've made up my mind. Tom must feel secure. He has grown up as Tom Tate and we don't want any doubt regarding his legitimacy; and I want to do this. I was wrong to elope to France with Gideon, causing everyone such distress, and now this wedding can take place with the entire family's blessing," said Harriet. "John and Ivy are using the capital from the sale of their business to buy us a house near them in Hexham. To be honest, I'm going to be more of Gideon's nurse than his wife and I'm prepared for that. His lungs are so weak and he's expected to live long. I love Gideon, but not in the same way as before, and he knows that. I have forgiven him for his behaviour, and we are friends. The truth is, he's too frail to be a husband, in every sense. I am the stronger side of the partnership and we both want Tom to be secure. It's for the best."

"Well, I can't argue with that," replied Frederick. "But are you convinced that moving to Hexham is the best solution? We will miss you and Tom. Part of me wants to advise you against leaving for selfish reasons. Your mother is going to find it very hard, and Maria will too."

"I've thought about this, Fred. Yes, it's going to be a great wrench. Mama is upset, but she understands. She knows where I'll be living and has given me a long list of places where she used to walk and people she knew in Hexham. She promises to visit in the spring or summer next year when the weather is fine. She knows that the winters in Northumberland are too much for her painful joints. Besides, she's very settled here in Shepton. We've been such a happy family, but everything's changing. You and Maria are moving to Banwell. And you'll soon be back at Windsor or Carlton House or wherever the Prince of Wales summons you."

"Have you explained what's happening to Tom?"

"Yes, I have, and he sees it all as a huge adventure. He loves seeing new places and he knows he'll be with his mother and father, and grandparents who love him."

"Indeed, but if you are unhappy in Northumberland, or for any reason you need to leave, you can always return here. Maria and I will welcome you with open arms."

"Thank you, Fred. This is a good decision. I will marry Gideon."

"I remember you saying that to me before."

Harriet laughed. "Yes, I remember. We'll write to each other, and Gideon promises to make frequent portraits of Tom to send so you can see him grow. It's not as though we won't see each other again. However long my married life turns out to be, I intend to make the most of it."

"True, but Hexham is a very, very long way from Somerset. Maria and I will make plans to come and visit you all. Perhaps we'll travel with Aunt Margaret next spring."

Harriet smiled, clapping her hands together. "Indeed, I look forward to it. Thank you for agreeing to marry us here in the church, and thank you for giving us the paper mosaic by Mrs Delaney. I shall enjoy having it with me and think of those happy days we shared together in Dover Street. This wedding is going to be a wonderful occasion. Maria and Mama have worked so hard to arrange everything for the breakfast afterwards."

"It's the least we could do, Harriet. We want you to be happy."

"I am happy, Fred, thank you."

Chapter Forty
Sad News and a Royal Summons
February 1801

Six years after the royal wedding, the Prince of Wales had separated from Princess Caroline, having barely lived as man and wife in that time, and was reunited with Mrs Fitzherbert. Frederick felt relief that George was back with his 'wife', who knew well how to manage her restless lover whilst maintaining a deferential distance from him in her own home in Park Street.

In the winter, Mrs Fitzherbert entertained the Prince at her home in London and in the summer months she took a villa in Worthing. Each morning, the Prince mounted his horse from the stables at the almost complete pavilion at Brighton and galloped over the South Downs and along the shore to be with her. The Prince's letters to Frederick spoke of his contentment with this arrangement, repeating his regret that he had ever abandoned her to marry the dreadful woman whose name he would never commit to paper.

Released from his duties as Chaplain to the Prince of Wales at Windsor Castle, Frederick and Maria had spent the past five years permanently settled in the vicarage at Banwell, enjoying the spacious house and large garden next to St Andrew's Church in the centre of the town. Frederick appointed a new curate, Reverend Perkins, to maintain the spiritual welfare of the parish if he were called away. Compared to the Shepton Mallet Rectory, the vicarage at Banwell was airy and bright. Maria had insisted that the kitchen should be fitted with a new, modern range and that fresh water must be piped directly into the scullery, with no need for a well.

Frederick and Maria were sorry not to have the company of Aunt Margaret in Banwell. Protesting that the upheaval would be too much for her, she had decided to remain at the rectory in

Shepton Mallet. Besides, to everyone's surprise, she had struck up a friendly relationship with Reverend Rudge, spending hours with him discussing a shared love of literature.

Banwell was close enough to the coast that, during the summer months, Frederick and Maria enjoyed day trips to Weston-super-Mare to bathe and take the sea air. And to the east of the town lay the Mendip Hills where they could meet Aunt Margaret and friends who travelled with her from Shepton Mallet, to share picnics in the meadows and on riverbanks. Banwell was also close enough to Bath to allow them to visit the Floyer home to meet Maria's sisters and elderly mother.

For those few years, life was serene. At nearly forty years of age, Frederick was satisfied with the progress of his career and the income from his several livings and clerical appointments. He played his fiddle in St Andrew's Church every Sunday, rode his music-room carriage around Banwell and enjoyed giving and attending concerts. His only regret was that he and Maria had been unable to have children, yet they took pleasure in Maria's sister's children when they came to stay, especially Letitia's baby daughter, Anna. Then, in the space of a few days, early in 1801, everything changed. Aunt Margaret forwarded a letter she had received from Harriet.

To Mrs Margaret Poulton, The Rectory, Shepton Mallet
6th February 1801

My dearest Mama,

I have sad news. Gideon has died. It was not unexpected, but it grieves us all. Tom is very upset. He loved his father and now he misses him. I am happy to have been his true wife for over five years and I must be strong for Tom.

Doctor Simms, who attended Gideon, confirmed that his constitution was weak and there was a great congestion in his lungs, probably due to the damage from his broken ribs. Two weeks ago, he ceased eating, talking and did not rise from his bed. He took laudanum, to soothe the pain, and then he died.

The funeral is next week. I'm not expecting you to come. The weather is harsh, and the roads are very bad at present, making travel impossible.

So, Tom and I will continue to live in our house in Hexham. Ivy and John are very sorry for Gideon's loss but happy that we are close by. So, at forty-one years of age, I am now a widow with a home of my own and an inheritance from Gideon's estate. I still earn my own money from producing medicines.

Tom, at just twelve years old, is now taller than me and seems to grow higher each day. I enclose Gideon's last portrait of him. He is an able student and happy at school, though he's a lively and adventurous boy and loves being outdoors far more than sitting in a classroom.

Please do forward this news to Fred and Maria. Oh, Mama, I am sorry that Gideon's life turned out to be so different from the one he envisaged all those years ago. I remember with such happiness the times we would drink wine and talk long into the night about art and enlightenment – revolution, even! We were going to make so many changes in the world. Clearly God had some other plan for him.

I will write again very soon.

Fondest love from your daughter, Harriet

Saddened by the news about Gideon's death, Frederick and Maria were planning to visit Harriet in the spring when, a few days later, a horse bearing a royal messenger thundered into Banwell with an urgent summons from the Prince of Wales.

From George, Prince of Wales, Buckingham House, London
To Reverend Doctor Frederick Blomberg, Banwell Vicarage
24th February 1801

My dear F,

You must come at once. The King is gravely ill and may not survive. We fear it is a relapse of the same malady he suffered in '88, but this time it is far worse.

Father was out riding two weeks ago and, on returning to Buckingham House, complained of feeling ill. The doctors put him to bed, but he would not sleep. They filled a pillow with hops to sedate him and he slept, but when he woke he was raving again. I hope you'll be able to calm him down like you did before.

We have told all courtiers that he is suffering from gout and indisposed. It will soon be known that his madness has returned.

I wish to reinstate you as my personal chaplain so that we can confer more privately about the King's condition. Fred, I am fearful that my time to become king or regent may be approaching, and I need you by my side. Come quickly.

George, Prince of Wales

"Oh Maria, I'm so sorry," said Frederick as he finished reading the letter out loud. "You know this means I must go immediately. It's a longer journey from Banwell to London. Would you like to come with me as far as Bath and spend time with your sisters? I'm sure Barbara and the children would love to see you. And why not visit Letitia in Hampshire? You said you wanted to see our little niece, Anna, now that she's two and walking and talking. This could be your chance to be a good aunt and godmother to her. I don't know how long I will be away."

"Fred, I understand, though I'm sorry that it spoils our plans to travel north."

Maria sighed, barely disguising her annoyance that her husband, yet again, must attend to the royal family's needs rather than his own.

"And yes, I will go to Bath with you, as you suggest. Aunt Margaret might like to join us there, if she feels well enough. Then she and I can travel together to Hampshire and stay with Letitia in Alresford. I will write to her immediately. Clearly the Prince of Wales needs you urgently. Thank goodness that your new curate here at Banwell is so amenable. I far prefer Reverend Perkins to Reverend Rudge at Shepton, who always seemed so resentful when you were an absentee vicar. And I never liked the way he was always jotting things down in that notebook of his. At least Reverend Perkins, here, understands that you are an absentee vicar and doesn't question your absence."

"Thank you, my sweet," said Frederick. "And now you have an absentee husband too."

"Well, be sure to take your violin and cello with you, Fred. You might need the solace of music whilst you're in London and enjoy the chance to play with the Prince. The congregation here will miss your entertainment and will be eager to come to church when you return. Go and let the stable know you need the carriage prepared and I'll help us pack."

*

When Frederick arrived in early March, the occupants of Buckingham House were in uproar – the King had relapsed and this time his madness seemed out of control. Frederick followed a page to his apartment, where a servant unpacked his bags. From the window of his room, he surveyed a chilly garden, still dripping from a recent downpour with bare trees lifting their branches in supplication towards a leaden sky. Beyond the garden walls he could see the rooftops of mansions and chimneystacks and heard the clop of horses on The Mall.

The place smelled damp, and Frederick noticed a layer of mould on a tapestry hanging in the corridor. There were water stains on the wallpaper near the main door. If Prince George were appointed regent and chose to live here, he thought, then Buckingham House would need considerable refurbishment.

After changing his clothes, Frederick made his way to the Prince of Wales's private apartment and knocked. A page opened the door and Frederick entered. He bowed to the Prince, who strode towards him, wrapping his plump arms around him. Frederick felt George's large belly pressed against his own.

"Fred, thank goodness you're here. Oh, the poor king. He is a dreadful sight to behold," said George, wiping tears from his eyes. "I saw Father in his room yesterday. His eyes were yellow, like a tiger's, and his tongue dark and too large for his mouth. His limbs constantly trembled and all he could speak was gibberish. It was monstrous. We knew he was going blind before this last attack, but now he can barely see at all."

"George, I'm so sorry," said Frederick, loosening his white collar. "I'm not sure I'll be able to say or do anything which might assist, but of course I will try."

"Thank you, Fred. He still detests doctors and speaks only of clergymen he can trust, and of you in particular. I've insisted that Doctors Willis, Senior and Junior, are in charge. Willis Senior is a clergyman as well as a physician. These doctors treat the mind with kindness and tolerance rather than imposing physical torture on him like the quacks who had control of him before. Follow me, we will go to his room."

Frederick and George walked upstairs to a suite of rooms in Buckingham House where the King was kept secure and under constant watch.

"What should I expect when I go in?" Frederick asked the doctors as he stood by the door, hesitating.

"He may not recognise your voice at first," replied Doctor Willis Junior. "Be polite and respectful. He has been restrained. He can't harm you."

Frederick entered the King's chamber. The room was dark save for a few candles on the mantelpiece and the flickering light from a small fire in the grate. The King was in a chair with his back to the door. Frederick walked around the seated figure, tied up in a jacket, his arms crossed in an uncomfortable hug. He sat down in a chair in front of him.

"Your Majesty, sir, it is I, Frederick Blomberg, come to see you."

The King looked up at him. His eyes were dim in the light and Frederick remembered that he was blind. Frederick continued to talk in the hope that the King would recognise his voice.

"Sir, I have come to London from my latest parish in Somerset. I thank you, as my patron, for the new living at Banwell. My wife, Maria, and I are very comfortable there. It's close to the sea."

"Close to the sea, eh, like Weymouth, what, what," came the growled reply. "You're a man of God?"

"I am, sir. I have you to thank for my ordination and my livings."

"Then I am pleased for it, sir. Who are you?"

"I'm Frederick. The Reverend Doctor Frederick Blomberg, sir."

"You're a doctor?"

"No, sir, I'm a clergyman."

"Those doctors who torment me claim to be men of God, but they are not. They are quacks, false prophets and cannot be trusted."

Frederick could tell that his presence was unlikely to make any difference to the King. Doctor Willis Senior approached the King from the other side of the chair and reviewed his patient.

The King, turning towards Willis, shouted, "Who's there? I know you're there."

Willis indicated to Frederick with a shaking finger not to acknowledge him but to continue talking to the King.

"Sir, 'tis I, sir, Frederick, Master Frederick. Shall I read to you, or would you prefer to pray?"

"Argh, I remember now. I will not have the devil in my room. Get out, get out, what, what! You are the cause of my guilt."

Frederick recoiled in horror. The King struggled to release himself but was unable to loosen his arms. His mouth opened wide to reveal blackened teeth and an engorged tongue. The skin on his forehead was blotchy and peeling. His white beard straggled down his chin and spittle ran from his lips into it.

"I have a thirst and a hunger. Will no one feed me? Will nobody give me comfort? I am a thing, a beast. I'm at your mercy. God forgive me. I detest my treatment. I am surrounded by cruelty. What was your name?"

"Frederick, sir. I am sorry for your distress. I am Master Frederick. I came to you as a child." Frederick covered his mouth, finding the sight of the King upsetting.

"Frederick. Ah, now I know you, sweet Frederick, child of my loins. A comfort. You must save yourself. Leave me. I am beyond redemption." He struggled against the restraint but fell back in his chair, defeated.

"Where is my beloved, Meliza, mother of my child? I want her."

Frederick looked at Willis and shook his head. Seeing this man looking so powerless and crazed was distressing. Desperate to leave, with relief, he followed the doctor out of the room.

"Thank you, Reverend Blomberg," said Doctor Willis Senior. "Thank you for trying. His mania is not yet controlled. But rest assured, we will never administer the cupping, the bleeding and the leeches. Our approach is different. We treat the mind, not the body."

"I thank you for your care. If I can be of any further help, please let me know. I'm sorry that I could not do anything."

"You did help. You treated him with respect and without any form of attack. He may remember this. We believe he will become calmer when he is moved to the palace at Kew, and away from the city."

"Thank you, Doctor Willis. I trust you will do your best for him and sincerely hope that the King recovers. I bid you goodnight."

The next morning Frederick joined the Prince in his rooms to discuss the situation.

"Here, have a glass of small-beer," said George. "It's my current tipple and prevents me calling for wine. Can you see, I've lost weight?"

As he accepted the glass of beer, Frederick nodded, reluctant to reply, whilst viewing George's enormous girth. In truth, he was larger than ever. His belly was vast and even the cravat wound around his throat could not disguise the swollen and flaccid flesh below his chin.

"George, I don't believe I was any help at all when I saw the King last night. His mania is beyond my knowledge."

"And I am being told by advisors that I should prepare myself for the position of regent. Part of me relishes the prospect and at the same time I am fearful of the level of responsibility I will have to bear. A monarch's life is never his own."

"We need to wait and pray. But George, tell me about your life. I heard that you are moving Princess Charlotte to Windsor Castle. Do you see much of her?"

"A certain amount. I am very fond of my little daughter. She is a child of great character. I suppose it is natural, since she is mine. But I had to intervene and demand that she be moved from her mother's house in Blackheath. That woman is a terrible influence. From what I hear, the Princess of Wales – I can't bear to call her by her name – has been entertaining all manner of men. She's grown exceedingly large and coarse. Last year, my spies tell me, she produced a child, and nobody knows who the father is. She dotes on a feeble little boy called Willikin, keeping him close to her all the time. I ask you. She has no sense of decorum. She sleeps with whomsoever she wishes. She keeps a bawdy house open to any number of undesirables and foreigners. No, no, it's not at all suitable for an eight-year-old girl. She's been exposed to the most disgusting and improper people. She's in danger of being thoroughly corrupted."

Frederick had to turn away and smile to himself. The irony

of hearing George describing his wife this way amused him. Yes, Princess Caroline might not be providing a suitable environment for her young daughter, but was it any worse than the life George would offer?

"Presumably she'll have the company of the younger princesses at Windsor?" said Frederick. "They'll be entertainment for her."

"They're a much better influence than anyone. Certainly not my mother, the Queen! She is not the best guide for the girl and has become fat, oh so fat. She's bad-tempered all the time. Of course she's worried about Father. They lead separate lives now. It is a sad situation."

"And Maria Fitzherbert?"

"Ah, Fred, at least I still have the love of that most excellent woman."

"She's very understanding."

"Would that I could return to Brighton to be with her. She's rented a house in the town, and I have built a tunnel from the Pavilion to her home. We can meet in secret, but…" George held out his arms and let them fall to his sides in hopelessness, "alas, I am needed here. Fred, my spectacular new pavilion is nearly complete, and I so enjoy staying there. When things here are resolved, you must come to stay and bring your Maria to join us."

"She would like that, thank you."

"Any children, Fred? Any little Blomberg offspring?"

"No, George. After seventeen years of marriage, we've accepted that we will not be blessed."

"I'm sorry for it, Fred, sorry for it. And what of Cousin Harriet and her beau, the crippled artist?"

"Harriet and her son Tom are in Northumberland. Gideon, her husband, has just died."

"Ah, probably for the best."

Frederick struggled not to retort with offence or laugh at the insensitivity.

"Gideon's body was very weak after the accident."

"Well, well. I'm sorry for it, Fred. Indeed. What trials you do have. Will Harriet and the boy stay in the north country?"

"Yes, they're settled there. My aunt Margaret talks about leaving Shepton to visit them. She misses them so much. Tom is growing up and Harriet says he towers over her now. He's only twelve, but he talks about joining the army one day, which terrifies me. He wants adventure."

"Families, eh. My mother keeps her daughters close. Too close, I fear. They'd like to get married, but there's a terrible dearth of suitable young princes for them to marry, ha! So they mope around the castle like forlorn creatures from a fairy tale. It makes me sad to see them so unfulfilled."

"And would they have any choice in their husband if a suitable one were found?"

"Perhaps. The Princess Royal managed to get away, so there's always hope. But her husband is a brute, to my mind, a terrible brute. The other princesses must endure being cooped up with their mother. I do feel sorry for them."

"Indeed, I do too. George, I thank you for the beer." Frederick set down his half-finished glass and bowed.

"Thank you, Fred. It's good to have you near me. Makes me calm. I'll let you go."

*

The King's illness eventually subsided and for nine years an uneasy normality returned.

Resuming his role as monarch, and occasionally appearing in public, few of his subjects had any idea of the fluctuating state of the King's health and how suddenly he could slip into mania. Every few months he battled manic episodes and problems with his eyesight, yet each time he recovered, remaining lucid enough to maintain his role as monarch, being briefed by ministers on affairs at home and abroad and signing acts of Parliament.

Towards the end of 1809, celebrations to mark his fifty-year reign began and were scheduled to last for twelve months with a finale planned for 25th October 1810, the anniversary of his ascension to the throne.

In September 1810, Frederick travelled to London to join the last stage of the jubilee celebrations.

However, exactly fifty years since George III was declared king, the royal family suffered a tragic blow. Their youngest child, the much adored Princess Amelia, died of consumption at Windsor in early November. News of her sudden death plunged the King back into a fresh bout of his illness. Mourning his beloved daughter, imagining long conversations with her, and recalling the loss of his two young sons, Princes Alfred and Octavius, the symptoms of mania were now beyond control.

The King was removed to secure rooms at Windsor Castle where he roamed the suite in his sightless, crazed state, barely aware of those around him.

Anticipating that the parlous state of the King's health might finally demand that the heir to the throne should assume the role of regent, Prince George appointed Frederick his Clerk of the Closet, a more intimate role, as well as his chaplain.

Chapter Forty-One
Prince George Becomes Prince Regent
February 1811

By the New Year of 1811, the Government could no longer tolerate the situation. The country needed a lucid monarch, and doctors confirmed that the King's condition was now beyond redemption. He would not recover. The Regency Bill was passed by Parliament and on 6th February 1811 Prince George became prince regent. The first decision the country's new Head of State took was to throw a lavish Grand Fête on 19th June in celebration of the regency, at Carlton House. Frederick and Maria Blomberg were amongst the guests.

Carlton House Palace was ablaze with candles. Guests wearing their finest clothing arrived in the early evening, eager to view the interior of the new regent's palace and admire the decoration. Frederick knew that George had spent a fortune on furniture, flooring and pictures for the staterooms, plates for the sideboards and statuary for every alcove. An army of servants, dressed in blue and gold livery, marched around the palace offering guests glasses of champagne and trays of canapés.

Frederick held Maria's hand and led her up the steps to the colonnaded entrance on the north side of Carlton House, through the impressive entrance hall and into the staterooms where they marvelled at the rich decorations, painted wallpaper and gilded plaster, soft Turkish carpets underfoot and silk drapes hung at every window.

Progressing along the line to greet the new prince regent, Frederick and Maria approached George, standing upon a platform in the Gothic conservatory to greet his guests. Maria curtsied and

Frederick bowed before the Prince.

"How's this, Fred," said George with a grin, waving his hand, indicating the opulence of the stateroom. "And my dear Mrs Blomberg. A pleasure." He bowed to Maria.

"You look magnificent, sir," said Frederick with a smile. "The palace decorations are a triumph."

"It does look good, doesn't it? I am magnificent. It's all my own design! Must let you go, sir, ma'am."

Frederick and Maria moved on to allow the next guests to greet the new regent.

"Oh Fred, I'd no idea this place was so, so… much!" cried Maria. "And to think that you stay here and I'm a guest too. It's overwhelming."

"That's exactly the reaction George demands from his guests. He's waited a long time for this moment. At last he can enjoy calling himself prince regent."

"But might it all be taken from him by the King? What if the King recovers?"

"He won't recover. The King's mind is completely gone. I had a word with the older Doctor Willis earlier. He confirmed that it's hopeless. The poor man may live for years, but he's senile, completely blind and deaf. He doesn't know who anyone is. He plays the harpsichord all day and sings to himself. He believes he can see and talk to his dead son Octavius. He even cries for a woman called Meliza, the old pronunciation of my mother's name. I don't know if he means her, or someone else. It's very sad. However, George is delighted to have the power he's craved for years, but I doubt he relishes the work the position entails."

"That's what you always said about him. Well, he has taste. Unusual taste but very impressive."

"He wants to make a good impression and craves approval. Some of his brothers and uncles are here, but Queen Charlotte refused to come. She doesn't think it's right for George to be celebrating what is actually a terrible situation. So none of the princesses could come either."

"Wouldn't they'd have enjoyed it?"

"I'm sure they would, but there we are."

"And I assume the Princess of Wales was not invited?"

"Absolutely not. He has no contact with her. It's a shame for Princess Charlotte because she was desperate to come. George showed me the sweetest letter she wrote to him pleading for an invitation. She's fifteen now and a lively young lady. But it's for the best that she stays at Windsor until the novelty of the regency calms down."

"Well, Fred, I am very privileged to be in such splendid company. I will have to tug at your sleeve every time I see a lord or lady and you can tell me who they are. I can't believe that we are attending the most important party of the year."

Frederick patted his wife's hand and led her through the rooms to greet fellow guests. In the early hours of the morning, after the party had been roaring since eight o'clock at night, the new prince regent sat down for supper in the Gothic conservatory with two hundred favoured guests. Frederick and Maria gazed in astonishment at the dozens of round tables, exquisitely laid with fine china and gleaming cutlery. Dishes of cold meats, tureens of hot soup and salvers bearing all manner of fruits were offered to guests. Iced champagne flowed all through the night and other wines, chosen to complement the many dishes, filled the finest crystal glasses.

On a table in front of the Prince Regent, an audacious, decorative centrepiece attracted attention. Water from a tiny fountain trickled into lengths of silver dishes, shaped like a winding stream, flanked by mossy banks, adorned with pretty flowers and plants. Tiny fish swam up and down this miniature stream beneath arched bridges whilst small urns, placed along the stream's route, puffed out fragrant smoke.

The guests continued eating and drinking until the early hours when carriages collected weary revellers and Frederick and Maria finally retired to his rooms on the floor above.

By dawn most of the tiny fish in the silver stream were dead.

Chapter Forty-Two
Tragic News
20ᵗʰ June 1811

The following morning, Frederick and Maria were preparing to take a carriage ride around London when a messenger arrived with a letter addressed to Maria, care of Reverend Blomberg. It had been forwarded from Aunt Margaret in Shepton Mallet.

Opening it, Maria swiftly read the contents, emitting a loud shriek, and handed the letter to Frederick.

"No, no, not Letitia, I can't believe it. No, it's not true."

The letter from Aunt Margaret contained the tragic news that Letitia, Maria's younger sister, had suddenly died. Edward Woolls sent word to both Banwell and Shepton Mallet a few days ago and Aunt Margaret was anxious to forward the news to Maria. Frederick bit the tip of his tongue to stay tears pricking his eyes. Letitia was such an attractive woman, always full of life and laughter. Where Maria was thoughtful and measured, Letitia was adventurous and fun. Yet she was always considerate, kind and devoted to her young daughter, Anna.

Maria sobbed uncontrollably into her handkerchief. "How can someone develop a fever like that simply after a cut to the hand?" she cried. "Edward says, in the letter, she was consumed by it. Poor little Anna, this is dreadful for her. We must go to Alresford. Oh, I can't bear this."

Frederick felt torn. He had enjoyed being part of the huge party at Carlton House and was looking forward to spending time with the new regent in London. But, he realised, they must support the Floyer family and leave London immediately.

"We must attend the funeral," he said.

Maria looked up, her face streaked with tears. "Yes, may we? Will the Prince Regent be angry if you leave? Weren't you supposed to meet the Bishop?"

"I will write to him when we're back in Banwell." Frederick bit his lip and looked away. The Bishop of Bristol had recently appointed Frederick a prebend of the cathedral, yet another promotion and a further living to add to his collection.

"Maria, I'm sure George will understand. There are other people here to serve him. My responsibility is to you first. We must go to Hampshire."

*

On 30th June 1811, mourners filled St John's Church in Alresford at Letitia Woolls' funeral. They dabbed their eyes with handkerchiefs whilst the organist played a solemn anthem. Frederick and Maria took their seats in the front pew, nodding at the other two surviving sisters, their husbands and children. Aunt Margaret travelled separately from Shepton Mallet, joining them at the church.

Frederick observed with professional interest as the vicar conducted the service, describing Letitia tenderly. Clearly, he had known her well and was able to talk about her enthusiasm for dancing, music and love for her family.

Afterwards, at the Woolls' family home, Maria sat down with Anna in the drawing room. The girl's face was pale and tear-stained. She pressed herself close to Maria, who put her arms around her, waiting for the sobs to subside.

"Mama looked so perfect lying there in bed," she wept. "You couldn't see anything wrong with her. Then she stopped breathing. I can't believe it."

"My sweet girl. You must be brave. Your father will care for you, and we are all here to help."

"I don't think Papa knows what to do. He just stays in his study all day," Anna replied.

"He's in shock," replied Maria. "Your mama died so suddenly, and he is finding this very hard, as we all are. I'm sure he wants to look after you. He was so pleased when you were born. It took a long time for you to arrive, and you make him so happy."

"But he won't talk to me. I don't know what to do. I don't know how to keep house."

"Anna, you are loved by everyone in the family, and we are all here to look after you and your papa. Let's leave it a few days. Uncle Fred and I will stay here in Alresford and help you and your father decide what to do. But here is a suggestion. Perhaps you and Papa could come back with us to Banwell for a few weeks. There's plenty of room at the vicarage and we can look after you. I'm inviting you as your aunt and godmother, and with Uncle Fred's agreement."

"I would love to come with you, thank you, Aunt Maria."

"Good, we will talk to your papa. We will care for you."

*

Frederick doubted that joining his late wife's family in Banwell would salve Edward Woolls' overwhelming grief, but Maria was adamant. He accepted that Anna would benefit from the love of her aunt and godmother. He had always liked his little niece. At eleven years old she was pretty in an unusual way, thin and gangly with long black hair and dark, expressive eyes glowing beneath thick, almost horizontal eyebrows. Her skin was dusky, as though she spent time in the fields in high summer in contrast to her mother's strawberries and cream pink complexion. She reminded him of a Spanish painting of the Madonna he had admired in a High-Church chapel somewhere.

So, a few days after the funeral, Frederick, Maria, Margaret, Anna and Edward Woolls travelled back to Somerset together, stopping at Shepton Mallet to see Aunt Margaret safely installed back in the rectory before continuing to Banwell.

At the age of seventy-four, after a lifetime spent caring for other people, Frederick could see his aunt looked tired. What Frederick also noticed in Aunt Margaret's face, as he watched her sink into her chair after the long journey, was the look of a woman approaching the end of her life. An irritating cough had become more persistent, and her eyes looked red-rimmed and weary. Her cheeks were pale, and she was thinner. Frederick recognised the signs from giving absolution to parishioners as they approached their final days. Setting off for Banwell, Frederick leant out of the carriage window as far as he could and waved at the woman who had tended him from his earliest days, instinctively knowing that he might never see her again.

Two weeks later, on 14th July, she died. According to Reverend Rudge, Margaret had complained of chest pains one afternoon after walking back to the rectory from the town bookshop. Hearing the clatter of books as they dropped onto the flagstone floor of the parlour, Rudge found Margaret collapsed in her chair by the fire. He summoned the doctor, but it was too late.

On 1st August, the day of Margaret Poulton's funeral, the church of St Peter and St Paul in Shepton Mallet was filled with mourners from the town and also many who had travelled from far away. Harriet and Tom made the journey from Hexham, the two Laing cousins, Sam and Noah, came from Kent.

Frederick conducted the funeral service in a professional manner, refusing to allow emotion to make his voice quaver or lose his place in his open prayer book. Despite hearing Harriet weeping loudly next to Maria and Anna, who buried their faces in handkerchiefs, he maintained his composure. Rather than give a eulogy, he sat down at his cello before his beloved aunt Margaret's coffin and played the *Lacrimosa* from Mozart's requiem. As the beautiful music soared to the rafters of the church, Frederick poured all his emotion into his playing, each searing chord commemorating his gratitude to a woman who had been a mother, aunt and devoted companion.

After the funeral, Frederick and Maria were delighted to welcome Harriet and Tom at the vicarage in Banwell. By now, Tom was a fine young man of twenty-two, tall, broad-chested and strong. With the inheritance from his late grandparents' will, he planned to visit America and see what opportunities the young country might offer.

However, Frederick did not have long to enjoy time with his family. In early September he received a summons to return to London. The Prince Regent needed him.

Chapter Forty-Three

The Prince Regent Gives Frederick a Gift
7th September 1811

Sitting with George on the south terrace outside Carlton House, the two men admired the gardens, enjoying the last of the summer sunshine. Every shrub had been trimmed and the grass neatly scythed; autumn flowers had been planted in the beds and a pair of peacocks strutted across the lawn, calling each other.

"We're a couple of old troopers, aren't we, Fred?" declared George, leaning back on the cushioned bench on the terrace, blowing out the smoke from his cigar. "Here we are, you are now fifty and I forty-nine. What a long way we've come. How hard we've worked."

"Speak for yourself, George," said Fred, puffing his own smoke up into the evening sky. "You spend your life in one palace or another with no end of servants to tend to your every need. I'm kept nimble and trim by rushing around the country. May I remind you that I have not stopped travelling these last few months? First I attended your Grand Fête in June, then dashed to Hampshire for Letitia's funeral, back to Shepton for my dear Aunt Margaret's funeral, to Banwell to settle the family and finally here I am back again at your service at Carlton House. My life is not my own. I am a servant to many masters."

"Are you saying that I have no masters?"

"No, sir, you must answer to God, like all of us. But you have the privilege of snapping your fingers and others will do your bidding. You are fortunate."

"I agree; I am fortunate. Fred, how much have you had to drink?"

"Quite a lot." Frederick burped.

"So have I. We are happy, drunken old troopers."

"We are indeed." Frederick took another sip of the excellent Madeira and held up his glass for a servant to refill it.

"I'm looking forward to the day my daughter Princess Charlotte gets married," said George. "I've been thinking a great deal about her. She may only be fifteen, but it's important to find the right person for her. I want her to be happy, have a child, or children, and secure this country with an heir, but only if she finds a suitable husband."

"That's a very generous approach for you to take, George. I thought the royal family believed that marriage was all about duty, not love."

"It is." George sighed. "When we live in such an exalted layer of society, duty must prevail. It is so hard to find love within duty."

"You seem to have found love, George, just not with your wife, alas."

"Indeed. Marriage has not been kind to me. And I have to accept that, even at my tremendous age, I am still attractive to the ladies. I can't help being the focus of their attention."

"George, it might have something to do with your position in life."

They both laughed out loud and clinked their glasses.

"Fred, you've been lucky. You love your Maria, don't you?"

"I do."

"But no children."

"No, George, as you keep reminding me. But, for the moment, we enjoy caring for Anna, the child of Maria's sister, Letitia, who died recently. Her father has found it very difficult to cope since his wife died. And Harriet and young Tom have stayed on with us at Banwell after my dear Aunt Margaret's funeral. Maria is very pleased to have her company. I have quite the family waiting for my return in Somerset."

"And what of the boy, Tom?"

"He plans to visit America seeking adventure."

"Adventure, in America!" exclaimed George. "The trouble that colony caused us. I dare say its loss contributed to Father's madness, but there we are. They chose to separate from us."

"It will be hard for Harriet when he goes, but she can see he has inherited her own bold spirit. He's an able young man, intelligent and full of energy. He will have a good life there. Harriet would have liked to keep him close in Northumberland but knows she must let him go. I reminded her that she chose adventure too when she was young."

"That's all you want for your children, that they should be happy. My mother will be especially happy if we find a good husband for Princess Charlotte. Oh, Mama has become such a cantankerous old biddy lately. It's very hard to please her. I'd like to make her proud. I've always craved parental approval."

"Really, George? I wasn't aware that parental approval ever bothered you."

"Fred, how can you say that? Of course it does. I do love the old woman, despite being irritated by her. And I love Father, in my fashion. I only wish we were able to converse with him, but he's withdrawn from us forever, the doctors say."

"It's a very sad situation. I too should like to see him again, even though he would not know me."

"Oh, but he might, Fred. He always loved you more than the rest of us. The number of times we would hear him saying, 'oh, Master Frederick this, Master Frederick that… he is my friend' and singing your praises as a man of the cloth. It was very wearing."

"I'm sure you're making that up, George. I know he loved you and the other princes and princesses when you were young children."

"Yes, when we were small, had no opinions and didn't create trouble. Then we all grew up, didn't we, and started having ideas and wanting to do things. You know, Fred, he controlled all of us most cruelly."

"In what way?"

"Well, remember, he enforced all those rules for us at the Princes' House, restricted food and limited playtime. Then he wouldn't let me go abroad when I wanted to. Yet he let Princes Frederick, William and Edward go off on adventures, sending them abroad and into the army and navy. Even Prince Ernest was let loose. And then he wouldn't allow the princesses to marry when they were desperate to. Those houses at Windsor and Kew must be like nunneries. They're now filled with hysterical women who are longing to break out and wed the first man they encounter."

"You paint a sad picture." Fred took his final puff and stubbed out the cigar. "Will you change their situation when you become king?"

"I will do what I can. The King has been mad for nearly ten years. I mean, how much longer can he live? How much longer can I live?"

"I think, George, if you look after yourself, you can enjoy a long and healthy life. Maybe eat and drink a little less?"

"Oh, you sound like Lady Hertford."

"And you still love her over all other women in London?"

"Indeed. I adore her. She has the most beautiful house in Manchester Square, keeps an excellent wine cellar and has a talented cook. You must come and dine with us there, Fred."

Frederick pondered George's fascination with Lady Hertford. He had met her at Carlton House dinners; she had been at his side for the Grand Fête. Older than the Prince, with a portly figure, she was immensely rich and proud, having little in the way of interesting conversation or strong views. She was not fun or witty like Mrs Fitzherbert, yet somehow she offered George the comfort he craved, as if she were the mother whose love he longed for. Frederick shook his head, a small laugh escaping his lips.

"What are you chuckling about, Fred?" said George. "You've had a thought and it's usually because you're about to mock me."

"No, sir, I wouldn't dream of mocking you."

"Ah, Fred, I almost forgot. I have something for you. A present."

"A present, George? You are too kind."

"You're going to love this." Struggling to his feet, George waddled inside to his study, returning with a large scroll tied up with a dusty pink ribbon.

"What's this?"

"Have a look. Pull the ribbon."

Fred spread out the large piece of curved parchment on his lap. There was a royal seal at the bottom, its red wax cracked and dusty.

"Good heavens, deeds to an estate!"

"To Kirby Misperton in Yorkshire."

"Are you giving me this?"

"The property was always in the gift of the Crown. Some years ago I asked the archivist to review the situation. He reminded me yesterday that he'd found the deeds. The property did belong to one of your many Blomberg forebears. It seems to have come down the generations and ended up with a clergyman and his eccentric wife. Their son died. No apparent heirs, so the property now belongs to the Crown. I'm gifting it to you."

"George, this is extraordinary. Thank you so much. I'd given up on ever inheriting it. As you know, the case ruined Coaty and I decided not to pursue it further. As a young man I was selfish and wanted to be a gentleman, not a priest. I thought I needed property to be comfortable and not have to follow a profession. But, as things have turned out, my life is comfortable, and I enjoy this profession. And now you're giving Kirby Misperton to me. Just like that?"

"Just like that," said George, beaming. He waved to a nearby servant to pour some more Madeira. "I couldn't do this when I was Prince of Wales, but now I'm regent I have access to everything, absolute power over the Crown Estates. I can do anything."

"George, I don't know what to say."

"You can say thank you, George, and never say I don't do things for you."

"I've never said you don't do things for me. Thanks to the King, I've risen through the ranks of the church and thanks to you I've been given palace positions and now you are giving me this."

"Well, be happy with it."

"I am very happy with it. I've often wondered about the other Blombergs," mused Fred. "But they're all dead. Except me."

"There are no other living claimants, Fred. Don't you think your ghostly Blomberg parent would be pleased? Oh, I still enjoy telling that story; it's got me through countless tedious dinners. Few of us get an apparition's message from beyond the grave to set us on our way."

"No, indeed." Frederick pressed his lips together, nodding.

"I want you to have this, Fred. I know Father did too. In one of his last lucid moments, he confirmed that he wanted you to have Blomberg's inheritance. I think he remembered more from his youth than anything that happened a week, a day or an hour ago."

"I'm overwhelmed. Thank you, George."

"It was always yours, Fred, not even mine to give. But I'm glad I've been able to help. You must take your beloved Maria and show her your estate. I'm told it has farms and cottages and many acres of land producing a goodly income. You can call yourself a baron too. You've always wanted a title. I would attest that you're a very rich man now, Baron Blomberg."

*

In October 1811, Frederick, Maria and Anna made the long journey from Somerset to North Yorkshire, stopping for three nights at inns along the way, finally arriving at Kirby Misperton.

Along the drive to the hall, oak leaves fluttered down through the damp air, landing on the surface of the lake then sinking under the water. Crunching over gravel, the carriage drew up outside the front door. Frederick, Maria and Anna stepped out of the carriage and a grey-haired woman emerged from the house in greeting.

"Good afternoon, Baron Blomberg," she said in a broad Yorkshire accent. "We are very pleased to welcome you to Kirby Misperton. Come in out of the cold. There's a good fire in the drawing room and I will bring you all some tea. Sir, do you remember meeting me when you last came here, though it was thirty years ago and I was a young maid in the household?"

"Indeed, Mrs Troughton. Thank you for your kind welcome," said Frederick as he ushered the women into their new home.

The trio entered the hallway and looked around. Recalling the layout of the house and his memory of that meeting with Ursula Blomberg made him shudder. He followed Mrs Troughton into the drawing room. The house had been cleaned and polished in anticipation of their visit. Frederick could see Maria assessing the tired furniture and knew she would be making a mental list of replacements. Running her shoe over a few threadbare areas of the rugs, she caught Frederick's eye with an expression he knew well, and he smiled, recognising that changes would be made.

Mrs Troughton returned to the room with a tray of tea things, setting it down on the Pembroke table by the window before handing round teacups to everyone.

"Mrs Troughton, please do sit down with us," said Frederick.

"Ooh, Baron Blomberg, I don't know that I should."

"Please, Mrs Troughton," added Maria, "we would very much like to talk to you. This is our first visit – well, it's mine and Anna's first visit – to Kirby Misperton. We know very little about the place. Will you give us an idea of the estate and the people who live here?"

Perching on a chaise longue, Mrs Troughton gave them a lengthy account of the local families, farmers and professionals. She seemed to be related to most of the people in the village and assured her new employers that there would be plenty of willing workers, should they need more staff.

"Baron Blomberg, sir, I remember when you and your cousin visited, when old Mrs Blomberg was alive. I'm sorry she was not friendly. That was her way."

"She had no interest in my claim, and I'm not surprised."

"And I remember another visitor from your family who came here a few years ago, Mrs Poulton, your cousin's mother."

Frederick swallowed hard. "My aunt, Mrs Poulton, has sadly died."

An awkward silence descended on the little party and Maria intervened. "Mrs Troughton, thank you for the tea. Now, I would very much like a tour of the house to review the rooms. We have bedrooms to choose."

Frederick, Maria and Anna explored every room, peering out of each window. They took in the valley and the lakes, small streams and copses surrounding the estate and viewed acres of woodland merging with the misty hills.

Maria put her hat down on the quilt of the ancient four-poster in the master bedroom. "Fred," she whispered, "this is a wonderful place, a proper home to call our own. We are so lucky."

"I've waited for this property and title all my life," said Frederick. "I've always wanted to be a man of consequence. But most of all I wanted my own home and family."

"You were always a man of consequence, Fred," said Maria. "We've always created our own homes and family, but this place will be splendid for us."

*

In March, the following year, Harriet arrived at Kirby Misperton, welcomed in by Mrs Troughton. Shaking back the hood of her cloak, she smoothed her hair and looked around the hall of the mansion. The door to the left opened and Frederick rushed forward, embracing her.

"Oh Fred," she whispered. "It's wonderful to see you. And in your own home, at last."

Maria and Anna approached from the opposite room and joined in the greeting.

"Here," said Maria, "let Mrs Troughton take your cloak and come into the drawing room."

Maria had redecorated the room with new furniture and fabrics. Fresh paper covered the walls and colourful rugs lay upon the polished floorboards. Elegant tables bearing fine porcelain vases and ornaments were dotted around the room and large landscape paintings and a few portraits hung upon the walls.

"I'm so pleased to see you, Harriet," said Maria. "Come, let me show you to your room and when you've had a chance to wash and change, then we can talk."

The dining table was laid for a family banquet and Frederick declared that, if Maria had been able to find a fatted calf, they would have cooked it for this feast. Instead, they had a joint of roast beef and Mrs Troughton's best Yorkshire pudding.

Conversation was lively and full of news, tinged by sadness when they all recalled her mother Margaret's funeral the previous August.

"And what news of Tom?" said Frederick.

Harriet paused, dabbing her mouth with her linen napkin, closing her eyes and taking a deep breath.

"I think he's enjoying America. He's only been there for six months, but I've had two letters from him and have brought them with me for you to read."

"Where is he living?" asked Frederick.

"In a city called Savannah in a region called Georgia. He appears very settled there and has found work in a brewery. He makes beer."

"He's a brewer!" cried Frederick, Maria and Anna.

"Yes, he enjoys the work very much. He says he's learning all about the process. His plan is to buy some land and establish a hop garden, so they don't have to be imported from England."

"Hops!" cried Frederick with delight, recalling the far-off days of his flight to Kent.

"And he's taken the lease on a large, newly-built house in the centre of the town," continued Harriet. "A housekeeper looks after him and he even rents out two spare rooms to lodgers, men who work with him. The house has a covered wooden deck space at the front where, he says, they all like to sit on warm evenings. For a young man of twenty-three, I feel very proud of him."

"How long will he stay in America?" asked Anna. "I liked meeting Tom last summer. Will he return and visit us?"

"I don't know, Anna," replied Harriet, biting her lip and looking up at the ornate plaster ceiling of the dining room. "He's doing so well and is loving the adventure. I hope he'll come back, but I doubt it will be for many years. It's only me in Hexham now. Tom is using his inheritance well and investing in his new life. But I do miss him so much."

"Tom was always an adventurous boy," said Maria. "He's very like you, Harriet."

"Perhaps. As his mother, I wanted to keep him close, but he was always such an active child, curious about everything. I'm not surprised that he's chosen to do this. I'm considering making the journey there to visit him one day."

"Yes, you should," cried Anna. "How long does it take to sail to America?"

"I think it's at least a month, from Liverpool to a place called Washington. And Tom says in his letter that he found the passage on the ship very rough at times. Then there's quite a journey south to the town of Savannah which takes a further week."

Anna nodded her head, absorbing this information. "So, it takes a letter at least two months to arrive? I will write to him," she added.

"He would like that, I'm sure. I send letters every two weeks, just with news about my life in Hexham, the family and his old school friends. Sometimes I include newspaper cuttings. He's never been one to sit down and stay still for very long, so we can't expect him to be a great correspondent. He knows about my visit here and will be delighted that we are together again. Oh, but I miss him."

"Of course you do," said Maria, "but it sounds perfect for him. Perhaps he'll marry an American and start a family in Savannah."

"Yes," replied Harriet, "in which case, I shall definitely sail to America and attend his wedding!"

"Are you still making potions, Aunt Harriet?" asked Anna.

"I am, just as I did before in Shepton. I scour the countryside finding wild herbs and plants and make tinctures and creams."

"And do you make potions to smooth a complexion?"

Harriet looked at the young girl's eager face. "Of course. But I also make a very good hair lotion from rosemary you might like. You rub in the oil, and it brightens and strengthens your hair. I will make you some if you have any rosemary in the garden here."

"There's an entire kitchen garden," put in Maria. "Harriet, if you've no pressing need to return to Hexham, please stay with us as long as you wish. You'll find plenty of herbs in the fields. Of course, it is very early spring and there's less growing, but I know how expert you are."

"Thank you." Harriet smiled and sat up straight. "I will stay until the summer, then return to Hexham. Thank you. I'm so happy to be here with my family."

Chapter Forty-Four
A Royal Wedding
Spring 1816

Still officially Chaplain and Clerk of the Closet to the Prince Regent, Frederick decided to concentrate on the management of his estate. So, he resigned his three Somerset livings, only keeping his prebendary role at Bristol Cathedral, and continued regularly travelling between his home in Kirby Misperton and Carlton House.

After five years in residence, the Blombergs had turned Kirby Misperton Hall into a comfortable home where they regularly entertained family and visitors. Maria and Anna remained in Yorkshire, taking their place in county society, and every summer, Harriet visited from Hexham. Frederick enjoyed inviting friends with a shared interest in music to form quartets or give impromptu concerts in the large drawing room.

The highlight of spring 1816 was the wedding of the Prince Regent's only daughter, Princess Charlotte, to Prince Leopold of Saxe-Coburg. Anxious that she should find a husband she could love, the Prince Regent agreed to her marriage with the young prince, despite regarding him as an inconsequential man from an unimportant German principality, bringing little money to the union. But Princess Charlotte loved him and was determined to marry him, so her father approved the match.

The wedding took place on 2nd May 1816 at Carlton House and crowds of well-wishers lined The Mall as the bride approached the palace in her carriage. Princess Charlotte wore a shimmering silver wedding dress and a garland of diamond roses upon her head. The bride's mother, Princess Caroline, was, at this time, living in Italy and not invited. Unable to bear being in the same room as his estranged wife, the Prince Regent would have refused to allow her attendance at any cost.

Standing near the altar with the other clerics in the chapel at Carlton House, Frederick was amused to hear the Princess snort with laughter during the vows when Prince Leopold promised to endow her with all his 'worldly goods', for he had none.

The following year, in April 1817, the royal family was delighted when Princess Charlotte and Prince Leopold announced that they were expecting a child. Anxious for the pregnancy to go smoothly and considering that sea air would be good for the young mother-to-be, the Prince Regent invited the newlyweds to stay at the now completed Brighton Pavilion. He instructed his Pavilion staff to give his daughter their best attention.

Frederick was commanded to join the royal party and given rooms at the Pavilion. For entertainment, George and Frederick organised theatrical performances and musical soirées in the ornate music room where they both played vigorous cello and violin duets. The royal couple enjoyed their seaside sojourn, finally departing, some two months later, to their home at Claremont, in Surrey, awaiting the arrival of the future heir to the throne.

The day after the young couple left Brighton, George and Frederick rode out along the West Cliff overlooking the sea in the company of an admiral, chief equerry and two grooms. Whilst pausing on the crest of a hill to admire the view, the Prince's horse was spooked, bucked and kicked Frederick twice in the leg, causing him to fall from his saddle clutching his broken limb and crying out in pain.

Horrified at the injuries the horse had inflicted, the Prince Regent dismounted immediately, shouting at the grooms to find the nearest doctor and calling loudly for assistance from local people. George fretted over Frederick as he was carefully conveyed back to the Pavilion, sending to London for expert surgeons.

The Prince Regent insisted that Frederick should remain in his care in Brighton until his fractures had healed.

By late June, he had recovered enough to walk unaided. With relief, Frederick returned to Carlton House and thence home to Yorkshire and the care of his wife.

Princess Charlotte remained confined at Claremont, awaiting the birth of her child due in mid-October. By the end of that month, anxiety increased as the baby refused to appear. Surgeons, doctors and experts were called and, in early November, after a fifty-hour labour, a very large boy was delivered, still-born. The princess failed to recover from the devastating birth, complaining that the brandy Doctor Croft had given her made her feel tipsy. A few hours later she too was dead.

The whole country was shocked by the death of the twenty-one-year-old princess and her baby boy. Women wept openly in the streets, shops shut, restaurants closed, race meetings were cancelled and parties postponed. Black bands were fixed to clothing as the population mourned the tragic loss of the young princess.

The country came to a halt on 19th November, the day of Princess Charlotte's funeral. A public subscription was swiftly set up to raise money for a monument to be commissioned and set in place above her tomb in St George's Chapel, Windsor. Prostrate with grief, and unable to bear the pain of attending the ceremony, the Prince Regent retreated to his rooms at Carlton House, refusing to receive visitors.

Regarded as a neglectful father, the Prince Regent became the focus of resentment, blaming him for the awful loss of his daughter and her baby. When he finally visited his daughter's tomb at Windsor, and later returned to Carlton House, an angry mob pelted his carriage with stones and shouted insults.

There was little the Prince Regent could have done to avoid the dreadful outcome, but combined with anger at his treatment of his wife, Princess Caroline, the future queen, public opinion turned against him and his damaged reputation plummeted even further.

Unable to bear the constant heckling from crowds outside Carlton House in London, the Prince Regent decamped to Windsor Castle to mourn his daughter and try to come to terms with the loss of his grandson and heir. During Christmas of 1817 and New Year of 1818, he was rarely seen in society, too grief-stricken and wracked with guilt to enjoy his longed-for regency. For comfort and solace he turned to Frederick, his chaplain, and invited him to the castle in late February.

Heavy rain clouds hung over Windsor Great Park as George and Frederick rode out one afternoon, galloping through the castle gates and into the park.

"Come on, Fred, keep up," yelled George, urging his horse across the sodden turf. Clods of mud flew up from his horse's hind legs, battering Frederick in the face. He felt tired and his injured leg ached, but he knew that a vigorous ride was the only way for George to deal with his grief. Frederick kept up the pace until both horses and riders grew weary. Cantering to a halt at the edge of a wood, they spotted a small hunting pavilion amongst the trees. Dismounting and tethering their horses outside the wooden building, they climbed the few steps to the open veranda and sat down upon a bench, gazing out at the wintery park.

"Did you hear, Doctor Croft killed himself last week?" said George with a deep sigh. "I'd told him I didn't blame him. I would never have wanted him to do that. Now it's three people dead."

"I heard, and I'm sorry for it," said Frederick. "I'm not sure I could have borne responsibility for dear Princess Charlotte's death and failure to save the baby. Sometimes forgiveness can be more painful than blame."

"You know, Fred, we've been over it countless times with all the experts. They knew the baby was overdue. We don't know what went wrong. Prince Leopold paced around outside the room where poor Charlotte suffered so dreadfully. He couldn't help or do anything. He's distraught to have lost his wife and child. He'll never be king consort now."

"I'm very sorry for Prince Leopold and Doctor Croft and his family, as I am for your family," said Frederick. "The agony he must have been in to shoot himself. We must have faith in our experts. Sometimes things go wrong and we have to come to terms with loss."

"I hope you're not going to call it God's will?"

"No. I can't believe that it's God's will to lose the life of a young mother and her baby boy. It is a tragedy."

"A tragedy. And now it's a tragedy for me because I have no heir. I loved Charlotte, despite her hateful mother. That baby boy was my hope and salvation. All lost. Now, who will produce an heir for the Hanover line? My brothers are useless. Prince Frederick's not well and his duchess can't have children. William's had two dead babies, and you can't keep count of the children he's had with his mistress. Edward has yet to find a legal wife; he likes his mistress too much."

"You can't blame your brothers for loving women who aren't accepted as royal consorts or are unable to produce children," said Frederick. "You were exactly the same with Mrs Fitzherbert."

"I know. This system is madness. It bullies people into behaving the wrong way. Love is important."

The men stared up at the low clouds on the horizon and approaching rain fizzed in the sky.

Frederick thought of Coaty, Aunt Margaret, Letitia and the many friends who had died. Death seemed to be more and more a part of his life. Was this the burden of reaching the age of fifty-six? He was familiar with death, witnessing it on a daily basis as a cleric. He had learnt to be professional and pragmatic. The deceased person did not need his help; those who were left behind were the sufferers.

The two men sat in silence for a while as rain began to pelt down, battering the roof of the veranda.

"How's your Yorkshire home, Fred?"

"It's extremely comfortable, thank you. We're very happy at Kirby Misperton. You should come and visit us. Maria loves it and we've formally adopted her niece, Anna, since her father has died."

"That's kind of you. Fred, do you want to move there permanently?"

"What, and leave you all to yourself in London? Never! Are you trying to get rid of me?"

"No, I'm being generous for once. I like having you as my chaplain and Clerk of the Closet; it allows me to call upon you whenever I wish. But I'm aware that you might like to be somewhere else."

"George, our arrangement suits me very well. Much as I love Kirby Misperton, I don't have to be in Yorkshire all the time. The summer months there suit me fine. I like London, Carlton House and enjoy being close to Windsor, and to you. There's so much to do here. In our lines of work, it's very hard to retire. You will be king one day and that will bring even greater responsibility. Maybe, when I'm older, I might make Yorkshire my permanent home."

"And tell me, Fred, how is your leg? I forgot you might still be in pain after that time we rode out in Brighton. I was shocked to see how injured you were. I beat the horse afterwards to punish it. I've caused you enough pain in the past. I thought, what if I'd killed you?"

"My leg has mended well, thank you. Those surgeons in Brighton were very good. Not all doctors get it wrong. Now I can ride quite as well as you, if not better."

"Better than me? Ha, Fred, you dare mock my riding?"

"Never," replied Frederick, laughing.

George sighed, patting his fleshy knee. "I'm glad we've done this. Chases the cobwebs. Hasn't healed the wound though. Let's get back to my study and drink hot brandies."

The pair mounted their horses and, kicking their flanks, galloped back to the castle.

Chapter Forty-Five
The Death of Queen Charlotte
November 1818

In early November 1818, the Prince Regent summoned Frederick to the palace at Kew because his mother, Queen Charlotte, was dying.

Entering the door to his former home, Frederick felt overwhelmed by the memories he associated with the place. Each time he visited, he remembered himself as a small boy, bewildered by the tutors, eager to play music with George or running outside in the park with his greyhound, Jupiter. Recalling Coaty's funeral, and the meeting with so many of his old associates, he realised that few of them were alive now. Lady Charlotte Finch had died five years earlier and he had attended her funeral at St James's Palace, and most of the staff from his day had retired.

Climbing the stairs to the Queen's private suite, he felt a sense of dread that yet another important figure in his life was about to depart. Bowing to the Queen, he sat down opposite her. She was seated in a black chair in her drawing room, squinting at him through red-rimmed, rheumy eyes. Her face was swollen, and she seemed to be chewing at something invisible in her mouth when she spoke before closing her lips in an expression of displeasure.

Her deafness made it very difficult to converse. Frederick did his best by offering easy conversation and friendly company to soothe the Queen, aware that her irritability was borne from physical discomfort. Recalling the days when he and the children were young, and how the entire family might sit together in the gardens at Richmond or Kew enjoying the sunshine, he was pleased to see her nod her head and smile briefly. Then, pointing at the Brompton portraits of himself, Prince George and Prince Frederick on the wall nearby, he reminded her how reluctant to pose the boys had been. She smiled again at the memory, her head drooping as if she were drifting off to sleep. He was relieved when the attending doctor indicated that the audience was over and he should take his leave.

Writing to Maria, he said:
19th November 1818

> *My dearest Maria,*
>
> *I write to you from Carlton House. This has been a sad time. George was with Queen Charlotte at the end. She died on 17th November, seated in her chair in her room at Kew. She was disappointed with her princes and princesses and furious with her husband for withdrawing from her so long ago through madness. I gather the King has no idea she's died, and can't even remember who she is, or was.*
>
> *I can only confess this to you, my dearest wife, but seeing her in her dying state, I felt rather frightened of her. Quite a confession for a man of fifty-seven years and a priest! It was like being a small child again in her presence.*
>
> *Her death has been yet another huge blow for Prince George. Staying with him at Carlton House, he insists on drinking himself into a state of collapse or working until past midnight arranging the funeral. He is so contrary. I recall the times when he and his mother were openly hostile to one another but, as we know, people deal with death in their own way. He's been publicly grieving and spending hours comforting his brothers and sisters.*
>
> *He has gone through all her things, working out who should receive various tokens. He's given me the magnificent Brompton portrait with Jupiter. It pleases me to know that she kept it close in her rooms all her life. George has sent the other Brompton portraits of himself and Prince Frederick to the home of one of Charlotte Finch's daughters. He's also given me Hamilton's portrait, made in '79, when I was just seven years old.*
>
> *I thank you for the warm socks, which have been a boon to my poor feet in these freezing days. I fear I am prone to the same gout afflicting George. Oh, the pain that assaults the big toe on my left foot when it feels*

*inflamed. George will take to his bed at the slightest discomfort and call
for laudanum. I soldier on and wear your socks for comfort. I will see you
in a few weeks' time.*

My love to you and Anna,
Your loving husband, Fred

*

Frederick returned to Kirby Misperton and his family, and a further
two years elapsed before he received another urgent summons.

In early January 1820, the doctors attending the monarch sent
word that King George III's health was declining rapidly and
Reverend Frederick Blomberg's presence was requested at Windsor.
Once again, Frederick made the journey south to join the family at
the castle.

One evening, George and Frederick visited the apartment where
their father had been incarcerated for nearly a decade. Peering
through a peephole in the door, they watched the old man slowly
prowling the space like a caged animal, feeling his way around the
furniture, picking up objects and setting them down again. For
years, he refused to be shaved or allow his hair to be cut. A long
wispy beard, like a food-encrusted bib, dripped down upon his
chest and strands of white hair flowed down his back. Muttering
to himself and holding imaginary conversations with his long-dead
children, he tapped at the keys of the harpsichord or stood at the
window feeling the breeze.

A few weeks later, in late January, the Prince Regent was
informed that the end was near. Once more, George and Frederick
crept into the apartment to see the King. This time, their father lay
upon his bed, eyes shut, hands crossed upon his chest, emitting the
rattling noise Frederick had heard countless times when offering
the last rites.

Within hours, news filtered swiftly from the corridors of Windsor

Castle that King George III had died at the age of eighty-one. Few people, except his small coterie of doctors, personal servants and closest members of the family, had seen him outside his castle prison for ten years.

As the day of the funeral approached, George took to his bed. Visiting George in his suite at Carlton House, Frederick could see that the new king was very sick and breathing with difficulty. At the height of his illness, he spent the day sweating in his bed, fretting about his new status and dreading the return of Princess Caroline from exile in Italy. He was tormented by the likelihood that the Government, courtiers and subjects regarded her as the rightful new queen and that she should be entitled to return to England and claim her throne. Frederick knew that the prospect of enduring a coronation with 'that woman' by his side felt even worse than his illness and George would never allow it.

The King's funeral took place on 16th February 1820 at St George's Chapel, Windsor. The Prince Regent did not attend. George was still genuinely ill with pleurisy and being tended by doctors at Carlton House. But Frederick was concerned that the new king's absence from his father's funeral would only intensify his widespread unpopularity.

Two weeks after the King's funeral, once King George IV had recovered from illness, he and Frederick picked their way through piles of newspapers, magazines and pamphlets spread out on the desk in his study at Carlton House.

"How do I make my subjects love me?" wailed George, batting the pages of *The Times*. "Look at these eulogies!" he cried. "My father commands their love even though he's not been seen in public for years and years. Do people realise he no longer recognised his queen, his children? Me! This outpouring of affection is absurd. The people of this country should be used to me by now. Why can't they accept me as king with love and gratitude? I've been prince regent for ten years. It must count for something."

George and Frederick scanned more papers.

"And look at this!" shouted George, stabbing with a finger at the inside pages of the *Morning Chronicle*. "The cartoonists have no respect. They represent me as grossly fat and depict me in the company of huge women. They make me sound like a selfish, fatuous spendthrift."

Frederick chewed his lower lip and glanced over another paper. He sympathised with George but understood that he had gained a bad reputation after a lifetime of selfish and self-serving behaviour. It was not surprising that the illustrators and sketch writers mocked him. George wore extravagant clothes and consorted with many mistresses. He had been greedy, grasping and self-regarding. Frederick shook his head at the harsh words but understood their source.

Caroline, the Princess of Wales, was also the subject of much ribald teasing, but now that the old king was dead, there was greater support for her as the wife of King George IV. The public regarded her as Queen of England, even though she wasn't in the country.

"I'm king, but I don't have an heir," spat George. "How will people remember me? I must divorce Caroline. Surely it's not too late for me to marry again?"

"George, it's not in your power to change the constitution. You might try to divorce her, but it would be difficult and an embarrassing process. And I really don't think you would be successful."

"Henry VIII managed it."

"Those times were different, George. The monarch is answerable to Parliament these days."

"Oh, I'm so furious. And now Prince Edward's new wife is with child. Why should he be granted an heir and not me? It's not right."

Frederick nodded in appeasement. He had been pleased to officiate at the marriage of Prince Edward, The Duke of Kent, to

Princess Marie Louise Victoria of Saxe-Coburg at Kew Palace in the summer of 1818. At last there was a glimmer of hope that a legitimate child would be born to the House of Hanover. If the expected child arrived without mishap, he, or she, might become the heir to the throne. Frederick could see that the prospect was eating George up with envy.

And, as if to distract himself from the agony of acknowledging the wife he detested, George had wholeheartedly thrown himself into the redecoration of Buckingham House. Frederick was fond of the old mansion, depicted in the background of Brompton's portrait of him. With a mixture of sorrow and excitement, he presumed that the next time he saw the place, George would have imposed his stamp on it, and the house be changed into a palace.

Frederick remained in London as the winter months of 1820 turned to spring and plans were made for the coronation of George IV to take place in June. Courtiers and administrators worked hard on the guest list, decoration of Westminster Abbey and the management of crowds expected to throng the capital in celebration. Now that he was king, George was busy with the politics of the country and in constant negotiation with Parliament so that he would receive sufficient funds to ensure that the coronation would be an impressive event and that he could maintain his lavish lifestyle.

On June 15th, a few weeks before the coronation, the King summoned Frederick to his study at Carlton House. Wearing his best new black jacket and a fresh white collar, he made sure his shoes were shined in readiness for the meeting. He was looking forward to seeing the King. The summons had mentioned the prospect of new responsibility. Frederick imagined that he might be granted a new role, keeping him close to the royal family and confirming his status as a respected member of the new monarch's court.

"Master Frederick," said George as Frederick entered his study and approached the vast desk, covered in papers, architectural drawings and clothing designs. "Thank you for coming, Fred, sit down. As you know, I value you greatly. We've been through so much together."

"Indeed we have, sir," replied Frederick, "and I am pleased to be by your side at the start of your reign. I've no doubt you'll be an exemplary king, and I look forward to helping you."

"Thank you, thank you. The thing is, I am compelled to make changes. This is not my choice, but Knighton, the new Keeper of the Privy Purse, has insisted. Fred, it pains me to do this, but I'm relieving you of your role as my personal chaplain and Clerk of the Closet."

"What!" cried, Frederick, recoiling in shock. "After your father's funeral you assured me that I would remain at your side in these roles, as I have been all these years."

"And so I would have wished but, alas, these things are beyond my control. Now I'm king, my expenses are under more scrutiny than ever, and Parliament has insisted that they put Knighton in charge of my budget. I like Knighton; he's a seasoned money manager and his approach makes a lot of sense. He's been appointed to make cuts and get the Privy Purse back into some order. He says I spend too much. So, amongst other savings, he's cutting down the number of clergy and staff we have in the royal household, including giving up your apartment at Carlton House."

Frederick felt his throat constrict. The news was like a blow to his chest, rendering him mute.

"But Fred," continued George, in jocular style, "I do have good news, and this is what I wanted to tell you. I'm making you a prebendary canon of St Paul's Cathedral. It's another rung up your clerical ladder. I know you wanted to be a bishop and Father blocked it. I'm making amends. I'm also granting you the living at St Giles in Cripplegate. I gather it's the most lucrative in the City of London.

Fred, it should see you through. Let's call it a parting gift."

"What do you mean, a parting gift? George," said Frederick, swallowing hard, "we've come this far together. I can't imagine not being by your side. Maria and I are prepared to move from Yorkshire to London. You have my absolute devotion."

"I don't doubt it, Fred, but it has to be done. I thought you might appreciate the change and withdraw from all the hard work I make you do."

"Thank you, George," replied Frederick more out of habit and politeness than gratitude or comprehension. Frederick was unsure whether these two additional livings were the result of George being thoughtful or that he'd simply found a way to get rid of him. Frederick felt hurt and deflated and was unable to question George further. This was not what he'd expected.

He stood up. "Is there anything else, sir?" said Frederick.

"I thank you, Fred, for your understanding. You are the best of men." George came round to Frederick's side of the desk and patted his shoulder.

"No, sir," said Frederick quietly, "I'm merely a clergyman and a close relation. I have your best interests at heart. Thank you for the position at St Paul's and Cripplegate," he added, bowing. "You, and your father, have been very generous to me."

"No, no, Fred, it's no less than you deserve. On coronation day I shall look out for you in the abbey amongst my highest clergy. There's a fitting for my robes next week. Oh, the ermine, the weight of velvet; it's all so perfect." He kissed his lips with finger and thumb. "I hope it isn't too hot on the day. I will suffer for my brilliance. What will you be wearing?"

Frederick was too crestfallen to even think about it. "I'll be wearing a Benedictine habit. It's black."

George stretched his arms above his head, placing an imaginary crown upon his head with his hands.

"Fred, I've waited so long for my father to die and now everyone must be made happy that I am finally king. I want my coronation to mean something."

"We are happy for you, George. You'll be a very good king."

"Oh Fred, what a cruel system it is that it takes one man's death to start another man's life. I want to be a good king and also to be loved."

Chapter Forty-Six
A Coronation and a Separation
19th July 1821

On the day of the coronation, the temperature in Westminster Abbey was unbearably hot. Wearing his habit of thick black wool, Frederick could only imagine the heat the King must be enduring in his many layers of fine cloth, velvet robes and rich fur trim, combined with the weight of the heavy crown upon his head.

There had been much speculation about the Princess of Wales and whether she would be crowned 'Queen Caroline' next to her husband. For years, King George had been adamant that 'that woman' would never be admitted. He refused to allow a throne to be set in place for her in the abbey and deployed his guards to ensure that she could not enter.

Frederick was concerned about this risky approach. Where George was not popular, and had rarely been approved by his subjects, Caroline acquired the reputation of wronged woman and was admired and supported, despite being detested by her husband. Many people regarded her as the rightful queen and should be crowned as the constitution stipulated.

As the coronation ceremony began, all the doors to Westminster Abbey were firmly barred. Those inside the ancient church, sweltering in the summer heat, could hear loud hammering at all the entrances as 'Queen Caroline', and her supporters, battered the doors, shouting for admittance. She was not admitted.

Afterwards, Frederick joined the huge coronation feast in Westminster Hall. Illustrious guests were served wave upon wave of delicious food whilst spectators in the gallery above could only look on with hungry envy.

Frederick was amused when, to his surprise, he felt hot wax dripping upon his wig. The cheap candles in the candelabra above the tables had burnt down too fast, flooding their holders. Some of the guests' fine clothes were ruined.

Observing the new king from a distance, Frederick felt detachment from his brother; it was as though some invisible cord connecting them all through childhood, youth and age had been severed. No longer would he be at George's side at important moments in his life. The coronation signalled a new coolness in their relationship. Surrounded by Knighton, Keeper of the Privy Purse, and fawning courtiers, the new monarch was now prey to influential players eager to please him, if possible, and influence him to their own advantage.

The King had a new mistress too, the unpleasant Lady Conyngham. Frederick could not understand why, yet again, George had chosen a proud, vain, portly woman, just seven years his junior, to be his consort. Her husband seemed untroubled by his cuckold status and the family's association with the King worked to their advantage, providing her sons and daughters with titles, good marriages and favours. At the coronation, Frederick noticed that Lady Conyngham was wearing jewels once owned by Queen Charlotte, feeling affronted that this woman should benefit so blatantly from her position.

But, throughout the coronation ceremony, what hurt Frederick most of all was the sense of dismissal. George had let him go. It was not just an expression all kings used when a meeting was at its end; there was purpose and action within the phrase. Frederick had been 'let go'. He had been dropped and the pain of this revelation cut him to the quick.

Soon after the coronation, Frederick gathered up all his belongings from the Carlton House apartment, which he had been asked to vacate, and took them to his new home in Cripplegate.

The vicarage was at least a century old with low beams and creaking floors. Situated in Well Street, a few steps away from St Giles, one of the oldest churches in the City of London, he toured his new home, wishing that Maria were there with him to review the house. Wandering the empty rooms, he considered how best to improve and redecorate the old building, anticipating that Maria would want changes in the kitchen, thicker drapes at the windows and comfortable furniture.

Stepping out of the study door into the garden, he stood on a small terrace, surveying the charming garden before him. A large lawn sloped down to a bastion section of the old Roman wall overlooking a large pond flanked by tall grasses and willow. A vast fig tree to the right of the lawn cast welcome shade onto the grass, and tangled honeysuckle, jasmine and climbing roses mingled together across a high flint wall. Well, he thought to himself, walking towards the fig tree, this vicarage and garden was a very pleasant place if it was, indeed, a parting gift and he should be thankful for it.

However, when he sat down on a bench in the shade, he gave way to the grief he had buried in his heart the day of King George's careless dismissal. Hot tears coursed down his cheeks unchecked. He may be fifty-nine years old, a baron, a respected cleric and close contact of the royal family, but the suddenness of this parting hurt him more than any childhood beating or broken limbs. He didn't know how to ease the pain. He craved the love of his younger brother and also wanted to protect him in the way he had done for years. It hurt him to know that so many of the new people surrounding the King would now work the situation to their own advantage, influencing him with flattery in order to extract personal favours.

Then there was Sir William Knighton, a clever, charming man, who had wormed his way into the new king's affection and was now Keeper of the Privy Purse, manager of his accounts and self-appointed advisor. Frederick did not trust the man, though he admired his intellect and organisational skills. He understood why George would choose him as a close associate. Knighton was a physician, and Frederick knew that he used his medical knowledge to offer constant sympathy to George for his many ailments whilst providing him with unlimited amounts of laudanum or other palliatives whenever he called for them.

No, thought Frederick, taking his handkerchief from his pocket, drying his eyes and mopping his brow in the summer heat. Whatever influence over his brother he might once have enjoyed, that was now finished. The King no longer needed him.

Frederick looked up at the canopy of large, fleshy leaves through the fig tree to the blue sky above and breathed in the sweet air of this pleasant garden. He looked forward to showing Maria and Anna their new home in London, away from the royal household.

It was time to return to Yorkshire and the company of his wife and family.

*

In May 1822, Harriet sent the family in Kirby Misperton a letter, together with an invitation to her wedding in Hexham. She had formed a connection with Doctor John Simms, a physician in Hexham, and their marriage was to take place in the summer. The betrothed couple had known each other for many years, since he had been closely involved with Gideon's treatment in the latter years of his life, and had been present at his death. A widower of some ten years, wrote Harriet, John Simms had two grown-up sons, one of whom still lived in Hexham with his wife and three small daughters, Celia, Lorna and Grace. Harriet sounded delighted to have become stepmother and grandmother to this family.

In August 1822, Frederick, Maria and Anna spent three days journeying to Hexham, stopping for two nights at Auckland Castle, home of the Bishop of Durham, William Van Mildert, whom Frederick knew from his role within the Deanery of St Paul's Cathedral. Following two very convivial evenings in the ancient castle, their carriage took them up and over the vast, bleak moors of Northumbria, across a treeless terrain of grass and heather before descending towards the town of Hexham, nestling in the Tyne valley below.

The Blomberg family stayed with Harriet in her comfortable house in the centre of the town; she was determined to keep the property as inheritance for Tom, should he ever return from America.

The wedding took place at Hexham Abbey. At Harriet's insistence, Frederick agreed to share the ceremony with the rector, and it was he who completed the vows, announcing that the couple were now man and wife. The new Mr and Mrs Simms emerged into the sunshine of a summer's day to the loud cheering of townspeople in the market square.

The wedding breakfast was held in the dining room of Doctor Simms' house on Battle Hill, now Harriet's new home. Harriet embraced Frederick, Maria and Anna as they entered the house after the wedding, introducing them to her new husband.

"Baron Blomberg," said Doctor Simms, bowing to his new wife's closest relative, "we are honoured to see you and your family. Thank you for making the journey."

Doctor Simms was a man of about sixty years, with a portly stomach, short of stature with a shiny bald pate, ringed by tufts of curling grey hair. His default expression was one of concern and ready smiles.

"Maria and I are delighted to attend," replied Frederick. "It seems you have a great deal in common with my cousin. She has always been an exemplary herbalist and doctor of natural medicine. Indeed, she was always searching our estate in Yorkshire for herbs to ease my troublesome gout."

"Ah, gout, the most difficult of ailments. I commend her attempts. She is remarkably knowledgeable and has taught me a great deal," replied John Simms. "It was our medical discussions which brought us together. She is an instinctive maker of medicine where I am more inclined to the disciplines I acquired during my training in Edinburgh. Much of the teaching there encouraged the use of drugs to numb pain rather than finding treatments to ease the cause of the problem."

"That reminds me of the approach of Doctors Willis, father and son physicians, who treated the late King George III," replied Frederick.

"I gather from my dear wife that you have a close association with the late king as well as the current monarch?"

Frederick nodded, certain that Harriet would have shared the truth of his parentage. "Indeed, I was brought up in the household of the old king and the late Queen Charlotte. I am, or was, a close associate of the current king, George IV."

"Yes, I have heard much about him too from Harriet. Let me introduce you to my brother, Doctor James Simms. He and I both studied medicine at Edinburgh, and he remained in the city to establish his practice. I have seated you and your wife opposite him at our wedding feast. He met the King just recently when he visited in Edinburgh earlier this month."

"Really!" Frederick could barely contain his excitement at the prospect of hearing first-hand news about George. "Your brother treated the King?"

Frederick spent most of the wedding breakfast deep in conversation with Doctor James Simms. The doctor had been summoned to attend the King during his Scottish tour.

"The King was very gracious when I attended him," said Doctor James Simms. "I believe his stomach was upset from four days of poor weather at sea, followed by a drenching in our highland rain. His personal physicians, who had travelled with him, had not brought a large enough supply of suitable medicines. I was honoured to meet His Majesty but could only prescribe an emetic to help with the sickness. As I left his room, I heard him calling for cherry brandy. I believe that may have revived him more than any other medicine."

Frederick chuckled at the story, envisaging the needy king's demands so easily satisfied by food or drink. He continued bombarding Doctor Simms with further questions, delighting in his stories about the King's enthusiasm for Scottish reels at the Caledonian Ball. Despite his gouty legs, the King had joined in with the revelry, dancing with many of the Scottish ladies in the ballroom.

Frederick also laughed out loud at Doctor Simms' description of the King's pink pantaloons, worn beneath his Stewart tartan kilt together with the many badges and orders he had pinned and draped across his expansive chest. Doctor Simms continued his descriptions of the King's visit until he had exhausted every detail.

Towards the end of the wedding feast, Frederick took out his fiddle and played a series of jigs and the three little Simms granddaughters enchanted guests with their improvised dances.

Maria and Frederick remained in Harriet's house in Hexham for a week, venturing to the famous Hadrian's Wall that Aunt Margaret had so enjoyed exploring. Picking their way over the ruins of Roman buildings, visiting towns and villages along the River Tyne, they enjoyed the last of the late summer weather high upon the majestic hills. Frederick felt invigorated by the journey to Northumberland and was delighted to see Harriet so happy and settled. He liked her new husband and his family but most of all he had enjoyed the contact with someone who had recently encountered George. He wondered if he would ever see his brother again.

Chapter Forty-Seven
An Invitation to Brighton Pavilion
December 1823

As Christmas approached, Frederick was busy planning celebrations and events at the St Giles' Vicarage in Cripplegate when a stiff, white envelope from King George IV arrived. It contained an invitation to attend a private concert on 20th December of music composed and conducted by the Italian composer Rossini in the music room at Brighton Pavilion.

The sight of the card requesting his presence made Frederick's heart palpitate with excitement. It was not a direct, personal summons from George, but it was a request that he should be there. Might this surprise invitation signal the rekindling of their friendship, especially at a music event?

Maria viewed the invitation and declared it a splendid opportunity for Frederick to speak to the King at last, but she declined to accompany him in the carriage to the concert in Brighton. There was too much for her to do at the vicarage in preparation for visitors, parties and events so close to Christmas, she said. It would be irresponsible for her to leave.

Feeling a little guilty at leaving the parish of St Giles so close to such an important festival, Frederick was excited to go. Briefing his curate, Reverend Bates, in the rectory study, he promised to return by 22nd December at the latest, unless, perchance, the King needed his further attendance.

Putting up at a hotel in the centre of Brighton, Frederick prepared for his appearance at the Pavilion. A barber in the town was summoned to cut his hair and he paid a boy to shine his shoes. Maria had suggested that he should take his violin with him, in case he would be called upon to perform a duet with George. Holding his beloved instrument tightly in his hand, he entered the ornate hallway of the Pavilion, following the throng of excited guests to the music room where he took his seat close to the front. Nodding to some familiar faces in the audience, he waited, with mounting excitement, for the King and the much-lauded composer to appear.

With a great roar of approval, the doors at the far end of the music room opened and the King strode forth with the diminutive Rossini to his right and Lady Conyngham to his left. Taking his place upon a throne-like seat in front of the orchestra, George settled himself whilst the composer took to the rostrum, tapped the music stand with his baton, and the concert began.

Straining his neck to view the King, Frederick watched George nodding his head and slapping his hand on his knee in time to the music. The orchestra's performance of a newly composed valse ended to rapturous applause. Then, to everyone's astonishment, the King leapt upon the rostrum, nudging Rossini aside, insisting that the orchestra should play the piece all over again under his own baton.

The King then sat with the musicians on the stage and played a violin solo of the overture to *The Barber of Seville*, which, Frederick thought, needed further rehearsal and polish. The assembled audience clapped and cheered their approval as the King stood and bowed before taking his seat in the audience again.

At the end of the concert, Frederick stood up, aching to be seen by the King and raising his hand across the room in greeting. George saw him, nodding and smiling in recognition, and appeared to raise his hand to summon Frederick closer. At that moment, witnessing the exchange, Lady Conyngham took the King's arm, directing him away from the music room, through a door and into an anteroom to the side of the stage. The King disappeared into the private throng and the door closed.

Disappointed, Frederick realised that he was not going to see George. He would not be beckoned to join the King's party and take his place within the inner sanctum of his closest entourage. He was merely a member of the invited audience at the concert. Much as he had enjoyed Rossini's cheerful, soaring music and the bold operatic singing, the sensation of exclusion was overwhelming, and Frederick was engulfed by depression.

He returned to his hotel and, after a sleepless night, hastened home to London.

*

Three years elapsed and there was no further contact from the King. Then, in early January 1827, Frederick read the announcement in the papers of Prince Frederick's death. He was not surprised by the news, having seen the Duke of York some six months earlier at an event at St James's Palace and noticed he had not looked well. Suffering from dropsy, resulting in heart failure, the sixty-three-year-old prince died on 5th January.

Frederick sent a heartfelt note to the King expressing his sorrow at the loss of their brother, and recalled events of their shared childhood which he thought George might find touching.

King George III and Queen Charlotte had determined that the second of their sons should be a soldier. Packed off to a military life in Hanover in his teens, Prince Frederick had risen through the ranks and was respected by fellow commanders for his organisational skills and establishment of training schemes. However, he had never been a natural leader or an imaginative strategist, making inferior decisions in skirmishes, wars and armed engagements across Europe. Poorly rated by the generals of the British Army, the 'Grand Old Duke of York', as he was known, had been reluctantly married to a Prussian princess, Frederica Charlotte, and there had been no children.

The King and Prince Frederick had been close when they were children, but the two brothers rarely saw one another in adulthood and quarrelled frequently. As prince regent, George had grudgingly paid off his brother's frequent gambling debts. However, since his coronation, King George and his brother had been on more friendly terms.

The Duke of York's funeral took place at Windsor Castle on 20th January, a bitterly cold day. With no heating in St George's Chapel, the assembled mourners, including most of the royal family, government ministers and the highest clerics, shivered through the ceremony and blew into their hands for warmth. Frederick took his place in the chapel and mourned the loss of yet another member of his blood family. Gazing at George, standing at the front of the chapel, near the coffin, overcome with grief, Frederick longed to offer solace and speak of their shared loss.

George, suffering with a heavy cold, had insisted on rising from his sickbed to take his place at the funeral and physicians were nervous that the icy temperatures in the chapel might impair his recovery. As soon as the funeral was over, the King was hastily bundled into his carriage, back to the warmth of his quarters at Royal Lodge, Windsor.

Yet again, Frederick had exchanged a solemn nod with the monarch but had not spoken to him. He returned to his family at the Cripplegate vicarage with a heavy heart.

Chapter Forty-Eight

Life at Kirby Misperton
Early September 1827

"He's been playing that solemn music for hours now," said Anna, shutting the door of the drawing room to muffle the sound of requiems and plaintive tunes. "Even the dog can't bear it. Look at her," said Anna, pointing at Prinny, the elderly whippet who slumbered in the drawing room on a rug close to the unlit fireplace. "I swear she's put her paws over her ears so she can't hear it."

"He's sad, Anna," said Maria. "He thought that this morning's message from the King would be an invitation or a summons, but it was only a cursory greeting and kind wishes for his sixty-sixth birthday sent by a private secretary. It's hurtful and he's depressed. You've seen him like this before, Anna; he's expressing his emotion in the only way he knows, by playing this music."

Anna shrugged and carried on with her sewing. Setting down the book she'd been reading, Maria leant across her chair to pat Anna's hand. "Surely you remember how you felt when your dear mama died? I realise George, I mean, the King, hasn't died, but he's withdrawn his association and Uncle Fred is sad about it. The birthday greeting was disappointing."

Anna cast down her needlework on a table nearby and picked up a magazine, flicking through the pages. "Aunt Maria, it says in the *Gentleman's Magazine* that the King spends all his time having parties at Windsor Castle. And if he's not having parties, he's entertaining that hideous Lady Conyngham."

Batting at a page in the magazine, she said, "Have you seen this picture of her? Look at the cartoons. She looks awful, and she's always pictured wearing the most massive jewels. There's a drawing somewhere in here which calls her a king-fisher. That's quite funny. Apparently she and the King go fishing near Windsor and he is shown here like a big fish that's been caught by Lady Conyngham's rod. Look at those huge lips!"

"Anna, you mustn't mock the King. You must be sensitive to Uncle Fred's grief. We want him to be happy whilst he's here in Yorkshire or else he'll fret about what's going on at court without him. Besides, we'll be travelling back to Cripplegate in a few days for the winter."

"But is the constant gloomy music necessary?" replied Anna, waving her arm in the direction of the mournful sound. "Why is he still so beholden to the royal family? He's hardly seen the King since the coronation – that's nearly seven years – even though we've been in London and Uncle Fred has let him know when we're at the vicarage. I thought they were his family – doesn't the King care?"

Maria smiled and shook her head. "I'm sure the King cares, in his fashion, but he's busy and surrounded by people who control his life. Uncle Fred understands the royal family; he's of their blood and feels drawn to them, despite their indifference. If circumstances had been different, he might have been king. He was George III's firstborn son."

Anna shook her head. "It's such a peculiar thought. Oh, I'm weary of this sewing, Aunt Maria. I can't settle on anything. I'll go outside and find some more comfrey. Harriet taught me how to make a very good face cream with the herb. I only wish she'd succeeded in finding a cure for Uncle Fred's gout."

"We'd all be very pleased if anyone could cure that," replied Maria, smiling. "By the way, Anna, your complexion is particularly good at the moment. You look very fresh and bright-eyed."

"Oh, does it, do I?" Anna smoothed her cheeks with her fingers. "It must be the comfrey face cream. My friends in Malton are all clamouring for me to make another batch."

"And I don't suppose your bright eyes have anything to do with Captain Newbery coming to call this afternoon?"

"Possibly," replied Anna, blushing. "I'm looking forward to

seeing him. Mrs Troughton said she would bake her special rock cakes with almonds for him. He likes them very much."

"And I dare say he likes you very much too."

"I am hopeful," said Anna. "I find it a curious coincidence that the Newbery family not only lives close to us here in Yorkshire but in Cripplegate too. We seem to occupy exactly the same neighbourhoods."

"I'm sure it is a fine coincidence, Anna," said Maria, enjoying the sight of her niece's glowing face. "Go on, hunt down some more comfrey. Though I still think the light in your eyes is due entirely to a certain Captain Newbery."

"You may be right," replied Anna, laughing as she skipped out of the room.

Maria followed Anna into the hall and listened to the mournful sounds of cello music seeping from Frederick's study.

Seated in front of his music stand, his cello before him, Frederick turned the page of Allegri's *Miserere* and began playing the next line. Just when he thought he had come to terms with his separation from George, something new would hit him hard and plunge him back into a slough of despondency. The cursory birthday message from King George had disappointed him. Since George had become king in 1820, Frederick had diligently sent him birthday greetings for every 12th August. His suggestions for duets or soirées had elicited no response, and he must now accept that the King no longer desired his company. If he did, he would be summoned, and Frederick would attend, just as he had always done for over sixty years.

Every autumn, when he left Yorkshire to resume his duties at St Paul's Cathedral and as vicar of St Giles in Cripplegate, he would send a message to the King announcing his return to London. He only ever received a cursory acknowledgement, sent by a private secretary. It was time to stop bothering.

Frederick knew he would always be welcomed by his fellow

clerics at St James's Palace or Windsor Castle, but he missed the easy access to King George he had enjoyed during those days as his private secretary. And now, he learnt, Carlton House was about to be demolished. The King had turned the focus of his building zeal towards the rebuilding of Buckingham House with remodelling by the architect Nash, expanding it into a palace more fitting for a monarch. Meanwhile, over at Windsor, the castle had been rebuilt in the Gothic style.

Frederick was torn between his love for his own family, his delight at finally gaining his Blomberg inheritance and his strong attachment to his blood relations. Now that the old king and queen were dead, George was the only one left who might care for him or could recall a shared experience. The other royal princes and princesses were polite when they met him at the royal residences, but Frederick knew that the siblings were driven by self-serving instincts. Each one of them had desires of their own and wanted their brother, the King, to assist with their plans. The princesses wanted the freedom to marry and live in their own households, and the princes always wanted more money and titles.

Frederick worried about the six princesses who'd spent their lives trapped within the prison of the royal palaces. Those who had not married minor aristocrats from Germany continued to live in the gilded cage of royal homes as middle-aged women with little to do. He was sorry for them.

*

On a balmy September day, Frederick and Anna took an afternoon walk around Kirby Misperton shortly before the family's return to London for the winter.

Supported by his stick, Frederick followed the route past the stables and the outhouses, through the gate to the meadow and around the lake. Heading for the bench close to the small mound topped by the obelisk, he whistled to Prinny to slow down. The dog bounded back to his side and sat, tongue lolling, whilst Frederick sat down. The recent attack of gout had subsided, but his joints still felt stiff and painful. Anna perched on the bench next to him.

"I gather you enjoyed last night's ball at Malton, Anna?"

"I did, very much, thank you, Uncle Fred," said Anna.

"And Maria tells me your young Captain Newbery will be calling later before he too travels back to London."

"Yes, he will join us for tea. Uncle Fred, he wants to talk to you."

"Talk to me. I see. Could this be a conversation of some importance? You know, Anna, we will give you a very good marriage portion when the time comes."

"Oh, Uncle Fred, he hasn't even proposed yet, but he may. We have an understanding."

"And this afternoon he may share his intentions with me?"

"Yes, hopefully."

"I see. Thank you, Anna, for alerting me. Then I shall be prepared for my talk with Captain Newbery and will agree to his request for your hand, if you approve."

"I do approve. Thank you, Uncle Fred. Shall we carry on the walk?"

"No, I would like to pause here a bit longer. Just sit and stare." Frederick breathed deeply and raised his hand to his forehead to shield the sun as his gaze travelled up the full length of the obelisk standing before them.

"Tell me again why you built that obelisk, Uncle Fred," said Anna, squinting as she followed his view. "I can't understand what the Latin on the plaque says."

"It says thank you; that's all," Frederick replied. "I commissioned this obelisk soon after taking possession of Kirby Misperton in 1812. It says thank you to the King, both kings, for their generosity. They gifted this place to me although it was mine anyway, but the history of it was complicated. I wanted to acknowledge the gift and leave a lasting monument."

"And that's what the Latin says?"

"Yes, I wrote it in Latin because I didn't want everyone to understand. It's a personal message from me to the King."

"But has King George ever seen it? Does he know it's here?"

"He's never visited, but yes, he knows. I commissioned an engraving of it and sent him a copy. But I doubt he'll ever travel to Yorkshire. From what I hear he doesn't leave London at all now and he certainly wouldn't travel any distance by carriage. I don't think he's in very good health. But then he's always claimed not to be in good health," Frederick said to himself with a small chuckle.

"It was a very generous gesture to say thank you. But if it belonged to your family anyway, what was the need?"

"Because, in the end, all it took was a signature by the Prince Regent, as he was at the time, and it became mine. I've a lot to thank him for."

"And now he does not see you," said Anna.

"Well, it's not quite like that, but yes, we are not in touch. He's the king and surrounded by new people. Some courtiers were envious of my closeness to him. For the moment, other people are more important to him than me."

"Even though you've been friends since you were children?"

"Anna, life as the king is not a normal existence. You don't have the freedom to choose what you do or whom you see. I am happy to be an ordinary person."

"You're not ordinary, Uncle Fred. You're a brilliant musician, but I do wish you'd play more cheerful music."

"Ha!" Frederick laughed out loud. "You are right, Miss Woolls. Well, I'm looking forward to a concert in London in two weeks' time. If your friend, Captain Newbery, is also in London, perhaps he'd like to join us?"

"Oh, yes." Anna clapped her hands and tapped her feet on the ground. "I will ask him at tea. I'm sure he'd love to come. I'm sorry we're all leaving Yorkshire soon but look forward to seeing him in London again next week. He says he'll have to return to his regiment soon. I do think that being a captain in the army sounds tedious, especially when there's no war to fight." Then she added, "Thank heavens there isn't a war to fight."

"And has he told you whether he intends to join the Newbery medicine business in St Paul's Churchyard after giving up his commission?"

"Probably. But he's still hoping to inherit part of the Newbery estate in Sussex. He might move there."

"And I take it that's why you've become interested in Aunt Harriet's herbal remedies?"

"Oh, I'm always eager to learn about nature, Uncle Fred. Harriet taught me so much. Look at all the natural plants that surround us," said Anna, waving her arms around. "Surely God would like us to understand how all these natural gifts can make our lives better."

"Indeed, Miss Anna, you are right."

Chapter Forty-Nine
A Wedding in London
24th June 1828

The morning sun beamed through the stained glass windows of St Martin's Church on Ludgate Hill, throwing geometric patterns of colour onto the pale stone floor. Frederick took Anna's arm and walked her down the aisle whilst the organist played Bach's *Toccata and Fugue*. Anna held Frederick tightly as they approached the altar where Captain George Newbery was waiting for his bride.

Together Frederick and George's father witnessed the marriage certificate. Beaming with delight, the bride and groom and all the wedding guests, including Harriet and her husband, who had travelled from Hexham, emerged from the church and gathered for the wedding breakfast at the deanery, close to St Paul's Cathedral.

Maria had embraced the role of 'godmother and aunt of the bride' with enthusiasm, helping Anna to find the most flattering dress in fine white muslin, whilst Harriet created a garland of wild flowers and herbs for her headdress.

Anna smiled with happiness as she was introduced to more members of the Newbery family, many of whom had come to the wedding from their estate in Sussex. The groom looked resplendent in his military uniform, greeting everyone with a gracious bow or tentative kiss, and was introduced to members of the lively Floyer family.

Choosing to resign his army commission, George Newbery had decided to begin married life with a role in the family medicine business and that he and his wife would set up home in London, close to St Paul's Cathedral. The Blombergs' generous marriage portion also enabled George Newbery to lease the Old Abbey in Malton so that Anna would enjoy being close to her family when they were in residence at Kirby Misperton.

Aunts twittered with delight over the bride. What a beautiful dress, how lovely her hair looked in the floral garland, and what a handsome husband.

"You've been a wonderful father to Anna," said Elizabeth Powney to Frederick, leaning towards his ear so that she could be heard over the chatter.

"I'm glad to have helped. I'm sorry that Edward Woolls did not live to see his daughter wed, God rest his soul," replied Frederick.

"Fred, I must tell you something," continued Elizabeth, leaning even closer. "My youngest son, Richard, is an officer in the army as you know, and his regiment was invited to Windsor for some farewell event before they sail for India."

"Oh," said Frederick. "Congratulations to Richard. I'm sure my dear friend Peniston would have been very proud of him. I do miss him, as must you, I'm sure."

Frederick was not surprised to hear that the son of his old friend, Peniston Portlock Powney, had found his way into Windsor. Peniston had always been anxious to see his children introduced at court.

"But Fred," continued Elizabeth, "when Richard met the King, he asked after you. There, isn't that impressive! He knew exactly who Richard was and the family relationship with you, Richard's uncle."

"He asked after me?" Frederick was overwhelmed. In his mind he'd concluded that George no longer wanted anything to do with him. This little flame of connection ignited a fierce beacon of hope in his heart, making him quake with excitement. He'd not seen George since they exchanged nods at the funeral of Prince Frederick, the Duke of York, on that freezing cold day in February nearly eighteen months ago. They'd hardly spoken in the eight years that George had been king, apart from the occasional pleasantries at court events. The letters of acknowledgement and birthday greetings from George had seemed perfunctory and insincere. There were no invitations to tea or royal summons to attend the King.

Frederick felt his heart beating faster in his chest. This scrap of news triggered a fresh desire to make contact. He resolved to write to George.

All through the wedding feast, he mentally composed the letter he would send to the King. Having been chaplain, private secretary and Clerk of the Closet, his name would be known to the courtiers surrounding the monarch. Surely a letter would get through to him? The possibility of a reply made him giddy with pleasure. Enthusiastically quaffing his wine, he made cheerful conversation with members of the Newbery family and his own, but all he could think about was reuniting with his brother.

Tapping his wine glass with vigour before standing up at the table after the wedding breakfast, he made a surprisingly amusing speech. Later, he took out his violin and played a jig. Everyone tapped their feet and clapped their hands to the tune. A few of the younger guests danced.

Maria, Harriet and the newlyweds were delighted to see him so merry.

After Anna's wedding to Captain Newbery, Frederick and Maria chose not to return to Yorkshire but remained at the vicarage in Cripplegate, close to the young couple's new home in London.

All through the summer and autumn of 1828, following the heartfelt letter he had written to George after the wedding, Frederick waited for word from Windsor. Finally, in late November, the King's messenger delivered a stiff white envelope to the vicarage in Well Street. With trembling hands, Frederick opened it in his study and read the contents:

From King George IV, Windsor Castle
To Reverend Doctor Frederick Blomberg D.D., The Vicarage,
St Giles, Cripplegate, London
23rd November 1828

Dear Reverend Blomberg,

I was very pleased to receive your letter in July. I apologise for the tardy reply. My health has not been good. I congratulate you on the wedding of your niece. I gather you and your family are settled in London for the winter. I would like to invite you, your wife and Captain and Mrs Newbery to tea at Windsor Castle on January 14th next year, 1829. It would also please me if you would stay the night at the castle and take divine service at St George's Chapel the following day. Details will follow from my office.

Yours etc

George IV

PS My dear F, it has been far too long. Please bring the Mozart Violin Concerto Number 5.

Here it was at last! Frederick smiled at the letter, reviewing the postscript over and over. Yes, the last line was definitely in George's own hand, and he sounded sincere in his desire to see him again. Euphoria overwhelmed him and, picking up his violin, he played Purcell's *Allegro and Andante* followed by a blast of Vivaldi and then some lively Rossini. Frederick played the music with such vitality that Maria came rushing into his study from the parlour to check on him. Showing her the letter, his beaming face told her all she needed to know.

"We're all invited," she cried. "Well, our Captain Newbery will be very impressed by this. Have you heard any more about the King's health?"

"I hear a little from my clerical colleagues at St James's Palace. He's been difficult to manage, I gather. Always demanding laudanum and calling to be bled."

"I'm so pleased he has responded to you at last. What a long time you've waited and now this. I've always found the King a very contrary person."

"It's possible that I'm one of the few people who understands him. I almost feel sorry for his many long-suffering mistresses."

"Is that dreadful Lady Conyngham still at his side?"

"Apparently he's fallen out with her. I read the same magazines and papers as you and Anna. He's come to blows with many of the people who surround him. They've all left."

"Including Sir William Knighton?"

"Yes, even Knighton. And I'm relieved to hear it. We'll see the situation more clearly when we are there. Well, Maria, I realise this invitation is two months away, but we must plan the visit and review our wardrobes. We'll all need new clothes if we're to be presented at court." Frederick thrust back his shoulders. "I will order the Mozart score he requested."

Chapter Fifty
A Visit to Windsor
14ᵗʰ January 1829

There were butterflies in Frederick's stomach. The carriage rumbled under the arched entrance to Windsor Castle and was guided towards the main entrance. Great layers of crenelated stone now topped the once plain apartments. Turrets and towers had been built on top of the ancient walls and roofs. The castle looked far more polished and regal than it had done in George III's day.

Recognising some of the corridors in the castle, Frederick and his family were led through newly decorated staterooms, and he noticed paintings he had never seen before. They were given time to change and prepare for their audience before being led along the carpeted passages into the King's drawing room.

Filling the broad armchair in his drawing room, George made no attempt to get up when his guests arrived. His clothes looked unkempt and dirty, and his hair was wiry and tousled. George's stomach strained at the fabric on his waistcoat and his fleshy legs bulged through his breeches at the knee.

Frederick was horrified by George's appearance. Resembling an inflated bladder or some shocking deep-water pufferfish, his full lips opened and shut without emitting sound and his swollen eyes were surrounded by sagging flesh, one of them filmy with cataracts. Seeping through chafed skin on his swollen ankles, a puddle of moisture collected around his feet, staining the carpet.

The King nodded in acknowledgement of his guests with a feeble wave before his hand slumped back onto his distended stomach.

Frederick felt overwhelming sadness for this once vital man who used to stride the city in search of entertainment. Now he was truly in very poor health. Frederick could tell that his guests shared his horror at the sight but did their best to disguise their reaction.

Bowing low to the King, Frederick introduced Maria and Captain and Mrs George Newbery, who also bowed and curtsied.

After a few minutes of polite conversation, George held out his hand and Frederick took it. Pulling him closer, George whispered, "Fred, as you see, I am ill. I suspect I will die soon, but I wanted to see you."

"I'm pleased to see you too, George. It's been many years since we last conversed properly."

"Indeed, too long, too long. Fred, I want to show you something. It's in my study. Your family may remain here, sir. Some tea will arrive. Come with me."

George summoned the two pages standing sentry by the door, and they hurried forward to lift him under each armpit to an upright position before shifting him into a large wheelchair.

Frederick followed as the pages wheeled George through a door into his study. The room contained another large armchair and, emitting a great whoosh of breath, George was lowered into it.

Pointing to an instrument case on a table nearby, George said, "Go on, Fred, open it. It's for you."

"For me?"

Opening the case, Frederick took a breath of surprise before picking up the violin. It was beautiful.

"It's not the Stradivarius you wanted all those years ago, Fred, but it's a Stainer – every bit as good and just as rare. It's for you. Please sit down; try it out. It's been tuned in readiness for you."

Frederick sat down on a chair opposite George. He held the violin to his chin and picked up the bow lying next to it in the box, drawing it across the strings before playing a familiar tune from the Purcell piece they had learnt together as boys.

Frederick then played a piece of the Glück which always gave him such pleasure.

"It's the most magnificent violin I've ever played. The tone is remarkable. What a wonderful instrument. Thank you, George, is this really for me?'

"It is, Fred. Take it."

"No, it's far too rare a gift, George."

"It's for playing, not admiring. I've been wanting to give you this for years."

"Years?"

"Yes, I bought it for you about five years ago when Rossini came to the Pavilion. Many rare violins were displayed at the concert, and I bought this for you then. Would that it was that Stradivarius, but I thought that this Stainer would give you pleasure."

"It does give me pleasure, George. This is so generous. I can't thank you enough. I had hoped to talk to you at the Pavilion that day of the concert, but you were surrounded by people."

"I saw you, Fred. I wanted to beckon you over, but then Lady Conyngham and others took me away. I was sorry for it."

"I was sorry for it too, George. But I'm here now. I wasn't sure you still played, but I have brought you some new scores, including that Mozart you wanted and other pieces, assuming you don't have them already."

"Fred, look at my fingers; I cannot play."

Frederick looked at the bloated hands, crabbed with arthritis and covered in flaking skin. His fingers were blue at the tips, his nails ridged with strange horizontal lines.

"But I still take pleasure in hearing music. Your hair may be white like mine, and your face somewhat lined, but you appear to be in good health. Are you well, Fred?"

"I'm very well, George, thank you, and all the better for seeing you. I found our separation very hard. We've been apart for eight years – too long. I've always said we are like a tally stick, you and I. We need to be together to make the piece whole. Although, you were always the larger piece."

"Are you insulting your monarch, Fred?" replied George. His good eye was bright with a familiar twinkle.

"I would not dare, sir. You are the same person you always were. I confess you are a little altered in appearance, but I see your spirit is unchanged."

"Oh, I need these words, Fred. The truth is, there's no one else who can talk to me without artifice. It's always been the case. Ever since we were boys, I never had to pretend to you. You could see inside me. And I know what you saw was not always good or wholesome. But I could depend on you. I've not been a good brother."

"You can always depend on me, George. I am so sorry you are suffering. Can the doctors help?"

"There is nothing they can do. I am at ease with the suffering. It's what I deserve."

"You don't deserve to be in pain."

"I do. I've reviewed my life and am not pleased with it. I failed in my duty as a son, didn't satisfy my parents and showed no respect or love to my true 'wife', Maria. I was a bad husband to an impossible woman and failed as a father and as a king. All my riches have been given to unworthy men and women. My grandson died before he could begin his life. I was unkind to you when we were boys."

"You were a child, George."

"I allowed you to take those beatings and this is my punishment." He waved his crippled hands around his face.

Frederick could see that the King was depressed and changed the subject.

"Do you see much of young Princess Victoria, Edward's child? We're all presuming she will be the heir, a future queen for this country."

"She is an excellent young lady, though she does not like me. Ha! I took her for a gallop in the landau when she was ten years old and terrified her mother, who thought she was in danger of being thrown from the carriage. I had total control, and she enjoyed the ride. When inviting her to kiss me goodbye, she refused, declaring my face to be too slimy. I was wearing greasepaint in a bid to look younger, and she saw straight through my artifice.

"I have another request."

"Of course, what is it?"

"To reappoint you as a working chaplain here at Windsor. It won't involve much work, of course, but it will keep you closer to me. Would you consider spending your time in London and coming to Windsor regularly?"

"Of course, George. It would be an honour. We are happy at my parish at St Giles in Cripplegate and will remain in London at your command. Much as we enjoy our Yorkshire home, we are not compelled to be there all the time."

"It's entirely selfish on my part, but I would like to have you near for what little time I have left on earth and spend it in the company of my oldest friend."

Frederick squeezed his eyes and bit the tip of his tongue harder. He didn't want to weep in front of George, but a single tear escaped, which he wiped away.

"And another thing, Fred. I have a further present for you."

"More! You've already given me the violin."

"Look in that pouch on the table."

Frederick picked up the small velvet pouch and opened it. Inside was a newly minted half sovereign. The shiny gold coin bore the pristine left-facing profile of King George IV, looking youthful, with a head of curled hair.

"Not a tally stick, Fred," said George in a rasping voice, "as you see, but a coin. Ha, ha. We are two sides of the same coin. I'm the head and you're the tails. I thought it would amuse you."

Frederick chuckled but was unable to prevent tears gathering in his eyes. George was right; they had always been two sides of the same coin, the half sovereign. He could see that George was getting tired.

"George, sir, you need to rest now."

"Yes, Fred, I will let you go. I may see you at dinner but will see you tomorrow morning after divine service and look forward to your attendance. It gives me great peace to know you are near me."

"And I share that peace."

Frederick bowed, touching George on the hand before walking backwards to the door.

Chapter Fifty-One
Brothers Reunited
June 1830

Since Frederick's reappointment as chaplain in January, life in London turned full circle. He and Maria enjoyed permanently living in the Vicarage of St Giles and Frederick made regular visits to the King at Windsor. On each occasion that he saw George, Frederick could tell that the King's health was failing.

By the summer of that year, the King had not been seen in public or beyond the walls of Windsor Castle for over four years. Only a handful of privileged courtiers or visitors ever saw him. The papers and commentators were not inclined to be kind towards the sixty-seven-year-old monarch who was deeply unpopular, poorly regarded and considered to have neglected his duty. Too often, the court reports in newspapers announced: 'The King was indisposed', 'The King was uncomfortable', that his health was 'not good' or 'The King would not attend'.

In mid-June, Frederick paid what would turn out to be his last visit to the King at Windsor. The day was hot, and a hazy heat shimmered over the thick stonework of the castle with barely a breath of wind for relief. Grooms ran round the stable yard bringing great buckets of water to the thirsty horses.

Taking the now familiar route through the castle to the King's bedroom, Frederick saw that windows were open onto the southeast terrace and gardens, but the air in the room was stale with the smell of sickness.

The sight that greeted him was grim and painful to behold. Frederick approached George's chair where he sat, like a giant walrus, propped up on either side by bolsters and pillows. His right arm was still streaked with blood from a recent letting. His face was pale and drawn and his throat so bloated that his head disappeared into it, the folds of skin below his chin resembling proving dough, soft, pitted and oozing sweat.

Frederick bowed, gazing at the sickly king. It was a while before George opened his bloodshot eyes, his lips forming a stressful smile over toothless gums. Fred could see he was trying to focus on him as he waved a hand to his right where Fred sat down.

"I don't have long, Fred."

"Is that what the doctors say, George?"

"I don't need doctors to tell me that my life is ending."

Frederick noticed that George's pebble spectacles sat upon a large-print Bible on the nearby table. "Have you been reading the Bible?"

"I have, with what little sight I have left. Religion never interested me when I was younger, but I have been taking comfort from reading the parables or having them read to me. I begin to understand my father's affection for the Bible and his belief in the church. I have had time to think deeply about things."

"I'm pleased to hear it."

"Do you believe in God, Fred?"

"What a thing to ask, especially of your chaplain!"

"No, I've been thinking about it. Not all clergy are men of God. You must know this?"

"Yes, I know this. And I'm not sure that I did believe in God in the beginning. I learnt to love him and allow my life to be formed to his praise."

George's eyes narrowed. "Are you mocking me again?"

"Never, George. I don't agree with everything that's written in the Bible. I've learnt more about human nature from the people around me than in the scriptures. I believe we have free will, and that humans, generally, want to do good rather than bad. I believe that love, especially within families, is the highest form of love."

"So many of my family, friends and associates are dead," said George, his voice croaky with the strain of talking. "You must experience this. I have strange conversations in my mind with people who are no longer alive. My mother and father appear to me. I see them as I see you, sitting there."

"I'm glad for it, George. You do look tired."

"I am tired but pleased you came to see me. Did you bring your violin, the Stainer?"

"Yes. Would you like me to play something?"

"In a while, but first I have a request."

"What is it?"

"In the bottom drawer of my desk is a box. Inside the box is a small locket with a black ribbon. Would you fetch it for me?"

Delving into the drawer, Frederick found the box with the locket and snapped open the cover to see a miniature portrait.

"Do you recognise her?" asked King George.

Frederick sighed, pushing his spectacles up his nose to focus on the picture, peering at the attractive woman with lustrous hair piled upon her head. "Of course I do."

"Maria Fitzherbert," whispered George. "She won't come and see me. It is my wish to be buried with that miniature. Please, will you tie it round my neck? I want it fixed in place, to have her with me when I die."

Frederick positioned the tiny locket on George's breast, pushing his hands behind the soft clay of his fleshy neck and grappling with his fingers to fasten it. The smell of decay rising from the King's body almost made him gag.

"Thank you. I have her near my heart at last." George patted the locket and sighed.

"You are welcome, George."

Frederick smiled at his childhood confederate, old friend and foe. He could see that his life was ebbing away.

"You know, George, sitting here in your chamber with you makes me feel like a boy again," said Frederick. "We could be plotting an assault upon the kitchen to steal food or planning mischief to annoy our tutors."

"Indeed, that gives me comfort. Just stay with me. That's enough. Whilst you are here I feel safe. No other brother or sister can give me such comfort. You were always Father's most beloved boy, the most fortunate son, Fred. I envy you."

"Envy me! How can you say that? You were always the heir. You became king. You have a place in history and will be remembered. That is fortunate. My life will just end. No one will remember me."

"Fred, I have spent many hours considering this," George whispered. "We may have shared the same father and grown up in the same environment, but I did not make good use of my advantages. I was granted many gifts, and I squandered them, disappointing my parents."

"George, you have been kind. You are generous."

"But I am not loved. You are loved, Fred. You have led a good life, remained married to a woman you love and are surrounded by people who love and respect you. Master Frederick, you have gained and maintained a worthy role in society and created a comfortable home. You are a man of God and a man of status. Yes, I envy you."

Frederick felt overwhelmed that George had thought about him so deeply and had so accurately described him. He may have had a painful childhood, but it was true, he had enjoyed a good life.

"George, we are very different characters. When we were children, I just remember wanting to be loved, whilst you were desperate to be king."

"Because I was born to be king, wasn't I? I had no choice. That was made clear to me when I was a tiny boy when all I wanted was to be free. You achieved freedom."

"But George, I was always the poor relation, your 'whipping boy', remember? I envied you for your status and your natural confidence, the way people looked up to you."

"You were jealous of me, Fred?"

"Yes, at times I was."

"Did you think that you should have become king?"

"There were times when I might have imagined it and yes, if I'm honest, I sometimes felt jealous of your privilege, envying the attention you were given, always in your shadow. But, in truth, I never desired the crown." Frederick shook his head, patting George's hand. "I desired respect. Yes, I wanted to be a gentleman but, as an adult, I discovered that respect had to be earned. It wouldn't just come my way because I desired it."

"Fred, you wanted to be royal?"

"I wanted to be a member of the royal family and that's different. It is as much my family as the one I was born into with my cousin and aunt. Remember how young I was when I came to you? How could I not want to be part of your family and to be loved, as a child should be, by the King and Queen? They were both kind and remote in equal measure. It was a puzzling time."

"Fred, you have been loved by your royal family, most of all by me. And you are fortunate. You may not have been blessed with children, and I am sorry for it, but you have the strong and protective love of a family. I had a daughter, but she died. I have no family."

Frederick listened to the King's words and felt a stone weight in his stomach dissolve and disappear. George was right. He had been the more fortunate brother.

Frederick looked at George seated uncomfortably in his chair. His eyes were drooping, but the fingers of his left hand indicated that he wished to hear music.

Frederick opened the case containing the violin, and holding it under his chin, he lifted the bow to the strings and began to play.

The End.

Epilogue

George IV died at Windsor on 26th June 1830. His body lay in state at the castle until his funeral on 15th July. Frederick was amongst the mourners. By all accounts, the funeral was not a respectful occasion. Since Prince Frederick, the next in line, had died in 1827, Prince William, Duke of Clarence, became King William IV. The new king talked loudly throughout his brother's funeral service and left before it was over. People demonstrated little grief for a monarch who never inspired affection or respect.

William IV turned out to be a popular king for the seven years of his reign. He was confident enough to walk freely around the streets of London or Windsor, enjoying the spontaneous approval of crowds who saw him. At his death in 1837, the crown passed to Victoria, the eighteen-year-old daughter of Edward, Duke of Kent, who had died soon after Victoria's birth. Queen Victoria reigned from 1837 until her death in 1901.

Frederick Blomberg outlived George by seventeen years. Dividing his time between his home at Kirby Misperton and his work as a parish priest at St Giles in Cripplegate, he continued his association with the royal family and was a chaplain to both King William IV and Queen Victoria.

Frederick and Maria modernised the ancient vicarage on Well Street and created a comfortable and spacious home with large reception rooms where they allowed parishioners to celebrate baptisms, weddings and funerals. The verdant garden, bordering the ancient Roman Wall of London, with its pleasant pond and vast fig tree, was ideal for garden parties. Renowned for his generous hospitality and impressive wine cellar, Frederick was a popular priest. His parishioners commissioned a silver candelabra in celebration of his eightieth birthday in 1841.

There are several stories relating to Reverend Blomberg in his sunset years in London. According to *A History of Cripplegate*, published in 1888, Frederick is described as: *A man of most charitable disposition and universally esteemed. A tablet in the south aisle of the church states that he gave the munificent sum of £750 during the first three years of his pastorate, towards relieving the necessities of his poor parishioners.* The account added that a well-executed painting of him hung in the Vestry Room of Quest House, Cripplegate (demolished in 1903).

However, despite being a popular priest, a disgruntled servant at the vicarage, dismissed for some misdemeanour, and knowing how to injure his former employer, stole Blomberg's three precious violins. Distraught, Frederick sought help from the newly formed police force, the Bow Street Runners. The violins were tracked to a pawnshop in Cock Lane in East London and Frederick parted with five pounds to retrieve his precious instruments. He was quoted as saying that no price would have been too great to have them restored to him.

Meanwhile, when based at Kirby Misperton, Frederick enjoyed the status of local celebrity in Yorkshire. George Newbery's family business manufactured Doctor James's Powders, which claimed to cure gout, a condition which dogged poor Frederick for years. The *Yorkshire Press* of the day regularly featured advertisements trumpeting the curative powers of these powders and cited *Baron Blomberg of Kirby Misperton Hall* as an enthusiastic consumer.

In 1837, the story of Major William Blomberg's apparition hit the headlines again. Reverend Doctor James Rudge, Frederick's old curate from Shepton Mallet, published a volume of anecdotes including the story of the ghost. His book became a bestseller of the day and Frederick became the subject of curiosity again, though, to my knowledge, he never gave interviews or publicly repeated the story. Further accounts of the apparition were published in *The Unseen World* (1847), *Recollections and Reflections from Bristol Cathedral by Rev L. W. Gulley* (1849) and *The Journal and Memories of Thomas Walley* (1863). These are useful sources, but each telling of the tale is different. There are so many versions of the Blomberg ghost story now that it's hard to know which might be the original, or the truth.

Reverend Doctor Frederick Blomberg D.D. never retired. He was still vicar of St Giles in Cripplegate when he died at the vicarage on 23rd March 1847 aged 85. Prince Adolphus, the Duke of Cambridge, attended his funeral.

Maria Blomberg died two years later on 13th February 1849, aged 92. She was interred next to her husband in the crypt of St Giles, Cripplegate.

At the back of St Giles, Frederick Blomberg's name can be seen on a plaque recording all the vicars of the parish. It's the only surviving reference to him there. His tomb has disappeared along with the tablet recording his generosity to the poor. In 1897 a fire started in a peacock feather warehouse, swiftly spreading across the area. The church was badly damaged and vicarage destroyed in the 'Great Fire of Cripplegate'.

In the Blitz of 1940, bombs destroyed the replacement vicarage, its handsome garden and the church roof was burnt out. Later repairs restored the roof to its original glory. The Well Street site, where the vicarage had stood, was absorbed into the new Barbican development in the 1960s.

On Baron Frederick Blomberg's death, Anna and George Newbery inherited Kirby Misperton, its contents and all the family wealth. They sold the estate at auction in 1847 and moved to West Sussex, purchasing a large house in Brunswick Square, Brighton. They lived there until George Newbery died in 1854 and Anna in 1857. They had no children.

The Blomberg/Newbery estate went to members of the Newbery family, nephews and nieces of George. Some of the family moved into the house in Brunswick Square.

*

All the figures from the royal family and household who appear in this novel existed in real life. Henrietta Cotesworth, Coaty, is well recorded thanks to her closeness to Lady Charlotte Finch, the head governess of the royal nursery. Letters in the Royal Archive from Queen Charlotte to Lady Charlotte Finch suggest that Mrs Cotesworth had a drink problem. The Floyer family of Bath, Frederick's in-laws, including Peniston Portlock Powney, his brother-in-law, all existed.

Other characters, including Margaret, Harriet and the Laing and Tate families were created for the novel.

However, the main players in this book are Prince George and Master Frederick. Historians of Georgian royalty generally give Frederick a cursory reference, if they mention him at all. Some call him the 'charity boy', 'whipping boy', 'adopted son' or 'foster brother'. References to Frederick and George's similarity in appearance are well recorded.

Yet I believe Frederick was a far more important player in the life of George III's family than he is given credit for. He has been hiding in plain sight all this time. If you revisit historical references to George III and his family through a 'Blomberg lens', his place becomes clear. Documents in the Royal Archives and in the newspapers of the day confirm that Frederick Blomberg was close to the royal family throughout his long life and his name is frequently included in guest lists at palace drawing rooms and levees.

Fanny Burney, the novelist and diarist, mentions him. Fanny Burney was Keeper of the Robes, a dresser to Queen Charlotte for four years between 1786 and 1790. During that time she wrote a vivid diary giving us a clear and moving account of the onset of the King's madness and its impact on the family and court at Windsor.

Spending hours poring over newspaper records and lists of guests present at royal or society events, I discovered that Frederick

Blomberg was frequently 'in the room where it happened'. As chaplain at Windsor he was a familiar figure within the castle. He officiated at several weddings of George IV's brothers. On 11th July 1818, at Kew Palace, he conducted the marriage of Prince Edward to his German wife, Princess Victoria of Saxe-Coburg-Saalfeld, who later gave birth to the future Queen Victoria. Frederick is listed amongst the guests at countless palace events. He was at George IV's coronation amongst the clerics. He is often referenced as playing the violin or cello with the Prince of Wales.

King George III supported Frederick through his education and both he and King George IV were instrumental in overseeing the granting of Frederick's lucrative livings. Livings (clerical salaries) were funded by local taxation within a parish and rent from church-owned land or property. Some parishes generated huge incomes. Shepton Mallet, Bradford on Avon and Banwell were very wealthy towns. Major landowners (or the King) would appoint the vicar or rector. A clergyman's living came with a vicarage, rectory or parsonage, which guaranteed a home. If the clergyman chose to be absent, the property could be rented out. An absentee vicar or rector could appoint a curate to do the work. By all accounts, Reverend Blomberg was a generous employer and cared for his curates though he was regarded in clerical circles as an 'unashamed pluralist', in that he accepted several livings at the same time, pocketing the salary that went with them.

What started out for me as an investigation into a sensational ghost story has developed into a fascinating odyssey into Georgian history. At the heart of the story is the 'bromance' between two men, half-brothers, who happened to have had a king for a father.

In this novel I have avoided reference to the turbulent world events and domestic crises going on at the time. These years – 1761–1847 – saw major upheavals, such as the American War of Independence, the French Revolution, the abolition of slavery, the Industrial Revolution, the Age of Enlightenment, development of education and complex English politics. I could not weave these great events into my book, so I limited my novel to the few characters at the heart of the story, following their lives and seeing the world from their perspective.

I've discovered a few images of Frederick Blomberg to bring him to life. On the front cover are details from two spectacular royal portraits Queen Charlotte commissioned from the court painter Richard Brompton of her sons. One shows the young Prince of Wales in Garter robes with Windsor Castle in the background, the other is a portrait of Frederick Blomberg wearing a glorious rust-coloured outfit and posing with his greyhound. It shows a beautiful boy of about eleven years old with Buckingham House in the background and it is painted as grandly as the two other royal children of the day, Prince George and Prince Frederick. I thank The Royal Collection / King Charles III for his kind permission for me to use a detail from the Brompton portrait of Prince George as a boy on the front cover. I thank the Austin Auction Gallery in Texas for granting me use of photography of the Blomberg portrait.

The Brompton portraits of Princes George and Frederick currently hang on the walls of the 1844 Room at Buckingham Palace. The Brompton portrait of Blomberg must have been given to Frederick by the Prince Regent after Queen Charlotte died. When it was auctioned in 1983 and again in 2023, the name Newbery, as owner, is referenced on the back of the painting.

Photographs from the recent auction reveal that there is an inscription on Frederick's portrait. In the space between the dog's belly and Blomberg's left leg is a message, in Latin, telling the viewer that, following the death of his father in America, Frederick William Blomberg was brought up in the household of George III and his wife Queen Charlotte.

I have also tracked a further image of Frederick as a boy. In 1769 Queen Charlotte commissioned the Irish artist Hugh Douglas Hamilton to make portraits of the entire family. He created distinctive drawings of all the children in his trademark round frame. Frederick Blomberg is included amongst the portraits, recorded, in graphite, chalk and watercolour, looking serious, in profile, with a sketch of a violin at the base. This portrait was recently purchased by the Royal Collection and is now kept safely with Hamilton's other portraits of Princes George, Frederick, William and Edward in a box in the Print Room at Windsor Castle.

There's another fascinating image which can be seen on the website of King Charles III's Royal Collection at Windsor. It's a watercolour by the court artist Paul Sandby dated 1771 and it shows George III's oldest children with their governess in the garden at Kew outside the redbrick mansion, which is now called the Dutch House but in Frederick's day was called the Princes' House. In the foreground of the painting is a group of children playing with a small carriage. In 1771, George, Prince of Wales, would have been nine and can be identified because he's wearing a blue sash and cracking the whip. Two other children are in the carriage: Prince Frederick (future Duke of York), eight, Prince William (future Duke of Clarence and King William IV), six, and four-year-old Prince Edward (future Duke of Kent and father of Queen Victoria) is trailing along after them. Another child is pulling the carriage. Could this have been Master Frederick Blomberg? The boy is wearing the same livery as the others under the watchful eye of their governess, Coaty, perhaps?

Postscript

Why did I choose to write this novel? Well, there's always been this story in my family that we, on my mother's side, were related to George III. The story had trickled down the generations and, like that game, *Chinese Whispers*, details had been lost in the telling.

Establishing that Frederick had no children, I'm satisfied that my family is not related to the royal family. The link, I believe, is my family's connection with Kirby Misperton in Yorkshire, the estate Blomberg was gifted by George IV.

My great-grandfather, James Robert Twentyman, bought Kirby Misperton, the estate and the grand mansion house, in the late 1890s. He came from County Durham and trained as an engineer in the ship-building industries on the Tyne. Clever and ambitious, he travelled to China and set up a successful business in Shanghai building the docks and maintaining ships. He also became fascinated by oriental art and shipped back a huge collection to adorn his Yorkshire home.

In the 1880s he married Ada Minns, the middle daughter of a publican who lived in the mining town of Easington in Durham. They had five children and, after several years of ex-pat life in China, returned to England and set up home in Yorkshire.

My grandmother, Verna, grew up at Kirby Misperton. As a child I used to love hearing her telling stories about life in the grand house in the early 1900s.

I have a very hazy memory of visiting Kirby Misperton with my family when I was about five years old, walking along the drive towards the house, past the lake, its surface thick with duckweed. The place looked very sorry for itself, overgrown and neglected. It was ready for a new life.

In the mid-1960s, Kirby Misperton became Flamingo Park Zoo and was later expanded into Flamingo Land, a theme park, which is now a tourist destination for North Yorkshire. The Hall is still there, in the shadow of the hectic rides, next to the children's zoo. It's called The Mansion, and you can have tea there or even get married.

And yes, the obelisk built by Blomberg to commemorate the gift of the estate from the King is still there. It's close to the flamingo lake and dwarfed by one of the rollercoaster rides. The bronze plaque Frederick Blomberg placed on the obelisk has been removed and is now kept safely within the office of Flamingo Land in the former vicarage next door to the Hall.

The inscription on the plaque reads:
Georgio Wallice Principi
Britanniarum Imperium
Pro Rege
Pie ac feliciter sustinenti
Ob agrum
Diu alienatum
Minificentia sua
Nuper restitutum
Columnam hannce
Grati animi monumentum
Dicavit
Fr Gul Blomberg MDCCCXII

My interpretation of the Latin (not for purists) is:
Praise to George, Prince of Wales, King and ruler of the British Empire
In recognition of his generosity that this place, long estranged, Has been restored to me.
I erect this column in gratitude.
So says: Frederick William Blomberg 1812

Acknowledgements

As any author will attest, the production of a book is not a solitary matter. Yes, the writing may be done alone, but the input, advice and guidance forming the finished product comes from many contributors. I thank my daughter Matilda Battersby for her early read of the text and her kind but firm pointers regarding structure and pace. I thank Venessa Pugh for her generous observations and my sister Liz Freeborn for her sound advice. I thank Eleanor Smith for her very thorough reading of the text and remarkable tidy-up.

I am supremely grateful to Janet Weitz, Publishing Director of Alliance Publishing Press, who saw the potential in this book and devoted hours of forensic reading of the text and provided an immeasurable editorial contribution whilst wielding her trusty red pen. I am so grateful to her and I also thank her excellent team at APP, Mark James for his jacket & book design and Jo James for her expert help with the book description.

To research the novel, I visited Kirby Misperton in Yorkshire, now Flamingo Land, and, thanks to Helen Brown, toured the Hall, saw the Blomberg obelisk in the grounds of the estate and handled the bronze plaque with the Latin inscription. I appreciated being given access to St Lawrence's Church in Kirby Misperton to see the Blomberg memorials to Ursula and her son William high upon the wall.

Fr Jack Noble, at St Giles in Cripplegate, kindly showed me the plaque at the back of the church commemorating Blomberg's tenure as vicar in the roster of clerics. I thank the art curators at Buckingham Palace and Windsor Castle for showing me fascinating royal paintings and drawings confirming that Master Frederick Blomberg was very much a member of the royal family.

Most of all I would like to thank Simon Battersby, my husband, for providing unerring support throughout this project. He endured endless discussions about Georgian history and regency life during the writing of this 'Georgian Royal Family Saga'. He tolerated my constant references to George IV, Frederick and the Blomberg family (real and imagined), who seem to have moved into our home and cluttered up the rooms like guests who never leave. They are still around but now safely contained between the covers of this book. I thank you for reading it.

Rosalind Freeborn.

Milton Keynes UK
Ingram Content Group UK Ltd.
UKHW021935311024
450473UK00010B/128